ŚIRĀ
THE ABANDONED CHILD

Meera Vyas

INDIA · SINGAPORE · MALAYSIA

Notion Press Media Pvt Ltd

No. 50, Chettiyar Agaram Main Road,
Vanagaram, Chennai, Tamil Nadu – 600 095

First Published by Notion Press 2021
Copyright © Meera Vyas 2021
All Rights Reserved.

ISBN 978-1-63940-388-2

DISCLAIMER

In loving memory of my grandfather

CONTENTS

Contents

'Power is never evil or good.
It's the man using it.'

CHAPTER I

WITCHES

Dark, horrific waves of the 1692 Salem witch trials reached the peaceful town of Drgaan, Massachusetts. The unofficial killings began in the name of witchcraft. Thousands of innocent women were burnt alive cruelly on the outskirts of town. Residents of the town convicted many women under false charges of practicing witchcraft. But in reality, most of those women were mental patients, and the rest were anarchists who dared to demand their basic human rights.

Amidst all that emerging chaos, Amaraya Bayer and her husband, George Bayer, lived with their two infant daughters Ablina and Raylina, on the riverside of Drgaan town. Amaraya and beings like her were what the world was hunting for, a "witch," and so did her two daughters.

"Some stories are reality written in a way to make people believe that they aren't real—because the truth always scares the non-believers," Amaraya read, closing the book knowing the last line by heart of her favorite book, '*The Tour to Nightmare*' written by Aryaraj Saud, to her 6-month-old daughters. "Night girls," she kissed them goodnight.

Amaraya snapped her fingers, and all at once, the flames glowing in the lanterns hanging in each corner of the room blew out. One more time she looked at her daughters sleeping peacefully in their cribs and quietly closed the door. "Are they asleep?" A husky voice startled her from behind. "Yes," Amaraya said with relief, wrapping her woolen nightgown around her shivering body, walking towards her husband, standing near the corridor window.

"George, I am afraid. I think we should go back to India," Amaraya said in her dulcet voice, looking outside the window. George kissed her forehead, burying her face into his chest, and said, "No, we can't, and you know that, Ami." "Oh lord," George muttered fearfully, staring out of the window at thousands of men prowling in the street with deadly weapons in one hand and a fire torch in the other, like hungry lions searching for prey in the dark forest.

Amaraya's heart shattered seeing a man heinously dragging a young girl by her hair towards the pyre stand. "Burn... Bur... Burn the filthy witch alive," the angry mass hollered. The harrowing screams of the young girl shriveled her throat. Amaraya held George's shoulders, and said, "George, please, let me help her." "Ami, you know it's not safe," George said and stopped her from going out to help the poor girl.

Amaraya regretted the day when she decided not to practice her magic anymore. Her powers were more than rustic; they were in deep hibernation, and reigniting them now would burn the whole town to the ground.

Laws were changing, and the world they all lived in was not the same anymore. Only God had the mighty power in their world, and the rest who held power were all evil. The humans discovered the witches' existence, and the fact that they resided in their very neighborhoods terrified them.

***

The next morning, Amaraya and George packed up their belongings to leave town. Amaraya went upstairs and gently lifted her twin daughters from their cribs. She placed them in their strollers and walked outside the Bayer Mansion.

George, for one last time, looked at the empty hall of his house. A tear dropped down on his wrist while locking the door of his childhood home. His heart sank, and the pain of letting go added an extra burden to his poor sunken heart. Amaraya benevolently kept her hand on George's shoulder to comfort him and said, "We'll build one together." George smiled forcefully, and without talking further, he carried the bags, and they left "Drgaan town," his home, forever.

After traveling for days, George and Amaraya took refuge in their dear friend Lord Fredrick Dhamiko's castle. Lord Fredrick welcomed the Bayers with open arms. He treated them like his family. He knew magic too, just like Amaraya and her daughters, but he was royalty, so he dodged the eyes of the witch hunters.

***

It was 1694, the somber era of witch-hunting was coming to an end, but the impact of 1692, the Salem trials, forewarned the witches all around the globe. The people who died in the Salem trials of 1692 were harmless humans. The real witches escaped and went underground before it all started, and those who failed to flee were killed by the witch hunters.

After spending two years and a half at Lord Dhamiko's castle, the Bayers bought their small farm at the town's edge. Amaraya and George weaved their dreams on the peace of the dead land with little magic spells and endless love. The two-floored dark brown timber house, surrounded by a beautiful garden with a teensy fish pond in the backyard, made their sweet home wonderfully magical. Life got normal. The Bayers found the peace they were looking for.

***

Amaraya was a witch by birth, and so were her daughters, while her husband, George, acquired witchcraft skills through intensive training under Amaraya's father in India. George considered magic an art of liberation, a medium for going beyond. For Amaraya, magic brought nothing but fear and death, and being raised in a land where magic was considered an art of the devil, would have done no right to her daughters. Therefore Amaraya and George decided to keep their daughters least exposed to their magical roots.

Amaraya and George homeschooled their daughters; together, they briefly taught their daughters about magic and thoroughly about other normal human subjects. Their days began with art and science lessons and were completed with warm, sugary milk. The Bayers were having the time of their lives, away from the world, in their little world.

***

As the years passed, Ablina Bayer and Raylina Bayer turned from little angels to beautiful young girls. The Bayer sisters were raised together, but they grew up completely different from each other.

Ablina was like a cool breeze of calm nights, an optimistic, vibrant soul loaded with wisdom and a heart blazing with passion. Raylina believed that Ablina was what you would call "a walking ray of hope" and not just because of her kindness or compassion for other people, but because Ablina firmly believed that good existed, not just in her fantasy books but also in real life. She was that true friend who would sit with you in the dark until the light reaches in.

At the same time, Raylina was a chaos bringer, impetuous, someone who would prefer war over adjustment, yet pure-hearted. Her head and heart worked in different directions. She claimed that she was different from the rest of the world. Still, deep down, she knew that she was just like any other normal girl striving hard to make it independently.

Despite their different personalities, they shared an unbreakable bond, a bond deeper than the blood running through their veins, a bond of "Love." And love trumps all.

***

The unbearable heat and humidity had deprived the life out of the "Kaike plant." Amaraya poured water on the plant and chanted, "Vin." The cool breeze revived the dried, discolored dead plant, turning it back into its faded green color. She kissed the tip of the conical miniature tree-like "Kaike plant," fondling the leaves, smiling, remembering what conjuring real magic felt like.

"It's beautiful, Ma," Ablina said in her sweet voice, nuzzling the velvety leaves of Kaike. "They die fast and come back to life even faster," Amaraya explained. "Ami, it's 2:00. I am going to town to buy some ingredients for the medicine," George informed and headed out, carrying white cloth bags folded between his arms. "Wait,

I am coming too," Amaraya said and tip-toed her way out through the thorns lying in the yard.

***

The blissful town of "Rau" was scantily populated. Rau had few shops, a church, and one dispensary. George worked as a physician at the town's dispensary; his medicinal herbs' expertise made him immensely popular. His little knowledge of magic and science helped many underprivileged people of the town. He treated them for free. He was an angel sent from God for the people of Rau. But, on the other hand, Amaraya chose to be as unnoticeable as she could for her family's sake.

Amaraya and George visited the general store and picked up the groceries for their home. "Honey, is there anything else left?" George asked. "We got everything except the ginger root," Amaraya read out from the list. "No... I am not going there... That man is a maniac," George said. "Stop acting like Raylina," Amaraya said, furrowing her eyebrows in annoyance. "Okay, anything for you, Ami. But I won't let you slide away from this easily," George said in a dramatic tone, and they headed towards the Greenhouse located in the middle of town.

"Barriet's Greenhouse" was established in 1605 by Elov Barriet, who came to the town of Rau with his family in 1601. As an immigrant, Elov faced many adversities in finding a proper job, so after trying his hands on everything, he built Barriet's Greenhouse. Since then, the Barriet family became the rulers of the agriculture market by selling and growing the world's most delicate, top-class breed of crops.

As a medicinal herb specialist, George mostly grew his own vegetables, fruit, and herbs in his backyard. However, some rare plants needed a specific environment to grow, so the Bayers bought a little space at Barriet's Greenhouse.

Mr. Barriet saw George and Amaraya walking towards him. "Afternoon," Mr. Barriet greeted Amaraya and intentionally ignored George. Mr. Barriet envied Amaraya and loathed George for some unknown reason. "Hello, Mr. Barriet," George said in a mocking tone. Amaraya pinched George's back and said, "Enough." "I was polite," he mumbled, stepping aside to the corner. Amaraya and Mr. Barriet chatted about the new plant species found on the banks of the Amazon River.

George was bored with their detailed discussion about herbs, so he walked out of the store letting his wife and her weird friend continue their serious, life-altering conversation. After 30 long minutes, Amaraya finally came out and instantly apologized to George.

George acted riled off to tease Amaraya for making him wait, but as he saw the tears rushing into her eyes, he gave up his act and said, "Sorry, please don't cry, honey." She smiled. Amaraya was George's world, and the only thing he wanted was to make her happy. He would do anything for that smile, anything, he thought, gazing at his beautiful wife. Infinity seemed little in front of his love for her.

***

George put his arm around Amaraya's shoulders and said, "Let's get those pastries for our girls." "Okay, but don't be late," she said. He chuckled as he walked towards the bakery.

Through the bakery's glass door, Amaraya saw her husband taking his time to taste every new arrival and finally choosing the obvious, regular chocolate cake. Amaraya smiled, as she knew it was his way of getting back at her from taking her time at Mr. Barriet's Greenhouse, but she let him play his trick on her and patiently waited for him.

"Here you go, Mr. Bayer," said Miss Jackson and handed him the pink pastry box. "Thank you!" George said and walked out of the shop.

Crack, Crack… Two shots fired. Amaraya saw George hitting the ground on his back in front of her eyes. The pink box dropped. The cake fell out and got spilled all over the place. Miss Jackson ran to see what happened, "Oh my god," she bawled.

"Take the girls out of here," George panted and shut his eyes, once and forever. "No… No, wake up, George, please… please wake up," Amaraya begged. She lifted him in her arms, and the blood started splashing out from his back. The scent of his blood caused a throbbing pain in her head, blurring her ability to think.

Amaraya was in a deep state of shock, unresponsive, just like George. She forgot that she was still alive. She thought she was in one of her nightmares, but one more gunshot snapped her right back into reality.

"Alvriya Casindes," Amaraya screamed wrathfully, and the dry leaves started whirling around her, the hoarding of the bakery quaked. "Booyimo," she yelped, and the gust of wind threw the shooter 8 feet high in the air. The shooter saw Amaraya walking towards him, and he fired again. She backed, and the bullet glazed by her right shoulder. The shooter pressed his hands vigorously onto the rough concrete road to stand up and ran from there as fast as possible. Amaraya ran after the shooter to chase him down, but a familiar voice stopped her. "Mrs. Bayer," she heard from behind. She turned back and saw Mr. Barriet calling her, standing near George's dead body.

"No… George," Amaraya yelped, running back to him. "George… please come back to me, love," Amaraya sniveled, falling on her knees, and lifted his fallen body into her warm embrace again, hoping for it to revivify. But he was gone. Her George was gone. She held him tightly against her chest, mourning in anger.

Amaraya remembered her father's advice, "But men ain't Kaikes, Ami. Once gone, they are gone." Her faith didn't let her believe her father's words, so she raised her hand with focus and chanted "Herclusiaso." But nothing changed. He was still dead, and just like her father said, he wasn't coming back.

Amaraya kissed George's lips with a heavy heart; it took her a minute to pull herself away from his cold lips, as it was their last kiss. "Faraliyaeisis," she said with agonizing pain, and his body was on fire. She stood there watching her life burn away in those dense orange flames.

Miss Jackson and a few others who witnessed Amaraya casting magic darted out from there like a bat out of hell. Mr. Barriet's views changed about Amaraya. He started fearing the woman he once respected and adored. But Mr. Barriet still was her friend. So with little courage, he walked towards Amaraya, and kept his hand on her shoulders with empathy, and said, "My dear, your daughters are alone." His words reminded her of her daughters, so she ran as fast as she could to the farm.

***

Amaraya arrived home and saw her daughters playing in the yard. "Abby, Ray," Amaraya yelled. The Bayer sisters came running to their mother. "What happened? Where is Papa?" Raylina asked in her soft voice. Amaraya didn't answer; she took them to the basement and locked the doors.

Ablina saw the peril on her mother's face, but she didn't ask her. "Where is Papa?" Raylina asked again in a firm tone. "He is dead," Amaraya said without empathy. Amaraya knew the hour needed her to be like that; her shattering soul would have destroyed her daughters, so she chose to be as cold-hearted as she could be.

Amaraya took the knife and cut her hand; she poured her fresh blood into the old brass bowl and chanted, "Domdisvaisous… Domdisvaisous… Domdisvaisous… Domdisvaisous." The mysterious red fog started appearing out of thin air. She hugged her daughters coldly and said, "Don't worry, I am still here, and I will protect you."

Amaraya, Ablina, and Raylina walked towards the brown coffins. There were four coffins nailed to the ground; they were meant to be used in desperate times for all the family members to hide. Amaraya opened it and asked them to lay down in it. She closed the coffins of Ablina and Raylina.

Amaraya kissed the top of George's empty coffin and said, "I will avenge the man who did this to our family." She laid down in hers and closed the door. "Finjoliy," she chanted, and their bodies started to turn into stones. Before the spell ascended to her face, she said, "Lvisi," hurriedly. The mystical red fog circumnavigated the coffins. And the coffins disappeared.

CHAPTER 2

REVENGE WILL TAKE WHAT'S LEFT OF HER

Why the "summer" is so parched,
And why is the "winter" always so cold and cruel.
Will you please tell me why the "monsoon" cries and
destructs?

I smile and say they are the victims of unrequited love.
The summer chooses the heat to make people leave,
The winter chooses the cold to bury her soul,
And the monsoon never learned how to keep it in, so she
poured her heart out heavily.

And just like her daughters, with every revolution, the
Earth made around her lover—the Sun;
In the hope of touching him one day, she returned with
nothing but got miles away.

He lifted his right arm to his face and gently pressed his thumb and index finger, to wipe his watery eyes. He then picked up the peacock feather from the pocket of his berry blue-colored blazer, kept it as a bookmark on the next page, and shut the book. "Drop me right here, and off you go," the man said in his intense, heavy voice. "Okay, Sir," the driver said.

The man walked for a while and stopped at the old rickety gates; he sighed deeply as he scanned the area. He headed towards the dilapidated two-floored dark brown timber house. He pulled his phone out of his blazer pocket and dialed. "I am here," the man said while standing at the house's front door. "Protect them with your life," the man on the other side of the phone commanded. "Fine," the man replied and headed straight to the hoary basement.

The room was filled with nothing but emptiness. The man felt their auras but couldn't see them. He tried endless spells to undo Amaraya's magic, but her style of practicing magic was different from other witches, and only the people closest to her knew the hacks and cracks of it.

The man pulled up his loosened low-waist jeans and walked imperturbably out of the basement. He spotted the dead Kaike plants in the yard and got his clue. He dug a little and found a broken bottle covered in soil. He smiled and took out the tiny scrolled paper from the bottle.

***

"Lvisi Cano," the man said, and just like that, the coffins reappeared. He opened the coffins and found their stone-frozen bodies. "Varenelia Veresia Gav," the man cantillated the spell, and with every repetition, the crack in the stone increased. The ritual continued for two days, and because of it, his body was giving up. Magic was slowly sucking the energy out of him. It was not easy for him to withstand the power of such a herculean spell.

At the dawn of the third day, his continuous efforts paid off, and the stony layer sedimented on their bodies broke. Gazillion pieces of stone scattered around the room, resembling an after-effect of warfare. "And so it begins," the man smiled and fell sharply on his face to the floor. Exhaustion was finally taking its toll on him. After ten minutes, the man forcefully stood up from the ground, wiping his nose bleed.

The man carefully lifted them one by one and took them to their beds. Amaraya, Ablina, and Raylina were unconscious, and as per the written instructions in the scroll, it was clear, "Do not wake them up; let them rise," so he waited for another 4 days.

As the days passed, their bodies were slowly rejuvenating; the blood in their veins was running again naturally, and the pale ivory color of their skins was coming back from the white cold. The man stood there watching them come back to life. It was spectacular for him, as he had never seen such magic before. "Indeed, it was beautiful," he thought and left the room.

***

They opened their eyes together. Amaraya stood up first, and after her, Ablina and Raylina.

Amaraya kept her hand on her beating heart, staring vacantly at Ablina and Raylina. "Girls," her words stumbled as she tried not to fall apart in front of her daughters. "Ma…," Ablina whimpered, running into her mother's arms. Raylina looked away stoically to hide her mournful eyes from her sister and mother.

"Ami," he said, and their eyes turned to the man. He walked in like the house owner, went near the dirty blue curtains, and tore them. The curtains dropped with pelmet. His almost 5 feet 8 inches height, smug smile, and bad attitude irked Raylina instantly. The smile on her mother's face added fuel to the fire.

"Alisar," said Amaraya and hugged him. She instantly pulled herself back, "How did you find us? Who sent you?" she asked in an interrogative tone. Alisar understood that it was a delicate situation, so he held her hands and said, "Your father sent me, Ami." She decided to keep quiet, as Alisar's loyalty towards her father was unquestionable, and rebelling at that moment was stupid.

"Who killed him, Ma?" Raylina questioned in an unhesitant tone, not paying any attention to who dragged them out of the coffin or why. The crushing pain inside Raylina's heart urged her to punch the universe. She wanted to weep the world out of her, but she couldn't. The loss hardened her; she became emotionally deprived, just like her mother.

Amaraya fleetingly described the events, trying not to dwell on the painful memories of the day when she lost the love of her life. Raylina felt that her mother was hiding something, that bits and pieces of what had happened were purposely leaped by her mother. "Ma," she cried sourly, expecting anything but silence. Amaraya shifted her eyes to Alisar, to dodge Raylina's upcoming questions, "Girls, meet Alisar Vasaga," she introduced, and fortunately dodged the questions.

Alisar Vasaga was 405 years old. However, he looked like a young man in his early 20s. His luscious, ash-like complexion, sharp jawline, and well-toned body made him look like a sensational, handsome prince from a dark fairytale. His seraphic smile and mysterious personality made ladies of all ages, young or old, fall in love with him no matter his age.

In the 17th century, Alisar secretly started selling immortality tonics to affluent witches and human communities. The tonic gave immortality to witches and humans by inhibiting their aging process. In addition to eternal life, the tonic made the consumers incomparably beautiful. By the 19th century, he launched the "Aqua Medicinals Company," which made him a celebrity in both the witch and the human worlds. As his fame and popularity grew, people began paying him in unthinkable ways for a dab of immortality tonic, making him the world's wealthiest man.

"One of the finest tonic makers of the world, it's because of his immortality tonic that we are immortal...

practically," Amaraya said. "Oh… stop being so generous. I have learned from the legend himself," Alisar said. Amaraya's smile narrowed. "Your grandfather taught me," Alisar said, looking at the Bayer sisters.

Raylina was already fed up with her mother's constant lying and Alisar—her newfound scapegoat. She knew that no matter how much she begged and wailed in front of her mother, she was never going to get anything out of her. She aggressively pulled out the old satchel from under the bed, dusted it roughly with her hands, "I am out of this," she said rudely, and stormed out of the room.

Ablina softly held her mother's hand and stopped her from going after Raylina. Amaraya and Raylina's temperaments were always fragile, one wrong word, and their anger could blast out like a bomb. George was the flag-bearer of peace in the family, but with him gone, the duty passed down to Ablina.

"You all must be hungry?" Alisar asked, breaking the wave of silence in the room. "Yes, I feel like I am carrying a volcano in my stomach," Ablina replied. "Alright, then let's go, ladies," he smiled at her. Ablina and Amaraya took a few of their belongings from their rooms while Alisar went down.

Raylina walked into the living room and stared at the family portrait blankly. Before a drop of her tear could fall from her right eye, she roughly rubbed them off. She learned that from her mother. The 17-year-old felt that it was in the family's best interest. She clenched her old satchel with fury and said, "Papa, I will make sure to burn the person responsible for your death alive."

Alisar quietly walked towards Amaraya, who was hiding behind the partly opened door of the living room, worriedly watching her daughter. "Amaraya," He called her in a hushed tone. Amaraya shifted her eyes from Raylina to Alisar. "We should leave now. But before that, take a bath," Alisar said and left.

***

They stood behind the frontline of the entrance door. Amaraya inspected the area twice, just to be sure it was safe to walk out again. She saw the high building and other prodigal establishments developed around her home. The world she knew once had changed completely. While Ablina was riveted by the new changes, Raylina didn't bother because, for her, it was all wasteful.

Amaraya, Ablina, and Raylina stepped out together in the new world of the year 2012. "It's much scarier than when you left," Alisar said to Amaraya and went out. They patiently waited in the porch area. "Ma, I don't think he is trustworthy," Raylina said. "Ray, we don't exactly have a choice. I have to trust him or at least have to pretend that I do," Amaraya said. "You know he is here at your father's command," Raylina reminded her. "I am well aware of that. We are still alive, in one piece, and that means my father does not want him to kill us," Amaraya said.

Beep… Beep… A loud galling sound interrupted their intense conversation. "What is this?" Ablina asked, her eyes widening with surprise, glued to the strange-looking buggy on four wheels without a horse hauling it. Alisar lowered the window of his red Volvo and smirked at her, "Welcome to the future. Climb in!"

They walked towards the car, and after a century, the sunlight touched their bodies, and their oldest friend, the Sun, suddenly became a foe. The beauty of darkness lured them in. Their bodies craved to run back into the arms of the peaceful night again. But the "Carriers of Light" had to bear the unbearable. Amaraya rolled her tongue and blew the air out of her mouth, lightly. "Vayuokoi," she chanted, and the blast of icy magical wind blew the hot, humid air away.

They sat in the Volvo, and one last time looked at their home from the car's back window. Their hearts bled as they swallowed the sight of their old lives.

On their journey, Alisar introduced the new world to the Bayers. There was a lot to take in, horses replaced by metal cars, plastic water bottles, high-rise buildings, mobile phones, airplanes; women openly wearing skin-tight trousers just like men, and what more women standing equal to men just like they were supposed to.

Ablina was all impressed with the new world. Raylina wanted revenge and justice; nothing else mattered to her. The background change hardly affected her in any way. She was not yet ready to open her eyes to the change.

Amaraya pretended to be interested, but deep inside, she, too, was preparing the list of potential suspects.

***

Alisar stopped at Malisia's Diner on the sidelines of the highway. As they walked inside, their eldritch dresses and exceptional beauty grabbed the attention of everyone present at the diner. The people at the diner stared at them with strange expressions. The Bayers vetted the diner thoroughly; the dark yellow stripes on the walls, ugly red tables, and black chairs creeped them out.

"Why are they looking at us like that?" Ablina asked innocently. Alisar chuckled and said, "Well, look around and look at yourselves… you girls look like 16th-century gothic princesses, and Amaraya… don't get me started." "It's not our fault that we spent 300-plus-something years in the tomb," Raylina said with irritation in her voice. Alisar simply nodded. "I think he is crazy, Abby," Raylina whispered. "Shhhh… don't say that… he's a witch too. He can hear us," Ablina said nervously. "Or maybe because he has ears, you crazy girl," Raylina chuckled.

Alisar looked at the girls with his judgy eyes, but then he realized that he was the mature one, so he ignored them. He ordered for Ablina and Amaraya. Raylina scared the waitress but managed to get what she wanted to eat on her own.

They waited for their food to arrive while Alisar went out to fill the gas. "Ma, why is grandpa involved in this?" Raylina asked. "I don't know, Ray, that's why we are going to play along, so shut up and behave," Amaraya ordered. "Yes, ma'am," Raylina said, giving up. Alisar came back, and they simply stared at him. The waitress came in with their orders, which broke the silence. "Nice," Amaraya said, taking a bite from her burger.

***

The front gates opened automatically, and Alisar drove the car inside, which wowed Amaraya. "Girls, wake up," Amaraya said with excitement. The house was shaped like a half triangle, and the walls were covered in glass, making it look dream-like. "Welcome to my home," he said to Amaraya.

Alisar was a choosey man; he liked things to be done his way, so he designed the house himself. The girls and Amaraya were carefully looking at the home with amazement, and Alisar liked showing off his creations, so he showed them every corner of his house.

"Mr. Vasaga, I am sorry for being late. I missed my train," said the woman. "Ohhh! Eraa, you are here, finally. Ladies, this is Eraa. She will help you out with your outfits and everything," Alisar said. "Is it?" Amaraya spoke with tension. "Don't worry. She knows, I trust her," Alisar said.

Raylina lacked many things, but she believed that she had mastered studying people through their eyes. It was her specialty, which she was very proud of. Eraa's honest dark brown eyes, delightful smile, slim rose-beige-colored body, and the slightly visible greys in her straightened hair made her appear to be a perfectly harmless mundane. Raylina summed up Eraa in two words—"simple woman."

Eraa briefly outlined herself and her family to the Bayers. She told them that she was a devoted mother and one of the most trusted friends of Alisar. She said that Alisar trusted her blindly, and she made sure never to break his trust.

The Bayers bonded with Eraa in a short time because of her simplicity and good nature. "Ladies, these are some outfits I picked up for you three. Alisar specifically told me to make you look acceptable in this world, so just go ahead and try the dresses. Oh yes, and Dmitri is here. He will take care of your makeover," Eraa stated.

***

Amaraya, Raylina, and Ablina's tastes were specific and unique. Amaraya picked up the grey formal sleeveless dress, which was elegant and simple; it perfectly fitted her curvy body. Raylina's dressing style was different; she always liked wearing her father's pants over her skirts, so she went with dark blue jeans and a white off-shoulder top with a clean black colored leather jacket. Ablina, on the other hand, was stylish; she fancied dressing up, so she picked up the chic yellow lacy flare dress from a hanger.

Dmitri arrived with his 2 assistants in the room. He looked at them with curiosity and discomfort. He asked them to sit on the chairs for the makeover. Their medieval attires and hairstyles scared him a little. He wanted to talk, but he was reluctant to do so.

"Look at them, OMG… they are hideous," Dmitri said with disgust. "Careful, Dmitri," Eraa warned him to mind his tongue. "Apologies, Ma'am," Dmitri said. Dmitri directed his assistants to take care of their hair and faces. The makeover was a big challenge for Dmitri, but he managed somehow.

Ablina decided to keep her long black hair. So, Dmitri gave her hair subtle layers with caramel highlights to make them look posher. She wore a pastel-green scarf to cover her sensitive, pale-colored neck. Her bright, innocent, honey-dipped eyes gave a clear idea of kindness running through her veins.

Ablina flaunted her new look in front of her sister. Raylina smiled and said, "Abby, in your case, the appearance couldn't deceive anyone."

Amaraya looked at her stunning, naive daughters, and for a moment, she forgot about the burning fire of revenge inside her. Then she looked at herself through her breathtaking dark brown eyes in the mirror and admired her new, elegant, medium-thick feathered haircut; she liked the way it suited her warm, almond-dipped skin.

"Amaraya Shaurayaveer Bayer, you can do this, you have to do this," she mumbled with sheer determination, and suddenly her head started recalling the headlines of her past. **"Princess of Shaurayaveer Dynasty eloped with a commoner—Amaraya Shaurayaveer married George Bayer! The all-time scandalous couple finally**

officiated! 'All ties cut, from our end,' said the
Shaurayaveer family."

Raylina spotted Alisar alone in the swimming pool
from the window. She rushed down to meet him.

***

Alisar's hypnotizing cobalt eyes followed Raylina as she
walked in his direction. He noticed her long brunette
hair chopped down and replaced with a medium-layered
haircut. Her outfit made him think of her as a beautiful
swan draped in a warrior's suit.

Raylina saw Alisar watching her, so she hastily wore
her jacket to cover her shiny red-rose skin. His gaze made
her uncomfortable. He came out of the pool and wrapped
a dark blue bathrobe around his masculine body. He
flipped his wet, dark brown hair back and walked closer
to her.

Alisar stared into Raylina's cognac eyes, which purely
screamed her fierceness out loud; they intimidated him,
but at the same time, they dethroned Alisar's heart in
every way. "You're a vicious man who talks dreamily; you
can fool my grandfather and my mother, but you cannot
fool me," she said in a serious tone. "I like the way you
think," he said and took a step back from her.

Alisar sat on the pool chair and looked up at Raylina's
face. "According to Eraa, people worship you, but for me,
you're just a man who manages my family affairs, nothing
else," she said clearly. Alisar stood up from the chair. He

held her by her arms and said, "It's true I am here to manage your family affairs. Your grandfather and mother have lots of unresolved issues, and my only work here is to patch that broken bond, and I will do anything for that." "I don't trust you," she said again.

Alisar loosened his grip on Raylina's arms and let her go, "Raylina, every part of you screams nothing but revenge. Don't drag revenge into your family's lives." He paused and hurtfully looked down. "It will destroy you in ways you cannot even imagine," he advised. She walked back into the house.

CHAPTER 3

DESOVIR

Change is misery, initially. Adapting to change is painful, and eventually, after fully accepting it, the change becomes regular. Starting life after a leap of a century was an arduous job; learning new things and technologies made the Bayers' lives a bit more complicated than it was before. But like Charles Darwin said, "Survival is Everything."

So, the Bayers adapted to the new world and learned new things, few of them with the help of Eraa and many with magic. Also, Alisar's memory potion assisted them in updating their knowledge of the new world. And the rest of the information was readily available on the "Internet."

Raylina caught Ablina splatting her clothes inside Raylina's suitcase. "Hey Ablina, you cannot just put everything in my bag," Raylina shouted angrily. "Ray, you have only packed four pairs. I could use a little bit of extra space," Ablina begged. "Girls, it's time. Alisar is waiting," said Amaraya. "Mother, these bags, I need help," Ablina pleaded as she dragged her overloaded suitcase to the door. Raylina swung her index finger and her luggage started moving by itself.

"Ray, you don't have to use your powers for small things like this," Ablina panted, pulling her suitcase onto the floor. "Abby darling, these little magic tricks are the only way to use our gifts. As our dearest mother will never teach us the real stuff, and even if she does, she won't let us use it anyway, right Ma?" Raylina taunted Amaraya purposely. "Look, Raylina, I don't care what you say. I am your mother, and you both will do as I say," Amaraya said furiously, using her veto authority.

"Ma… Ray… please stop all of this," Ablina begged, holding herself back from saying something regretful. "Aww… my sweet little obedient Abby. I know, as usual, you will not question Ma, but just so you know… our mommy dearest is planning to pay a visit to our Grandpa, whom we never meet. Who also happens to be on our who-killed-our-father/her husband suspect list," Raylina said it all in one breath. "I am going alone, and that's final. So scream all you want, Ray… you are not going," Amaraya said, taking a sip from a brown portable coffee mug. "Ridiculous," Raylina said and furiously left the room.

Ablina was quiet; she was more of a convincer than an arguer. She liked being reasonable and calm in the moments of cut-throat battles. "Abby, you understand, right?" Amaraya asked, hoping for Ablina to be on her side. "Ma, I do not always agree with Ray, but I think she is right this time. It's not safe for you to go alone. But if you really want to go to India, then please let us come with you," Ablina said as calmly as she could to convince Amaraya.

Alisar overheard their bitter and tense conversation. He thought it was better to blow off the spark before it turned into fire. "Hey, ladies, we should go," Alisar informed hesitantly, and without speaking any further, he swayed his fingers and moved their bags downstairs.

***

The deadly silence in the car was like a nuclear winter, cold and everlasting. Amaraya was always a strict parent. Her guidebook to parenting was filled with rules and restrictions. She hated her father for being a draconian follower of discipline and regulations, but she was just like her father—headstrong and lived her life by very strong principles. And no matter how much Raylina would disagree, she was obstinate and arrogant, just like her mother. "So, where are we heading?" Ablina asked. "Desovir," Amaraya informed.

Raylina blew out a resounding "I don't care" exhalation and laid her head down on Ablina's lap. "Alisar, thank you so much for helping us with everything," Ablina said to avoid the upcoming wrangle between Raylina and Amaraya. "No need, sweetheart," Alisar responded with a smirk and winked at Ablina from the rearview mirror. "Stop blushing. He's old and friends with Grandpa and probably a Grandpa," Raylina whispered. "Well, granny Ray, all thanks to his tonic, in our case, age literally doesn't matter," Ablina said.

Raylina briskly stood up and said, "Hey, I could definitely beat Alisar's silly tonic. It's not my fault that our sagacious mother doesn't let us explore." "Sagacious... hmmm... look who is finally reading," Ablina said in a mocking tone. Raylina frowned and moved to the edge of the seat.

"She is doing this to protect us, and she didn't want us to explore because magic brings death," Ablina explained. "I want to know the truth, Abby, plain, simple truth," Raylina reasoned and looked outside the window.

During the rest of their journey, Ablina and Raylina slept as there was not much to do or talk about. Amaraya read the book she had brought to kill boredom. While Alisar kept his eyes focused on the slippery mountain roads, trying to reach Desovir safely before night struck.

***

"Welcome to Desovir" was written in blue bold italic letters on a small white billboard on the roadside. "Here we are," Alisar said with relief. Raylina was still dizzy and uninterested. Ablina looked outside the window. Her traveler's heart started to jump up and down. The joy on her face was priceless. Alisar was peeking at her from the mirror, trying not to get caught; her innocent face reminded him of someone he lost a long time ago.

Desovir was a beautiful small town surrounded by high mountains and dense forest, isolated from the world. The town seemed to be very organized and disciplined. The houses in Desovir were built in a uniform line with huge gardens in the front. The town's center was marvelously architected, and every store had its own parking space.

Raylina had to let people think that she was ignorant, so she was covertly observing every detail of the town. She resisted a little, but then she couldn't stop herself from commenting, "Desovir... Nah, this town should be named Ablina," Raylina said, laughing at Ablina.

Alisar parked the car in front of a medium-sized white house with ample outer space and a garage. Amaraya saw the nameplate, and it bought a genuine smile on her face. "Bayer's Home," she read out loud. "Hey, don't be mushy; I have done everything as per your request, Ma'am. Now let's go and check out," Alisar said, and they all stepped out of the car.

The Bayers stood in the front yard, admiring the captivating view of their elegantly sculpted new home. The artist who designed the Bayer house was one of the greatest warlocks of all time. He manually carved the protection spells with real gold on the white-colored house walls. The detailing on the walls was magnificent yet undetected. Alisar personally looked over the house designs to make sure the house had its unique style. He did his best for the Bayers.

"Well, you have done good work, old man," Raylina said and winked at Alisar. Alisar was embarrassed and didn't speak back. "Ray Behave!" Amaraya said in a stern tone. The rising anger on her mother's face and Raylina's determination to annoy her mother more gave Ablina her clue that it was time to distract everyone. "I am excited to see the house from inside," Ablina said and successfully halted the big battle between her sister and mother for the time being. "Okay!" Alisar smiled, and they headed inside.

***

"Splendid," said Amaraya looking at the living room designed with a perfect blend of two different styles, Scandinavian and mid-century modern; the light-orange-colored couch was the highlight of the living room. The fireplace built in the corner of the room was rounded with big dark yellow pillows, making the whole setup look warm and cozy. Raylina praised the exquisite and ancient paintings hanging on the stair wall. "Upstairs is way better than this," Alisar said, and they all went up to see their rooms.

***

The first floor of Bayer's home had three rooms, each designed exclusively to match their taste.

Amaraya's room seemed like a traditional art gallery with a giant artistic wooden bed in the middle. Her room had limited furniture and more windows to let every ray of the light shine in. The hand-painted art piece on the warm jewel-toned wall was the masterwork of her room.

Ablina's room was colored in baby pink with white-themed bed stuff and furniture. It looked like a princess's room. Raylina's room, on the other hand, was a polar opposite to her sister's room. The room was designed with a modern approach. It had a large bed attached to the sidewalls and a big black and gold chandelier hanging in the middle of the room, giving the room a contrasting effect. It was stylish and refreshing.

Amaraya, Ablina, Raylina were stunned. The look on their faces was satisfying for Alisar. "Seems like you love it, Raylina," Alisar ridiculed. Raylina gave the death stare to Alisar, but he neglected it; he developed this particular response from Ablina and Amaraya. Raylina noticed that her rude behavior was not repelling him anymore; instead, he was having fun.

"Alisar, you are the best. I loved it," Amaraya said. "Anything for you, Amaraya, and your daughters," Alisar said, glancing at Ablina. Alisar gave them a black card with one golden strip on it and said, "Here's your credit card, use it to buy anything and the limit is… well, use it till it stops working," Alisar instructed them on how to use it.

"Thank you, Alisar," Ablina said cordially, trying to hide her happiness. "FYI, you know that… that's our money," Raylina specified. "Yes, indeed," he replied.

"Girls, magic is off-limits," Amaraya warned. "The world we live in will never accept us for who we are, so we have to keep our gifts a secret. Am I clear, Ray?" Amaraya asked. "What, Mother, I am not the only one with the… gifts! And when do we ever use it, I barely know any real spells," Raylina angrily argued.

"Well, honey, it's always the impulsive one who gets everyone killed," Alisar taunted. "You OLD MANNNNN… Pereliso," Raylina said. Alisar started puking blood. Alisar didn't counter-attack. Instead, he kept on suffering. "You are right, my dear old man. I am impulsive," she laughed. "Raylinaaaa no," Amaraya shouted in anger.

"Revfieliyekta," Amaraya said, and Alisar's blood vomit stopped. In the heat of the moment, Amaraya slapped Raylina. "Are you insane, Ray? How could you do this to him? He helped us, he saved us, and this is how you repay him?" She scolded. "It's alright, Amaraya, she cannot trust anyone, and that's not her fault. If someone had shot my father, I would have behaved just like her," Alisar said.

Alisar's words touched Raylina's heart. She was ashamed of what had just happened. She could not control her anger. Her soul was suffocating, and Alisar's words made her realize that. "I am sorry, Alisar. I shouldn't have done that," Raylina said, feeling embarrassed. Alisar smiled sweetly and said, "Apology accepted." It was the beginning of their friendship. "I think it would be healthy if we all rest now; we had enough for today," said Alisar. "I'll walk you out," Raylina said.

Raylina walked him to the door. She held the door open for him and waited for him to say something. "I am sorry, I almost bled you to death," she spoke restlessly, incapable of resisting herself from talking. "It's okay," he smiled lightly. "You are vicious, and there is something wrong about you, but you have a genuine reason, Alisar Vasaga, for whatever you are doing, and trust me… it's you who should start trusting people more," Raylina advised.

Alisar looked at Raylina's radiant face, shining bright as the moonlight fell on it, and then into her eyes that were brimming with nothing but pure emotions—anger but also love; confusion mixed with kindness, questions, but unmatched loyalty, all in one. "Good night," Alisar said and left from there, smiling.

***

Raylina locked the front door and went up to her room. She took off her old burgundy satchel from her shoulder and gently placed it on her bed. She took out a book wrapped in red silk cloth. She closed her eyes, and bowed her head down to the holy book, and prayed.

"Ya Enam Vetti Hantaram Yash Chainam Manyate Hatam. Ubhau tau Na Vijanito Nayam Hanti Na Hanyate (Those who think that the soul can be killed or can kill; both are ignorant. For truly, the soul does not kill, nor can it be killed)," Raylina heard her father's voice, reciting a verse from the world's oldest scripture, "The Bhagavad Gita." She opened her eyes, and the view brought her back to reality.

Until now, the burning anger in Raylina's heart dried out the tears her eyes made, but a small glimpse of her father's love cracked the cloud of her grief, setting it free from the cage of strength, showering down on her burning rage, letting the flood in her eyes flow.

CHAPTER 4

A DAY IN HELL

Raylina stared blankly in the mirror. "Raylina Bayer, why do you always lose your head?" she spoke to herself while untangling her miserable hair. Finally, after thoroughly combing her hair, Raylina looked back in the mirror. "Ugh, this is more pathetic," she said, messing up her well-combed hair, cursing at her decent and presentable self.

At a snail's pace, Raylina took each step. She was a brave person, indeed, but like any other person, there was one thing which she feared in this whole wide world, and it was her mother. "Hell isn't that bad," Raylina thought and marched forward until she saw her mother arguing with Alisar at the dining table.

Raylina stopped. She hid behind the nearest wall and started eavesdropping. "That's absurd, you are lying, you know it's not the case, my father killed him, and I am going to prove that," Amaraya said firmly. "Ami, if your father wanted to kill you and your girls, do you think he would have waited 305 years? Huh?" Alisar said with annoyance. "You and my father want me to believe that a mythological freak 'Vaylar' is involved in killing my husband? Bravo, I like your creativity, Alisar," Amaraya angrily taunted. "Well, he comes off as real," Alisar said.

"Ray, this is next-level bad," Ablina says in a hushed tone from behind. "Abby," Raylina gasped, holding her chest to calm down. She held Ablina by her arm and said, "You gave me a heart attack." Amaraya heard their whispering and instantly refrained from talking further. "Girls," Amaraya said, pouring herself a cup of ginger tea.

Raylina and Ablina rambled towards the breakfast table as though nothing had happened. Alisar greeted joyfully, and Amaraya requested Raylina to get plates for everyone. Ablina felt a little odd, seeing her mother sitting peacefully and enjoying her tea. She wondered why her mother was not scolding Raylina for what she did to Alisar last night. It was like her mother's memories were wiped out, which was good, though, she thought.

Raylina came and sat beside Ablina, setting the plates for everyone for breakfast. "Ray, what's happening?" Ablina said, trying to maintain a fake smile on her face. "I don't know," Raylina said, looking at Alisar and her mother.

Alisar pressed his left elbow on the table, rested his face on his palms, and stared at the Bayers. "Ami, you should tell them," he said in a stern tone. Ablina feared that something wasn't right. "Ma, what's happening?" Ablina asked nervously. "Girls, Alisar knows who killed your father," Amaraya said.

Raylina knew the name, but she wanted to discern the story, so she bottled up her know-it-all self and pretended to be clueless. "Who is it, Mother?" Raylina asked. "Vaylar Scandios," Amaraya said lightly. "Vaylar, it's just a name. How could he? Why would he?" Ablina asked. "Wait, you know?" Raylina said with amusement. "I read Sister," Ablina bragged.

Alisar folded his arms, resting his back on the orange back post of the chair, and began, "The magic which flows in your veins is different from that of other people." "Different... how? What do you mean by that?" Ablina asked curiously. "It is because you both come from a special line of..." Alisar hesitated. "Of Śirā Ragata," he completed. "What is that?" Ablina asked dimly. "Something out of your syllabus and completely useless," Amaraya said and abruptly cut off the discussion. "Ma, don't keep us hanging. It's our right," Raylina insisted. "You will know what I want you to know. Now get up, and go to school," Amaraya ordered.

Amaraya threw a death stare at Alisar for revealing too much. "May I have a word with you, Alisar?" Amaraya said, trying to hide her emotions. Alisar cleared his throat and said, "Of course." He followed Amaraya to the living room.

Raylina was still sitting at the dining table, waiting for her mother to give her proper answers. But Ablina knew that now was not the time to poke the bear, so she dragged Raylina out of the dining room. "Ablina, what is your problem?" Raylina said with irritation. "Don't provoke Ma. She is already mad. She will skin you alive," Ablina warned. Raylina rolled her eyes and said, "I am not scared of her." "Ya, I know, but I am scared, so please," Ablina begged.

***

"Are you out of your mind?" Amaraya's caged anger busted out. "I thought you told them," Alisar said calmly. "We already discussed that I would tell them about this… So, why did you put your nose in between?" Amaraya said rudely. "They should know about it… it's their legacy; hell, they are legacies," Alisar said. "I didn't spend 3 centuries in that dark, suffocating coffin to get them killed… I am not taking my kids to India, and that's final," Amaraya said firmly.

"You know, if that man we are talking about exists, then the only man who can protect you and your daughters is your father, Ami," Alisar said, trying to pour some sense into her. Amaraya looked out of the window and saw Ablina and Raylina talking near the car, and said, "I am not taking them… ever."

***

Alisar wore his gladiator glasses as he stepped into the sun. He unhooked his bright red coat with one hand and walked towards the Bayer sisters. "Look, Abby, Alisar is walking out alive! Or should we say, Mr. Lucky, since he survived mother's wrath," Raylina laughed at her witty comment. "Please stop," Ablina said, stopping Raylina from starting another war-like situation with Alisar. "Let's go, girls," Alisar said, ignoring Raylina's snide comments.

"So, our dear family friend, tell me something. According to you, Vaylar wants to take away our powers?" Raylina asked. "No, it's not about the powers, it's more than that," Alisar answered, after a long silence. "More than what?" Raylina asked impatiently. Alisar looked away and pretended not to hear her question.

Day by day, the mystery was getting messier. The Bayer sisters were marching towards a maze from which the only way out was not to get inside it in the first place. "Why kill my father?" Raylina questioned in a low tone. "Let's get you both to school," Alisar said and opened the door for Raylina. She raised her eyebrows, sighed, and sat in. Alisar deliberately ignored her questions as the beans weren't his to spill.

***

"Desovir Public School" Ablina read out loud with excitement in her eyes and her voice. "Alisar, thank you so much for dropping us," Ablina said. "You're always welcome, princess," Alisar said.

"God…" Raylina mumbled, staring with the least interest at the school's name board. "Good luck," Alisar scoffed. "Get lost," Raylina said with a half-smile. Ablina saw the strange connection building up between her sister and Alisar. She wanted to ask Raylina about it, but she remained silent. "Bye," Alisar winked at Raylina, which made her blush. "Bye," Raylina said sweetly. Alisar left, and the girls headed to school.

***

Raylina and Ablina stood before the crimson red, box-like building with creepers rolling around its windows and a huge playground in the middle. Jocks, nerds, losers, and cheerleaders dressed up funny, loitering around in their various social covens. "Death isn't life's only flaw," Raylina said while observing the perfect high school framework.

Ablina was ebullient about going to school. For her, it was like a dream come true. Before ages, she never really had a chance to study like an average child. Now that she finally had the chance, she was planning to gather the feel of being at high school as much as possible.

Raylina, on the other hand, hated any mode of education; her goal was to find her father's killer, and high school was more than a deviation—it was an unwanted disaster. "This is going to be amazing," Ablina said with excitement. "You are impossible, Abby. Look at them; they all smell and suck," Raylina said with a nauseated face. "This time, we will make some friends for real and be social, so stop being so repellent, Ray," Ablina said.

"Abby, go ahead. I always have your back; just don't get knocked up. We might be immortals, but our organs work just fine, which makes us fertile for life," Raylina laughed wickedly. "I am your sister, Ray," Ablina said in an angry tone. "Darling, I am meant to be your life's reality check guru. I was born with you for it," Raylina said sarcastically.

Raylina and Ablina continued their little fight schedule of the day. Raylina always thought her daily fights with her sister brought her a stroke of good luck, so like a cultic ritual, she followed it scrupulously. Ablina and Raylina somehow managed to find the counselor's chamber and waited for the counselor.

***

A middle-aged plumpish man entered the chamber. He pulled out his rolling chair from under the table and finally noticed them. He adjusted the tilted nameplate on his table for them to see. "Derik Whinhart, counselor," Raylina read in her mind.

"Good morning, Raylina and Ablina Bayer," Derik Whinhart said while looking at their names in their files. He waited for their response, but Ablina was blanked out, and Raylina was in no mood to talk.

Due to extreme nervousness, Ablina's body began shivering, and the cold sweats in her hands wetted the blue file folder she was holding. She clenched her maroon floral dress to reduce the tension. But it didn't help her either, so instantly, she unclenched the dress and kept her hands on the table. Raylina saw her sister freaking out and said, "Abby, he is just a counselor."

Mr. Whinhart stamped their files, handed them their schedules, and asked them to resume their routine at Desovir High.

***

Raylina already hated the place, and Ablina was imagining the future. Raylina started walking out to the main door. "Where are you going? You cannot bunk class," Ablina said worriedly. "Raylina, please, Ma will kill you," Ablina begged. "Good for you, Abby," Raylina said and kept on walking.

"Wait, Ray," Ablina said, walking hurriedly behind Raylina, trying to keep up with Raylina's speed. Ablina's high heels restricted her speed; she struggled to walk, but she was desperate to fit in the new world, so she was ready to go all the way. "Ray," she thundered.

Raylina stopped after hearing her sister's distress call. She turned her head and saw her sister on the floor. "I told you not to wear these," Raylina said, pointing at Ablina's black heels. Raylina caught everyone laughing at Ablina. She saw Ablina's tears dropping down on her hand, and that was it for her. Raylina helped Ablina stand up and yelled, "Walk away," to the crowd making fun of her sister.

Ablina instantly forgave Raylina because she agreed with her; the heels were too high. "You're hurt; let's get you out of here," Raylina said. "Yes to the class. Pleaseeee," Ablina asked with a pouty face and puppy eyes. "You owe me, no nagging for the next 20 minutes," Raylina chuckled softly. "Done," Ablina said, holding her sister's arm as a crutch, and limped towards their first class.

Ablina's happiness was Raylina's top priority. Raylina never said it aloud, but Ablina was the "tie" that connected her to the world. And after their father's death, Ablina was the reason that kept her ongoing. Without her, Raylina would have given up a long time ago.

Ablina identified the classroom and directed Raylina towards it. As they walked, they suddenly ran into a moderately tall, good-looking guy wearing a black tank top with a green sewed lion logo on it. His burgundy angular fringes highlighted his compelling black eyes and heavenly olive-toned complexion.

"Astor, love, the game is about to begin," said a girl wearing a matching outfit, black skirt, and white stripe crop top with the same logo. Ablina figured out that they were together and that his name was "Astor," an unusual name, she thought, spellbound by his handsome face. "You must be the new sisters joining us. Hello, I am Olivia Mark, the head cheerleader, and student president," she bragged in her fake throaty voice.

"Hi, I am Ablina Bayer, and this is my sister, Raylina," Ablina said nervously. "God, Abby, you are a 300-plus-something-year-old witch," Raylina whispered. "Raylina, huh," Astor said with a mischievous look on his face.

"What... is something wrong with my name? Do you find it funny?" Raylina said aggressively and moved closer to him.

"Angry much..." Astor said playfully. Raylina clasped her hands behind her back and said, "Don't mess with me." The unnecessary addition of high school drama was getting on Raylina's nerves. She was annoyed about not having enough time to process everything happening around her. Ablina drooling over a random high school guy, her mother being a complete tyrant, and on top of all, her father's killer roaming free was making her more frustrated than she already was.

"Raylina, please calm down," Ablina said and pulled her away from Astor. "I am sorry, Astor. Let's go, Ray," Ablina excused, and they went into the classroom. Raylina wanted to run out of that place as fast as possible, but Ablina was angry and angry Ablina was scarier than her mother; so, she sat beside Ablina quietly, opened her notebook, and started scribbling in it.

Vaylar... Vaylar... Vaylar...

"Professor Angelina Markoff" entered the classroom. Ablina was deeply and instantly inspired by Miss Markoff's personality and confidence. Her model-like slim figure, her stunning strawberry-colored vest, and her admiral hairdo were so good that the most beautiful girls in the school were nothing in front of her.

"What are you doing, Ray? The professor is already here," Ablina said pleadingly. "Okay, fine, Mom. By the way, we are in school—drop the professor thing," Raylina said.

The professor wrote "1692 Salem witch trials" on the green board in capitals. Ablina and Raylina read it, and the real stories of witch hunters killing witches started to boil up in their heads' cauldron.

"Students, we are going to talk about one of history's most dreadful event, where many innocent lives were taken on just mere suspicion," Miss Markoff said. "Innocent… many of them were actual witches!" The guy sitting in the corner interrupted the class.

Raylina and Ablina looked at him. He was wearing a light blue jersey and ripped jeans; his glossy black textured bangs covered his broad forehead, and he looked like he came straight from his bed. His piercing electric blue eyes were hard to ignore, but his opinion towards the topic scored him a second spot on Raylina's kill list.

"Mr. Visac Levin, do you have something to say?" Miss Markoff asked. "You called them innocent, and I agree that some of them were, but not all," Visac said in an unwavering tone. "I think killing in the name of superstition is wrong," Miss Markoff stated. "So, you think witches aren't real?" Visac questioned her. "So, you think they are?" Miss Markoff countered his question with a question.

"Real, or not, burning people like some leg piece is inhuman and unjustifiable," Ablina said furiously.

The heat in the room escalated to the next level. The tension between them was increasing with each stare. Ablina was never the type to lose temper, but hearing Visac speak ridiculous things about her species became personal. Visac managed to disturb her inner peace. She wanted to go all nuclear on him with all the magic spells she had ever learned, but then he was right. Not all of them were spotless.

"Mr. Levin and Miss. Bayer, let's not turn this classroom into a battlefield," Miss Markoff said to stop the rising war. Ablina's first day was officially ruined because of Visac. She gloomily sat on her bench, without any interest in the class for the next 30 minutes.

CHAPTER 5

FORBIDDEN JUNK

On her way home, all Ablina could think of was what had happened in Miss Markoff's class. Her equanimous nature was disturbed by Visac Levin. She wanted to forget it all, but could not seem to do so. Her excitement died on day one, and she equally started hating Desovir High like her sister. Meanwhile, Raylina was unruffled by what had happened at school, as she never had any expectations of people or places. Her attitude helped her survive the first day of high school.

Ablina opened the door rigorously and went straight to her room. "Abby," Amaraya called her, but Ablina didn't answer. "What happened to her?" Amaraya asked Raylina tensely. Though the worried look on Amaraya's face bothered Raylina, deep down, she appreciated Ablina for not behaving like a goody-two-shoe in front of their mother.

Raylina smiled sarcastically and said, "Disappointed, Ma?" "Well, yes, I thought she was the decent one in the family," Amaraya said scornfully. Her mother's snide comment got to her. "Don't worry, she is still the same, just occupied with a little boy drama," Raylina said, dropping the boy bomb, and left before Amaraya could answer her back.

Raylina opened her room and saw a cardboard box pack on her bed. She smiled as she read the "Forbidden Junk" labeled on the side of the box written in her handwriting. She removed the tapes pasted on the box and picked up the only thing in it that was most dear to her, an old iron-grey-colored diary.

Raylina turned the diary's cover to view inside. Her fingertips felt the roughness of the stony paper as she touched the letters randomly engraved in black-gold ink. The moistened magic of ink printed on her fingers, emanating the scent of mist. She smiled, recalling how happy she was before all of this happened, and said, "Dad, I wanted Grandma's miniature diamond crossbow as a family heirloom, not a book called 'Diary of Chryorold.' Now I need to ask your nerd daughter how to access this."

***

Ablina was resting on her bed with earplugs on. She was scrolling through Visac's social media profile. "*Skydiver, Traveler, Carpe diem.* Huh," Ablina said in a tone of disbelief while reading his "Bio."

Visac's shirtless photo appeared, and the scrolling stopped. Ablina's eyes gawked at his toned muscular body. "Whatever," she grumbled and looked away from her phone screen. After a minute, she looked back at her phone, and this time her eyes caught something else which weirdly shook her heart. It was a picture of Visac and Olivia Mark with the caption *"Madly in love!"* on it.

Ablina stopped scrolling, and threw her phone aside carefully on the bed, and closed her eyes. She wasn't exactly sure why she was feeling that way, but something moved inside her.

"Ablina, get up. We need to go," Raylina came rushing into her room and muddled Ablina's deep thinking. "Where? What happened?" Ablina asked vacuously. "Remember, Chryorold?" Raylina questioned. "Yes, Papa lost it during his visit to Spain," Ablina answered.

Raylina grinned and leaned closer to Ablina. She kept her arm around Ablina's shoulders to comfort her for what she was about to tell. "What if I tell you that I stole it?" Raylina unveiled. "You did what? Raylina…" Ablina snorted and almost choked on her saliva.

"I was angry at him for scolding me because I failed that stupid test he made us take, so I went in and stole his favorite diary," she said casually. "Papa was depressed for months because of it," Ablina yelled at her loudly. "Well, I was depressed too, because of him," Raylina clarified.

Ablina reprimanded Raylina for about 10 minutes. She tried her best to make Raylina understand that the sinful crime she committed was immature and horrible. On the other side, Raylina rolled her eyes to a point where her eye balls and lids became stagnant.

Ablina saw no sign of guilt on her sister's face, so she quit talking. Raylina puckered her lips, took a deep breath, and cautiously said, "If you are done chastising me, can you please tell me how to use this?" Ablina stared at her in disbelief, wondering what her parents did wrong while raising Raylina. "You are brilliant, my sister; you stole things and didn't even know how to use them, Bravo!" Ablina said furiously. "Ya, let's go now," Raylina replied, sassing her way out of Ablina's room.

***

Raylina and Ablina went into Raylina's room; they locked the door, and Raylina handed her the diary. "Ablina Bayer, I would appreciate it if you could," Raylina simpered wickedly.

"You know I will," Ablina said, rolling her eyes. "Diary of Chryorold is a search engine. Every detail about magic can be accessed from this diary," Ablina said. "You mean Book," Raylina interrupted. "One more word, and I will tell Ma about this," Ablina threatened. Raylina mimed about zipping her mouth and agreed to Ablina's threat.

"Chryorold" can only be accessed by the heir of Shaurayaveer. It needs a secret magical word chanted by the Shaurayaveer bloodline and a drop of blood to get the information," Ablina stated. Raylina raised her hand to ask a question like an obedient little girl. "Yes," Ablina said. "Okay, so if I am correct, Papa needs Ma's blood to use it?" Raylina asked. "Yes," Ablina replied. "What's the word?" Raylina asked. "Varnadoveresias," Ablina said.

"Varnadoveresias," Raylina said, dropping her blood droplets on the stony paper. As the drops of her blood touched the paper, the random letters engraved on the stony paper started to jumble up. "What do we do now?" Raylina asked. "What do you think I am?" Ablina said, giving a blank stare at Raylina. "Dude, you are a bookworm. Aren't you supposed to know about this? I thought you listened to his boring heavy lectures," Raylina said. "That is insulting; you are not the only one who sleeps with open eyes in the classroom," Ablina said.

Ablina tried her best to bury her rage, but Raylina's devil-may-care attitude made that impossible. "Okay, looks like we have to figure it out now," Raylina said, studying the book. "Ya," Ablina spoke in her head. "Vaylar," Raylina said with her closed eyes, and information started to appear on the pages. It was handwritten with the footnotes. "Classy Man," Raylina said, looking at footnotes with a big smile on her face.

"He traveled to a mystical world; he found strength, but lost himself."

"He returned home with a lost soul and a magical seed."

"Vaylar Alisoyar Madrianil Scandios," a self-proclaimed God of Magic, was said to be born somewhere in the world's northern region. For some people, Vaylar is nothing but a

tale of fickle imagination, but he is as real as the oceans and mountains for those who have seen him with their eyes. Those who believe he exists say that before he became the most dangerous warlock in the world, he was a simple homely peasant boy who loved the stories of magic.

One thousand years ago, Vaylar began his search for ultimate power. He traveled miles to find the answer, and at last, he found what he was looking for: "Magic." And after a long hustle, he managed to bring magic from the other world to our world, but he paid the price for it.

The power Vaylar carried within him was beyond what his human form could handle. The only way to survive was to share the magic with others, so he chose the men he trusted the most and shared the poison flowing through his veins. But the magic he passed on was said to be the magic of the devil. Only a few of his men survived the poison.

Dark magic gave Vaylar everything, and in return, he gave his everything to dark magic. His hunger for power turned into madness, and to feed the growing madness inside him, he began a never-ending blood bath. He slaughtered masses of witches and sacrificed many innocent human lives. Many men tried hunting down Vaylar, but no one ever succeeded.

A piece of advice, if you are looking for him, stop the quest.

PS: It is okay to live with half-knowledge rather than knowing the devastating truth.

Note: *Some bloodlines carry the magical gene which can control the universe if brought together.*

"That's it. Well, this is insufficient, nonsensical crap! This man just wasted a rare paper," Raylina said, staring at the page, expecting more information to pop up. "Managed to bring the magic..." Ablina said with confusion.

Raylina kept staring at the page with her mouth open. "So..., he got magic from the other world we don't know about, and he was not able to contain it, so he passed it on, and then he killed our father. Why?" Raylina maundered. "I don't know, Ray, but I think we have to rule out this man," Ablina said. "This Vaylar guy sounds like a poorly written character from a flop TV soap opera," Raylina mumbled, furiously closing the diary.

Raylina kept the diary on the bed and tensely sat on the floor. Ablina sat alongside her and said, "Ray, please don't be disheartened. We will find that person who killed Papa." Ablina tried to console her sister, but Raylina's heart was dipped in sadness, and it needed more than comforting words from her sister—it wanted answers. Raylina laid her head down on Ablina's shoulder. "Ray, you cannot let yourself down with this," Ablina said, thinking about "Vaylar."

"Ting Tong" the Bayer sisters heard the doorbell ring. "I'll go check," Raylina said, and she cached the diary in her closet. Raylina grabbed Ablina's hand and asked her to stay behind.

***

"What are you doing here?" Raylina said loudly to the man standing at the door. "Astor," Ablina said, gawking at him in surprise. Astor was about to explain, but someone came from behind and said, "Little Brother." "Alisar," Ablina said, staring at Alisar with her mouth wide open in shock. "Astor and you... Brothers... You guys are freakishly old," Raylina said with astonishment.

Raylina was okay with the newfound fact. Ablina was still in shock, trying to process the whole moment; she was nervous, and the little butterfly for her recent crush pinked her cheeks. "That's what I was trying to tell you guys earlier," Astor cleared. "I am sorry about the morning, Astor," Ablina stuttered.

Raylina noticed Ablina's red cheekbones, which suddenly started shining brighter than the sun. The tiny sweat droplets on her upper lips, continuously playing with a strand of her hair, were obvious clues of Ablina developing a little crush. "Not again," Raylina mumbled, squinting her eyes in irritation. Alisar patted Astor's back hard and said, "No need to apologize to this fool." "Whatever, loser," Astor said annoyingly.

Amaraya stood there watching them. Alisar understood her animosity, so before she could say anything, he said, "This is my little brother, Astor." Amaraya was deeply puzzled, hundreds of decades spent, and she had no clue that Alisar had a brother. Alisar read her doubt-filled expressions, but he didn't over-explain; he acted placidly. "Nice to meet you," Amaraya said after a long, suspenseful pause. Amaraya served tea to them, and they chatted casually about world affairs.

Astor sensed the stress on his brother's face, so he jumped in to rescue his older brother. "I am here to invite you to the party; it's a bonfire, and you guys are new, so I thought you should come with me," Astor suggested.

"Let's go," Ablina instantly agreed, trying to act cool in front of Astor. However, Raylina resisted because her mind was still thinking about "Vaylar." After some begging and crying, Raylina agreed to go.

Raylina noticed Alisar trying to slip away from the conversation, so before he could duck his way out, she grabbed his car keys from his pants' side-pocket. "You are coming with us, old man. I am not going alone to their stupid party," she said in an ordering tone. Alisar, with a lack of enthusiasm, said, "Okay, princess, but please ask Amaraya first."

"I don't mind, just be careful, and stay close to Alisar. Back by 11," Amaraya instructed. "Why don't you join us?" Alisar invited. "You look like 18. I don't," Amaraya chuckled. "Come on, Ami, you still got that juvenile charm," he winked.

The Bayer sisters looked at their mother with confusion. "What is he saying?" Raylina asked. "Nothing," Amaraya laughed. Alisar, in a desultory fashion, followed them out to the car, and they left for the bonfire.

CHAPTER 6

THE BONFIRE

The way nature's light blended with manmade fire had a particular effect on Raylina. The overwhelming view of the stars and the moon clubbing up with the bonfire to stir away the night's darkness made her feel the ataraxia it produced. Rock music playing aloud on the woofer irked her a little at first, but the song's meaningful lyrics comforted her heart. After spending 2 weeks in the new era, she began to feel like she belonged in that century. The setting succeeded in distracting her from reality, at least for a while.

Ablina was thrilled to be there. She wanted to be in a social group, and this place was the perfect opportunity to fit in. Everyone stared at them as they entered the party with Astor. "So, Ablina, what is your specialty?" Astor asked. "Well, I can sing," Ablina said innocently, trying to give Astor the satisfying answer. She wanted to be more than a typical, centuries-year-old teenager.

Astor cried out of laughter. He flirtingly tucked the strand of Ablina's hair behind her left ear, trying to look away from her pink lips, but epically failing to do so. Her childish actions were slowly growing on him, "What I meant was your specialty in magic," he described. "Ohh, that, well, I don't use magic regularly. Our mother is not okay with us using magic," Ablina said restlessly. "And yet she doesn't mind drinking immortality tonic now, and then. Bit of hypocrite. Eh?" He said bluntly.

Raylina's eyebrows came closer, and the vertical lines on her forehead started surfacing, "Don't cross your line, Astor," Raylina warned in a soft tone. "I am sorry. I didn't mean in that way," he said crisply. "And one more thing, Astor, our grandfather, he taught your brother to make those tonics," Ablina said bitterly. "Hey, guys, don't fight like this," Alisar said to break it off.

Ablina and Raylina gave Astor a baleful stare like they wanted to rip his head off. "Hey, Ablina," said Olivia and interrupted their conversation. "We are starting the game. Why don't you guys join us?" Olivia asked. "I am out of this, Abby. You can go," Raylina said. "Ya, let us get out of here," Alisar said and walked away with Raylina. "Yes, I would love to, let's go," Ablina said, lacking enthusiasm and left with Olivia and Astor.

The roulette was set, and people circled around it. Olivia took the megaphone and asked everyone to listen keenly. "So, folks, Let it BEGINNN…" and the crowd cheered loudly.

Ablina was deeply offended by Astor's snide comments. Her dreams of being a part of the new world were squashed in a minute by Astor's behavior. For her, a person was either good or bad; there was no in-between, but what naive Ablina didn't understand was that the world was not as simple as she believed it to be—it was both dark and light ruling the world together.

Astor read what was written on Ablina's dim face, but he wasn't sure how to fix the mistake he had made. But the mistake was made, and the only way to fix it was to apologize, which Astor felt he was bad at, especially when it involved him being utterly genuine. He sighed deeply and bent a little to reach her height, "I am sorry. Please forgive me. I didn't mean to disrespect you or your family." Ablina smiled a little, letting go of her anger, forgiving him, "I don't know how to play this." "Can you teach me?" She asked. "Follow my lead," Astor winked.

***

Raylina and Alisar were sitting close on the bench near the lakeside, gazing at the reflection of the full white moon and the hot, bright red-yellow bonfire entwining in each other, creating a perfect contrast on the black canvas of the lake. It looked like the sun and the moon, making love in the darkness of the lake, emanating the flames of their passion, screaming to the world that it's worth falling in love and getting destroyed.

Raylina turned her head towards him and said, "What are you thinking?" Alisar didn't answer her question. He laughed, and tears came rolling down his cheeks. He was terrified of the words he held inside him, as they were slowly rebelling against him, urging him to come out and crush him.

Alisar rested his head on Raylina's shoulder. She felt his unspoken pain. Before this, Raylina deemed that she was the most courageous amongst the Bayers, but it changed right at that moment. Her courage was challenged by Alisar's pain. She chuckled softly and said, "And that's why we are alike." They found company in each other's solitude.

***

People randomly kissing each other, girls going topless, and giving guys lap dances made Ablina uncomfortable. She wanted to mingle in, but she couldn't. She wanted to embrace the ways of the modern world, but her skepticism became an unwanted hurdle.

Olivia was sitting on Astor's lap. His hands were traveling to all the inappropriate places on her body as he kissed her. Their little public display of affection annoyed Ablina. She felt abandoned and a little jealous. Her excitement for the night was slowly deflating as it progressed.

"Hey, Astor, I am feeling a little tired. Can you give me the car keys?" Ablina asked gently, looking everywhere, but at him. "Is everything alright? I'll come with you," he said with concern. "No," she started to explain.

Olivia's eyes broadened as she saw Astor's worried face. She wrapped his arms around her waist to show Ablina that Astor was hers and said, "Oh, come on, Astor, she is a big girl. She can take care of herself, let her go." "Yes, it is alright," Ablina said tiredly. Astor gave her the car keys and said, "I am coming in 15 minutes. And then we'll leave." "Okay," she said and left from there back to the car.

Ablina jadedly headed to the parking lot. "Which one is Astor's?" she mumbled, staring at the similar-looking 20 black cars parked in line. She was all drained out. Her exhausted mind failed to remember that the car had an automatic lock system; one button pressed, and she could have easily spotted the vehicle.

Ablina closed her eyes to remember the number plate. But she didn't exactly recall the number plate. However, she was able to recognize the directions. She started pacing and finally spotted her white jacket on the car's dashboard. "Yeah, that's it," she said cheerily.

Ablina took the car keys from her rugged white jeans. She opened the door, and as she sat in, someone grabbed her hand. Thud… the man slammed the car's door with drastic force and thrust her back on the door, covering her mouth with his black leathery gloved hands.

Ablina struggled hard to see his face but was incapable of removing his mask. Her anxiety made her forget the two elemental fighting spells she knew, so she chose to go with the original defensive approach.

Ablina punched her elbows back in full power and hit the man on his chest. He jerked back a little. Ablina used these two seconds of release. "HELPPP…" she cried. He rapidly grabbed her and covered her mouth. This time he was gazing at her with his wild, bloody red eyes.

Ablina stopped struggling; it was like her body was paralyzed in fear by staring into his wild, bloody red eyes. She was terrified and regretted coming alone. Ablina was losing her hope of getting free from this man, but then she heard a sharp sound of metal striking his back. The masked man stumbled a little, trying not to fall down. Ablina slightly tilted her head and saw "Visac Levin" holding a metal rod in his hand. She was shocked to see him there, as she never expected someone like him to rescue someone like her.

Visac raised the metal rod again to hit the masked man, but the man ran away before it. Ablina breathed with relief and fainted in his arms. "Ablina, wake up… hey… wake up…" Visac repeatedly said to regain her consciousness.

Visac hurriedly retracted his everlasting gaze from her angelic face as she opened her eyes. "Ablina, are you okay?" Visac asked. His concerned face melted the layer of hate in her heart. Ablina smiled and nodded faintly. The sign of relaxation on Visac's face was crystal clear. Their little feud was resolved at that moment.

Visac lifted Ablina and took her in the car. "Thank you, I don't know what I would have done without your help," she said. "Ohhh simple, you would have gotten yourself kidnapped," Visac replied with the devilish smile on his face. "HAHAHA, so you really want to start this again?" Ablina asked sneeringly. Visac bent down his head a little, came closer to Ablina, and said, "I don't mind."

Visac and Ablina stared into each other's eyes, and their denying rebellious teenage minds started to waver for a moment. Visac pulled himself away from Ablina as he heard someone coming. It was Raylina and Alisar. Ablina quickly put on her artificial smile to hide the incident from her sister.

Raylina examined the look on their faces; she figured out that it was terrible timing. "Looks like we disturbed Ablina and Visac," Raylina smirked teasingly. "Nothing is going on," Ablina immediately responded. "I have to go," Visac said to dodge the awkwardness, and he left. "What is wrong with you? Did I say anything about you disappearing with Alisar?" Ablina asked quietly.

Raylina's facial expression abruptly changed from taunting to blank; she was given a taste of her own medicine. Raylina knew that whatever happened today at lakeside was something she had never felt in her life. Maybe it was because she had never dated anyone before. But whatever it was, it was different and felt right. "I think we should leave. It's late," Alisar insisted.

They all headed home. Astor kept talking about Olivia's strip dance at the bonfire, unaware of the weird quietness in the car. Raylina ignored Astor's nonsense, lost in watching the city passes by, breathing the country air.

Ablina was strangely quiet. Her mind was in a dilemma. She wasn't sure whether to tell this to her mother and sister or not. Ablina never imagined that she could get attacked like this, and Visac would be the one saving her. It was hard for her to forget about those fierce red eyes, his touch, the helplessness; everything was too much for her.

***

Ablina went straight to her room, picked out her lemon-green comfy shorts and blue crop top from the closet, and stepped into the bathroom. She stood under the shower with her eyes closed, trying to wash the night out of her system. And for a moment, the water did seem to wash away her thoughts.

After standing in the hot shower for 10 minutes, Ablina opened her eyes and saw the red water on the tiles. As she looked closely, she realized that it was her own blood coming out of her arms. The wounds on her arms were at the exact spot where the masked man had grabbed her.

Ablina quickly got out of the shower and looked at her arms in the mirror, "It's impossible," she said to herself, wondering how she got the wound marks on her arms, as she clearly remembered that the man was wearing gloves. She wrapped the towel around her body and rushed out of the bathroom.

***

Ablina went to Raylina's room and quietly opened the closet to pull out the Chryorold hidden between Raylina's clothes. She silently walked out of Raylina's room and headed back to her room.

Ablina locked the door and opened the diary, thinking about the man who attacked her at the bonfire. "No, I cannot do this right now. I need some time to process all of this," she said and closed the book instantly.

Ablina lay down on her bed, trying to sleep, but the more she tried to avoid her thoughts, the more restless she became. "Ahhhhhh… Mind works faster when you want it to slow down," Ablina said, covering her face with the soft pillow.

The cold wind blew, and the vase near the window table fell. Ablina stumped out of her bed quickly and walked towards the windows. While locking the windows, she felt a presence in her room, like someone was watching from behind. She turned around, breathing shakily, wishing that it was all in her head and nothing was standing behind her. But her prayers were unanswered, and there he was, standing in front of her, staring at her with his wild, bloody red eyes.

This time the man didn't cover Ablina's mouth. It was already deadened with terror. The man removed his hood and let his short, wavy, messy black hair fall out like a waterfall. He then unmasked himself, and an innocent face behind those wild, bloody red eyes made her think of the word "unbelievable."

CHAPTER 7

GRAYMANOS

The man picked up the "Diary of Chryorold" from the bed's side table and handed the book to Ablina. "Darker their soul gets—the redness in their eyes brightens," he said with a voice croaky as a storm. Ablina was quivering and sweating. She wanted to run away as fast as she could, but her frozen feet didn't let her. He stepped back when he realized that he was frightening her. "They call us the 'Graymanos'—the Descendants of Nature. The oldest creatures to roam on Earth before mankind existed," he said humbly. "Graymanos," she vacantly repeated.

"I have a message for you, Ablina," the man said in a grave tone. "What?" Ablina asked, her pulse rising in fear. "Do not let him open it again, or this time the world will collapse," he stated. "Who?" She asked with horror. "Vaylar," he answered, gazing at her innocent face with his wild, bloody red eyes.

"Ablina, your grandfather needs you," The man told her tersely and jumped out of the window. She inspected outside her house from the window, but he was gone. Within a blink of a second, he had vanished into thin air, like a ghost.

Ablina subliminally shut the windows and locked her door. She sat on her bed, draping herself into a warm blanket, and lay down. Her head was spinning with information that the Graymanos gave. Her theories involving multiple suspects were just thrown away by one name, "Vaylar."

Ablina stood up and sat down on the carpet; it was freezing up, but her body temperature leveled with the floor. She took out her phone, plugged the earphones into it, and tuned in her favorite song. The name "Vaylar" was hardwired into her brain. "Vaylar," Ablina absentmindedly typed into the search engine. "What the hell is that?" She shouted and stood up quickly. Her eyes didn't believe what she saw, and her mind exploded. "This can't be true," she said and sprinted to Raylina's room.

***

Ablina stormed into Raylina's room like a maniac. "Raylina, WAKE UPPPP," Ablina said. She almost sat on Raylina's face to wake her up. "What is it, Abby?" Raylina said, still in bed with her closed eyes. "Wake up!" Ablina said loudly, roughly shaking Raylina's shoulder. "I will rip up your head, Abby," Raylina threatened and fell back to sleep.

Ablina pulled off Raylina's blanket and said, "Ray, wake up. Check this out." Raylina pushed her arms on the bed to lift her up. She sat and rubbed her eyes to examine the information on Ablina's phone.

Raylina was stunned. She couldn't believe it either; the information about Vaylar matched word by word, and even the commas and full stops were blindly copied from the diary. "This is serious," Raylina said, habitually scratching her nose. "Ray, I need to tell you something else," Ablina said. Ablina recounted everything that happened at the bonfire.

"Ray," Ablina sighed, and kept her hand on Raylina's. "I don't know if Vaylar killed our father or not, but there is definitely something going on with this Vaylar."

Raylina stood up from her bed and distraughtly walked towards her room's window. She vacantly stared at the flickering lights of street lamps from the window, getting hold of the events. "Maybe we should talk to Ma about all of this," she spoke with her eyes fixed to streetlights. "No, we cannot, Ray. We cannot talk about this to anyone, not until we figure out what is actually going on," Ablina explained.

Ablina talked Raylina out of telling their mother about it, as she thought it was too soon to scare her mother with this newfound deadly information. "I think you are right. Telling Ma is risky. Once she knows about this attack and the rest, she will straight away send our asses back to the tomb," Raylina said, hugging her shivering chest, walking back to her bed.

"Let's go back to sleep. We will talk about this tomorrow," Raylina said and hopped back in her bed. "Okay, good night," Ablina said slowly, standing there like a little child scared of monsters under her bed.

Raylina blew hot air from her nostrils and said, "No matter how colder it gets. In their arms..." Ablina swiftly lay down beside Raylina and tucked herself in a blanket. "You'll find your warmth," Ablina said cutely, finishing their family slogan, and hugged Raylina like a lost puppy. "Whatever," Raylina puffed, pulling the blanket away.

***

Raylina smoothly moved Ablina's hand away from her and quietly sneaked out of the room, heading to the kitchen. Some people go to therapy; some prefer a great spa massage, and some like a bottle of wine to handle their problems. But for Raylina, the solution to her problems was simple—FOOD. So she opened the fridge, took out the leftover bowl of pasta, and placed it in the microwave.

The dullness on Raylina's face slowly started to diminish, seeing the bowl whirling in the microwave. She was amused by how efficiently it worked and considered it the best device ever invented by mankind. She ate the whole bowl and dozed off with diet coke over the dining table.

***

Amaraya switched on the kitchen lights and saw Raylina slouching on the dining chair. "Raylinaaaa, wake up. I am so done with you," Amaraya said, trying to hold off her anger. Raylina's head was heavy as a stone; she could barely open her eyes. Amaraya gently shook her, and Raylina woke up in shock, falling down from the chair. "Ma… What…," Raylina shrieked in pain.

"What is wrong with you all?" Ablina came rushing down to the kitchen. "Why are you guys shouting?" Ablina asked waspishly.

"What is going on with you two? Ray, what is this? Sleeping at our dinner table and Ablina, getting angry for no reason," Amaraya yelled at them furiously. "Mother, you need to chill out a bit," Raylina said in a sleepy voice. "Chill out! OH, Honey, parents don't have that privilege," Amaraya responded deliberately. "Sarcastic much," Raylina said, rubbing sleep off from her eyes. "Please stop it. Both of you," Ablina begged.

The tug of war between who is right and who is wrong went on for an hour. Raylina and Amaraya both claimed to be correct. And neither of them was ready to give up. Ablina sat in the chair and had her breakfast, listening to their bickering. "I hate to interrupt this epic tussle of righteousness, but Ray, we are late for school," Ablina informed and went up into her room to get ready for the day. "Oh crap," Raylina said and ran to her room to get changed. "And I'll be the doorman," Amaraya mumbled and went to answer the door.

Amaraya unlocked the door. It was Astor holding the Kaike plant pot in his hands. "Good morning," Astor greeted her respectfully and handed her the Kaike plant. He read the signs of disapproval written all over Amaraya's face. "You again," she uttered, walking inside. Astor pursed his lips and followed her inside.

It was evident that Amaraya disliked the Vasaga brothers. Their constant appearing out of nowhere, trying to be a knight in shining armor for her daughters, was irritating and super inappropriate. She never considered them her friends. They were more like her acquaintances. Amaraya tolerated them because she wanted to unravel her father's plans for her. And keeping Alisar close was the best way to do it.

"Girls, Astor's here," Amaraya asked the girls to hurry up. Astor prayed for them to come fast, but it was not his lucky day. "So, Astor, why are you here?" Amaraya questioned directly. "Alisar asked me to come, and protect them, your daughters at school, they are new to all of this, so I am like their man-servant," he said tensely. Amaraya's expressions intimidated him. He felt like he checked into hell on a bad day.

"I am really grateful for all this, but you know I didn't ask for it," Amaraya exclaimed, trying to mask her rudeness, her eyebrows rising in suppressed anger and sarcasm. "Alisar promised your father that he will keep you all safe. Alisar wanted my help, as he felt outnumbered by you three, so he called me up," Astor said nervously.

Astor took a breath of relief as he saw Raylina and Ablina coming down from the stairs. He thanked God for the first time in his life that day. "Hey! Finally, I thought we would miss the first half of school," Astor teased. "And good morning to you, too, Astor," Raylina answered. Raylina's spontaneity made him laugh, "We have a witty witch in our town," Astor said in his flirty tone. "Can we go now?" Ablina said with irritation.

On a regular day, Ablina would behave like an optimistic dove. But with Graymanos and Vaylar at the plate, it was hard for her to be her usual self. "Okay, grumpy princess," Raylina said as she realized that Ablina was in no mood for more bullshit. That's the thing about sisters; they read the hidden subtitles.

"Girls," Amaraya stopped them and announced, "Next week, I am going to India." "India... next week..." Raylina responded with great shock on her face. "Vaylar," Ablina quavered. "Yes, I need to start from somewhere. The only person who can really help us is your grandfather. The old man knows it all," Amaraya nervously tried explaining to them. "Ma, but he wanted to kill you and Papa for marrying against his wishes. Why tell the grim reaper the location!" Raylina asserted. "Honey, I know, but if he is behind this, I have to go and find it by myself," Amaraya reasoned.

"Abby, Ray, we will discuss this once you guys are back from school," Amaraya insisted. "This is a suicide mission. Ma, and after losing Papa, I cannot believe you want to hop on the board of this charade," Raylina said furiously and stomped out of the house.

***

Astor and the Bayer sisters arrived at school. Astor silently watched Ablina's furrowed forehead in the rear-view mirror. Then he turned his head to the left and saw Raylina's sulking face. He understood that Amaraya's decision about going to India disturbed them. "Girls, I need to see Olivia. Lock the doors and keep the keys with you. We will meet at lunchtime," Astor said, and left them alone to sort it out.

The Bayer sisters were still in the car, not talking. Their heads were immersed in how to deal with the problems reaching their way. First Graymanos message and now Amaraya's announcement of going to India was like getting diagnosed with liver failure and cancer at the same time.

Raylina got out of the front seat and opened the back door of the vehicle. She dragged Ablina out and kept her hands on Ablina's hands. "Abby, we will get through this," Raylina assured her. "What about Graymanos?" Ablina asked, raising an eyebrow.

Raylina pressed Ablina's hand tightly. "I am also freaking out here. I get it, Abby. We don't even know the basics of protecting ourselves, and some bizarre creatures think we can save the world... Look at us, Abby. I am an angry girl with zero fighting skills, and you... Well, look at your nails," Raylina said nervously in one breath and pressed her back against the car's door, folding her arms across her chest in despair.

Ablina overlooked Raylina's comment on her well-maintained manicured nails, as her mind was crowded with worries. "What if something happens to Ma?" Ablina said with a horrified face. "Nothing will happen. Throw that thought out of your system, Abby. We will not lose her," Raylina affirmed. "We have to go with her," Ablina said. Raylina, with a smarty smirk on her face, said, "I think you are right, Abby. It's time to say Namaste to Grandpa." They both nodded their heads in unison.

CHAPTER 8

SOMETHING'S FISHILY

The scent of the freshly painted library cheered Ablina. The light lemongrass-washed walls and the contrasting sky-blue-colored bookshelves organized genre-wise seemed to settle her formless world. But then the thought of Visac took her breath away. Her eyes fervidly searched for him.

Raylina caught her sister secretly scanning for a man. "He is not on your hit list anymore... Good to know," Raylina sarcastically chuckled. The wicked looks on Raylina's face irritated Ablina. But she was not ready to start a pointless argument with Raylina. Thus she buried her resentment under the impassive face and said, "I don't have a hit list. That's more like you, Ray," and drowned her embarrassed head into the book.

"*The world is a wonderful place, but there are people who like to wreck this adjective.*' Deep stuff, Ablina," Astor read loudly, drawing everyone's attention to him. "Astor, this is a library, not a cafeteria. Keep your voice down," Ablina said awkwardly.

Raylina's malicious smile puffed her upper cheeks as she saw Visac walking into the library. "His presence in the room was enough to unsettle her heart," Raylina said dramatically. Ablina's heart's rhythm changed its course as he walked towards her table.

Visac saw the eagerness in Ablina's eyes, but he was not ready to face her. To avoid the encounter, he sat at a distant table and buried himself in the math textbook. The mathematical equations of the book looked easy compared to talking to her.

Visac was tempted to take a glance at Ablina's honeyed eyes and her lovely face, but he didn't. The situation was challenging, but he had to do what he thought was right for her. At last, his will gave up, and he peeped at her. Ablina laughed softly as he turned his eyes back to the math textbook. She understood what he was doing, "Whatever," she mumbled and resumed her reading.

An hour went by, Visac's ignorant behavior kept Ablina occupied. He peeked at her every second to catch a glimpse of her, and she caught him every time when he did that. It was superficial, worthless, and futile. It was her "immeasurable pride" and his "false manly ego" which restrained them. "But those who surrender live longer," she mumbled to herself and stood up from her chair. She thumped her soft, manicured hands on the table and walked straight towards him.

Ablina stood over Visac's head. He knew that she was there, waiting for him to look up, but he pretended to be captivated by the textbook. "Visac, we need to talk," Ablina said. Visac looked up, and her ravishing jawline caught his eye. "What?" He asked in his cynical tone. "Not here, get up," she said in an ordering manner. The expression on his face changed from downbeat to confused.

Visac stood up, and Ablina instantly stepped back to evade the closeness, but she stumbled. Visac clasped her in his arms. "Some things are inevitable," Ablina mumbled, staring into his electric blue eyes. The world around him unpaused as he released her from his embrace. They looked at each other in awkwardness, not sure what to say or do next. Visac was never a shy person, but in her presence, he was becoming one. "Not here," Visac said and dragged Ablina out of the library in front of everyone.

***

"What do you want to talk about?" Visac asked impatiently, moving close to her. After a moment of quietude, Ablina rallied her spirits and drove him away with her index finger. "Nothing," Ablina said anxiously and started to walk away. "Hey… Hey, Ablina… Ablina… wait," Visac ran behind her.

Ablina halted. Visac came and stood there in front of her, quietly. "What?" Ablina asked softly. Ablina's pink-glossed lips distracted him. For a moment, he forgot how to speak. Visac tried his best to act cool and said, "I am sorry for being a jerk, but I just don't know what to say to you. What happened back at the library was so sudden… I just…" He paused. "What? Why don't you complete it?" Ablina said, raising a sardonic eyebrow. "That guy who attacked you last night, did you tell your folks about him?" Visac asked and smoothly changed the subject. "Yes, I told my sister about it," Ablina said. "You should take this to the cops. I mean, that guy was scary. His eyes were scary," he said and took a step closer to Ablina. "No, I can't, Visac," she said and unconsciously stepped closer to him.

Ablina brushed her fingers over Visac's hair gently and said, "Sanvitigmilo." "Was that in Spanish?" He questioned, muddled by her strange behavior. "Do you remember about last night?" Ablina asked. "Yes, I do. I don't have Alzheimer's, Ablina," he answered. Visac's answer befuddled Ablina. "What are you?" Ablina said with terror on her face. "Are you okay? You look like you have seen a ghost," Visac asked concernedly. "I have to go," Ablina said and ran out of there. Visac was still standing, feeling disoriented.

***

Ablina kept on running until she was in the parking lot. She took her phone and dialed Raylina.

"What?…I'm in this stupid Math class," Raylina murmured.

90

"Ray, need you. Come to the parking area," Ablina spoke in a quavering voice.

"On my way," Raylina said, and hung up the call.

Ablina was restless about what had just happened. She did not understand how the spell went wrong; she mastered it. The forgetting enchantment, "Birsada," was one of the most primary and uncomplicated spells of all time. 8,000 years ago, a 9-year-old witch girl from Nepal accidentally invented a "Birsada enchantment" while trying to flee from Ghana's slave traders.

"Look back into their eyes filled with innocence, and touch a part of them gently, and utter 'Sanvitigmilo.'" Ablina replayed the instructions her mother taught them during their sorcery and spells classes. The spell was conjured accurately with perfection. There was nothing wrong with it. She wondered why it did not work on Visac. The magic was supposed to make him forget everything about the previous night, but he remembered everything.

Raylina came rushing to the parking lot. "What's up, Abby?" Raylina asked. "There is something fishily about Visac," Ablina said tensely. "It's fishy, Abby," Raylina said. "This is not the time to expand your grammar knowledge, but fishily is a word," Ablina said rapidly in one breath. "Vooo—Calm down, Abby. What on earth happened?" Raylina asked calmly.

"I cast the forgetting spell on Visac, but he still remembers everything," Ablina said nervously. "First, stop pacing around me. Second, you are paranoid. Is it possible that you made some mistake in chanting that?" Raylina queried in breaks, trying not to shoot up Ablina's anxiety. "No, Ray. I don't make mistakes, especially when I am using magic on someone's brain," Ablina said. She described what exactly went on when she tried erasing the memory of last night from Visac's head.

"I thought you guys went out for a little make-out session; I am disappointed in you, Abby," Raylina teased. "Ray, this is serious," Ablina said furiously, still thinking about Visac.

Raylina talked Ablina out of it, and they agreed not to think about it till the India trip.

***

The Bayer sisters went back to class, and the moment Ablina walked in, Visac's eyes caught her. His eyes followed her every move, even the ones she didn't make.

Ablina and Visac kept on playing hide and seek with their eyes. Ablina was embarrassed, and Visac's head was stuck with a whirlpool of questions. The bell rang, and Miss Shelia gave all the students last-minute instructions about what to bring while visiting the "Desovir Museum." Ablina left quickly, and Visac followed her.

"Ablina…" Visac ran after her in the hallway. She kept on walking, not paying attention to him. "Ablina," Visac caught her wrist, tugging her close to him. "Let me go," Ablina said, jerking her tiny wrist out of his clasp. "Wait," he said, grabbing her by her waist, and pulling her aside into a corner to talk.

"What," Ablina asked, staring into his eyes. "What is your problem Ablina?" Visac demanded, his eyes finding its way back to her lips. Ablina's breathing rate started to shoot up; the only thing she wanted was to run away as far as she could, but her body refused even to move an inch away from him. "I have a boyfriend," she lied, jolting her way out from his arm fence. Visac stood there watching her leave, wondering why he was bothered by Ablina and her problems.

***

The journey home was full of self-confrontations. Ablina repeatedly asked the answers for her stupidity. She was convinced that there was something shady about Visac. However, a tiny part of hers was still in a dilemma. She thought that maybe she had made some mistake while casting the enchantment on him. Maybe his eyes distracted her, but then again, why was she distracted by his eyes?

These questions messed up Ablina's head. They raised multiple storms with deadly thunder in her heart. "I like him, but after hearing what he thinks about the witches, how will he react once he knows we exist?" Ablina cried in her head, and the tears of doubt and terror rolled down her cheeks. She wiped the tears and went straight up to her room.

Amaraya saw Ablina heading upstairs without saying a word. She thought about asking Raylina first, but talking to her would have given her the impression that she was forgiven about the morning fight. So, she headed up to check on Ablina.

"Ablina, hey darling, what happened? Is everything alright?" Amaraya asked with concern. "Hey, Ma," she answered gloomily. "What happened, honey?" Amaraya asked again. "Nothing, Ma," Ablina said, laying her head down on Amaraya's lap. "You know I am your mother, and I don't like to remind this every time to you guys," said Amaraya and tucked Ablina's hairs backward.

Amaraya kissed Ablina's forehead with all the affection she had in her. Ablina rose up from her mother's lap and gave her a tight hug. "It's okay, honey, it will get better," Amaraya said, gently patting Ablina's shoulders. Sometimes, all we need is to show an equal amount of empathy, to let people know that we care for them.

"Ma, how do you stop liking someone?" Ablina asked naively. Amaraya smiled and said, "Well, you cannot, but you can always move on." "But what if I don't want to move on?" Ablina questioned. "Then you can always go and let that person know how you feel about them," Amaraya advised.

"How can I just go and tell them that?" Ablina puffed. "You can. With a little bit of courage in your heart, a pinch in your head. And… oh yes… a parsec of it in your soul. That'll work, I think," Amaraya said. Ablina smiled and said, "You are the best, but I guess time will help me too." "No, darling, I disagree. Time will bury it for a while, but it always comes rushing back, and that will make the whole thing regretful," Amaraya explained. "You are right, I guess. The trip to India will give me both time to think and the courage to say it," Ablina said smartly.

Amaraya proudly looked at her daughter. She loved Ablina's negotiation skills. Her command at explaining things reminded her of her brother. "No, there is nothing you can say that will change my mind," Amaraya said and smoothly rejected Ablina's request. "Ma, we have never met any of our relatives. I think we deserve to know about them. It's our right," Ablina argued in a soft tone.

Amaraya ignored Ablina's words as much as she could. Still, Ablina was her mother's daughter. Her determination was more powerful than her mother's. Ablina laid her head on Amaraya's knee, "Ma, we are just asking you to take us to India. You can meet grandpa first, and if things work out between you and him, we will meet him. If not, we can always visit the Taj Mahal," Ablina pleaded. "Okay, fine," Amaraya let out a sigh and finally agreed. "YEAH," Ablina jumped out of joy and ran to Raylina's room to give her the good news.

CHAPTER 9

DIVULGED

The crystal blue sky was seized by hundreds of birds hustling their way to find the meal of the day. The brightest and the only star, Sun, shined upon the Bayer sisters sitting on the abandoned railroads.

"The sovereignty of kind words can melt the most rigid hearts."

Ablina read lines from her father's diary aloud. "I miss him and his weird philosophies," Raylina said, looking at the yellow flowers blooming between the railway sleepers. "Me too," Ablina said and gave Raylina a side hug.

"Abby, I intent to ask you this," Raylina said sincerely. "Yes, anything," Ablina said. "Why does she always listen to you? Did you use magic to convince our old lady?" Raylina asked curiously. "No, I am not you. I don't use magic for selfish reasons," Ablina replied with hubris.

"Ouch, I am offended, Sister," Raylina said, trying to balance on the old rail tracks.

Ablina walked behind Raylina, playing football with a medium-sized round stone. "It's effortless, Ray. You can always ask nicely with puppy eyes," Ablina answered, with a complete focus on her game. Raylina turned around and said, "WOW." Ablina winked at her and grinned. Raylina quickly hugged her and rejoiced, "Ohhh, you are like my peanut butter. I can always rub you on people when things get hard." "Ewe, Ray, that's gross. Ahh! I love our morning walks," Ablina said and pushed Raylina away.

The morning walk was a ritual started by George. He took his daughters for a morning walk every day. It was his way to get to know what was going on in their lives. He allowed them to be as open as possible; their thoughts, doubts, fears, and troubles, he welcomed it all. It was like an open, non-judging talk show. Raylina and Ablina continued this after his death. It made them feel closer to their father; it was a way of keeping his memories alive.

***

The Bayer sisters walked in and saw their mother and Alisar having a serious discussion about something. It was intense and felt like an aftereffect of the blast. "Hey," Raylina said to catch their attention. "Hello, ladies, back from a walk?" Alisar asked. "No, we went to hatch our eggs," Raylina said sarcastically. "So, would you mind making me an omelet?" Alisar flirted. Raylina broke into a smile. Their wavelength was flawless; despite spending so little time together, their understanding was like they had known each other for centuries. Alisar stood up to leave, and the Bayer family went along with him to escort him to the door.

"Amaraya, I am in no position to interfere, but I think you should go alone. Taking them will only complicate things," Alisar advised. Raylina's eyes started to boil with anger. "Yes, Alisar, you are right, my dearest. You shouldn't interfere. Stay the fuck out of it," Raylina lashed out. "Raylina Bayer apologized now," Amaraya ordered angrily. Raylina did not want to, but she did and then left from there to her room.

Amaraya once again apologized for Raylina's behavior towards Alisar. Alisar humbly explained the risks of taking the girls to India. He knew Amaraya's ways of handling things. He just wanted to avoid the family feud turning into a war. But Amaraya was bound by her word to Ablina, and she intended to keep it. "Alisar... My daughters have never met their grandfather. Hell, it's been centuries since I saw him. I think it will be best for them and for me," she said.

"Okay, but I can't let you go alone. Astor will come with you," Alisar said. "Well, I don't mind, a bell boy at my service," Amaraya giggled. "At your service, Madam, but before that, I would love a cup of ginger tea," Astor said, appearing out of nowhere, which startled Amaraya.

Amaraya stared at Astor with a grim face; she wanted to punch him for petrifying her like that, but she decided to let go this time, looking at the circumstances. "How did you get in?" Amaraya asked seriously. "Magic milady," Astor winked. "Okay, I will get your tea, but no more magic tricks in my house," Amaraya warned. They all went back in for tea.

***

They say it's a mother's job to hear her child's inaudible conflicts, but if it's true, then why it can't be the same for her child. Amaraya watched Ablina silently work alongside her, waiting for her to give her final decision about going to India. She tried hard to ignore her daughter's repeated actions to find out the results. "Ablina, stop it," Amaraya irked.

Ablina stopped whipping the cream for her hot chocolate and looked at her mother's face questionably. Amaraya deeply inhaled the humid air into her lungs and gradually released it, "Abby, we are going, as I promised." Ablina nodded happily. Amaraya heard the knocking on the door; she smiled at Ablina and said, "Start packing," and went out to answer the door.

Amaraya opened the door, and it was Eraa with her son. "Hello, Eraa," Amaraya welcomed them into her house. "This is my son, Visac. He is in the same class as your daughters," Eraa said. "Hello, Mrs. Bayer," Visac greeted her with humbleness. "Hello," Amaraya smiled with delight and called Ablina to meet her classmate.

After a couple of minutes, Ablina came out of the kitchen. The sight of Visac shook her system upside down. "Ablina, how are you?" Eraa said in her sweet voice. "I-I-m-Fine," she replied anxiously. "Where is Raylina?" Eraa asked. "Eraa, Visac, would you like tea, coffee, or anything else?" Amaraya said to distract them with their beverage preferences, dodging Eraa's question. "No thanks," Visac said restlessly. "I would love some ginger tea," Eraa replied.

Visac perceived that his presence was making Ablina jittery. To stop her hands from shivering, she hugged her breast, but it didn't work. The tremors and flutters worsened. Her phone slipped out of her hand, and as she bent down to pick up her phone, the strap of her purple-pink stripe tank top fell off. She lifted the strap and caught Visac staring at the tiny black mole on her left collar bone.

Visac swiftly looked away, but his eyes came back to the place from where he started. He tried looking away, but he could not help himself. All of this increased tension in the Bayers' living room. At that moment, he admitted to himself that he was attracted to Ablina.

Ablina's face turned red out of embarrassment. She tried hiding her blush, but it didn't work. She thought that the best way out of that situation was to escape from there. So she excused herself under the pretense of making ginger tea and hightailed out of the room.

***

Ablina watched the water bubbling in the kettle as if the boiling water had all the answers she was looking for. Her mind considered throwing the boiling water along with the kettle on Visac's head. But the question still puzzled her, why does he affect her so much?

"Honey, I think it's overheated," Amaraya said. "Sorry, Mom, just taken up with something," she said and closed the stove. She turned her face around as she wanted to hide the turbulence his presence was creating in her heart. Amaraya poured the tea in traditional Japanese teacups and carried them out in a tray.

Ablina was rearranging the dishes in the closet, which was therapeutic for her. She heard footsteps approaching. The familiarity of the sound raised her pulses. At this point, she could identify Visac by his footsteps, and this annoyed her. "Visac," she murmured and turned around. His face secretly snatched away the anger from her face. "Ablina…" Visac said. "Let's not go there," she insisted.

In the battle of pride and who gives in first, their wounded hearts were the victims, suffering endlessly. Ablina wanted Visac to explain his actions, but she didn't want him to talk to her. "I want to tell you why I think like that," Visac tried to convince her to listen to him. "Did you know… About us?… So, you hate us, then why aren't you burning us at stake? Like you meant in our history class," Ablina started shooting. "Don't say that," Visac begged, finding ways to answer her.

He looked at her with hurt in his eyes; he flipped his hand with a dramatic light swing in an odd manner, and the fire flames started to come out of his right palm. "For some people, magic is a curse, and Ablina, I am one of them," he revealed in a despaired voice.

"Visac, I don't know what happened to you, but I know one thing," Ablina said in an empathetic tone. She took a step closer to him and kept her hand on his face, "Cursed or not, you are a good person. You saved me at the bonfire, and that incident sums up my thinking about you. Let me help you, Visac."

Visac let his helpless self fall in love with Ablina, and the unseen guard he had kept up started to liquefy. "Ahamm," Alisar said, interrupting their moment. "Alisar," Visac said in a disappointed tone. Ablina pulled her hand away from his face, and Visac wiped his eyes with his long sleeves. "Wrong timing," Alisar said in a playful tone. "I should go," Visac said, and he left. Ablina ducked in embarrassment and went up.

***

Ablina entered Raylina's room and found Raylina lying on her stomach on the bed. "Raylina, we need to go to the museum," Ablina said. "I am not going, Abby; fuck off," Raylina said in vexation. "Language, girl. And what have I done? Why are you mad at me?" Ablina asked. "Abby, please, I don't want to talk. Please leave me alone," Raylina irked, still infuriated by Amaraya and Alisar.

"Can I come in?" Alisar asked, but before they answered, he marched in, like always. Raylina was incensed by Alisar's view regarding going to India. Ablina sensed the tension between the two of them, so she suggested, "Alisar, I think you guys need to talk," and she left them alone in the room.

Alisar sat on his knees and softly held Raylina's hands, "Ray, I am sorry, I shouldn't have said that. I am just concerned about you and only you." Their eyes had the rest of the unsaid conversation. "I know that," she said, and her smile hoisted the flag of peace. "You should stand up now, old man, or your knees will hurt badly," Raylina chuckled hard.

Alisar looked in her eyes alluringly and said, "I think you're falling for this old man, so you should stop calling me that." "I like your confidence, old man," Raylina flirted. "I know you're a skeptic in this field, especially hostile in the emotional genre, but I would be lying if I said that you are the only one falling in this," Alisar said, still sitting on his knees.

The grave silence took over the room after Alisar's odd confession. The world stopped revolving for a moment around them. Raylina looked back in his eyes, and her mightiness started to dissolve in his humility. The pride she carried so graciously was turned down by his simplicity.

"I-I..." Raylina stammered. It never occurred to her that she would ever fall short of words, but Alisar made that possible. "I hate it when you guys fight," Ablina came into the room with a big smile on her face. Their moment was broken with her entry, but that's the thing about families; you can blame them but got to love them, no matter what.

"Raylina, now we are seriously late for the visit. Astor is waiting for us," said Ablina. "Okay, nerd, let's go," Raylina said. And they all merrily left Raylina's room as a team.

***

While walking down the stairs, Raylina saw Amaraya's face from between the two stair railings. The disappointment on her mother's face was so intense that it could be spotted clearly even from afar. Raylina broke the ice first and said, "Mama, before you start, I apologized, and we are good now." "I don't know what to say to you anymore, Raylina. I raised you to be a better person," Amaraya said sadly, sighing. "What do you want me to do, Mother? I already apologized," Raylina said obstinately.

The height of Amaraya's disappointment in Raylina was continuously increasing, and Raylina made sure not to do anything about it, at any cost. "Maybe we can discuss this matter later?" Ablina said to stop Raylina and Amaraya from making a scene in front of everyone.

"Have to take this," Astor said and went outside the house to answer his phone. "Eraa help them with the passport stuff. I have something to be taken care of," Alisar said and hurriedly left. The Bayer sisters and

Amaraya quickly filled the passport process documents with Eraa's help; meanwhile, Visac sat there like a little boy waiting for them.

***

"Astor!" Alisar said in anger and violently knocked him down to the ground. He hauled Astor up through his collar and said, "I asked you to do one thing, Astor." "One fucking thing," Alisar roared and punched him on his face again.

"Alisar, listen, brother, I did as you asked," Astor replied faintly. "You fucked up punk. I took care of you for centuries. I gave you this life you are living so lavishly, and in return, I asked for one freaking thing, and you screwed up like always," Alisar lashed out.

"I was pretty clear, Astor. Ablina was yours to be taken care of," Alisar said, concealing his urge to kill Astor. "I am doing exactly as you asked me to do. Trust me on this," Astor pleaded. "Oh really? Aha!!! Astor, Bravo, she is getting closer to that prick-Visac… They were freaking romancing in the kitchen," Alisar shouted.

"Hey guys, is everything alright?" Visac interrupted their aggressive conversation. Alisar was shocked; he didn't know what to say, and it was like his mask had fallen off. "Nothing, Visac, mind your own business," Astor piqued. "Rude much," Visac said, and he left from there in his metallic grey SUV jeep.

Visac, not reacting to what happened, gave Alisar relief. He became assured that Visac didn't hear anything.

The Bayer sisters came out of the house with Amaraya, and the Vasaga brothers quickly cleared the air of hostility. Alisar opened the door for Raylina. Astor did the same for Ablina. "Where's Visac? Isn't he coming?" Ablina asked. "No, he left,' Alisar said, climbing behind the wheels, and started the car.

***

Astor was quiet, which was unlikely of him. His mind was all taken up by what happened in the Bayers' front yard. For Astor, Alisar was an ideal big brother, an overachiever who got everything he put his eye on. On the other hand, Astor was a carefree soul thriving his way into the world, living like every day was his last. Astor always looked up to his elder brother. He religiously followed Alisar's path. But with every effort Astor made to prove himself in Alisar's eyes, the rift between them widened.

Alisar, Astor, and the Bayer sisters reached the museum of Desovir. Alisar dropped them at the front gate and left for his business meeting. They spotted that their classmates were already standing outside, and Mr. Patel was directing kids to stand in line and maintain discipline, so the Bayer sisters and Astor ran and joined the group.

Ablina saw Visac was already there, standing next to Olivia Mark, his ex-girlfriend. Visac knew that Ablina was looking at him. Still, he purposely avoided her. This made Ablina more determined to go and talk to him.

Ablina slightly moved towards Visac, but as she was getting closer, Visac moved back further.

Finally, Ablina managed to stand next to him, but he acted like that didn't bother him. "What is up with you, Ablina? Stop this," Visac said in an annoyed tone. "I am trying to talk, Visac," she said. "I don't want to, please leave me alone," Visac said bluntly and switched places with the guy standing in front of him.

Ablina moved back with Astor and Raylina. She was done for the day, so she started to observe people around her. Weirdly, it relaxed her. Ablina watched Raylina and figured out that Raylina was lost in her dreamland, which Ablina assumed might be due to her little chat with Alisar.

Astor was not in the mood to joke around; he was hiding away from Olivia. "Astor, hey, you okay? Is something troubling you?" Ablina asked. "Nothing, Abby, I am just exhausted," he said lowly and walked away from her.

"Attention, kids. The tour will start in five, and any type of indiscipline will be subject to direct suspension, so think before unleashing the wild inside you," Mr. Patel warned them. They all went inside the museum in line, as they were instructed by Mr. Patel.

"Why is everything here dead?" Raylina said, looking at the stuffed deer. "That's the whole idea of the museum," Ablina chuckled. "What's up with Astor? Why is he sulking?" Ablina asked. "I think he was born disturbed," Raylina mumbled, staring at the dead deer. "Not funny,"

Ablina said. "Okay, sorry, but don't you think the way they have described this place is a little bit overrated," Raylina said, now staring at the deer's antlers.

Visac was standing on the first-floor balcony staring at the hellfire portrait. Astor was sitting in the corner, staring at a kid. "Visac or Astor," Ablina asked herself while looking at them. Ablina decided to talk to Astor as he seemed more depressed. Also, Ablina felt a little obligated to help him because he and Alisar helped them through everything.

"Hey," Ablina said and sat next to him. Astor nodded. "Looks like you're having a tough day," Ablina said, and gently kept her hand on his. "You never give up, do you?" He smiled lightly. "Nope, never ever," Ablina said sweetly and chuckled. "Tell me, Abby, are you always like this?" he asked. "No, I just don't want people I care about staring strangely at other people's kids without any legit reason," she responded. He laughed. Their laughing caught everyone's attention, including Visac's.

"OKAY, you win, it's nothing big—I just had an argument with Alisar, and I know we will be normal after some time, but I am just mad right now," Astor said. "Look, I have no right to meddle in between you two. Literally, if someone would speak in between Ray and me, we would probably kill them. Nevertheless, I think I should give you this little tip to quickly get over this sibling fight," Ablina said and paused.

"What?" Astor asked. "Do nothing," Ablina answered. "What do you mean by that?" He posed curiously. She beamed, and her honest eyes shined out like a firefly in the dark forest. "Well, that's the tip, Astor. This relation, the relation between siblings, is manufactured to withstand any adversity. So the only thing to do is to do nothing," she explained.

Astor gazed at her in wonderment, and he smiled somewhat. Her wise words stopped his brain cells from exploding. "Abby, I simply adore you, but this sucks, it's so used up and old," he said to tease her. "Wait, when did I say it's original? I just reminded you of that," Ablina said wittily. "You know what?" Astor asked. "What?" Ablina asked. "You should run for president," he said, and they burst into laughter.

Astor realized that Ablina was not just some random girl to mess around with. She was unique and, moreover, a good person/witch. He felt like he had a genuine conversation with a real person after a decade. Their conversation liberated him. After a long time in his lifetime, he felt lighter and better. "Ablina thank you!" Astor said seriously. "No need," she smiled and rolled her eyes.

Ablina saw Visac gazing at her and decrypted his looks. He was jealous of her and Astor talking. "I need to find Ray," she made an excuse and went upstairs where he was standing.

CHAPTER 10

THE FIERY BUTTERFLIES

Love brings inevitable chaos, and it did the same to Ablina. Each step she took towards Visac broke her nerve by nerve. Ablina believed that a person's past tells you many things about their present. And she wanted to know everything about Visac's past, present, and above all, why he was keeping himself distant from any source of happiness.

"Hey, can we talk?" Ablina asked with an aching heart. "What? There is nothing to talk about," Visac said with utmost disinterest. Ablina disregarded his incivility and said, "Not here," and dragged him by his hand towards the fancy metal gate.

Ablina pushed the metal door, and it opened inwardly. They both overlooked the "Do not enter" sign hanging around the Shoebill Stork's beak carved on the right-side panel of a metal door.

Ablina and Visac walked through the crescent-like pathway, which opened into an enormous hall. They were confounded with surprise. It was all very surreal. Ablina curiously inspected the subtle pearl-white room. "I never knew we had this room in our museum," Visac said, which interrupted Ablina's deep contemplation of the room.

The spotless, white-themed huge room lured their minds into thinking. Ablina and Visac individually cooked up multiple theories in their heads. But they fell short of an explanation after using every neuron in their nervous system. "Emptiness," a deep voice spoke. They turned around and saw an old man standing behind them. "Emptiness?" Ablina asked. "Yes, this room was created to describe what emptiness looks like," the old man answered. "But why is it in white? Shouldn't it be painted black?" Visac asked with earnestness. "It's a perception, son. For some, emptiness looks dark, and for some—white," the old man answered.

Their eyes vigilantly followed the old man as he moved slowly to the room's left corner, "You know what I think about this," he panted, staring at the whitewashed room. "I think it's not about the color. It's about the matter that resides in a person's heart—evil, good, bad, jealousy, hatred, love. And when you don't have that matter inside your heart, it just looks like this... Empty. And when someone...," he paused to catch his breath. "And when someone reaches this level, they either become the creator or bring the apocalypse to the world," he spoke softly.

Ablina was deeply impressed with what the old man said. She couldn't keep herself from mumbling, "WOW!!... I am Ablina Bayer," she said and walked towards him. He continued smiling with his fading sight, and suddenly the lights went out. The darkness took over the entire room. "Visac..." she searched for him in the room.

Visac held her by the shoulders to stop her from recklessly moving in the dark. "Calm down. Lights will come back any minute," he assured her. The warmth in his voice gave her comfort. "Where did he go? Hello, Sir?" Ablina asked. "I think he is not here," Visac stated. She sighed deeply and held his hand. "I... I was scared... for you, Visac," she said worriedly. "Why?" Visac demanded. "Because... I don't know, maybe I care about you," she replied nervously.

Visac could hear Ablina's heart beating faster with every passing second. He was still holding her in his arms, and he wanted her to stay, but his inner conflicts said otherwise, "I am a strong man. I can take care of myself." "There is no doubt about it, but being strong doesn't mean you have to be alone," she reasoned and softly touched his left cheek.

Visac gently removed Ablina's hand from his cheek and gloomily said, "I am better off this way, and it will be best for you to stay away from me." "You and I both know I am incapable of doing that. I cannot leave someone who needs my help. I owe you, Visac, so let me help you. You were there that night to save my life, let me help you out," she said with adamance. Ablina kept on forcing him to talk, but he firmly refused to do so.

Visac's stubbornness was pushing her strong will away. But Ablina refused to give up. She kept on pushing him to speak, which made him more anxious. "I am a killer, Ablina," he said aggressively, failing to keep the strong facade. "I killed my sister in her crib. I set the cradle on fire. I burned her to death," Visac screamed in distress. His agony snatched his strength away, and he fell to the ground on his knees.

Ablina sat down gingerly beside him, trying not to fall on him in the dark; she kept both her hands on his shoulders and said, "Tell me what happened." "I didn't mean to, Ablina. She was my baby sister. I loved her," he sobbed. Ablina patiently waited for him to talk, and after a long minute, he continued, "I had an argument with my father over some toy, and I couldn't control it. I tried… I tried."

Ablina hugged him, and he rested his head on her shoulders. "Hey… Visac… Breathe, it was an accident," Ablina said, trying to calm him down. "No, it wasn't, Abby. I killed her. My rage swallowed an innocent soul," he wailed.

"Listen to me," Ablina said in an ordering tone. Visac looked at her even though he couldn't see her face. "You are not a killer, Visac Levin. Don't blame yourself. You are a good person who saved my life that night, and what happened to your sister was an accident," she spoke clearly. "You have to forgive yourself," Ablina said. Visac stopped crying and hugged her. His feelings of loneliness, guilt, and hopelessness went away like magic.

Little hazy, fiery balls, which vaguely looked like butterflies, started coming out of Ablina's fingertips. Those fiery balls started to swallow the darkness in the room. Ablina wondered how she was doing it. She didn't know that she was capable of casting this type of magic. It was like the magic inside her was speaking to her. It was bizarre and breathtaking at the same time. She could have dwelled on her brain to overthink the phenomena, but she let it go because, for the first time, she wanted to be there in the moment.

Visac's eyes brightened up from the light of those tiny fiery balls. His heart filled up with hope he never thought he deserved. He looked at her with affection. No matter how much she denied it, she was in love with him entirely from that moment forward—they both were.

One tiny fiery butterfly came between them, they looked at it together, and their eyes met. "Visac... let me be your fiery butterfly," she said hopefully. He laughed, she smiled, and the lights came on. "You know you are insane," Visac chuckled. "Well, you are smiling, so I guess my job is done here," she beamed.

"Got to go. Ray must be looking for me," Ablina said and started to walk away from Visac. He ran a little to catch up with her. They reached the entrance together, but soon they parted ways because high school was still scary, and coming into the limelight was always the wrong idea. Ablina saw her sister waiting outside, and she speedily went to her.

"Where were you? The trip ended an hour ago," Raylina curiously asked. "I got lost," Ablina fibbed to her. Raylina understood that her sister was trying to keep the encounter with Visac hush, so she let her, for one whole second. "Come on girl, learn to lie better. Abby, you are a freaking witch, you are a disgrace to our whole clan," Raylina mocked. "Whatever," Ablina replied. They continued their teasing and chatting on their way home.

***

Visac dimly walked into his house. He saw his mother, Eraa, watching TV and chopping vegetables for dinner. He removed his shoes and placed them neatly in the shoe rack. Being the neat freak he was, he donned his home slippers. He entered his room and lay down on his bed.

An hour passed by, and Visac was unmoved. He blinked his eyes every time he thought of her. It was like she had become the master of his eyes. Her words poured down like rain on his burning soul. He closed his eyes to get some rest as the thoughts of her were driving him crazy, but her face wouldn't let him. He restlessly stood up from his bed and went downstairs.

Visac stood there in front of his mother, soaked in sweat, exhausted. "What happened?" Eraa asked worriedly. "Mom, I want to go to India with them," Visac announced. "What?" Eraa snorted. "I feel that something is going to happen, something bad. The Bayers are in danger. I need to go," he pleaded. "Visac, Alisar is sending Astor with them. They are in good hands," Eraa argued.

"No, mom, you don't understand," Visac growled. "Calm down, son. And yes, I do know where this all is going... You like that girl," Eraa said, breaking the ice. "What? NO... NO," he said, trying to hide the truth but failing miserably. "Lying is not one of your greatest strengths, Visac. I am your mother, and I saw the way you were staring at her," Eraa said.

Eraa and Visac stared at each other for a moment. "Ohh come on mom. Stop being so imaginative," Visac said. "Ablina comes from a very powerful family, Visac. You and I are nothing in front of them. If they know about this, they will murder you just like they killed George Bayer, Ablina's father. They are ruthless when it comes to their daughters," Eraa tried explaining. "You are wrong, mom," he snarled. "You are not going," Eraa stated clearly. Visac stomped his feet on the floor and left.

Visac rushed out of his house, feeling a little embarrassed. His mind was benumbed. He had never felt like that before. Ablina touched something inside of him, which he had tried very hard to keep out of reach. Love arrived at his door, knocking, but he was undecided whether to open the door or not. Visac's horrible past haunted him every moment; he could never come out of his miseries, and the only thing that kept him breathing was his mother.

Visac hated magic; he believed that the magic he carried within his veins was demonic. He felt that darkness was slowly leeching away the goodness in him. He closed his eyes for a second. Ablina's image moved him, and he opened his eyes quickly. Visac couldn't believe what he saw. Was it the universe trying to warn him? Or was it just a dream? "Ablina, I cannot let you be alone there," he mumbled, and he started his car.

***

Visac gently touched the name "Venus" carved on the tombstone. His tears dampened the soil. He kept the fresh pink roses on her grave, and said, "I am sorry, Venus." "I know you probably won't understand what I am saying, but please forgive me," he sobbed silently. He sat beside her grave for hours.

Visac thought his wailing and begging would bring his little sister back, but life doesn't work like that. People think that the hard part of life is to lose someone you love, but they're wrong; the hard part is to carry on without them.

The blend of warmth and the cold evening brought nostalgia; it filled Visac's head with the blurry memories of Venus. He smiled, and rested his head back on his sister's tombstone to feel closer to her. Suddenly his eyes fell on the tombstone across him. He walked to the grave and started clearing the dirt deposited on the tombstone with his jacket sleeves to read what was written.

"Death brings out the hidden wisdom in people"

"We realize that the things humans run after are a complete waste"

Visac understood and felt the lines he read. He captured it on his phone. It never really happens in a place like this, but he carried something back from that graveyard. He carried forgiveness, he carried the wisdom of life, and he carried his second chance.

CHAPTER 11

NAMASTE INDIA!!!

Two weeks passed since Amaraya decided to go to India with her daughters. But now that she was on her way to the airport, she was re-thinking her decision about returning to her homeland. The thought of meeting her family after centuries gave her a zillion breakdowns. She knew she was still not welcomed back. But, there was no other way out of it. "Ma… Ma," Ablina nudged lightly on Amaraya's shoulders to wake her up. "We have arrived at the airport."

The Bayers and the Vasaga brothers stepped out of the car and walked across the street to meet Eraa, who had already been there, waiting for them for an hour. "Hello," Eraa greeted them politely. "These are your tickets, and please keep your IDs handy," Eraa said and gave them their tickets.

"Ray, we'll need another trolley to fit these," Ablina said, stuffing her bags into the baggage trolley. "I'll get them for you," Astor said and went to get one. "This looks better than the baggage I carry inside me," Amaraya mumbled, staring at Ablina and Astor, arranging Ablina's bags into the trolley.

"Ray, let's get some coffee for everyone," Alisar said. Raylina nodded and walked with him to the airport's coffee bar. Raylina was upset with Alisar for not coming with her to India. Her cold behavior tormented Alisar; he wanted to talk to her, but she was in no mood to listen. "Ray…," he said, breaking the silence. "I really want to come along, but I cannot." "Whatever," Raylina said, rolling her eyes at his excuses.

"Ray… at least give me a chance to explain," Alisar said. "Alisar, it's simple, when I need my friends around, I expect them to be around… This is a big deal for me—bigger than your stupid meetings with clients," Raylina said rudely. "I am sorry, Ray," he said in a low tone. "What will I do if things get ugly with Grandpa? What if that Vaylar guy actually exists?" Raylina said, speaking her fears out loud. "I will be there once this is over," he assured, holding her shoulders. "Okay fine, if something happens, I know whom to blame," she said and walked away from him.

Raylina went back empty-handed, and no one noticed except Ablina. "Where's coffee, Ray?" Ablina teased. "Not now, Abby," Raylina said gloomily. They waited for the boarding to start. Amaraya was standing alone, far from everyone, in a corner. She still thought that bringing the girls with her was a bad idea. She felt that this was all just the beginning of something terrible.

Amaraya rubbed the golden necklace she was wearing, and the memories of George started to run like film in front of her eyes. The mere thought of George brightened her up. Then she saw her daughters smiling openly, without any fear of the future, for that matter, anything. She looked above and said, "We did great," and smiled.

"Mother, boarding's started," Ablina informed. "Oh yes, honey," Amaraya replied, gathering her wandering mind back to reality. "Ma, is everything alright?" Ablina asked, staring at her mother's dull, worried face. "It's all good, Abby," Amaraya said and gave Ablina an assuring smile.

Raylina walked behind her sister and mother to a security check. Her phone rang. She picked up and said, "What?" in a deadpan voice. "Look to your left," Alisar said. She turned as he asked her to, to her left, and there she saw him, holding white-colored cardboard with "*I am Sorry*" written on it, in his perfect scrawl. "I will be there, Ray," he promised. "I know, you have to," she beamed vividly. At last, Alisar waved goodbye and went home with Raylina's forgiving smile.

***

"All passengers are requested to switch off their phones and electronics while takeoff," the air hostess dressed in a bottle-green skirt with a shiny white shirt announced. "Raylina, I am freaking out," Ablina said in a terrified tone as she clenched the seat handle tightly. "Don't worry, Abby, you can always hold on to my hand," Astor said.

Ablina quickly held Raylina's and Astor's hands. She didn't feel ashamed of doing it, which mortified Raylina. "Abby, you are a witch. Stop behaving like a goat," Raylina said. "Yes, I know, Ray, but I still can die," Ablina said fearfully and pressed their hands more tightly. "She is right," Astor supported Ablina's point.

Amaraya was sitting on the other side of them. She was frightened too, but there was no one to hold her hand because the one who had promised forever was gone, so she went up to the world's best saviour, where everybody goes to escape from reality—Chocolate. She pulled the chocolate bar from her purse and ate it like she had all the leisure in the world.

The plane took off, and Amaraya realized that the jitters were only for a few minutes. Everything went back to normal after the first 5 minutes of take-off. It was as steady as water in a pond. She looked outside and saw the ocean of snowy clouds; it amazed her. It was dreamlike. Her head was clear as crystal for the first time in the past two weeks. The theories, Vaylar, her father, and everything else were lost somewhere, just like the plane in the clouds.

Amaraya took out George's old diary from her bag. She held it and felt George's presence. The pages of the old book started to resurrect the parts of her which had died with the love of her life. It's weird how people say don't invest in objects, in materials, but once they are gone, in the end, it's all we are left with.

"'Things' are permanent even after they're broken, but people aren't—they die. Therefore, objects can be loved, as they will always be there," Amaraya recalled a verse from her favorite book, The Tour to Nightmare by Aryaraj Saud.

23 September 1689,

I stood there. I couldn't move. I forgot my name and all the things I knew so proudly. You have bewitched me completely. I don't want it to be a dalliance; I want us to be forever. My fathomless love has turned me into a complete "Amorist." I thought I was whole and enough, but I was wrong. You washed my arrogance away with a simple smile. I remember my mother used to talk about soulmates—now, I know what she meant.

I want to remember this day. Before today, I never penned down anything about my life, but you said yes! And I never want to forget this moment, so here I am writing my first and last entry about you, Ami, because just like this entry, you are my first and last.

Amaraya, I love you. Thank you for loving me back.

G. Bayer

When someone dies, all the memories and things of that person become our crutch. We depend on the support it provides us. As Amaraya touched the paper, the memories of her and George started flooding back. She thought, "It's funny how words on a piece of paper can make you feel what the words coming out of a person's mouth sometimes fail to convey." "I miss you," Amaraya cried silently.

Amaraya wiped her tears before they could fall on the paper and spread the precious ink on George's presence. She closed the diary and put it back in her ivory-colored purse. She rested her weary head on the headrest, letting her heavy eyes fall into arms of dark, empty peace. The grip of a controlled mind loosened, and bad memories locked up in her brain's attic sprang up.

"Papa, please, I beg you, let him go," Amaraya cried. The loyal disciples of the Shaurayaveers clan, led by Amaraya's brother, kept on beating George brutally, one after one, mercilessly. "No, he is not a witch. You cannot marry him. Not till I live and breathe," her father said relentlessly. Amaraya kept on screaming, begging her father to let George go, but the ruthless, loyal men of Shaurayaveers dared listen.

The Shaurayaveers ruffians left, and so did Amaraya's brother. George was lying on the ground in his own blood, severely wounded. But he was a stubborn man, and more than that, he was not leaving without Amaraya. Period.

Amaraya ran to George and embraced him. She felt like the distance between them choked her; she held him like a little child clinging to a toy. She softly put his head on her lap and said, "George, please look at me," she cried as she sponged the blood coming out of his head. "Stay with me, please, Herclusiaso, Herclusiaso, Herclusiaso," she chanted, and the bleeding stopped. "I am so sorry they did this to you," Amaraya wept.

Amaraya's father stood there, disheartened and infuriated, watching his only daughter defy him for a commoner who had just come into her life. The indignation rose after every tear she shed for the man. He wanted to kill him — the man who stole away his daughter, both of them on the spot. But he didn't. "Amaraya, I disown you; you are no longer a Shaurayaveer. You are free to go with this man, but don't ever come back, and if you do, I will make sure to spread your ashes in the sacred Ganges, myself," he declared and left.

It was nearing sundown. Amaraya was still sitting on the veranda, holding George's injured body in her arms. She was lost and indecisive. It was hard for her to leave her family, but letting George go was even more heart-wrenching. But Amaraya had to make a choice, so she made one.

Amaraya opened her eyes from the appalling flashback. It was nighttime. She looked back to check on her kids; their peaceful, sleepy faces gave her relief, and she let sleep overpower her.

***

"Good morning, Ma'am! What would you like to have for breakfast?" The air hostess asked politely. "I'll have

125

coffee," Raylina said. "Same for me," Astor said. "Okay, Ma'am, and what about you, Ma'am?" she asked Ablina. "I'll have tea," Ablina replied excitedly. "Okay, anything else?" The air hostess asked respectfully. "No, thank you," Astor said.

Raylina and Ablina were nervous. They were impatiently waiting for the flight to land. Ablina distracted her fear of flight by observing the air hostess. She was amazed at how the air hostess always listened and humbly helped with every silly thing. Raylina looked outside the window seat, lost in her thoughts.

"Ladies and gentlemen, we will be landing soon. Fasten your seatbelts. Kindly switch off all electronic devices," the pilot announced. Ablina did as she was instructed, and for additional safety, she held Astor's and Raylina's hands.

The landing was pretty rough; it scared the hell out of Ablina. Raylina was playing it cool, but she was screaming loudly in her head. Being witches, the concept of flying was common for them. Yet, they were not comfortable risking their precious lives in the hands of a giant piece of flying metal.

"Woahhh… I am never, ever going back on that," Ablina sighed. "Me too," Amaraya said as they boarded the bus, taking them to the airport from the runway.

After spending two hours in the arrival proceedings at the Bagdogra airport in India, the Bayers and Astor finally got their security clearance. They wearily assembled all their bags in one trolley and walked towards the airport's exit gate.

***

"OH MY GOD," Amaraya mumbled, staring at her brother coming towards them. As usual, he wasn't walking alone. Behind him, there were 20 men covered with bizarre tattoos all over them, except their faces.

"After a long, long time... Amaraya," Aamirah said in his wind-like gravelly voice. "Aamirah," she responded with an attitude. Aamirah was Amaraya's younger brother. Their equation had been quite good until Amaraya picked George over her family.

Aamirah was a tall, middle-aged, bald man who always preferred to dress in white. His eyes were just like his sister's, dark brown. His noble presence and uptight walking made him distinctive. Hundreds of suns combined would have failed to match his brightness. He was prudent and harsh from the outside, but he was a really sensitive and compassionate human being from the inside.

Aamirah mastered the magic of astronomy; in other words, he was an astrophysicist. His precise astral calculation made him the first warlock to reach the sun and come back alive by the mode of astral traveling.

Amaraya ordered the girls and Astor to stay back, and then she moved forward to talk to him.

Single-word games made the Bayer sisters confused about what was happening. The man looked like their mother, so they put their money on him being their uncle. "He doesn't look bad," Ablina whispered near Raylina's ears. "Ablina, you are not good at judging stuff. He might look delightful from the outside, but I know he's hiding his urge to kill us," Raylina said. "I don't think so, Ray, if he wanted to kill us, he wouldn't have waited to exchange words with Ma," Ablina countered.

"Amaraya, Papa has been waiting for your arrival," Aamirah stated. "Good for him," she swaggered. Aamirah's nose wrinkled as he pulled his eyebrows down. "Let's go then," he declared and ordered his guards to fetch their bags. "Aamirah, wait, my kids are not coming with us," Amaraya said in a stern voice.

"Do you want them to wander here at the airport?" Aamirah said coldly. "No, they are going to stay in the hotel. Astor, take them with you," she directed. "No… No, he wants to see you and your daughters, and you can't leave them in a hotel," Aamirah argued. Their discussion was so heated that the fire could have flamed out. Neither was ready to do what the other wanted. It seemed like Amaraya and Aamirah had pre-decided in their heads not to do what the other said, just like Ablina and Raylina.

Ablina couldn't take it anymore, so she barged in the middle of their heated arguments and introduced herself, "Hello, Aamirah, I am Ablina." Aamirah looked at her in shock and was speechless. "That's what you taught your girls?"Aamirah said. "Don't start this," Amaraya said, trying to bury her anger.

Raylina tried to maintain her first impression, but it started to go beyond her control. "What's wrong?" she said in an irritated tone, interrupting their public quibbling. "And you must be Raylina. Well, let me see. Oh yes! We don't call our elders by their names; we don't greet them with a hello. We bow our heads to show them our respect and touch their feet. It looks like Amaraya, you missed teaching them the basics," Aamirah answered arrogantly, glowering at Raylina.

Raylina clenched her fist, trying to be as civil as possible. But she had to speak up as her uncle openly humiliated her mother and sister. "And sir, you are a really opinionated man and especially when your opinions are neither wanted nor required," Raylina answered blatantly. "Raylina, back off, honey," Amaraya said and pulled her away.

"Let's not do this here, Amaraya, in the middle of the airport's exit gate. We can continue our healthy discussion with everyone's opinion on board at home," Aamirah said, looking at the people staring at them at the airport. "Whatever," Raylina mumbled and began walking.

"Namaste India!" Raylina screamed, dragging her two bags towards the SUV car parked across the road. She politely asked the driver to open the door for her. Amaraya, Aamirah, Ablina, and Astor gaped at Raylina like she was some kind of alien roaming on earth freely wearing an orange dungaree.

CHAPTER 12

THE SHAURAYAVEERS

As the Bayers and Aamirah drove up on the mountain hill in their white SUV car, the world beneath them started to seem tiny and conquerable. But that's life all about, you see things from afar and judge them to be uncomplicated and orderly, but as you come closer, the mess and complications become visible.

Amaraya, Aamirah, Ablina, and Raylina were all lost in their own worldly battles. The physical distance was lessened between the family members—but the emotional distance remained intact and impenetrable.

As they say, "Everyone wishes to be powerful, but power doesn't guarantee love."

The Shaurayaveers had everything—wealth, power beyond imagination, royalty status, unchallenged loyalty of people, and much more. To sum it up, they had the world under their feet. Yet, deep down, these things couldn't fill the voids inside their hearts. Aamirah craved his father's validation. For him obeying his father blindly was alright, but for Amaraya, love was her weakness. For love, she could give up hundreds of thrones.

Though the chances of heartbreak were higher, Ablina preferred to follow her heart. And Raylina didn't really care about anything. For her, the world was a place where people lived, and when the time came, they died. The only ones she truly cared about were her sister and her parents.

Millions of wondrous towering pine trees embedded on high mountains, like an eiderdown made by heaven to specially protect the world from the "harsh winter." Raylina watched the glorious sun rays peeping through the meager spaces of dense forest, dreaming of coming out of it one day to prove its worth. It was extraordinary. It was nirvana. "Despite the world being an awful place, it manages to look absolutely beautiful," Raylina thought while admiring the landscape.

Amaraya was anxious. Her head was caught up again in the dark times of her life. And as the distance between her and her family home reduced, her blood pressure shot up. "Girls, remember when you meet him, you bow and touch his feet," Amaraya instructed. "No way," Raylina resisted stubbornly. "Darling, this is the way things are going to be. From now on, I say, you do," Amaraya decreed.

Raylina shrugged her shoulders and raised her eyebrows in fake astonishment, "Oh, really? When did we ever get to do what we wanted? It's always you bossing us around... Like damn puppets." "Enough, Ray. I am done talking," Amaraya said, ending the conversation in the middle, like always. But Raylina kept on blaming and complaining about how unfair Amaraya was to her.

Raylina and Amaraya's futile arguments were getting on Ablina's nerves. She was drained of being the referee of the family. "Please, you guys, enough. We haven't even reached yet, and you two are making all this worse," said Ablina irritatingly. "Abby, relax," Amaraya said.

Ablina took a long, tense pause for a while to prevent her head from exploding, but she was running out of patience. "Relax? You want me to relax... Look at yourselves; you both are behaving like kids. Do you even realize why we are here? Let me remind you, we are here to know what happened to our father slash your husband," Ablina busted out and started weeping. "Abby, I am so sorry," Raylina apologized genuinely.

"We will not fight," Amaraya guaranteed and held her daughters hands, and they hugged each other. "By the way, Aamirah is your uncle, try to stay away from him, or you will end up just like him," Amaraya smiled. "Bald, you mean?" Raylina joked. The Bayers started laughing. It was the first time they laughed with a lighter heart in two days.

Aamirah felt humiliated, but he let it all slide; because it was not for the first time that his sister demeaned him publicly. So he pretended that he didn't hear them. Plus, he was there on his father's command, so completing the job was more important than his sister's childish mockery. "Why does he hate us already?" Ablina whispered, examining his bald head. "No, he doesn't hate you. He is just mad at me, and I know he looks like a stubborn mule, but these years with Papa must have been hard for him," Amaraya said in a hushed tone.

"It's like Ray and me, we fight, and sometimes Ray wants to kill me, but she doesn't," Ablina smiled. "Correct," Amaraya said. "Ma, you should talk to him without all that," Raylina said with multiple pauses. "What all that?" Amaraya asked. "The acerbity," Raylina said. Amaraya was tongue-tied; she knew her daughter was right this time.

They drove past the beguiling town of Darjeeling, located in the foothills of the humongous Himalayan. The appealing natural beauty of the town imprinted their minds forever. After 3 hours on the curvy mountain roads, they finally reached their destination, "the Yama Castle."

***

The massive gates opened, and they drove inside the Yama Castle. The castle was built on the highest peak, and it covered half of the mountain's area. It stood there, alone and omnipotent, amidst trees, bushes, and the zillion little cascades flowing through the mountain's thin cracks.

Raylina and Ablina were inarticulate and dumbstruck. They didn't believe that the castle standing up on the mountain was their home.

As they drove closer to Yama Castle, the castle's wall became more visible. The bloody red sandstone, incredibly conjugated with green limestone, made the wall uniquely archaic and regal. The four towers of the castle were standing in each direction—east, west, north, and south—touching the skies. Each tower was bounded together by golden air bridges.

Aamirah stepped out of the car. "We are home," he said, looking back at Amaraya. Amaraya's eyes moistened, seeing her home, but she quickly looked away. "Being strong all the time is tiring," she thought, hiding her tears from her brother. Aamirah saw his sister's emotional face, but he ignored her. His issues with his sister were still there, and a few drops of water from Amaraya's eyes weren't going to solve them.

Astor was in another car, so they were waiting for him at the entrance door. "This tiny glitch was totally avoidable," Aamirah thought, getting impatient because of this slight delay. Aamirah was a perfectionist at the core, he liked things to be in order, and this quality of his was both his strength and weakness.

"Wonderful!" Ablina gasped, staring at the brown tree branches cloaking around the entrance door. "In records and books, the colonization of Darjeeling began back in the 19th century by British Raj. But in reality, we, 'the Shaurayaveers', laid the foundation of this range in the 16th century. These are no ordinary mountains, girls. Magic lives here in these mountains, every tree, every flower, every leaf—everywhere. Even the wind that flows here is magical… Breathe in the magic," Amaraya said, closing her eyes, breathing in the magical cold air of the mountains. Ablina and Raylina followed their mother and stood there, with closed eyes, breathing in the cold air of Darjeeling, feeling every stroke of wind flowing over their skin, spreading in their veins, and rejuvenating their souls.

Aamirah's ears alerted. One thing in the whole wide world he disliked the most was spreading the wrong information. "Sorry, but here you are wrong, Ami," Aamirah finally interrupted. Aamirah waited for his sister's response, but her expressions stated clearly that she was in no mood to argue, so he took the torch of enlightenment and began.

"The Yama Castle was built by the great Swastik Shaurayaveer in the 15th century. Not in 16th century. Swastik Shaurayaveer was the first warlock to master the 'Ragata' magic. He then came to Darjeeling and built it for his family. Yama is not just a castle. It is a school for everyone who wishes to learn the magic called 'Life,'" Aamirah said with pride. "Ragata… as in 'Śirā Ragata,'" Ablina said.

Aamirah looked at his nescient nieces and wondered how they could be so clueless about such basic knowledge. "And here I thought your mother was raising you two to be the powerful witches of the next generation," Aamirah said. "What does that mean?" Ablina asked again. "Well, there is no hurry. Now that we are here, Papa will make sure to teach you both some true magic," he taunted, glancing at Amaraya. "Balls... Bravo," Raylina grinned, slow clapping, enjoying and appreciating the captious comments of Aamirah. She saw her mother's nostrils flare from barely repressed anger, and the cold death stare she gave, made Raylina shut up. After 10 minutes, Astor's car reached in. They all went together inside the castle.

***

The interior of the castle raised the impact the exterior had made on them. A legion of Banyan tree branches rose to form the center of the main hall and scattered in all four "Yama castle" directions. The branches resembled the veins, and together it all looked like a dense network of the human venous system. "What is that red flower?" Raylina asked cluelessly, gazing at the beautiful red flowers which surrounded the trunk of the Banyan tree.

Ablina was astounded. She identified what it was but couldn't believe it. "The Ragata Flower," she gasped. "The what?" Raylina asked. "The deadliest flower of the witch world, the 'Ragata Flower,' or the 'Blood Flower,' or also called the 'Flower of Darkness,' 'The Flower which cannot be touched,'" Aamirah answered.

"But... Ragata flower is a myth just like Vaylar," Ablina mumbled in doubt, not ready to accept the fact. According to her, books don't lie, except if they are fiction work, but she was one hundred percent sure that the book she read was not fiction. "But they aren't real? It must be a replica or something," Ablina argued. "You should ask your mother," Aamirah said, staring at Amaraya.

"This is indeed the Ragata flower," Amaraya revealed. "Śirā Ragata," Ablina spoke with dramatic pauses. "What does Śirā mean?" Ablina asked directly. "We will teach you thoroughly, Ablina. Have patience," Aamirah said and walked out to answer his phone. Ablina looked at her mother to answer her question, but like always, Amaraya waved her off.

Aamirah was waiting for someone, but he was too proud to talk. "Ray, look at him," Ablina whispered. "What?" Raylina said. "That kid," Ablina pointed. "Standing over there." "Where?" she asked again. "Behind the tree," said Ablina. "Ohh, yes…," Raylina said and waved hello at the kid. He laughed and ran away. "Uncle A, how long are we going to stand here?" Raylina asked tiredly. Aamirah turned around and said nothing. Raylina realized that it was better to keep the lion rested, so she didn't speak further.

Astor slid back to where the girls were standing, "I used to think my family is weird," Astor said gingerly. They laughed at his statement. "At least you know your folks. These people are complete strangers, and that Aamirah, he is definitely the crazy one," Raylina murmured. "Yes, I agree. Just like you, strange and socially awkward," Ablina teased. "I like the guy," Astor said. "You both are illogical and unrealistic, and I am done with you guys," Raylina announced and moved away from them.

Ablina, Raylina, Astor, and Amaraya stood there for an hour, silently. Raylina kept staring at the ancient banyan tree and its offshoots, and Ablina's eyes were locked at the magnificent Ragata flower.

As time passed, the tsunami of questions related to Śirā Ragata kept on attacking Ablina's brain. She felt that it was high time for all the mysteries and secrets to come to the surface. And this time, no matter how much her mother tried to hide things from them, she was ascertained to find the truth.

Amaraya and Raylina were irritated, but they stood there quietly to avoid any quarrel between them internally and externally. "Now I know where you get all the torture ideas from," Raylina chuckled pungently. "Ray, if you don't stop, I am really feeling inspired today," Amaraya grin evilly. "Ohhh, I am scared," Raylina said in a fake tone. "Wait for it, Ray. Your grandfather is worse than me," Amaraya warned. "Mother, I think I am well immune," she replied. The threat chat kept going on for the next few minutes, but there was still no sign of the person they wanted to meet, "Artha Shaurayaveer."

Aamirah received a call, and he was ordered to take them to their rooms. Raylina gulped her anger and was astonished to see her sister so excited about the rooms. Amaraya asked the girls not to say anything or do anything to provoke Aamirah. But, on the inside, she was planning a cold-blooded murder of her brother and father. All four of them were escorted to their rooms.

Amaraya, Ablina, Raylina, and Astor were given the castle's entire right wing, almost like a well-decorated, lavish prison. Their rooms were specially designed as per their choices, which amused Raylina. She stopped complaining the moment she saw her big room with huge windows and a breathtaking view of the world's third-highest mountain peak, "Kanchenjunga." Ablina was well satisfied with her room. While Astor didn't care about the rooms, he was extremely jetlagged, and all he cared about was sleeping for the next 10 hours straight.

***

Amaraya walked into her old room and was shocked to see her room just as the way she had left it centuries ago. The deep red curtains with golden closures, the bed, her portraits, everything was untouched and unmoved; it was like no one came in except the cleaners with clear instructions. It amazed her; how they let her go or, in her words, threw her away but kept her memories intact.

Amaraya went into the balcony and saw an old broken bench in the corner. Bullets of nostalgia hit her head; the bench reminded her of her and George's bittersweet fights. It's strange how some people hold power over us even after they are no longer with us. Haunting us with their memories.

"Mother, look at this," Ablina rushed in. Amaraya quickly wiped her tears, and said, "Yes, Baby." "I found this picture. It was hanging in a corridor. Is that you?" Ablina said and showed the photo on her mobile. "Yes, it's me. It was made when I was 13, like real 13… not on immortality elixir," Amaraya said, watching her younger self, recalling the simpler times. "You look so pretty," Ablina smiled. "Thank you!" Amaraya blushed. "Ma, you okay? You look… sad," Ablina asked. "Just some old memories decided to knock on me," Amaraya said and hugged Ablina.

"Come on, Mother, Don't make it obvious," Raylina barged in and then joined the group hug. "What's obvious?" Amaraya asked. "That you love Abby more than me," Raylina laughed. Amaraya pulled Raylina's ear. "Ouch, Ma, please. It's inhumane," Raylina shrieked.

Aamirah walked in and interrupted their moment. "Dinner at 7. Sharp," he informed, looking at them turn by turn. "Okay, Aamirah," Amaraya acknowledge him. He left in an uptight fashion without saying anything further.

***

The Bayers and Astor marched together to the dining room. Ablina clasped Raylina's hand nervously as they entered the dining room. Raylina looked at her sister's face with side-eyes, "Grow up, child," she smirked. Ablina's face sulked, and she unclasped Raylina's hand.

The room was spacious; the reflection of a huge chandelier was all around the glass walls, and it looked all bright and glistening. The big flower vase loaded with fresh white lilies was kept on the center of the dining table. Amaraya guided everyone to their seats so that she didn't create any trouble from her end. All settled on their directed chairs and waited for the Artha Shaurayaveer.

Raylina kept her hands on the glassy top of the table and said, "Are we going to spend our entire night waiting for your father? Like we did in the morning? What is he, the president of the world?" Their mouths were hanging open in shock, staring at the daunting yet striking-looking man in his 70s wearing a high-neck kurta-pajama, standing behind Raylina's chair, staring back at them with his gleaming black eyes.

Raylina turned her head in the direction of what everyone was staring at. Her eyes bugged out in surprise as she looked back. She, too, had joined the terrified club of Astor, Ablina, and Amaraya. The atmosphere inside the room started to warm up from the waves of terror coming out of them, and they were rendered speechless.

Artha Shaurayaveer's sharp black eyes studied each of them meticulously. His know-it-all personality made him instantly unlikeable, but the kindness on his unwavering, brilliant face contradicted it. Artha's dense grey-black curly hair indicated that he was no longer on the immortality tonic.

Artha Shaurayaveer was kind, noble, fierce, courageous, a wonderful teacher, a devoted husband, and a great father. For him, his family was everything, because he grew up without one. Artha was 8 when he lost his mother and father in a tragic accident. After losing his family, the only thing which kept him alive was magic.

Young Artha spent his time learning all forms of magic, mastering it. He buried himself deeply into the world of magic and stayed there till the love of his life— his wife Anilsa—pulled him out. But his destiny took a different turn.

Artha lost his wife soon after their marriage, and a part of him died with her. But, fortunately, he had three reasons to carry on: his two children, Amaraya and Aamirah, and Magic. Artha channeled all his love, loss, and pain into magic and invented "Niyate magic," the magic of soul healing.

"Papa," Amaraya said as she stood up, feeling her words had frozen for an eternity. The girls and Astor followed her. "Amaraya," Artha said in his ocean-like deep voice. Amaraya and Artha stared at each other, and the years of unresolved issues started to crawl back on the surface from their head graves.

Aamirah came with his wife and daughter. Their entrance broke the moments of fiddly. "Gaurangi," Amaraya exclaimed, looking at Aamirah's wife. They hugged each other; their hugs hinted to Bayer sisters that they had been best friends.

Gaurangi Shaurayaveer was a great revolutionary witch of all time. She was well known for blending her remarkable medical skills with the "Jatur magic" — the magic of herbs. She never accessorized herself with expensive jewelry or branded clothes despite being a royal family's daughter-in-law. She was simple, kind, humble, and a visionary. She was in her 40s, and just like Artha and Aamirah, she too had stopped consuming the immortality tonic.

Gaurangi came from a very influential family of witches from a small village of Eoraki, Gujarat. Gaurangi and Aamirah married right after Amaraya eloped with George to re-establish the Shaurayaveer name. Their marriage was full of compromises and struggles until they had their first child—Ekani Shaurayaveer, 17 years ago.

"Ekani, meet your aunt," said Gaurangi, brimming with happiness. Ekani joined her hands together and said, "Namaste!" in her lovely voice and touched Amaraya's feet.

Ekani was a lively soul, a wanderer at heart. She enjoyed wandering in the lap of nature over parties and nightclubs. Her long layered hair, light brown skin, pleasant smile, and kind dark brown eyes made her the spitting image of Gaurangi, but a younger version. Even though Ekani was a royal Princess, she had a very down-to-earth personality and treated everyone equally.

"Meet Raylina and Ablina," Amaraya introduced her daughters. Raylina and Ablina greeted them in proper Indian customs. The Bayer sisters felt an instant connection with them. They were all delighted to meet each other.

Artha was standing there observing them quietly. He waited for Amaraya to introduce her daughters to him. Amaraya knew what her father wanted from the looks on his face. He wanted her to yield. But surrendering was against her nature. So, she waited for him to initiate the conversation.

It's hard to let go of your ego, and it's even harder to find the courage to do so.

Their silent war bothered Raylina. But she was courageous to the core and never thought about the consequences, so she went straight to Artha. She bowed her head down with humility and touched his feet. "I am Raylina Bayer," she presented herself. He beamed. He raised his right hand and kept it on her head, and said, "Jeete Raho (live on)." Ablina then went and did the same. He affectionately welcomed his granddaughters, and waited for his daughter to talk to him.

Families can be awkward, judgmental, forceful, messy, but they are always there when you need them, even if you come back after a millennium or so.

The Bayers, Shaurayaveers, and Astor sat on their chairs, and chefs started bringing the courses one after another. Potato curry, roasted garlic mint-coated naan (bread), dal tadka (Indian yellow lentils), baked cheese and paneer balls, spinach salad, oven-baked brussel sprouts, dried spicy okra, and many more lip-smacking Indian dishes were served.

Amaraya and Artha overlooked each other and minded their dinners. Their unbending pride restricted them from talking to each other. The rest of them bonded well. All except Artha and Amaraya chatted about mundane affairs, and the rest of the night went uneventful.

CHAPTER 13

NEW PEOPLE

The sunny rays barged through the windows and fell upon Raylina's face. She covered her face with a quilt, but her sleep was already disturbed, so she woke up from her bed and slipped her feet into the warm furry baby-blue slippers. She then pulled out the maroon woolen coat hanging on the coat rack and wrapped it around her shivering body.

Raylina sauntered into the Castle's halls to find her way to the kitchen. After some time, she realized that she was lost. "Oh no," she whined, scratching her right eyebrow unconsciously. She looked up helplessly, and her eyes caught on the inscriptions scribbled all over the Castle's roof.

"There is a loophole in the 'Book of Destiny,' and it's called 'Choices.'" Raylina read the quote in her head.

It was written all over the ceiling, millions of times. The outlandish design of the Castle's ceiling bewildered her mind. Her avidity to explore more kept her walking through the Yama's hallways.

***

After wandering for 20 minutes, Raylina stopped near the huge portrait. "It's big and unpleasant," she murmured while staring at the lady dressed in a red saree surrounded by lions. She pulled out her phone from the pocket of her woolen coat. "*Abby, I am lost. I am near this big painting; come get me,*" *she typed and sent it.*

Like always, Raylina started to lose her patience. She dawdled in the corridor to find her way back to her wing. But everything in the Castle looked the same; it was like a giant maze. She felt stupid for not remembering her way back. She sat down on her knees in forlornness.

The cold wind brushed Raylina's earlobes and whispered something to her. She stood up quickly and reconnoitered around, but no one was there. Her body numbed, but the blood flowing in her veins started to glow up. She felt like she carried the cosmos inside her. Raylina rubbed her ears with her index finger and thumb to restore her hearing senses. "Follow the branches," the whisper spoke again. She understood the message and searched for the branches.

Yama castle was the home of ancient witches. Everything in that place had its own meaning, so Raylina decided to follow the mystical whisper. She followed the branches spread on the edges of the ceiling, and they led her to Ablina.

Raylina saw Ablina and hugged her. "Ray, you okay?" Ablina asked worriedly. "I am fine," Raylina lied to Ablina's face. But it's difficult to lie when your face speaks the truth on your behalf. "My sister is not a hugger. Ray, spit it out," Ablina asked seriously. "I-I-I..." Raylina stammered. "What?" Ablina questioned in an interrogative tone.

"Leave me," the screams echoed through the castle walls. The Bayer sisters stopped their bickering and went running down to the main hall.

***

Ablina and Raylina reached there and saw a man wounded badly. He was begging the tattooed ruffians to stop beating him. At first, they couldn't figure out who it was, but as they moved closer to them, they saw Visac lying on the ground. They ran towards him.

"Visac," Ablina gasped, lifting up his bruised, broken face in her arms. Blood dripping from his wounded head, his olive green shirt soaked in blood, his body unable to move, was all too pitiful to watch. "Visac, oh my god... Please wake up," she wailed. His quivering lips gave Ablina relief.

The man standing behind Ablina tried to pull her back, but Raylina seized his arm, dragging him away from Ablina, and punched straight on his face. He fell against the wall and hit his head. He stood up, wiping off the blood coming from the top of his head, and walked towards Raylina, glaring at her with rage boiling up in his charming hazel eyes.

"Ray," Ablina cried. Raylina unglued her angry eyes from the tattooed ruffian she punched and shifted to her sister. "Abby, let's take him to Ma," Raylina said. They assisted Visac to get up. As they reached across the hall, they saw Artha. Amaraya and Aamirah came rushing down to the main hall, and just like that, the quietude took over the noise.

"Put that boy down," Artha ordered Ablina and Raylina. They carefully laid Visac down. Ablina put her glittery yellow scarf below Visac's head. Artha kept his fingers on Visac's head, and his wounds started to heal, just like that. The Bayer sisters were flabbergasted; they had never seen anyone heal someone without a spell, and they wondered if he had chanted in his mind.

Everyone in the hall was openmouthed. The magic Artha conjured was only studied in books, discussed amongst the witches groups, and heard about. But no one in the world had actually witnessed it. It was the first time any of them, including his own children, saw him conjure the "Ragata Magic."

Visac woke up like a new man. Ablina was overjoyed to see him in one piece. She hugged him in front of everyone. Amaraya went to Ablina and gently pulled her away from Visac. Raylina saw the embarrassment in her mother and sister's eyes, so she hugged Visac to save the so-called honor. "You owe me big time, V," she whispered in Visac's ear.

"Escort this young man to the guest room. His bones need rest. And rest of you, the show's over," Artha asked everyone to leave, and they did so, except Amaraya.

"Artha Shaurayaveer," Amaraya grinned, and he turned his back. "Amaraya Bayer," he taunted. "It's Amaraya Shaurayaveer Bayer," she proudly claimed. The wave of passive aggression flowed once again between father and daughter. "Papa, you can take away my family, but you can never take my identity away," she said, accusing him in an unwavering tone for casting her out of the family. "Ami," he bellowed. "Why did you kill my husband?" she asked angrily.

Artha remained silent. His strength was nabbed back by his honor prison, the strength he needed to continue. With hurt in his eyes and tired shoulders, he did what all parents do; he gathered himself to answer his disappointed child. "Ami, it wasn't me. It was Vaylar," he replied.

Amaraya stood there, crestfallen; like she wanted it to be her father. She started to walk away. "That day, you asked me to respect your decision," Artha said loudly. She stopped moving. He walked to her, and continued, "And I did what you asked for, Ami. But that does not mean I have to accept it," he said with a long pause.

Artha and Amaraya successfully inflicted the wounds they wanted to give each other to lessen their own pain.

"Papa, you abandoned me because I wanted to be happy? Because I wanted to marry the man I loved?" She sobbed. "Ami," he spoke with regret. "Don't, Papa. First, you beat George to death. Next, you wanted to kill me, and now your team of barbarians beat my daughter's friend," she said furiously.

"Ami, I was angry and hurt. No father in his right mind can think about killing his own child," Artha said in his defense. "You saw my anger that day, Ami, but you didn't see my worried face. You kids always want your parents to understand you, but when it comes to us, you all don't even bother to talk."

Amaraya laughed insanely. Artha's argument was pointless for her. She was not ready to listen or to talk. She started to walk away again. Artha stood there waiting for his daughter to come back like he did years ago. "Stubbornness cost you many things when you gave it a power over you," she recalled George's words and came rushing back to her father.

"I am not done talking," she said, and the frozen hope started to thaw. "I spent centuries in that hideous tomb with my daughters, your granddaughters, because some power-hungry maniac killed my husband, and you didn't even bother to come and check on us," she began firing. "It's been two days since our arrival, and you didn't even bother to say hello. You taught us about the ideals of forgiving… what about that, huh?" She said all of it in one breath.

Artha stared at her blankly. He took a deep, long breath and said, "You want me to give in first? Did you ever consider looking back, Ami? Years went by after you left, you had two daughters, but no, you didn't. And now you expect me to be normal with you."

"Ami, when you were born, I was the happiest man on this planet. But when I saw you, my daughter, leaving me, her family, to elope with a stranger she had known for 4 months… it broke my heart," Artha said in a painful voice. "Papa, you asked me to choose between my love and family," Amaraya said bitterly.

"Ami, we choose what we do not have. And I was not mad because you chose love over your family. I was furious because you were okay to walk away. That broke me," Artha said, gulping back his sorrow.

Amaraya's misunderstandings resolved after hearing Artha's side of the story. She realized that her father was just doing what a father should do; he was worried and protective of his little daughter. At that time, it all seemed intense and unjust, but it wasn't an unforgivable offense. And at that moment, Amaraya understood what she was about to lose because of her stubbornness.

"I love you, Ami, and I know I am too late, but I want to make it right," Artha said and kept his hand on her head. "Papa," Amaraya said with eyes full of longing love, and hugged her father without wasting a second. "It's late and chilly, Beta (my child). Let's go inside," he said and gave his cream shawl to Amaraya.

Parents, stand by you. They forgive you. They try to understand you, even if they don't believe in the things you do. Their efforts at making their child happy and safe never end.

The reconciliation of the relationship began at that moment. It's all about the effort one makes for you. Artha wanted his family back, so he decided to let go of his anger and let the tenderness of his heart for his children rule over his ego.

***

The sunrays crawled back, and the night expanded its dark claws all over the place. Raylina paced around in Visac's room with her head immersed in the thoughts about the whisper she heard in the morning, while Ablina sat beside Visac, not taking her eyes off his face, praying, waiting for him to wake up anytime.

"Hey," Visac faintly responded. "Visac, you okay?" Ablina asked worriedly, trying hard not to burst out into tears. "I am fine," Visac replied and kept his hand on Ablina's left shoulder. They both looked at each other like they were seeing each other after a century, completely ignoring Raylina standing there. "Why are you here?" Ablina asked directly. "I felt that something bad is going to happen, so I just…" he faltered, finding ways to tell her about his vision.

"Ahhhhhhem," Raylina cleared her throat and barged in their conversation. "Ray," Ablina said awkwardly.

"Okay, you guys do whatever you people do," Raylina said, and she left.

Raylina stood in the corridor, outside her sister's would-be boyfriend's room. She softly closed her eyes and rested her head back on the wall, still thinking about the whisper that guided her to Ablina in the morning. She wanted to hear that whisper again because it meant something to her. What she felt was more than magic. It was cosmically divine.

"Princess," the man said in his throaty voice, interrupting Raylina's deep pondering. She opened her eyes and saw the man she punched in the main hall in the morning, standing in front of her, with a smirk on his bodacious face. "It's Raylina," she said menacingly while gazing at his neck tattoo. "Śirā Ragata," he said while unbuttoning his black shirt to show her the rest of the tattoo.

"Śirā Ragata," Raylina repeated while scrutinizing the emerald green vein-like lines tattooed on his body. "It's..." she halted. "We all serve your family, who serve the 'Śirā Ragata,'" he said and lowered his eyes from her face to the ground. His decency touched her heart.

Raylina gently caressed his tattooed neck with her fingers. "'Śirā' means 'veins,' and 'Ragata' means 'blood,'" the man described, and he directed her fingers to the Ragata flower carved on his broad chest. "It's burned," Raylina said in wonder. "Well, most of us are," the man replied with subtlety. "What does that mean?" she asked. "Nothing, princess," he said, calmly.

The man looked at her through his piercing light hazel eyes while buttoning up his shirt. "I am glad that you punched me today," the man smiled. "You deserved it," Raylina said. "I am sorry," he said in a low tone. His apology established the foundation of their chaotic friendship. "Good night," he said, and walked in the opposite direction towards his room.

***

Raylina entered her room thinking about the man she punched; her head was captivated by his charismatic personality. She changed her clothes and slid into her bed. "No," she screeched and jumped out of her bed. "I didn't ask his name. Brilliant Ray!" she said to herself. She wore her slippers, wrapped herself in a long white woolen coat, and went out.

Raylina kept on walking hurriedly through the hallway. She was no wanderer, but to find her answers, she could go to any extent. She wanted to know his name, and it didn't matter to her if she had to search the whole castle to find his room or knock door to door.

The search for the charming hazel eyes went on for three hours. Raylina explored the entire castle to find the man she punched, but had no luck finding him. Her legs were aching, she wanted to go back, but she figured that the kitchen was nearby, so she headed there, per the roadmap her memory provided.

Raylina reached the correct destination. She stepped in, and the kitchen was bigger than her room. She spotted the fridge in the corner and said, "Ohhh, finally!" As she opened the fridge door, the pat on her back scared the hell out of her. "What the…" she bawled.

Raylina turned around instantly to see who it was. The man she punched held her by her shoulders and said, "Relax." "You scared me," Raylina mumbled. "I am sorry. I heard a noise," he stated. "I am here for coffee," she said, trying to avoid eye contact.

They stood there, not talking. The man she punched moved closer to her, and she stepped back. The man pointed his index finger at the opened fridge door and said, "It's open." "Huh," Raylina asked with her eyes wide open. "The door," he pointed again at the door. "Ohh…" She exclaimed nervously and moved aside from there. "Manashaya," he said. "Huh?" she asked. "I am Manashaya Rushik," he said, and he reached out his hand for a handshake.

Manashaya Rushik was a 20-year-old loyal devotee of the Shaurayaveer clan. Artha Shaurayaveer found him when he was 11 years old and brought him home. He followed Artha blindly like Aamirah. He was human by birth, but after undergoing intensive training under Artha's and Aamirah's guidance, he learned magical shielding skills and became one of the Shaurayaveer family's loyal soldiers.

Raylina tried to play it cool, but the dilemma of moving her hand or not to greet him made her intensely anxious. Manashaya took his hands back and put them in his trouser pockets. "I think I should go," Raylina said and left in a hurry. He stood there watching her leave.

***

Raylina scurried like she saw an untamed dragon hunting her. She reached her room and jumped into her bed, covering her head with a blanket. She was restless, wondering why she was behaving like that.

"Ah!" Raylina grunted, removing her blanket from her head. "What is wrong with you," she mumbled while clearing her messy hair from her face. She picked up her phone and called her best friend.

"Hello, Ray, it's 4:30 there. What happened? Is everything okay?" Alisar asked in a concerned voice.

"Alisar, calm down, you old man," she chuckled.

"Ray," he shrieked in annoyance.

"I want you here," she ordered.

"Ray, I am leaving next week. Hold on till then," he said.

"I miss you. I miss my best friend," she said without thinking.

"Best friend? Huh," he asked.

"I don't know, Alisar. Bye," she said and hung up the call.

CHAPTER 14

THE BEGINNING

Raylina woke up half asleep and walked to her balcony to check the noises coming from outside. She cleared her sleepy eyes and saw Artha standing in the garden, initiating his early morning class. His disciples were sitting down on the ground surrounding him.

"Our bodies and minds work together in harmony, but our souls don't. Our souls are meant to serve a greater purpose. Our souls are the light that brightens our existence. Though they are part of you, they are not part of you. They reside in you, and you become them," Artha explained to his students.

Raylina continued to watch Artha deliver an outstanding lecture on "the soul and its purposes" from her room's balcony. Raylina and Artha's disciples were completely hypnotized by Artha's speech, like a meteor could crash through and burn everything, but nobody would have noticed. It was like he was singing a melodious symphony of words. Their souls were deeply moved by Artha's wise words. At that moment, Artha held their souls in his very hands.

"Raylina, why don't you come down and join us?" Artha suddenly called her out loud. It took a few minutes for Raylina to apprehend that Artha was calling her. "Really?" she asked dubiously. "Yes, why not?" He smiled. "Okay, Grandpa," she beamed and ran down as fast as she could to the garden.

Raylina sat alongside Artha's disciples to attend Artha's lecture. Artha was happy to see Raylina taking a keen interest in his class. The lecture ended after 20 minutes. Everyone left but Raylina. She patiently waited for Artha to wind up his class.

"So, Raylina, what did you think of the lecture?" Artha asked her, wrapping a dark maroon shawl around him. "It was informative," Raylina replied. "I am glad that you think like that," Artha said brightly. "Grandpa is it true Vaylar killed our father?" She struck her question directly to Artha.

"How do you know? It was between…" Artha was visibly startled. "I was there, during the whole heart-touching confrontation between you and Ma. We all thought you were involved-in-murder…," Raylina hesitantly explained him in pieces. Artha wanted to explain his past actions to his granddaughter, but then there was no point in justifying it now, so he remained quiet and let Raylina speak.

The morose expression on her grandfather's face was hurting Raylina. She took a deep sigh to lighten her dour face and said, "I trust you, Grandpa, which is very rare for me." Artha gently nodded his head and said, "Thank you for trusting me, Raylina." "It's Ray, my people call me that," Raylina smiled. "Ray," he said, wearing a broad smile on his face. Artha and Raylina walked back towards the castle for breakfast.

Raylina placed her hand on Artha's arm and said, "Do you know, Grandpa? I did learn one thing from overhearing your dramatic conversation with Ma." "And what was that?" Artha asked softly. "It's difficult being a parent of a lunatic," she chuckled. Artha repressed his laugh for a moment, but he couldn't hold it any longer and burst out in laughter.

Amaraya was standing near the dining room waiting for Ablina. She saw Raylina and Artha walking towards her, chatting, laughing. She was happy to see her father making an effort to get to know her family. "Looks like you guys are getting along," Amaraya said hopefully. "Yes, Ma, Grandpa, and I agree on so many things," Raylina said and winked at Artha. "Amaraya, Ray is amazing," Artha praised.

"Ray... huh," Ablina came and interrupted their conversation. "Ma, they are really teaming up," Ablina added. "Breakfast's ready, we all should go and eat something," Artha suggested. "I am famished," Raylina said, and they all headed to the dining room.

***

Aamirah, Gaurangi, Ekani, Astor, and Visac were already at the breakfast table. Ablina came and innocently sat next to Visac. The elders in the room, gawked at them. In Indian families, the ultimate nightmare begins for boys and girls when they come under the family's suspicion radar.

Ekani saw the elders' judgmental faces and understood that it was time to distract everyone from Ablina and Visac, "Good morning, everyone!" she said zestfully. Everyone instantly greeted her back. Breakfast was served, and they all pretended to focus on it, but their main focus was still on Ablina and Visac.

Ablina realized that the awkwardness in the air was due to her. It freaked her out. Her leg started to shake restlessly. Visac noticed her pale face and her shaking legs, so he gently placed his hand on her thigh to stop the trembling before it started rocking the entire table. Her eyes widened, and the piece of paratha got stuck in her food pipe.

"Are you alright?" Raylina said while patting Ablina's back. "Yes... yes...," she coughed. Visac realized that his gesture made Ablina even more flustered than she was before. "I'll take your leave. I have some business in town," Aamirah said and left the breakfast table, not paying much attention to Ablina's brewing love story.

"Ekani, why don't you take your sisters out to see the town," Gaurangi suggested, diverting the attention from Ablina. "Ohh… Mumma, I would love to," Ekani said and turned to the Bayer sisters, "You guys, we should totally go. I think you will love it." "Sure Ekani. I am in," Raylina said. "Ma, why don't you accompany us," Ablina asked. "No, honey, you guys carry on. I have something to take care of," Amaraya declined the offer to visit the town.

"Ekani, take Manashaya with you," Gaurangi said and left for her daily meditative sessions in the Yama caves. "Girls, let's go," said Ekani with great enthusiasm, and the Bayer sisters went to Ekani's room.

It was weird for Ablina to digest the sudden change in Raylina's behavior. But she ignored it as her mind was taken up by Visac. Ablina somehow managed to sneak Visac away from the prying eyes of Ekani and Raylina to her room. Visac knew that he could not escape Ablina, and he had to find his courage and be honest about why he was there. "Visac," she started. There was tension igniting between the two of them. "Ablina, I know," Visac interrupted before Ablina could voice her question.

"I know what you are going to ask, but before I answer that question, I want you to know that maybe I'm wrong about this and there is a part of me that doesn't believe it… but if there is a slight possibility of this being true… the risk is too high," Visac said seriously. "What are you talking about? Stop talking in riddles. It's freaking me out," she said fearfully.

Visac held Ablina's shoulders and said, "I saw blood." "Blood, what does that mean Visac," Ablina's words trembled. "I saw you sitting in a pond of blood, your face… the agony… it all looked so real. I couldn't stop it. I don't know what it means," he painfully described. Ablina gently took his arms off of her shoulders and held them, "Visac, relax. It was just a dream."

"But it looked so real. I just could not sit idly after that. I had to see you," Visac said. His eyes looked as if he was reliving that terror. "It's okay," Ablina said and kissed Visac's forehead. Visac held her tightly, her warmth melting away his ice-cold panic state. He wrapped his hand around her neck, and slowly pulled her closer.

Visac's forehead pressed against Ablina's, their eyes closed. His lips softly pecked hers—two worlds merging into one. "No, we can't," Ablina said, pulling herself slightly back. Visac pursed his lips in embarrassment.

Visac silently stared into Ablina's honey-dipped eyes, wondering how to make this right, as he was falling in love for real. "Ablina, I love you," Visac said to break the grave silence between them. Ablina was tongue-tied, her heart knew the answer to Visac's questions, but her mind stopped her from saying it. "Visac," Ablina stuttered, breathing heavily. "I know…," Visac interrupted her. "I know Ablina," he said, clasping her tiny waist with his one hand, pulling her closer to him.

"I know," Visac said again, brushing his lips softly against her forehead and holding them there. Ablina held on to his waist tightly, and before she could decide between right and wrong, her hands moved on their own accord, putting pressure on Visac's neck. She leaned against him and pushed herself up slightly, letting her lips dive passionately into his. At last, their souls found each other amidst all the odds.

Ablina and Visac's wonderful moment was interrupted as they heard a knock on the door. "Oh my god, what do we do now?" Ablina panicked. "Relax, tell them I was here for notes," he said unmindfully. "Visac, very smart, we are not in school," she said in a sarcastic tone.

Ablina went and opened the door. It was Ekani and Raylina. "What is he doing here?" Raylina asked in her interrogative tone, looking at Visac standing inside Ablina's room. "Ray, we were just talking about joining Artha's classes," Visac said. Ablina sighed quietly and smirked lightly.

Raylina sniggered. "Well, I asked Abby, but I don't mind you being her spokesperson," she said and winked. "I think we should go," Ablina diverted the topic. "Oh, yes, we were thinking of wearing some Indian clothes," Raylina informed. "Indian outfits, cool, let's do it," Ablina said. The girls headed to Ekani's room. Ablina looked back at Visac and saw the lingering passion in his eyes. She blushed and gave him a small smile before disappearing down the hall with the girls.

***

Visac was spellbound as he saw Ablina walking towards him with Raylina and Ekani. His eyes were fixed on the tiny white pearls hanging downwardly on the metallic jumkhas (earrings). "Wow," Visac gasped, looking at Ablina's long floral magenta kurta. Ablina blushed like an 80s Bollywood heroine. Raylina was not okay with Ablina's newly founded dramatic expression, but she left her alone this time.

"Abby, look at you nailing this outfit," Astor said and interrupted Visac and Ablina's blooming slow-motion romance. "Thank you!" Ablina replied. "Well, I also look great," Raylina said, swirling off her light peach gathered top. "So do I," Ekani said, clearing the creases from her long purple dress. "You all look spectacularly beautiful," Manashaya pitched in and opened the door for Ekani.

Visac opened the door for Ablina, she climbed in the seat, and then he followed her and sat with her. Astor rolled his eyes furiously, he moved to the front seat, and Ekani took on the steering wheel. "Hey, where will I sit?" Raylina asked. "Ray, you can come with Manashaya. He is driving alone," Ekani suggested.

Raylina was not ready to go alone with Manashaya because she wanted to avoid the impending weird attraction brewing between them. "Can he drive this car? We can go in Manashaya's car," Raylina insisted to Ekani. "Ya sure," Ekani agreed. "No, I don't want him in this car, Ray," Ablina said angrily. "Okay, Relax, Abby. I will go with him," Raylina said. "No, you come here on this seat; there is space for one," Ablina said. "Okay," Raylina said and sat next to Ablina. Manashaya went alone in another car.

***

Amaraya's sky tore apart like paper, as the truth ripped out in the open, "Papa, what are you saying," Amaraya ranted. "It's true," Artha said solemnly. "Then why would you hide it, huh?" She sobbed, falling down on her knees on the living room's floor. "Ami, we never knew about George being a witch hunter. We started to dig out about him and his family after he was killed. Further, when we investigated your disappearance, we came across the man named Scodin Bayer, who happened to have a direct link with George, and the great Vandarlwan Bayer's bloodline, who you know was the first chief of 'Saith hunters,'" he revealed.

"George, a witch hunter, that too a Saith. No… No I don't believe this crap. You are lying," Amaraya said in disbelief, staring at her father, begging him to stop breaking her perfect heaven. "Bayers are witch hunters, Ami. And George was not any ordinary witch hunter. He was a Saith," Artha stated clearly. And hearing the truth again broke her into a million pieces. "Ami, he came to finish us, but then he fell in love with you, he learned our ways, and his perception about us changed with the time he spent here."

Saith hunters were a union of seven exceptional men of the human race with unique superhuman abilities such as eidetic memory, telepathy, telekinesis, and precognition, mostly similar to witches. They joined their forces to eradicate the witches' magical existence from the world. Saith hunters were as old as the witches. But, as time passed, just like the witches, they went into hiding as their superhuman abilities began to be seen as a threat to ordinary humans. In a way, they became the men they were hunting down.

The truth of George being the son of Saith Men shook Amaraya's perfect little world. She wanted to deny everything she heard, but the proof Artha presented against the Bayer family was strong enough to question her blind faith in her husband.

"Ami, George was a good man. He changed for you. He betrayed his own family for your love," Artha said, defending the man who took his daughter away from him. Amaraya wiped her tears and asked, "So his family killed him for marrying me, not ours?" "No, his curiosity got him killed. He was hunting Vaylar," Artha revealed. "What does Vaylar have to do with any of this?" Amaraya questioned dimly.

Artha sat alongside Amaraya and said, "Vaylar is not just a bedtime story, Ami. He is as real as the sun and the stars. He indeed opened the door of the other world." "What does Vaylar want, Papa?" she asked. "What he always wanted. The 'Crystal Rose,'" Artha replied grimly.

Amaraya chuckled caustically and mumbled, "BS." "What?" Artha asked in bafflement. "It's short form for bullshit. It's the new lingo people use," Amaraya mumbled inadvertently. Artha raised his eyebrows in hopelessness for his family and sighed. "Ami, we are the keepers of the 'Crystal Rose,'" he revealed.

Amaraya was unconvinced by her father's theory. She still believed that it all was just a big distraction created by the people who wanted to see George dead. "You don't believe it. Do you?" Artha asked looking at Amaraya's perplexed face. "But magic didn't kill him, Papa," she clarified. "It's easy to hire a hitman," he said.

Amaraya gripped her hand fiercely and declared, "If it's Vaylar who did this to George, I will kill him." "No, you will not do anything, Ami. Promise me you will stay out of this," Artha begged. "Papa, he killed my husband. I will not sit this out. No way," she avowed loudly.

"Don't be stubborn. This is not a game," Artha endeavored to convince Amaraya. "You are right, Papa, this isn't a game. It's a war," Amaraya enraged. "Ami, our entire family is at stake here, especially Raylina and Ablina. I won't let you do this," Artha stated clearly.

Amaraya was still trying to process the information her father had enlightened her with. The smoke rising from the fire of revenge was blurring her common sense. Amaraya's ferocity was burning her from within.

"Ami, Vaylar will be coming out of the shadows, and this time the whole world will burn to the ground. No one will survive. He is coming to get the 'Crystal Rose,'" Artha told her in a grave tone. "Where is it?" Amaraya asked. "Somewhere safe," he answered assuredly. "We cannot tell this to Abby and Ray. They mustn't know," Amaraya said in an intense tone. "Yes, I have that taken care of, Ami," Artha said. "We will take them to a safe hideout, all of you," he added. "Can we trust Alisar?" Amaraya asked seriously. "Yes," Artha guaranteed.

Amaraya and Artha commenced the preparation of necessary safety arrangements for their family. Aamirah and Gaurangi left the castle to gather all the possible help to stop Vaylar.

***

"Ami, there is someone you should meet," Artha said falteringly and nervously started walking towards the main hall. Amaraya followed him impatiently. They entered the main hall and what Amaraya saw blew her mind off. "Harvinya Bayer," Amaraya said with a disgusted face. The woman in her late 20s turned around and smirked viciously, "Amaraya." "So the traitor finally decided to show up," Amaraya said tauntingly.

Harvinya shrugged her shoulders and said, "Come on, sister-in-law. This is not the time to discuss the epic Bayer feud. We have better things to worry about." Amaraya walked near Harvinya and raised her one eyebrow, "Oh, Yes, Harvinya! We do have better things to talk about. So, tell me, exactly how did you manage to tip off the Drgaan town's people about us?" Amaraya questioned harshly.

Harvinya's wicked smirk narrowed, and she broke eye contact with Amaraya. "Come on, don't be shy. It must have felt really good, planning the cold execution of your brother and his family," Amaraya taunted. Amaraya folded her arms and added, "And I know the Bayers are Saith hunters." Harvinya went closer with confidence and snickered, "Amaraya, I will happily kill your entire family, including my nieces, once we save the land we are standing on."

Amaraya rushed to hit Harvinya's face, but Artha pulled her away. "Ami, calm down… We need her. In fact, we need all the aid we can get," Artha explained. "Papa, this woman is not trustworthy. She is vile, and she is here to destroy us all over again. She made us leave our home. She tried to kill her own brother," Amaraya pleaded. "I will gladly do it again," Harvinya said playfully, openly threatening them in their own home.

Amaraya lost it, she tried to hold herself back, but Harvinya's bad attitude made it impossible. Harvinya's face bothered her; the anger and frustration bubbling inside her came out. She picked up the flower vase next to her and threw it at Harvinya. "George had nothing to do with Scott's death, you bitch," Amaraya squealed.

Harvinya touched her forehead and pressed the wound with her fingers. "Done? Anything else you want to say or throw at me?" She shouted, wiping the blood dripping from her head. "Harvinya, you have my sympathies. What happened to Scott was not George's fault. Your son was one of the 'Takers,' he was killed by Vaylar," Artha uncovered the truth.

"Takers... What is that?" Amaraya questioned. "Enough, I don't believe you two. Artha you called me for this nonsense?" Harvinya said indignantly. "It's up to you to believe me or not, but there are things which we don't tell anyone, not even ourselves. Many men have lost themselves in the quest to be invincible. But they forget that power like that is just an illusion," Artha said.

"Don't mess with my head with your rubbish words, old man," Harvinya said, waving off everything she just heard. "Harvinya, don't cross your limit," Amaraya warned. "What are Takers?" Amaraya asked Artha again. "Takers are the men who shared Vaylar's power. The powers which he passed down," Artha answered.

Harvinya and Amaraya were speechless and disoriented. It was hard to digest for both of them that suddenly the most enjoyed bedtime story was becoming real and was turning into their worst nightmare. "Amaraya, if Artha is right about Vaylar, then I have to protect the only thing I care about," Harvinya said in a serious tone and went outside.

Harvinya came in with her 7-year-old child. "This is Kyle. He is my son, and I will go to any extent to protect him," she announced. Amaraya looked at him and smiled. Kyle's innocence melted her burning heart. She sat down on her knees and said, "Hello Kyle, I am your aunt." "Hi Auntie Ami," Kyle said in his peachy voice, and smiled, showing his crooked teeth.

Amaraya forgave Harvinya and welcomed her and Kyle with an open heart into her home. Amaraya asked the helper to escort Harvinya and her son to the guest room. Then she went to the kitchen to check on the dinner preparations. Artha went out to get some air. He fell asleep on the swing in the porch area while waiting for the kids.

***

Artha felt someone's presence around him, so he opened his weary eyes to see who it was. He gripped the swing's rope as support and stood up gently. "Artha… Why aren't you using the immortality tonic?" The man spoke from behind in his intense, heavy voice. Artha turned around and smiled with contentment, like he felt he could finally rest for a second. It was his old friend, his only friend, Alisar Vasaga. "I am officially retiring," Artha said.

"The magic we carry inside is not for us," Alisar cited, staring at Artha's wrinkly face. "You still remember?" Artha asked in surprise. "Yes, you never forget your first lesson with Yama's most learned Guru," he answered. "Indeed, Alisar," Artha said, embracing his old friend, and suddenly the war looked like a small affair.

It's rare luck to find a good friend in our world, and when you find one, lock them up in whatever dungeon you can find, they are too precious to lose, and Artha was lucky to find such a friend.

Artha and Alisar went into the garden, and they walked till it ended. "Together…" Artha said.

"Together…" Alisar repeated. "Bhumsaiya," Alisar chanted, and Artha kept his palms on the ground. An old dusty yellow box emerged from the little crack in the ground. Alisar took the box in his hands. He opened the lid, and a straight, bright light came out of it. The light was so powerful that it lightened up the whole town.

"The heavenly light can only be seen by a witch's eye," Alisar narrated and smiled brightly. He warily picked up the shiny white Crystal Rose from the box, and the white visible radiation coming out of Crystal Rose burnt his hand, including his bones. His hand turned into ashes and sprinkled down on the ground. Artha quickly caught the falling Crystal Rose from Alisar's hands and kept it back in the box.

Artha touched Alisar's hand, and his hands started to grow back. "Alisar, have you gone mad?" Artha said angrily. "You know this is our only chance against catching Vaylar," Artha yelled at Alisar. "I know… I know… Artha, you know history was my favorite subject," Alisar said plainly. "I was there when we burnt the whole valley in the name of finding our favorite person, Vaylar, remember?" Alisar said. "Yes," Artha replied with remorse.

"We need to be more vigilant, Alisar. Because we both know Vaylar is coming for my granddaughters," Artha said tensely. "Ohh yes, I know, Artha," Alisar affirmed.

The white shawl Artha wrapped around himself turned red. He fell to the ground, not fighting back. The pain inflicted by the people we trust is the worst pain a person could feel, and at that moment, it stops being physical and becomes soul-wrenching.

Alisar cruelly pulled out the steel dagger from Artha's heart. "Artha, I always knew you were an emotional fool, but I never thought you were this naive," he mocked. Alisar kept his one foot on Artha's bleeding chest and said, "I mean, the first rule of family secrets is, it's limited only to the family members, and I ain't your family, brother."

Artha was lying on the ground, hopelessly, slowly losing his life, watching his best friend clean the dagger soaked in his blood. Everything was dark. Although his eyes were losing their sight, the world never seemed so clearer. "Nāyam hanti Na hanyate (Soul does not kill, nor can it be killed)," Artha cited, smiling faintly. Alisar stepped on his best friend's chest and walked away.

***

Alisar walked into the castle and saw Amaraya sitting in the living room. She stood up from the sofa to welcome him. "Where's Abby and Ray?" Alisar inquired. "Oh, they all went to town for sightseeing," she said. "Astor's with them?" He asked. "Yes, Papa also sent Manashaya with them for their protection," she assured. "That's great," he said and stabbed her with the same dagger he used to kill Artha.

Amaraya's screams echoed in the castle. The thought of a child in the house gave her the strength to stand up and run. "Alvriya Casindes," Amaraya roared, and Alisar drifted 10 feet away in the air and hit straight into the wall. A piece of the wall broke down and fell on Alisar. Amaraya ran to the garden in search of help.

Alisar cleared the dust off his black leather jacket and coolly walked out of the door. He saw Amaraya running barefoot to the yard. Alisar snapped his fingers, and Amaraya fell down on her face. "Come on, Ami, Papa, taught you better, use your Ragata crap," Alisar taunted.

"OOH... You can't... you... Aw, that's sad... Ragata magic is stupid, the only thing you can do with it is you can heal yourself and others. We have modern medicines for that. This ain't real magic. You don't do meditation for this shit," Alisar explained seriously.

"Why?" Amaraya cried, crawling down on the ground. "Like father like daughter," Alisar chuckled. "Even after spending centuries apart, you guys still ask the same dumb questions. Well... Not in a mood to answer," he said jeeringly. He grabbed her by her hair to pull her head up, and sliced her throat slowly. He left her there with Artha's dead body to bleed out.

Harvinya heard noises and came out of her room. Her son followed her. She reached into the main hall, and no one was there. She spotted blood on the carpet and followed the blood trail. As she reached into the garden, she saw Amaraya lying on the ground beside Artha.

Harvinya ran to Amaraya and checked Amaraya's pulse. But she was late; Amaraya was already dead. "Look who we have here. Our dearest Harvinya," Alisar said with surprise. She turned around and was stunned to see Alisar holding Kyle in his arms.

"Alisar," Harvinya screamed. "Please don't do this," she begged Alisar. "Ohh, Mother's love, don't worry, Kyle won't miss you. You both will be neighbors," Alisar said with a big smile. "What, you don't get it? Kyle is innocent, so he is going to heaven, and my dearest Harvi, you know where you will be heading," Alisar mocked. "Don't do this. He is everything I have," she wailed. "Melodrama," Alisar said.

Alisar closed his right fist to squash the invisible air. He pulled his fist towards himself, tightening the unseen air, and said, "Imfa." Harvinya and Kyle started to suffocate. Alisar enjoyed the begging and pleading. The stone-cold monster didn't feel anything except his hunger for power. Harvinya hit the floor, and Alisar threw Kyle's body on the ground with her. Harvinya was lying along with her son's lifeless body. Her tears froze; it was like she forgot how to cry. Then the little life left in her left forever.

Alisar went inside the castle and waited for the Bayer sisters to return. He went to the bar and poured himself a strong drink. He felt the sting on his tongue, but his heart was steady. He laughed, watching the bright red flames burning in the fireplace, recalling his heinous crimes.

"The purest evil, greater than the devil himself, once again conquering the pious land of Śirā Ragata... Now all I need is Ablina and Raylina," Alisar praised himself, raising his glass of whiskey in the air.

The sharp hit on Alisar's head made him dizzy; he turned around and saw the face of a man who hit him. His eyes were blurry, but were not blurry enough to not know who he was. "Artha," Alisar shrieked and fell down on the floor. "And yet you fall on my feet," Artha said calmly.

Artha was standing strong on his feet, holding his bloody shawl with one hand to cover his abdomen from bleeding out. "As long as I live, nothing can hurt my family," he growled in anger. The inhuman growl trembled the walls of Yama castle, making the castle seem like it was shivering with his pain.

Artha ran out to check on Amaraya. He checked her pulse repeatedly, hoping for a miracle, and he kept on healing her in vain. "Ami... Ami... beta (my child) wake up, open your eyes," he wept.

Artha used every magic he ever learned to bring her back. He used every drop of his blood to save his child, but her soul had left her body, and no magic or medicine could bring her back. Artha fell alongside her and left himself to bleed out. He saw no point in saving himself.

Alisar came out; he saw them lying dead next to each other. Alisar walked close to them. He sighed and said, "Aw... you stupid Artha. You shouldn't have told me about your granddaughters and the Crystal Rose... Anyways see you in the afterlife." "Oh, and don't worry

I'll take good care of your granddaughters… specially Raylina," he winked and left.

Kyle's coughing sound awakened Artha. He stood up after numerous efforts and finally walked towards them. Kyle was lying unconscious on the ground beside Harvinya's dead body. Artha bent down to check his wrist for the pulse, and luckily Kyle had some. He healed Kyle with his touch, and to do so, he vested all his powers into Kyle's body.

"Souls are like water and sand, shaped to slip away; but unlike water, and sand, souls have a supreme purpose of serving, and until the work is done, it sticks into the arms of its holder."

Artha fell on the ground, dead, and Kyle woke up all recovered. Kyle pulled Artha's shirt collar and dragged his dead body into the castle.

CHAPTER 15

THE LOSS AND THE LOST

After buying every piece of clothing and antiques from Darjeeling's market, the Bayer sisters, Ekani, and Visac headed back to the cars. Ekani sprinted towards Manashaya, who was standing by the car, waiting for them. "Manashaya, can I come with you," Ekani asked shyly, biting her lower lip. "It's your car," he said. "Oh! Ya," she chuckled nervously.

Raylina spotted Manashaya and Ekani talking, and her curiosity to know what they were talking about drew her feet towards them.

"What's up guys," Raylina said, trying to keep the jealousy out of her voice. Ekani swiftly stole a glance at Manashaya and uttered, "Nothing." "Hey Ray, Ekani, we are getting late. Let's go before Ma skins us alive," Ablina said, interrupting their awkward look away. "Okay," Raylina mumbled.

Visac and Astor waited for the girls in the other car. "I think I will go with Manashaya," Raylina said. "What? Why?" Ablina asked sharply. "Because Abby, I was really uncomfortable sitting like that between you and Visac," Raylina answered and sat in the car before Ablina could say anything. "Okay then, Ekani, let's go," Ablina said. Ekani hesitated at first but followed Ablina back to the other car.

Raylina saw Manashaya smiling in the rearview mirror. "What?" Raylina asked. "Nothing," Manashaya chuckled. Raylina blushed and looked down, trying to hide her tomato-red face, which she was sure she had by now. She nonchalantly flipped her hair and looked again in the mirror. Manashaya's eyes were glued to her broad smile and at her face, turning brighter red by every second. Their eyes met, and suddenly, Alisar's face crossed her mind; she broke eye contact and looked away. "What am I doing? Why am I attracted to Manashaya when I have feelings for Alisar?" Raylina thought to herself.

The battle between Alisar and Manashaya in her head was getting on her nerves. She concluded that there was nothing to think about it, plus these silly things were for Ablina. "It's okay, princess. We all are a little confused when it comes to making choices. And we always choose what we don't have," Manashaya spoke, looking at Raylina in the rearview mirror. "That obvious, huh?" Raylina asked with a nervous smirk. Manashaya nodded.

"How old are you again?" Raylina asked bluntly to change the subject. "I am 20," Manashaya answered. "Without the immortality tonic… I am really 20, in a normal way," Manashaya added. "I got it," she said. "I feel comfortable around him, but you, you are like a stomach ache. I mean, we just met. I don't know you the way I know him, and this little weirdness between us is freaking me out," Raylina explained weirdly. Manashaya sighed deeply and said, "Ouch, your head is pretty messed up."

Raylina's eyes were glued to the vein tattoo on Manashaya's back neck. "Let's go out on a date and see how it works out," Manashaya proposed. "Straight forward… hmmm. I admire that," she smiled. They both looked at each other from the rearview mirror. Manashaya wanted her to verbally confirm, but Raylina rolled her eyes away from him. He waited patiently, and she played innocent.

The unsaid and unsettled feelings inside Manashaya paralyzed his tongue. He was afraid to talk any further. He wondered what would happen if he was honest. Manashaya kept on driving. Raylina kept on replaying about the time she spent with Alisar in her head. But the questions featuring Manashaya kept on bursting out in the middle. The questions she didn't want answers to. Because acknowledging them would mean admitting the unresolved feelings she had for Manashaya.

The guilt of having confusion between the two men was eating Raylina up. She struggled, but at last, she did find something to blame other than herself, and it was her hormones. She relaxed and abysmally abused them. "And that's how humans and witches find solutions to their problems, instead of accepting; they blame," Raylina said in her mind and snorted with laughter.

Manashaya smiled broadly, looking at Raylina's puzzled, deep thinking, and slightly insane face. He was so sure that the girl he was falling for was a pure maniac. But then he thought that love itself was an undiscovered and uncategorized mental disorder. And slowly, he too, was becoming a victim of this famous disorder.

Manashaya glanced at Raylina, once again to look at her insanely beautiful face, still concentrated on whatever was going inside her head. "Stop it, Manashaya," He uttered under his breath, ordering his love-crazed eyes to stop staring at her, and looked away, focusing on the road.

***

"Peaches and Pumpkins," Ablina said on the phone, and hung up. For a minute, Raylina thought it was time to admit her sister to a mental asylum, but suddenly she recalled something. "Manashaya, stop the car," she ordered suddenly. "Why?... What happened?..." Manashaya wondered, but he did as he was asked; he stopped the car, and so did Ekani, who was driving behind them. Raylina stepped out of the car and asked Manashaya not to come out.

"What the hell, Abby," Raylina said, heading anxiously towards Ablina, wondering why Ablina had chosen today of all the days to test their stupid, childish code word. "Ray, thank god you remembered!" Ablina said with relief. "Abby, this is not the time to play 'Remember it,'" Raylina rebuked.

Ablina showed her the message, "*Get away from Astor.*" Raylina was stunned reading it. "What does that mean? And why would Grandpa send this?" Raylina asked. "Exactly, it's Astor," Ablina said. Their delicate state of mind couldn't decide what to do. "We should go and talk to Astor," Ablina suggested. "No, the message states clearly to get away from him," Raylina said.

"What's up, guys? All okay?" Visac asked in a concerned tone, looking at their troubled faces. Their heads were taken up by Artha's strange message. "Speak out, Abby," he demanded. "Nothing, big man," Raylina said coolly. "Do not lie to me, Raylina. Look at her face. Something is definitely wrong," he said. Seeing Ablina, Raylina, and Visac arguing, the rest of them came out of the car. "Raylina, all okay," Manashaya asked, curiously. Raylina's lips were sealed.

"Astor," Ablina said, walking towards him. "What are you hiding," she asked him upfront. "I... I," he hesitated, trying to find a lie to convince her. But this time, Ablina saw an evil glint she had missed before, leaving Astor with no choice but to attack them. "Lamar," Astor shouted to put a spell on them, and the bright blue color flashed from his hand. The Bayer sisters, Visac, Ekani, and Manashaya, were paralyzed, and their bodies hit the ground.

Astor looked at Ekani, wondering why Alisar wanted her instead of Raylina or Ablina. But orders were orders. "Forgive me," he said with a bleeding heart and carried Ekani's body to the car. He carefully placed Ekani into the backseat and said, "Afturkalla," sending Ekani into a deep coma and drove off.

The magic wore off naturally, after 5 minutes, and their bodies unfroze. "Jarðarbrestur," Raylina screamed, but nothing happened. She kept on chanting the word, but it didn't work. Raylina was burning from the inside because of her helplessness.

"Ray, stop. He's gone," Ablina cried and grabbed Raylina's hand. Raylina shoved Ablina's hand. "It's your fault, Abby. You shouldn't have talked to him," Raylina yelled at Ablina, ruthlessly blaming her for everything. "Ray, I thought there was some misunderstanding," Ablina tried to explain.

"Fuck off, Ablina," Raylina said furiously and rushed back to the car to follow Astor. Manashaya tried to stop her from going, but she kept on pushing him away. Raylina used all her power to sustain him, but his tactics were a lot more powerful due to constant everyday training, way more than Raylina, even though she was a witch by birth. She pulled herself back. "What is wrong with you all? Ekani's been kidnapped by the man who was supposed to protect us," Raylina shouted furiously. No one said anything.

Raylina stood there for 10 seconds, breathing heavily. "Ray, I am sorry," Ablina said remorsefully. "Let's go back," Raylina said, trying to gulp her raging fury. She violently opened the door and sat inside the car.

Ablina, Visac, and Manashaya sat in the car and headed back home.

The thought of Ekani's abduction saddened Raylina. She felt futile, powerless, and above all, unworthy of the power she carried inside her. Ablina felt guilty about making a rash decision and doubting her grandfather's message. She thought she was naive and stupid for believing that Astor was innocent, and all of this was just a misunderstanding.

Manashaya saw the volcanic expressions erupting on Raylina's face, waiting to explode. He wanted to stop it, and like every other fool falling in love, he caught Raylina's hand in his own to calm her down. Raylina took a deep sigh, closed her eyes, and put her head on the car's headrest.

"No... No... Ray... he is taking my seedlings," Ablina screaming in her sleep. "Abby... Abby... Ablina, wake up," Raylina said worriedly. "Calm down, it was just a nightmare, Abby," Raylina said and wrapped herself and Ablina's shivering body in a warm, light purple blanket.

Ablina finally fell asleep, and Raylina quietly slid out of the blanket. "Ray," said Ablina and held her hand. "What?" Raylina asked. "Thank you," Ablina said with emotions brimming in her voice. "We don't leave each other's side,"

Raylina reminded Ablina. "Yes," Ablina exclaimed. "Move," Raylina said, sliding back under the blanket. "Chilly..." Ablina shrieked.

"Seedlings... it's confirmed, Abby. It doesn't work in your dreams as well," Raylina chuckled. "What?" Ablina asked. "Your brain," Raylina said, and they burst out laughing. Raylina and Ablina talked about numerous pointless things. And as the night progressed, their eyes became heavy, and slowly, Raylina was swept under the shroud of sleep. The insomniac nerd owl inside Ablina still had some charge left; she walked into her room for a while, and then she tried again to sleep, but her brain was not ready to shut off.

The next day, as the first rays of the sun hit the earth, Ablina was out and rushing through the twin room she and Raylina shared. "Ray, wake up, good morning!" Ablina shook Raylina's shoulders, pulling the blanket away from her face. "What is it with you, Abby," Raylina said furiously. "I got it, Ray, we need a code word," Ablina said enthusiastically, ignoring her sister's I-will-murder-you face.

"Papa..." Raylina screamed in irritation, pushing Ablina's hands off her, ducking back under the blanket. "They are not at home; they went out," Ablina informed. "Why didn't they take you," Raylina asked grumpily. "I figured it out, Ray; when that man was taking my seedling, he threatened me not to say anything or else he will kill you all," Ablina said. "I see we still haven't moved on from that," Raylina said, getting up and leaning her back on the headboard, squishing the pillow to her chest.

Raylina tried being fair-minded, but now the water was not over her head; it was drowning her. "Abby, I really love you, but this has to stop. We need to talk to Papa about this," Raylina said seriously. "No, we need a code word," Ablina insisted. "Enough, we are taking this to Papa," Raylina berated Ablina. "Okay," Ablina agreed, with downcast eyes.

Seeing Ablina's upset face, Raylina decided to helplessly agree with her sister's childish plan to stop the nightmares. She held Ablina's arms in hers and said, "I am sorry, Abby, let's get your code word." "Okay, let me tell you what happened next," Ablina said. "No, spare me, just tell me the code," Raylina said.

The people we love have uncanny power over us; they make us do the things we never thought we would ever do. Raylina Bayer was a lot of things; she was a mean, complicated, stubborn, tantrum-throwing maniac, but above all, she was a great sister to Ablina.

"Peaches," Ablina said with great enthusiasm. "Done," Raylina agreed instantly. "No, Ray, this is our code word, not just mine. Come on now," Ablina forced. "Pumpkins," Raylina said dispassionately, throwing her hands up in the air, surrendering.

"Pumpkins? You don't even like pumpkins," Ablina disagreed. "Abby, you know I can travel oceans for you, but that doesn't mean you make me do it literally. You wanted a code word. You have one. Now get out of here before I kill myself, and I don't mean it poetically," Raylina said gravely.

Ablina chuckled, seeing Raylina's annoyed face. "Okay, sister. We have 'Peaches and Pumpkins' as our code word..." Ablina said, smiling warmly at Raylina.

"Raylina, we are home, wake up," Manashaya said. Raylina opened her eyes. "It felt like it happened yesterday," Raylina muttered, remembering the morning when they made their secret little code word.

Ablina, Raylina, and Visac waited for Manashaya in the parking area. Ablina was shattered thinking about Ekani. Raylina was stressed, as her head was constantly showing her the worst images of the things that could happen to Ekani. Visac was silently staring at the entrance gate, holding Ablina's hand. "Let's go," Manashaya said, and they walked towards the castle unknown of the devil's deed.

***

"No guards... Where is everyone?" Manashaya wondered, walking towards the castle. "It's weird, even no one was at the entrance," Visac said. Raylina was still quiet, not paying attention to Manashaya and Visac's conversation as her head was haunted by the thoughts of Ekani's whereabouts.

Ablina's thoughts blinded her. She kept on walking where her legs directed. "Ahhhhhh...," Ablina tripped and fell. Raylina, Manashaya, and Visac helped her stand up. "Ablina, are you okay?" Raylina asked in a concerned voice. "I tripped over something," she answered blankly.

"Hand… It's someone's hand," Manashaya said in a horrified tone, picking up the man's butchered hand. "Visac, I think there is something wrong, man," Manashaya said, still holding the ripped hand in his hand. "OHHHH Hell…" Visac gasped in fear, looking at the piles of bodies lying on the ground.

Few hands bound to the bodies, and their legs lying on the other side of the bloody garden.

Heads nowhere to be found, the attached ones unrecognizable,

Men opened inside out.

View worse than war;

Like a painter's attempt to paint his darkest dream an "extra dark."

An agonizing picture of a bloody massacre changed those innocent eyes.

The burden of death dropped upon their young shoulders.

It was time to be the men and women they were supposed to be.

It was time to grow up.

The violent mutilation of more than 1000 men lying dead on the bloody ground shook them from inside. Even the worst monster could not do such a monstrous thing; it was an act of pure evil. It looked like the evilest maniac was set free to hunt. The chilly breeze stroked their warm skins, and they felt the unendurable pain of those unheard screams.

Raylina was horrified. She stumbled a bit and took the support of Manashaya's shoulder. He helped her stand still. "It's beyond hell," Raylina murmured, not blinking once. Watching this gruesome view made everyone brain dead.

A thought hit Ablina's head, and she started running fast like she was being chased by lightning. "Ablina, stop," Visac said, running after her. But Ablina didn't listen. She stopped near the dead bodies, and began searching.

Raylina understood what Ablina was doing, but she didn't go in to help her sister. For once, Raylina was more optimistic than her sister. Like she said to Ablina, Raylina didn't let that thought come to her mind even for a second. She stood there firmly, waiting for a miracle.

"Noooooo…," Ablina screamed out. Raylina ran. Visac and Manashaya followed her. They saw Ablina sitting in the blood pool, staring blankly at her mother's face, waiting for her to speak up again. Raylina stood there, the nothingness took over her heart, and she looked like a breathing corpse. Her senses were lost over the loss.

Visac went near Ablina, and as he touched her, she screamed. The fiery sparks coming out of her started to burn his hand. He stepped back in terror. The bright golden flames coming out of Ablina's body became intensely colossal, and this view frightened them all. It was like the "Goddess of Wrath" was awakened, and the rage piled inside her was unleashing in the form of fire.

The wolves growled like they were celebrating the initiation of Ablina's revenge. She screamed again out of pain, and the energy emitting out of the scream was so powerful that the land she stood upon trembled with fear. At first, the mighty sky acted to absorb her grief, but the intensity of her wounded heart won, and at the end, the mighty sky bowed down and begged for her mercy.

Ablina screamed again, but this time it was not full of pain. It was full of anger. Her wrath conjured the bright blue-green light which came straight from the sky and started to burn the ground and the dead people on it. Every man lying there got a proper goodbye. A once beautiful garden was turned into a cremation ground. "I will burn him alive," she said furiously and clenched her fist. Slowly, the flames coming out of her stopped. Ablina was back in reality, and she fell to her knees, crushed by the weight of sorrow.

Raylina was lost in a very disturbing unknown world. Her eyes could see the horrors of this world, but she was unresponsive, standing there like a dead woman, watching their burning corpses. She was in deep trauma. Ablina was terrorized to see her like this, so she gave a sharp slap on Raylina's face to snap her out of her shocked state.

Raylina's eyes blinked, and Ablina got hope of bringing her sister back. Ablina slapped Raylina one more time, and finally, a drop of tear came rolling down her face. "Ma is dead, Ray, I need you... Come back to me." And these words suddenly brought Raylina fully back to her senses.

The hands that rose to beat her when she was wrong, and bless her always, were gone. The eyes, which glowered at her misbehavior and shone with pride at her victories, were closed forever. The person Raylina feared the most and loved equally, if not more, left her, robbing her of warmth and leaving only bone-deep coldness inside her heart. Her "Ma" was gone and was never coming back to scold her, judge her, criticize her, fight her, comfort her, love her, to just... to just be there. She was gone, forever.

"Ma," Raylina said, wiping off the only drop of tear she let fall from her eyes. She was strong but clueless, ready to fight, to kill, but felt directionless. Just as she was staring into space, thinking about sinking back into the arms of emptiness, she saw a bright orange light from the corner of her eyes. She came out of her daze when she saw a child standing behind the sky-scraping transparent, fiery flames burning her mother's corpse.

A skinny boy dressed in a red t-shirt and light blue jean shorts walked towards them. He looked at Raylina with his crystal blue-colored eyes drowned in empathy, holding her hands, and said, "I am sorry, Ray." Raylina sat down on her knees to match his height. She gently held the little boy's shoulders and asked, "Who are you?"

"I am Artha. And right now, I am in Kyle. Kyle is the son of Harvinya Scott, your aunt," the little boy answered in his boyish voice. "I am in Kyle… what? What does that mean?" Ablina gasped in wonder. "Grandpa," Raylina said, looking at Kyle's chubby cheeks turning red due to the chilly weather. "Ray, Abby, it's me. My body is lying in our living room, and Ray, I need you to put me back in my body," Artha said, walking back into the castle.

They all followed Artha, possessing little Kyle's body, into the Yama's living room. As they reached inside the hall, their eyes together fell upon Artha's soulless body lying in a blood pool. Manashaya and Visac carried Artha's body to the dining hall and placed him on the giant wooden table.

"Grandpa… sorry… I mean, Mr. Shaurayaveer, how did you… get into this kid's body?" Visac asked, rubbing his frozen palms together to warm them. "It's old magic. I will teach you all. But for that, I need my body back. I am afraid Kyle won't be able to hold two souls any longer in his body," Artha said worriedly, staring at his body, losing the life.

"I don't know how… How will I do this?… Abby set the ground on fire, Grandpa. Let her do this," Raylina suggested, thinking about how she failed miserably in saving Ekani. "No, Raylina, only you can do this, and Manashaya will guide you," Artha answered with utmost resoluteness.

Incognizant as they were, Raylina and Manashaya kept on staring at Kyle's face blankly. "Hurry up, kids," Artha charged them in his childish voice. "Hold on, I need to get this book which I don't remember," Manashaya said, striving to recall the book's name. "Great, and he doesn't remember," Ablina said faintly, in a way indicting the dark night. "Yes," Manashaya jumped with a dash of hopefulness and ran straight to the library.

Visac saw Kyle's body releasing whitish-blue rays. "What is that?" Visac asked, gazing at the bluish rays emitting from Kyle. "It's my soul," Artha said in his baby voice, lying next to his dead body. "Grandpa, when we were in Desovir, Graymanos came to me," Ablina spoke out of nowhere.

Artha was staggered, "It's not possible," he said. "No, it's true, Grandpa," Ablina said. "If he was Graymanos, you wouldn't be standing here in front of me," Artha denied. "He told me that Vaylar was coming. And that you need our help," Ablina said. "Whom did he approach? How did he approach?" Artha questioned. "He came to Ablina," Raylina replied. "Twice," Ablina added.

Raylina and Ablina waited for Artha to say something. Artha was hesitant; he never thought that he had to be the one to open the door when confrontations came knocking. Artha took a deep breath and began, "Abby… Ray." "Here," Manashaya interrupted Artha, and at that moment, he became Artha's lifesaver unknowingly.

Everyone ignored Manashaya's late coming except Ablina, who threw him an angry look. "I am sorry, ma'am," Manashaya said calmly. "Raylina, come. Give me your hand," he said. He took Raylina's hands and slightly cut her right wrist. "Ouch," she groaned. He asked her to put her hand above Kyle's forehead. Manashaya waited till his head was completely covered with blood. "Now what?" Raylina asked impatiently, wrapping the table cloth around her knife cut. "You close your eyes. And wait for the Śirā Whispers to tell you what to do next," Manashaya answered.

"Śirā whispers? What is that?" Ablina asked. "Your grandfather will explain everything. And Visac, Guruji lied. We cannot do this magic. Only a true descendant of the Shaurayaveers can," Manashaya explained. "Ohh, I was really looking forward to learning that," Visac said innocently.

Raylina recollected the memories of the morning when she heard those strange whispers in the castle's corridors leading her to Ablina. "I know, Ray. You can hear them. The whispers of magic... now focus... they will speak to you," Artha said. "What?... What are you saying?" Raylina asked, trying to find a sense of what Artha meant.

"Śirā whispers are the whispers of Śirā magic. How does it work, no one knows, but only a chosen Shaurayaveer can hear them. So far, there have been only two witches from our clan who can hear them—

you and your great-great-great-great-grandfather, Aagney Shaurayaveer," Artha explained.

Without any further ado, Raylina closed her eyes, but the thoughts of her mother's bloodied body distracted her. The world became quieter just for her, but the raging pain didn't let her hear the voices even in that pin-drop silence. She opened her eyes and closed them again.

"Abby, I don't think I am strong enough to do this," Raylina said with a hint of tears in her eyes and pain evident in her voice. "Yes, you can, Ray. Ma always believed you were the strongest of all, just like her, and I believe in you too, Ray," Ablina told Raylina.

Raylina took a deep breath and closed her eyes again to concentrate on hearing the Śirā whispers. And this time, she heard something, a familiar voice talking to her. The concerned tone and warmth of the words made Raylina smile. It was Amaraya's voice. She heard her mother for the one last time. No one in this world can ever be ready to say goodbye to the people they love.

Raylina kept on hearing her like she was capturing Amaraya's voice in her heart. It was like she was carving her mother's last words in her. It was a painful closure, but a much-needed one. She opened her eyes, and she whispered "Przenieś Duszę" in Artha's ears. Artha and Kyle opened their eyes together.

Raylina and Ablina lost both of their parents, but they had each other; they *only* had each other. They hugged each other tightly, dealing with loss in their own way.

Losing someone you love immensely teaches you many things. But the most important thing loss teaches you is to pretend that everything is okay, that you can go on without them. Ablina and Raylina pretended to be strong for each other; they did it to stop the other from falling apart, and they both played their part very well.

CHAPTER 16

THE LAST LIVING GRAYMANOS

They felt safe together, so they all spent the rest of the night in the living room. Each of them was sitting in a different corner, all lost and exhausted. The horrific night passed, but the morning didn't bring out the rays of light as it was supposed to. It was just the shiny, scorching rays of sunlight burning their wounded eyes and hearts.

"You flew away, far away to start afresh, and left me to live alone in this coldness," Ablina scribbled in her diary. The last drop of her tear dropped down from her tired eyes on the paper, smudging the black ink all over it. The swirling ink mirrored the dark state of her mind.

Ablina tore the page and started jotting down the questions which haunted her the whole night on the new page of her diary. Raylina often teased Ablina for being an old geek because she preferred to write everything on a piece of paper instead of using electronic modes. And every time Raylina teased her about being old and opposite, Ablina remembered her mother smiling and saying, "I like it how my daughters are Yin and Yang, opposite sides of the coin, whole as one, yet different on its own."

Ablina smiled, remembering her mother's face, and that brought instant tears to her eyes. She wiped them and concentrated on the questions in hand. Ablina patiently waited for everyone to deal with the loss, but now it was enough. She walked straight to Artha and said, "We need answers, Grandpa, enough with all the mysteries and secrets."

Artha stood up and laid Kyle comfortably on the sofa. He covered him with his shawl and went to the kitchen. Ablina, Raylina, Visac, and Manashaya followed him. Artha took out the bowl from the cabinet, and filled it with water, sugar, milk, tea leaves, and put the bowl on gas. Everyone stood there quietly, watching him make tea. It's crazy how sometimes extremely simple activities can calm the storm inside one's soul.

Artha took out 5 dark blue cups from the kitchen drawer and poured hot steaming tea into them. He served them one by one and then walked back to the living room. They followed Artha like ducks following their mama. "Grandpa," Ablina said with irritation. He asked them to sit, so they did. "You can ask now, Ablina," Artha said. Ablina looked at him furiously; it was his attitude that made her mad. "Ekani," Raylina said. "Aamirah and Gaurangi are already on that," he informed.

Ablina took out the diary as if she was going to interview her grandfather. Artha looked at her and said, "History is long, Ablina. Your eagerness won't help you get all the answers instantly." "Okay, let's be specific, then, is Chryorold real?" Ablina asked. "Chryorold is real but fabricated by our ancestors to mislead the world about us," Artha answered calmly. "Why?" Raylina said with confusion.

Artha gulped the tea sip and said, "Let's be clear, with one thing. Your father was not a witch, nor was anyone in the Bayer family. He came here to destroy people like us. He was a Saith hunter. And the Chryorold was fabricated to mislead people like him."

"Saith what?" Raylina gasped in confusion. "I don't believe it. It's BS," Ablina objected. "Wait, what is all this? Abby, you know about this... Sap?" Raylina asked in a surprised tone. "Ray, it's Saith... The Saith hunters were a group of witch hunters gifted with special superhuman abilities. Their powers were like ours, but they were not exactly witches," Ablina explained. "Correct, Ablina," Artha said.

"But this ain't true, Grandpa. Papa was not a Saith hunter," Ablina opposed. "Ablina, Raylina, hear me carefully," Artha spoke. "George did not come here to

200

learn magic. He was here to eradicate us all, but then he fell in love with your mother, and the rest is history."

Artha saw their faces turn pale because of the information he gave. It addled their minds. The truth moved them, and it was hard to digest, but running away from the reality would have made it worse, so they prepared their minds to accept the waves of truth reaching ashore, letting them wash away the dirt of the lies living between their feet.

"So, where were we," Artha continued. "George stole the book from our library, but he didn't know the book was fabricated. We do that with all of our students. For security purposes. The right knowledge in the wrong hands can put us all in jeopardy." "I knew it!" Manashaya exclaimed. Ablina and Raylina ignored him.

Visac waited for his number, as this interrogation had raised some doubts of his own. Ablina was still unconvinced that her father was a Saith hunter because she was sure that he didn't have any superhuman abilities. "But the book," Ablina said. "Abby, it's editable," Artha said, trying to convince Ablina. "Enough… with the book. No one cares about it except nerds," Raylina said in an annoyed tone. "The real question is who did this, Grandpa? Who killed them all?" Raylina asked. "Alisar," he replied in a gloomy voice.

Hearing his name left Raylina speechless and heartbroken. Alisar was her first real friend, practically the first person on earth she trusted after her parents and sister. She could have never imagined him, out of all people breaking her trust. "It was all a lie, then?" Raylina questioned in her mind, putting every moment she spent with him in doubt. Artha saw the pain on her face. He realized that Alisar not only played with him; he also betrayed his granddaughter in more ways than one.

Artha hugged Raylina and pledged in a stone-like voice, "We will not let him get away with this, Ray." Raylina held him like a little hopeless child who had nowhere to go, and in a way, she didn't, she and Amaraya might have their differences, but they were always there for each other.

The thing about being an emotionally crippled person is that you stop caring about losing anything.

"Let's go and end him," Raylina said vacantly. "I agree," Ablina said, looking at Raylina's fallen face. Ablina had never seen Raylina so fragile and vulnerable. "Abby, Ray, are you both ready to take down the man who walked in and killed everyone within just an hour," Artha questioned them about their decision. "Yes, I am. I'll either end this monster or die trying," Ablina said, trying not to raise her voice. Raylina remained silent.

"You don't get it, do you?" After a long pause, Artha spoke, "Alisar is working with Vaylar, Abby." "Does it matter, Grandpa?" Ablina said without thinking. Ablina was not ready to use her common sense; her thirst for revenge fogged her ability to think. Raylina didn't say anything as it looked pointless to speak in between.

Aamirah and Gaurangi returned with a few remaining men. Artha was relieved to see his son alive. "Papa... Ami," Aamirah said, trying not to fall apart in front of his father. "Son," Artha said. They stiffly hugged each other, trying not to show their soft side. "Ekani, Aamirah?" Artha asked in scattered words. Aamirah couldn't speak, and neither could Gaurangi; they were devastated. The thoughts of losing their only child made their hearts heavy as stone and minds dead.

"Step aside, son," Artha said suddenly and pushed Aamirah behind him, placing himself in the front to protect the group from the tall hooded man walking towards them. As the hooded man came closer, Artha saw him carrying someone familiar in his arms. It was Ekani. The hooded man walked past Artha and the others, and kept Ekani's unconscious body on the sofa.

Without wasting any moment, Artha, Aamirah, and Gaurangi attacked the hooded man. He fell on his back on the ground and stood back up immediately. His black-colored hood dropped off, letting his short, wavy, messy black hair fall down on his forehead like a waterfall, revealing the same innocent face behind those wild, bloody red eyes. "Red Eyes," Visac recognized the man. "Graymanos," Ablina said in a flat tone, staring at her nightmare, standing in front of her in broad daylight.

Artha, Aamirah, and Gaurangi struck at him again. He fell down again on his face, trying to hold himself from attacking back at them. He stood back up on his feet, like nothing had happened, and started walking towards Ablina. Before he could reach her, Visac threw a punch at him. "Stay away from her," Visac growled. The man looked at Visac with his wild, bright red eyes and snapped Visac on the floor with a complicated, smooth move no one understood. Visac felt the breath leaving his lungs, and he groaned in pain.

Ablina saw her nightmare trying to kill the love of her life, so she moved her hand in front unconsciously, as if she intended to push the man afar, and a sudden blast of energy from her hand threw the man straight up into the wall. The man with wild, red eyes was dumbfounded.

The man with wild, bright red eyes didn't believe what he witnessed. The clueless little girl conjured the oldest of old magic like she was the original creator. He stood up, panting. "Last living Graymanos," the man with red eyes stammered. "Graymanos," Ablina gasped. He looked at Ablina with compassion, and for a moment, the brightness of his eyes dimmed. The raging darkness inside him took a halt for a bit and returned to its true self—light filled with nothing but goodness. "I am Avyukt," he introduced himself.

"You lied to us, Artha," Avyukt said, trying to restrict his dark side from coming out. "You said the child could not make it," he infuriated. Artha ignored him and walked towards Ekani. He put his hand on her forehead. "Eanchainn Marbh," Artha muttered.

"This magic is like a lock and key, only the man who conjured it can undo it," Avyukt said. "Astor," Aamirah enraged. "Artha, you haven't answered my question," Avyukt came back to his question. "Yes, the child survived. I protected her, and now she is under my protection. She is my family. She is my granddaughter," Artha proclaimed as loudly as he could.

"You lied. You lied to us all. All these years, you have left us to live with no hope. You are a disgrace to the Shaurayaveer clan," Avyukt said in a peevish tone. "What is happening? What is this man saying, Grandpa?" Raylina asked, trying to conceal her agitated state of mind.

"Ray, Abby…," Artha sighed. "What?" Ablina asked firmly. "There are things I did to protect our family," Artha began gloomily. Ablina knew what was coming, but prayed for it to be untrue. Artha's silence made her heart collapse. "What things?" Ablina asked in a quavering voice.

Ablina understood from Artha's expressions that she was the granddaughter he was talking about. Her heart stopped beating for a moment. She fell to her knees like she'd never stand up again. "I know… No… this can't be… No…" Ablina burst out in tears. "Abby," Artha said. He kept his hand on her head, but she pushed it away. "I am not a fool," Ablina said furiously.

Ablina sat there with her lips sealed as she didn't want to confirm it. She dared to ask the questions but didn't have enough strength to hear the answers. Ablina's whole life was a big fat lie, and she waited for Artha to give her a valid reason why she shouldn't kill him. "Abby, listen to me," Artha begged. "No, Grandpa. I always knew that there was something wrong with me, and my doubt was cleared when you asked Raylina to talk to Śirā whisperers," Ablina cried in agony.

Artha went down on his knees in front of Ablina, and he took her hand in his and gently but firmly squeezed them, "You are my granddaughter, and no power in this world can deny that. What I did years back was selfish and ruthless, but I did it to protect the small child from dying a horrid death."

Raylina sat down next to Ablina and said, "No matter what anyone says, Abby. You will always be my sister. If not by blood, then by my soul. Nobody can say anything to change my mind." Raylina placed her hands on Ablina's shoulders and gave her a side hug. "Peaches and Pumpkins, remember?" Raylina said fiercely. Ablina broke into sobs and laid her head on Raylina's shoulder.

Artha held out his hand to Raylina, and Raylina placed one on Artha's hand and, with the other, held Ablina tightly. Visac came behind Ablina and placed his hand on her shoulder, offering her silent comfort. Ablina found the comfort she didn't even know she needed. Aamirah walked to the circle and sat beside Artha. He placed his hand on Ablina's knee and said, "Papa is right, Abby. You are the daughter of my sister and George, and you always will be. No power in the world can change that. You are our family. No matter your blood, you are a Shaurayaveer."

The family sat there in the circle in silence, only interrupted by Ablina's periodic sobs. They found comfort and strength in that silence which was much needed after the massacre. For it is true, even when the world is against you, your family will never turn their back on you.

"Hey Abby," Raylina called. Ablina looked up at Raylina questionably. "I always knew you were adopted. No way could somebody this nerdy be related to me by blood," Raylina said jokingly and teasingly. Ablina made a face and fake cried out, punching Raylina and then hugging her tight. Everybody laughed out, slightly relaxed like a heavyweight had been carried away, and they could breathe again.

Artha held their hands once again and said in a serious tone, "Ablina, Avyukt is right. You are the last living Graymanos."

Artha stood up from the floor with the support of Aamirah and walked towards the huge glass window. He gazed at the breathtaking view of the Kangchenjunga Mountain, took a deep sigh, and began, "It was the harsh winter of 1691. Every droplet of water had turned to ice, and the green trees had turned white. It was like the 'winter' was competing with itself, for how colder it could be. We walked for three days, constantly, day and night, to reach Yana Village. Vinaka Bondori, the chief of Yana, had sent me a message to come urgently, to help the villagers who were dying due to an unknown outbreak in the village. I was their last hope. I reached there, and I saw people's skin losing its natural color, turning bluish-grey. I instantly knew it was no disease. This was the work of some dark, powerful magic."

"I searched the town for a witch who might have cast the spell, but I failed. I used every trick in my book to find out who was behind it and why. As the weeks passed, many innocent people lost their lives. I called everyone I knew who could help me, even the best human physicians' of that time. But nothing worked. Everyone gave up, they all moved out, but I didn't. I kept on trying to find the cause and the cure," Artha said.

"On November 21, 1691, my assistant called. He asked me to visit a sick, pregnant woman. I rushed to her cottage as I had the pressure of saving two lives. I examined the woman, and I got my answers. The child she was carrying was not normal—it was magical. I asked for the father of the unborn child, and she directed me to her backyard. At first, I didn't get what she was pointing at, but then I saw the ground I was standing on. It had turned dark blue. I dug the ground and found the dead body buried under it. It was… Mihira Adivaraha," Artha said in a serious tone and paused.

"On the same day the woman went into labor, she cried in pain for hours. My assistant and I tried everything to save her and the child. But the pain of giving birth to a Graymanos offspring was beyond what her human body could bear. She died on the labor bed," Artha said remorsefully. "Graymanos," Ablina whispered unconsciously.

Artha looked at his granddaughters with his eyes filled with tears. He touched Ablina's face affectionately and said, "I held you in my arms, Abby, the most beautiful child, the hope bringer." "That night, I fed you, I sang more than 20 different lullabies to make you sleep, but you were tough like me. You finally fell asleep, and I put you in your bed. I kept my head on the bedside and slept, peacefully for some time," Artha chuckled softly.

"My assistant came and woke me up. He asked me to come out and see. I stepped out and saw an army of dark Graymanos waiting for me to hand over the child of Mihira Adivaraha. I couldn't bear the thought of handing you over to them. So, I lied to them, and the best thing that happened was they believed me. It was also the worst because if they believed me, that meant they had completely turned dark," Artha stated.

Artha looked at Avyukt's boiling red eyes and continued, "Darker than I have ever imagined. And if they had embraced the dark side, that meant they had given up their responsibility of protecting our Mother Earth and passed it on to Shaurayaveers' shoulders, on all of our shoulders, as they were incapable of using their own Ragata magic." "That's what I came for in Desovir. To bring all the help, we can get to defeat Vaylar," Avyukt said, looking at Ablina, justifying his reasons for visiting Desovir.

Artha sat down on the couch, and resumed, "I wanted to raise you as my own, Abby, but I couldn't risk anyone knowing that you were alive, so I quickly wrapped you up in a huge red blanket and left the Yana village. I went to the Drgaan town to ask Amaraya for help. When I got there, I realized that your mother was about to give birth to the twins. I took you to the infirmary where I saw George pacing in the balcony like a man about to lose his head. Looking at him took me back to the day when Amaraya was born. I was just as restless as George was. We both waited for the next 2 hours; George was outside the room, and I was standing behind the door, hiding from him, holding you in my arms."

"After spending one more hour behind the door, I was done. I went there. George was spooked; he took the gun out of his lousy coat, but immediately, he had to pull it away as the nurse came out and delivered the news. She told us that Amaraya had given birth to two girls, but only one girl survived," Artha said painfully.

Artha's bereft expressions frightened them all. "George and I switched Abby with the dead child, and we both made the pact of never telling anyone about this. Not even Ami," Artha said. Ablina sat beside Artha and asked, "Why didn't you just give me to the army of Graymanos?" "Because of your face, it reminded me of my Amaraya. In fact, when I saw you again all grown up, it was like my Ami walking back into my life. You are a lot like her, and since you were born, I have considered

210

you my child. My God and my soul didn't allow me to let an innocent child be raised by the army of dark creatures under any circumstances, and neither did my heart," he explained.

Ablina cried, and so did Artha and Raylina. Ablina hugged him. "Abby, I love you," Raylina said, and she joined in the hug. "For the record, I am older," Ablina said and hugged them tightly. "For the record, that doesn't change the fact that I'm smarter than you," Raylina teased and fought back with her sister, like always.

After all the questions were answered, the family was reunited. But the story is never a story without the twist. "Who is Mihira Adivaraha?" Manashaya asked and interrupted their happy moment. And everyone except Avyukt stared at Artha again, having no knowledge of who he was or how he was involved in the story.

CHAPTER 17

MIHIRA ADIVARAHA

"Mihira Adivaraha," the man declared his presence in his dynamic voice. All the eyes in the living room shifted from Artha to the man who had barged in. The man unmasked himself, and bowed down his head to Ablina, and said, "Mihira Adivaraha, The legend, your father, our leader, the master of Ragata Magic." Ablina looked into his compelling bright red eyes and was lost. "Abby," Artha said and tapped twice on her shoulders with his fingers. Artha pulled Ablina away from the man.

Ablina tilted her head a little, trying not to look into his bright red compelling eyes, and asked, "Who are you?" "I am Sangul," he said in his husky voice. "Are you Graymanos too?" Ablina asked, staring down at his dusky veined arms. "I am their leader. More of an acting leader," Sangul said.

Artha glared at him with angry eyes, like he was trying to burn down the man with his glare. "Artha seems like your granddaughters know nothing about us or their history," Sangul said tauntingly. Artha gulped his fuming fury and kept mum as he was aware of what Graymanos were capable of. "We forgive you, Artha. In fact, we owe you. You made the right decision by taking our princess away from us," Sangul said.

Sangul kept his hand on Artha's shoulders and said, "And sorry for your loss, Artha." "Why are you here? Why now?" Artha asked bluntly, cutting the chase. "To save our world," Sangul said.

Ablina and Raylina looked at each other. They could no longer hide their worried faces. They realized that being born with magic did not mean that they were qualified to save the world. "Shit just got real," Raylina murmured. Ablina tensely clenched Raylina's arm, thinking about the unknown approaching.

We protect the people we love so much that sometimes they forget that they are totally capable enough to protect themselves. Ablina and Raylina lived happily and under the protection of their mother and father all their lives, but their shields were gone. They were out in the open, exposed and vulnerable. "Who is Mihira Adivaraha?" Raylina asked the tempting question again. "Oh yes, Raylina, I will tell you everything about the man," Sangul said with assurance.

Sangul made himself comfortable at home. His behavior reminded Raylina of Alisar, but she rebuffed the thought from her head. She felt that even thinking about Alisar was befouling her body and soul. Sangul stretched his arms up in the air and said, "One fine day, our dear God decided to build all of this. Galaxies, planets, black holes, et cetera, and the land you are all standing on… the Earth. God was a wise man." "Sorry… Sir, but I have one question," Raylina politely interrupted.

"Manners… I am impressed. Yes, please, my dear, all ears," Sangul said. "Have you met God?" Raylina asked curiously. "No, my child, I haven't," he said. "You said God was a wise MAN," she questioned him wisely, trying not to offend him. Raylina's honesty and authentic way of questioning galvanized Sangul. It's been a long time since he had met someone so refreshing and open like her. "Are you sure, Artha, that Raylina isn't one of us?" Sangul asked bluntly.

Artha looked at him with his fierce eyes. "Perhaps I am mistaken. But, Artha, I must tell, you have one hell of a warrior here," Sangul said, smiling at Raylina. "Oh, you have no idea," Artha said with sheer pride written all over his face. "Well, princess. As far as I know, God has no gender, but one thing I am sure of is that God chose a woman to build the Earth," Sangul answered humbly.

"God knew that the task of creating something on the piece of nothingness was unique, and it required someone who had a creative eye. Thus, our beloved God went to the royal court and entrusted a 'Woman' to create this… all of this. You see, God was farsighted because he asked a woman to give a perfect touch to our world, not a man," Sangul explained. "So…" Ablina asked impatiently.

Sangul stood up and slowly walked towards Ablina. He looked at her and said, "Woman is born to be a creator, a nurturer. That's why we call our world 'Mother Earth,' and that's why every new life that comes into our world is from 'Her' and not 'Him.'"

Sangul's narration mesmerized everyone present in the room. And everyone nodded, hanging carefully on to Sangul's words, and eagerly waited for the next. "Then what happened," Visac asked. "We say women know it all, and it's correct. The woman who created this perfection was afraid of leaving it in the hands of men, as she was well aware of what they were capable of," Sangul halted.

"True, men are killers and often destroyers, but it is also true that we are protectors, so she birthed 'Graymanos.' She asked us to protect the world she created. One simple task… But we failed," Sangul said, lowering his eyes down to the ground in shame. "How did you fail?" Manashaya asked. "Love, my friend, Love. Isn't love the greatest weapon for creation and destruction of all time?" Sangul said with a soft grin. All nodded their head in understanding.

"Graymanos were constantly on the move. Whenever we found the word of any destruction or war, we would send our men to repair the damaged parts of the Earth, and this went on for eons. Everything and everyone worked according to the laws laid down by our creator until... Until one day, our leader, Lais, fell in love with a simple peasant girl," Sangul paused and glanced at their curious faces. "Lais was our leader, the first chief, appointed by Mother Nature herself. We followed him since the beginning of time; we worshiped him. In other words, he was our God," Sangul said, gazing at the sun setting behind the Kanchenjunga from the window.

"Call it fate, or call it an evil plan, we were called to a village named 'Danvinya.' It was a small village with hardly 200 men, women, and children. The villagers welcomed us with open arms, and we decided to spend the night there. Lais was an honorable man; he wanted to return the gratitude, so before departing, he went to meet and greet the villagers for one last time. And then he met Kailyn."

"Lais didn't know that the dainty, stubborn girl, with an angel-like face, was waiting for him to save her. She stole Lais's heart in less than a second. It was love at first sight," Sangul said with a smile. "A forbidden love blossomed. Lais forgot his purpose, blinded by the world's most powerful drug—love, his dedication now changed. And our mighty man fell for her like a fanatic," Sangul said with ambivalence.

"Their love disturbed nature's order. Lais was not a random man; he was a Graymanos. We were created to protect the world, not to mingle and mate with mankind.

Their union was unacceptable to humans, witches, and us. We all tried to stop it, but love defeated us. Lais respectfully walked to the royal court and surrendered his powers to be with Kailyn. They married each other against all the laws of nature and mankind, and when you take away something from nature, you have to pay it back. And that's what happened; Kailyn got pregnant," Sangul said sadly.

"Lais thought that if he had given up his power, he could live a simple life with Kailyn and have a family of his own, but the Ragata magic was still there, coursing through his veins, and the child Kailyn carried in her womb was not human, but a hybrid between human and Graymanos. At the beginning of her pregnancy, the couple glowed. But as the pregnancy matured, Kailyn's human body started shutting down. She was not strong enough to withstand such great power growing inside her."

"Lais couldn't see her in pain. He prayed, begged, killed to save her, but there was nothing he could do. His last resort was to knock on the doors of the Shaurayaveers, but they were as helpless as the rest of the world who tried to save Kailyn. Lais lost all his hope, and then he came," Sangul stopped. "He?" Raylina asked.

"Vaylar Alisoyar Madrianil Scandios," Sangul halted and looked at them. "Also known as 'Alisar Vasaga,'" Sangul unveiled, staring at Raylina. The shock was evident on everyone's faces, and they gasped loudly. "Shocking, right? I figured out when I saw Ekani's neck marks, the magic so old, out of the world, there is only one person on this planet who could pull that off... Vaylar. George was close about finding Vaylar's true identity, and that's why he was murdered," Sangul said, looking at Raylina and Ablina's exhausted faces.

"It's enough for today. You all should get some rest. We will continue tomorrow," Sangul said. "We are fine," Ablina said tiredly. "But, I am not," Sangul opposed and walked out from there without saying anything further. He ordered the other Graymanos to protect the castle. They all ate whatever they could find at that hour and slept. Artha was a headstrong man. He was not ready to trust anyone anymore, so he and Aamirah decided to take turns. They both had enough reasons not to trust anyone ever again.

***

Artha stared at the stygian ground covered in the ashes of his people. The devastating view wrenched his heart out. He was disturbed. He wondered how someone could inflict such cruelty for power. "Is power everything?" Artha questioned his muddled mind. "It all seems hopeless," Avyukt came and stood beside him, staring at the dark ground. Artha nodded slightly, thinking about the upcoming war.

"When we first came across Vaylar, he seemed so... weak, so human, one punch without real magic could take him down, but when he played, all our smart, wise brains didn't help," Avyukt chuckled. "Last time he won, because we let him, this time…" Artha paused. "This time, he will pay," Artha said with adamance, and he went in.

***

Ablina and Raylina entered the dining room, and they saw everyone was already assembled at the table for breakfast. "Where are Sangul and that other guy?" Ablina asked, pouring a cup of ginger tea for Raylina. "They are outside," Artha informed. "Aren't they hungry?" Ablina asked. "Abby, they don't eat," Gaurangi said. "What are they? They look like vampires without pointy canines," Raylina said. "No, they aren't. Vampires are limited to the fiction world," Artha answered.

"You okay," Visac asked Ablina. "Yes, I am fine," Ablina replied and softly caressed his hand; he looked at her, and he knew that she was not. "Where is Manashaya?" Raylina asked. "He is outside," Aamirah said. "Why is he not eating with us?" she questioned. "He is not family," Aamirah answered. "Oh yes, he works for us," Raylina said sarcastically, standing up from the chair and headed towards the main hall.

Raylina went out to look for Manashaya. She saw him standing staring at the massacred ground. She kept her hand on his shoulder, and said "Hey." He quickly turned his face the other way to hide his pain from her. She held his face and said, "You can talk to me." "I don't want to," he said bitterly. "If you say so," she said and left.

***

"Good morning, Raylina," Sangul greeted gleefully. Raylina bobbed her head a little out of curtsy and sat in the corner. "Shall we?" Ablina asked. "Yes, of course," Sangul exclaimed and resumed the story. "Vaylar was just a man, but he was a man with a motive; he knew that magic existed, and in search of magic, he went to every nook and corner of the world. Finally, his endless hunt ended at our doorsteps. Vaylar was not born with magic, and he had no patience or interest in learning other forms of magic. So, he used the second greatest weapon—Friendship—and won Lais's loyalty to obtain the power he longed for."

"Lais was the king, but he was a naive king. Lais dug his own grave by telling Vaylar about the lore of the land which breathes magic. 'Darno,'" Sangul said in a low tone. "Darno," Raylina repeated in dismay. "The world of magic, the place from where Vaylar borrowed his magic," Sangul answered. "Ray, the information recorded in the Chryorold about Vaylar is accurate," Artha stated. "How he managed to rent his power from Darno is still unknown, but we know how he opened the door," Sangul said.

Raylina had millions of questions bulging out in her head, but she didn't ask anything. She let Sangul continue. "Vaylar got what he wanted. He said his goodbyes, and we happily parted ways. He returned when Lais needed him the most," Sangul chuckled softly.

"Vaylar convinced Lais that Lais's blood was the only way to save Kailyn. With no other evidence, we were left with no choice but to believe him. And then Vaylar dragged us to India, where all of this began," Sangul said morosely. "Your great grandfather, Aagney Shaurayaveer, assisted us in finding a way to save Kailyn," Avyukt interrupted. Sangul gave a death stare to Avyukt for interrupting him, but Avyukt didn't care. It looked like the Graymanos were having their own internal feuds.

"Lais kept on giving his blood to Kailyn, it did keep her alive, but the pain persisted. Vaylar waited till Lais was weak, and then he stabbed through Lais's heart, but he lived. Graymanos were immortal, but Kailyn wasn't. So he briskly took her... to," Sangul said and pointed straight outside the open window towards the banyan tree, standing tall and proud in the middle of the castle. All eyes followed his finger and turned to the tree, "The center of the Earth." "More like the heart of the Earth," Avyukt corrected.

Avyukt's unwanted comments were getting on Sangul's nerves. He clenched his jaw in irritation and said, "My dear, if we are talking about body parts, then it's more like the stomach of the Earth." Artha sensed the unspoken tension between Avyukt and Sangul from their body language. "This castle was built to protect this door so that it cannot be reopened," Artha jumped in to avoid any further clashes between Avyukt and Sangul. "This piece of land opens the door to Darno," Artha added, gazing at the tree.

Greed is the second-worst enemy of humankind after hatred. "Vaylar's greed made him do unthinkable things. He was ready to take innocent lives on a hunch. He was not conscious of what he was doing or what the consequences could be. There were chances that it could go all wrong. Lais told him a tale he heard, and Vaylar was determined to find out about it. Kaiyln's child was born against the rules of nature and mankind, so the child's blood was the key to opening the door. It is said that when we break nature's law, the magic which lives within gets imbalanced, and imbalance is the first step to destruction," Sangul said.

"Vaylar slit Kaiyln's throat, which induced her labor. And within the snap of a moment, life and death came face to face; the child was born, but the excruciating pain of childbirth swallowed his mother's life. 'Kailyn…' Lais kept on screaming. A gut-wrenching view of his wife dying and his child still attached to his mother made him lose his mind. Lais forgot about the little child lying in his mother's blood. He ran and held her in his arms," Sangul said in an ominous tone, looking at their disturbed faces.

"Vaylar cut the child's cord, and took him to the center of the center. He brutally mutilated the little boy's thumb, and as the child's blood fell on the ground, 'the purest yet impure blood drops' evaporated the poison of Ragata flowers. The flowers burned, every last one of them, the Ragata flowers which guarded the door to a different world for eons, were gone," Sangul described.

"Purest yet impure?" Ablina asked quizzically. "Yes, the child was a pure soul, but the Ragata (Blood) running in his Śirā (Veins) became impure because of him being partially human. It is said that the Ragata flower was created by Mother Nature herself. Ragata magic was the purest and only form of divine magic that ever existed on Earth, and the kid's blood disrupted the pious magic of the Ragata flowers," Sangul answered.

"We reached there, but we were late. Vaylar had already opened the door. A tremendous amount of dark and light energy was emitting through the cracked door. We were there standing helpless, watching him destroy the world. It was like he opened Pandora's box, unknown of what it held. Real or not, simply satisfied with the illusion. Vaylar consumed the light and kept the darkness untouched," Sangul shrieked and broke down. It was like he was reliving the hell he was narrating.

Avyukt took the torch of narrating the story as Sangul was emotionally drained, recalling the horrific past, "And the only way we could think about was to consume the darkness coming out from the door, so we did that."

"We were limited editions of Mother Nature. Soon each one of us consumed the darkness more than our bodies could bear. Some of us died, our bodies started to burn out. Only 200 of us were left. But the darkness kept on coming out from the door. We begged Lais to come to his senses, and he did join us, but adding one Graymanos to the list was not enough to withhold the darkness coming out from the door," Avyukt said.

"The darkness was gobbling our land, our world. It was the end of the world. We beseeched to our Almighty and Mother Nature to save us, save us all, but all hope faded away in that darkness. Darkness spread like a plague. Everything the darkness touched became lifeless. It was a black world, a world without light, a world without humans," Sangul said in a painful tone.

"So, how did it end?" Raylina asked. Sangul smirked, looking at Raylina, and walked out of there. Everyone followed him towards the library. He reached the last section of the library and waved his hand in the air like he was asking the wind to open something. And all of a sudden, the wall behind the bookshelves began dividing into two halves, revealing a dark, narrow, hidden passage. Artha was amazed, as if he never knew that there was a secret passage in his castle. They all walked inside it.

The passage was like a never-ending, deeper, dark dungeon. "Why don't you use your magic to lighten up this place a bit," Ablina taunted Avyukt. "Ablina, we are here to help, not to kill the rest of you. Our magic is like a grenade bomb. If we use it, this place will blow up," Avyukt explained. "Sangul did fine," Ablina argued. "Ma'am, he knows the password," Avyukt said. Ablina gave a sharp grimace to him. Avyukt looked away with a little smirk.

They reached in a big dark hall. Sangul asked Raylina to shed a drop of blood on the ground. "Abby pin," Raylina demanded. "Do I look like your personal assistant," Ablina said while rummaging in her small red sling bag. "Yes, you are, Abby," Raylina smiled, and she pinched her fingertip.

Raylina dropped a drop of her blood on the ground, and suddenly, magically, the fire of the torchlights started to light up one by one. "Awesome! Seems like we are on a great treasure hunt," Raylina said. They observed the trunk of the banyan tree in the middle. "Where does it end?" Ablina asked. "It's deeper," Avyukt said. "It's attached to the earth's base, like a literal base," Sangul said. "Why are we here, Sangul?" Artha questioned. "Crystal Rose," he said.

Artha was ashamed because he knew that the Crystal Rose was gone, and it was Vaylar who took it. "We are here for the Crystal Rose," Sangul repeated, studying Artha's hesitant look. "But it's," Artha stuttered. "You see, trust is a very fragile subject. Betrayal is common for both the natural and the supernatural, my friend," Sangul said with a quirky smile. "We choose not to completely trust your ancestors. And… we were right," Sangul said. "He took it away from me," Artha confessed.

"You shouldn't have told him in the first place," Sangul said. "Crystal Rose is ours, Sangul," Artha said furiously. "Indeed, my friend. I was there when it all happened," Sangul said calmly. "The Crystal Rose, it's true," Manashaya said amusingly. "Manashaya, we don't teach useless things here," Aamirah intervened.

"What does it mean? What are you guys talking about?" Ablina asked in confusion. "The Crystal Rose, the world's most powerful flower. The possession of the flower makes you the living God of this planet," Avyukt answered. "I am still not getting it," Ablina said, trying to remain calm.

"Ablina, Raylina, we are the original keepers of both flowers. Ablina is the daughter of Mihira, which makes her a legitimate heir to the Ragata flower. And Raylina is our 'Śirā whisperer,' just like Aagney," Artha explained. "Grandpa, we got it. We are a family of florists. Ragata... Śirā... Whisperer... Crystal thing. Stop riddling and come to the main point," Raylina said in a highly perplexed state.

Artha took a deep sigh and said, "It is believed that our race was created along with the creation of Graymanos, and our great ancestor, 'Aagney Shaurayaveer,' was the first man created by Mother Nature." "Weren't Adam and Eve the only folks who came first on this planet? I mean, don't most of the humans believe that?" Raylina asked. "Ray, didn't you hear him? He said, the first man created by Mother Nature, not by God," Ablina described. "Plus, every religion has a different theory of who came first, so your question doesn't make any sense." Raylina scrunched her face and said, "Whatever, nerdy pants."

"When the darkness took over the world, Aagney Shaurayaveer, your great-great-great-grandfather, reached there with it... the 'Crystal Rose' or the 'Śirā Flower.'

This shocked everyone because Śirā was something we never knew existed. We only knew that Ragata existed. And only Graymanos could use this form of Magic until now," Avyukt said.

"Miracles don't just happen. Miracles are the results of our efforts. And Aagney made an effort. He planted the Crystal Rose on the decaying black ground. And suddenly, a straight, entrancing bright light came out from it, ripping off that huge cloak of darkness. The light emerged and fell on the newborn son of Lais and Kailyn like a spotlight, transforming him into a full-grown man from an infant," Sangul described.

"The son of Kailyn and Lais valiantly walked straight into the darkness, imbibing the dark fumes coming out the door. So quickly, the darkness disappeared like it never existed. He embraced the darkness; he embraced it all. The power of light slowly started to re-establish its roots, and so did the hope in our hearts that had faded long ago," Sangul smiled.

"The darkness and light stopped coming out, but the door was still open. The man was clueless about how to shut the door forever. He walked in front of the door and groaned thunderously, begging for help, and the sky trembled with his howling; everything around him became stagnant. Our bodies couldn't move, but our eyes could see the true sons of Mother Nature—Aagney and Lais's son, battling to find the right answers to close the door. It all looked so diaphanous," Sangul said.

"A child to her mother is like a detached organ of her body, it's not connected to her physically, but she still feels every pain her child feels. Mother Nature heard his wailing. She sent the cold wind to deliver the message to her second son, 'Aagney.' It is said that it was the first time Aagney heard the whispers from heaven, whispers of magic. The wind gently touched his ears and whispered two words 'Śirā Ragata.'"

"'Rudhh (Stop),' Aagney asked the man in his authoritative voice. The man did as he was asked, and the world resumed. Aagney took the man's wrist in his hands and carved it with bare nails. And let the drops of his Ragata (Blood) fall on the dead ground. Aagney then did the same with his wrist. The fallen blood mixed, magically, and suddenly, the gap between the doors started to get smaller and smaller, and eventually, it closed."

"Mihira Adivaraha," Aagney said, gazing at the full-grown man, the son of Lais and Kailyn, standing beside him. "Mihira Adivaraha," Mihira echoed his new given name, watching the small seedling growing into a sapling out from the closed door. Within a second, the tiny sapling turned into a giant banyan tree radiating the green and red colors of Śirā Ragata (Vein & Blood) magic onto the world. Soon, the branches of the tree spread worldwide and healed the damages completely," Sangul said.

"You mean, all over the world?" Ablina interrupted. "Yes, all over the world," Artha clarified. "The ancient magic of Śirā Ragata united and saved the world," Avyukt

228

said. "Mihira and Aagney then together traveled the world to hunt Vaylar down, but they never succeeded," Sangul said. "No one ever did," Artha added. "Despite evil playing its ways, the goodness in the world still remained untouched," Avyukt spoke avidly.

"I get the whole story about Mihira, the son of Lais and Kailyn, and Aagney saving the world, but I still don't understand what our roles are in saving the world this time," Ablina asked Avyukt. Avyukt looked at her and said, "You don't get it, do you?" "No," Ablina said calmly, hiding her irritation behind a fake smile. "You and Raylina can conjure the magic of Śirā and Ragata just like Mihira and Aagney. Because you, Ablina, you are half-Graymanos and half-human. And Raylina can hear the Śirā whispers, which means she controls the magic of the Crystal Rose," Avyukt answered.

"Okay… so this all has something to do with flowers, veins, and blood stuff, but how do we exactly pull this off," Raylina asked with a blank face. Sangul raised his arms, and suddenly the cottony cloud magically appeared. "Watch it," Sangul said hopelessly, looking at Raylina's and Ablina's perplexed expressions.

CHAPTER 18

ŚIRĀ RAGATA

The enchanting view of the endless Universe took her breath away; she realized that she was an immortal Goddess, and breathing was not important to her. The coruscating colors of infinite galaxies startled her. She wondered how God pulled it off. "The creator at its best," she thought, gluing her divine eyes to scrutinize the Universe. It took her a minute to go through every corner of the humongous ocean of the Universe. "I trust you and only you, Iraja," God said. "I will not disappoint you," she said with enthusiasm, without comprehending what she was assuring.

God touched Iraja's forehead, and they were transported to a piece of land. "Iraja, it's yours. You create it the way you want it to be," God said. "What do you want me to build?" Iraja asked, staring in dismay at the barren land. "That's up to you," God said and left Iraja there.

Iraja was clueless, and at the same time, she was envious of God's creations. Every thought was jumbled up in her head, except God's command. The faith God had in her doubled up the pressure. The creator of the Universe wanted an amateur prodigy to create a masterpiece.

"Iraja, you cannot match God's creation," a voice came from within. Iraja tensely bit her lower lip as she knew the voice was right. She sat down. The visionless mind watched the piece of land. The question of what to create on the blank land haunted divinity herself.

As the days passed, Iraja became more restless. The responsibility of creating something without knowing what to create made her impatient. But then she had to begin somewhere, so she started to design a prototype, and by each design, she compared it with God's creation. Iraja rejected every blueprint she made; they all looked incomplete and hollow. She knew she had to do her best, but she was unable to deliver it. Hundreds of years passed, and the land was still plain and unbuilt.

God observed Iraja's every effort and repeated failures, but he decided not to intervene like any other parent or guide. And it went on for ages. Finally, eight hundred thousand years later, God asked Iraja to come back home. Iraja did as she was asked.

Each journey has its own lessons to teach. As Iraja was traveling back home, her mind rested, and the thought of creating perfection stopped bothering her for a moment. She wandered like a free bird. She happily reached home.

"Welcome back, Iraja!" God said. "I am sorry, but I failed you," Iraja said with a dejected heart. "No, you didn't fail. Not entirely. What counts is that you tried your best," God said. Iraja smiled, and she ran back to the piece of land. God followed her. She reached there and looked at it again.

"What do you see?" God asked. "Life," Iraja said in a lively tone. God looked at her with pride and was glad to know he had chosen the correct candidate for the job. "But…" she hesitated. God knew what Iraja was going through. Iraja's self-doubt fouled the light within her; the lack of faith in her started to sink her self-belief again.

"Self-doubt is like a rotten seed, it dwells deep into us, but nothing comes out of it. Iraja, my child, I created you, and I have all the faith in you. And when I can, then why can't you?" God asked. "I just cannot match up to you. Look at this." Iraja said and pointed to the zillion blueprints lying on the sandy land.

"Why do you want to create something like me?" God asked. "Because… You are marvelous. You are God," she replied, gazing at the Universe. "If I wanted this piece of land like the rest of the Universe, then I could have built it myself. You know, I can do that within a blink of a second," God said, staring at the plain land. After a brief pause, God said, "Don't let uncertainty ruin the best in you. You know you can do it. It's all in there."

Iraja understood what God meant. The biggest hurdle in creating the world was her. Her doubts wrecked her own capability. "Soul lives behind one's heart, and in-between the power resides. The power of good, the power of bad, the power of evil, the power of justice, the power of destruction, the power of creation, the power of everything," Iraja said, taking a deep breath in, slashing the flesh which covered her heart.

The darkness hidden behind Iraja's heart started to fall out. As her darkened blood touched the ground, the color of her blood turned from dark black to shiny red. Slowly, after some time, the ground soaked the shiny red blood inside of it.

Iraja closed her eyes and touched the ground with her fingers. She felt something was trying to bulge out from the land. Tiny dark, bloody red petals started to grow out from the land where her dark blood touched. They phenomenally pleached together one after another, transforming into a beautiful bloody red, dark flower.

The bloody red, dark flowers grew everywhere her darkness fell. Iraja was disheartened as she knew that her darkness consumed the magic within the land. The destruction had started before creation, and it worried her. But suddenly, the veins in her wrist started to glow. The light was so powerful that it busted her veins and then fell on the plagued land. The light blinded her for a while, and as the shine went away, she saw a beautiful little white rose standing amongst the bloody red, dark flowers.

Iraja glanced at her healing veins, plucked the white rose, and said, "'Śirā' the 'Flower of Hope,' 'Flower of Veins.'" She then touched the bloody red, dark flowers and smiled, "'Ragata' as the darkness will always lead to creation." Iraja accepted her light and dark. She realized that her darkness was the beginning and her light was the journey.

Iraja closed her eyes and took a deep breath, and as she let go—the skies, trees, birds, animals, mountains, every beautiful thing she could imagine, she birthed it to make the Earth. It was more than perfect. It was her best. And at last, she made oceans. Their eyes gazed at the view and said, "Life" in unison. God appended one tiny thing to Iraja's epic portrait and added humans to the list.

God proudly said, "Iraja, you birthed 'Life.'" Iraja smiled and said, "And you made me."

The fluffy cloud disappeared, but beguiled by the incredible story of Iraja, everyone kept on staring up, wanting the cloud to project more. "You and only you, Raylina, can find the 'Śirā flower' or what you people call the 'Crystal Rose,'" Sangul spoke cautiously, trying not to spread panic in the group. "Find? What?" Raylina enquired in confusion.

"Find? You said that you had the Crystal Rose, and you switched the real with the fake one," Artha spoke tensely. "Well, we didn't take it or hide it or anything. Sorry for that, my friend," Sangul apologized, looking at the boiling wrath on Artha's face. Sangul hastily shifted to Raylina to evade Artha's aggression and said, "Aagney never told us where he got the Śirā flower in the first place. Even if we have the Śirā flower, the only person who can use it is the Śirā whisperer of the Shaurayaveer clan, which happens to be you, Raylina."

"Also I believe that the Śirā flower was used up during the first time when the door to Darno was opened, and if it is true, then only a true daughter or son of Iraja can grow the Śirā flowers," Sangul said. "And how do you think I can do this," Raylina asked. "Well, that we don't know," Sangul said.

"You are supposed to know, man, aren't you the oldest living creatures on this freaking planet," Raylina spoke rudely. "We all are trying to save the world here, Raylina," Sangul growled at her furiously. "Sangul, my family needs time, so let's end this today," Artha insisted before their heated argument turned into combat.

Rage and love are the only things that come out without warning. Raylina was piling her anger up. Her mother's death and Alisar being the murderer tormented her constantly. She felt guilty for trusting Alisar when she knew that the man yelled trouble from the beginning. "Your pathetic story is not helping me kill that man," Raylina uttered, staring at her shoe's eyelet. "We are here to help you," Sangul said sincerely.

Ablina understood the sensitivity of the matter, so she took a deep breath and calmly said, "I am sorry, Sangul. We want to save the world, and we need your help, but Alisar... I mean, Vaylar... Whatever his name is. He slaughtered men and witches like a joke. And we know that he will come back to kill us and get the Śirā flower, and this time I am afraid he will succeed." Sangul smirked and said, "No, he won't, because we have three live leverages." "Three?... How?... We know he wants me to open the door and close it back. And Raylina for the Crystal Rose. But who's the third?" Ablina asked, her eyebrows furrowed in confusion. "Visac," Sangul said solemnly.

Everybody grew quiet and stared at Visac questioningly. Visac himself had his mouth hanging open. "You are his son, Visac... You are Vaylar's son, and you and his brother Astor hold the last bit of Vaylar's magic," Sangul divulged, glancing at Visac, standing in the corner, barely processing why his name was suddenly popping out of nowhere in the story.

"It's unbelievable, no one survived that poison for more than a month, and Visac's been holding up since he was a little boy," Avyukt said with bafflement. "Well, you can, if you are a spawn of the devil himself," Sangul said. "What? No... no... this is not happening?" Ablina denied, staring worriedly at Visac's blank face.

"But Visac is not in the tracks. And how do you know he's Alis... Vaylar's son?" Avyukt questioned, with suspicion evident in his eyes, still adjusting to the truth that Alisar is Vaylar. "Yes, Avyukt, I am fully aware that his name is not documented in our tracks, and the reason Visac is not in the 'Tracks' is that I erased his name. And I did it because Alisar asked me to. Because before we knew he was Vaylar... he was Alisar... Our Alisar... our most loyal friend and whom we all trusted blindly," Sangul said, with his eyes locked at Artha, remembering his good days with Alisar, who turned out to be Vaylar— the biggest evil, power-hungry massacrist.

"Tracks?... What are Tracks?" Ablina asked curiously, wondering why she hadn't heard of this yet. "Tracks or, you can say records. We keep track of all the people other than us and the Shaurayaveers who practice magic, just to avoid a catastrophe," Sangul replied, staring at their perplexed faces.

Visac was deeply heartbroken. His thoughts were stuck on how he always felt that something about him was dark and evil but could never figure out why. And now that the truth was out in the open, he deliberately wanted it to be untrue. So he stood there, frozen, broken, traumatized, not knowing how to process it.

"Visac, son, you carry his last few drops of magic inside you; that's what makes you a really important pawn in this game. Now you've got two choices here, lad," Sangul halted, keeping his hand on Visac's shoulder to fake console him. "First is that you walk away and we kill you, and second, if you somehow make it out, Vaylar kills you." "The choice is all yours to make," Sangul warned, pulling his hands off his shoulder, giving him nothing to choose from.

"Stop it," Ablina enraged, intertwining her fingers with Visac's. His wet eyes said that he was lucky to have a girl like Ablina in his life, but his words fell short of expressing it. "Sangul is right, Ablina. Visac doesn't get to choose. And if he objects, we will snap him like a twig. We are not barbarians, Ablina, but we aren't saints either. So he better be with us," Avyukt threatened, giving him an ultimatum.

For some reason unknown to him, Avyukt disliked Ablina and Visac's togetherness. It left a bitter taste in his mouth, and right now, he had more pressing matters than to sort out his feelings. He hated the day when he went like a common hooligan to talk to Ablina. He regretted it all. "He could have done it in a more civilized manner," he thought while staring at their hand-holding.

"No... No, this ain't true. I am not Alisar's... Vaylar's son," Visac roared with rage, finally denying everything all at once. "It's true, son. The sooner you accept it, the better for all of us," Sangul said sternly.

The innocence in Visac's eyes was replaced with hatred. Visac was both shocked and angry. He was shocked because the man who had always been around as his mother's boss since he was a boy was actually his father. And he was angry because he didn't know about it. Now he was wondering if Eraa was his real mother or if he had been lied to about that too.

After all these years of pain and misery, the only good thing Visac had in his life were his parents—Kain and Eraa. Though his father, Kain, died when he was 10, his memories still lingered in his heart. From holding a pencil to catching his first fish, Kain taught Visac everything. His father made him the good man he was. But... Alisar... Vaylar... was the opposite of good. He was a pure monster, a monster without a heart. And Vaylar's monstrous, foul blood running through his veins disgusted Visac.

"How should we stop him?" Visac asked fretfully, gazing at the silver "Ouroboros" statue hanging above the fireplace. "We hide," Artha answered calmly.

"Hide? Why should we? We are not cowards," Manashaya said. "People say that there is a difference between being a coward and being stupid. We are fighting someone who has managed to hurt us all," Artha said, looking at Raylina. Artha's eyes turned to Visac, and he said, "Right now, our emotions are heightened, and a good soldier never goes to war wearing his wounded heart as armor. That's stupid, and we are not stupid."

"You are right, Artha. Raylina needs to find a way to create the Crystal Rose or perhaps find it," Sangul agreed. "Where will we go, Grandpa?" Ablina asked. "These mountains will protect us," Artha said. "They always have," Gaurangi maintained.

***

Tears dropped from Manashaya's eyes onto her cheeks. He affectionately kept his hand on hers and said, "I am sorry, Ekani." "She will be okay. We will find that bastard," Raylina said and clasped him in her arms. He pushed her away gently and said, "I think you should start packing."

Sometimes a simple soft gesture tells us exactly how a person feels about you. Raylina understood that Manashaya's hidden feelings for Ekani were surfacing. "Fool," she murmured and left. Raylina made a tough call at that moment. She realized that the world is not just complicated. It's messed up, and feelings are as useless as the appendix in a person's body.

"Feelings make you stupid," Raylina mumbled and went into her room's balcony. She tightly gripped the metal railings and clenched her hurt. She glared at the high and mighty Kanchenjunga Mountain and said, "I get it now… I get the whole lone wolf thing. When you are alone, you are stronger, and no one dares to mess with your mind… with your heart. From now on, the only thing that matters to me is my family's protection."

Being stubborn, arrogant, or misbehaved doesn't mean you're a bad person. It just makes you a little bit unapproachable. Ablina noticed the obvious change in Raylina's behavior. She saw that Raylina had already packed her bag without any help, which was a sign that something was going on with Raylina. And that meant only one thing that soon Raylina was going to transform into a cold-distant little brat.

Ablina, being Ablina, rechecked the wardrobe for one last time before leaving. She kept the things that Raylina forgot to pack in her bag, and while doing so, suddenly, a book fell down at her feet. It was the Chryorold. She touched the book and the memories of her days at Desovir flashed in front of her eyes. She missed how things were before coming to India. "Abby, it's time," Raylina said. They both headed to the main hall.

Raylina saw Manashaya across the main hall, coming out of the living room carrying Ekani in his arms; she rushed there and lifted Ekani's head a little. Manashaya looked at Raylina, and she looked away. They both went near the car, she opened the backdoor, and Manashaya gently kept Ekani in the car seat. "Raylina," he called. "Yes," she said. "I…" he hesitated. "Not now," she said and walked away.

Ablina witnessed the tension between them; she was worried about Raylina's condition, first Alisar and then Manashaya. "Once all this ends, we will get out of this place, Ray, we will go far… far away," Ablina said and held Raylina's hand firmly, reminding her that she would be there for her no matter what. Raylina patted Ablina's arm and said, "Let's go."

They all boarded into cars and headed towards the mountain caves. Ablina peeked out of the car window and saw Manashaya, Aamirah, and Gaurangi tailing behind in another car. Raylina kept her eyes fixed on the mountain road, lost in her thoughts, finding a way to heal her wounded heart. She knew that it was her who had to heal herself. The pain was hers to endure, it was hers to overcome, it was hers to be dealt with, and not anyone else's.

***

As they climbed higher, the cold, chilly wind and rainy snowfall fogged up the car windows. Ablina poured hot coffee for everyone. Raylina shifted her attention from staring at the road to scowling at the snowy mountains and then to the scary-looking man with piercing red eyes sitting beside her. "So, Avyukt, how old are you?" Raylina asked bluntly to goad him. "I stopped counting after 100," Avyukt said in a peeved tone.

"Did you ever date?" Raylina asked. "No," he mumbled. "Hey Abby, I guess I will survive. If he can live without someone for eons, I can surely live for 100 years. After we kill Alisar... Oops! I mean Vaylar, the only man who knows how to make classic age drugs, we will surely die," Raylina said, trying to pick a fight with Avyukt. "Your mockery doesn't affect me," Avyukt said in a calm voice.

Raylina laughed and said, "Don't give much importance to yourself, darling. We are side-actors, our lives are dependent on a ventilator, and we are just a plug-pull away." Avyukt rested his hand on hers, and whispered in her ear, "Don't be a bitch."

Raylina gently pulled her hand from below, and then she firmly gripped Avyukt's hand and whispered back,

"Ouch... I think I pressed the wrong button." Ablina's head slightly turned back to talk, and they quickly became distant. "Everything okay, Ray?" Ablina asked. "Ya, nerdy," Raylina said and rolled her eyes.

***

"Abby, here, take this coat. It's chilly," Raylina said and handed the furry grey coat to Ablina. "Thanks, Ray!" she said and gave a side hug to Raylina. "It's 9:30. Where's Grandpa?" Raylina asked, waiting near the car. "We are the ones to reach first," Avyukt said. "Where are Manashaya and all?" Visac asked. "Call them and find out," Ablina suggested. "Okay," Visac said and dialed Manashaya.

"They are just 30 minutes away. Uncle Aamirah asked us to wait inside the car," Visac informed them. "30 minutes? Great! Whatever, I am sleepy, going in," Raylina said with irritation, opening the car door and sat inside.

Raylina rested her achy body in the back seat of the car, trying to shut off her mind for a bit, but like always, it didn't, so she lay there with closed eyes, permitting her thoughts to take control over her already hopeless world.

"Let's wait inside the car," Ablina said. "Okay... Avyukt, you coming?" Visac asked, draping his arm around Ablina's shoulders. "I am good here. I don't feel anything. You both go and sit inside," Avyukt said.

Ablina and Visac sat in the front seats. Ablina saw Raylina sleeping and then turned her eyes back to Visac.

"I am afraid," Ablina said. "Hey Abby, you are the strongest witch/Graymanos in the whole world. You are my fiery butterfly, so chin up, babe. I know you will get through this with Raylina, with your family, with me," he said sincerely.

Ablina smiled lightly and said, "When did you become a pep talker?" "Well, I can't see you being gloomy. I promised Venus to take care of you," Visac said. "Sweet!" She blushed and gently pulled his cheeks. "I never thought I was cut off for romance," he said. "But I always knew," Ablina winked.

"Get a room, weirdoes," Raylina laughed. "Ray… You eavesdropper," Ablina said. "Abby… Visac… you guys…" Raylina paused. "What?" Ablina waited. Raylina began to tell them how happy she was for Ablina and Visac, but then she thought saying it out loud might jinx their epic love, so she smiled, and said, "Nothing," and left them alone in the car to give them some privacy.

***

Avyukt saw Raylina stepping out of the car and walking towards him. He chuckled. "Looks like your sister kicked you out," Avyukt taunted. "Well, it looks like you are jealous that the man inside that car isn't you," Raylina taunted him back. "Your deadly red eyes don't scare me," she added proudly. "Ohhh… you see Ray… lina, your pretending is as fake as you," Avyukt said, trying to channel all of his patience.

"Look at you being all high and mighty, got betrayed by one and dumped by another," Avyukt sneered. Raylina slapped him. He wiped the blood out from the corner of his lips and looked at Raylina. "Fuck off," Raylina said rudely and walked away to the cave, with her blood dripping on the white snow.

Avyukt gripped Raylina's injured hand and dragged her closer to him. He pulled out a black cloth from his pocket and wrapped it around her bleeding wound. Avyukt gazed into her fierce cognac eyes and said, "Aamirah will seal this up."

Avyukt's dark red stare made Raylina feel uneasy, as if they were taking over her mind. She pressed her fingers into his rugged chest to gently drive him away. Raylina stepped back, and took the support of the snowy wall, trying to warm her hands in the freezing cold while gazing at the starry sky. Another of their cars pulled up, and she saw Manashaya carrying Ekani in his arms towards the cave.

Aamirah walked towards the cave, and he stood before the slope. He touched the surface, and slowly the ice started to melt. The cave looked like a small burrow from outside, but it became whiter, shinier, bigger, and warmer as they went in. "A splendid hideout," Raylina said, gawking at the marbled floor.

"Girls, we got these sleeping bags for you, so... help yourself out. Visac, this one for you, and Manashaya, take this one," Gaurangi said, and handed them their sleeping bags. "I will sleep in the car," Raylina said and rushed out before anyone could say anything. "Ray..." Ablina said and started to walk behind Raylina. "Wait... I'll talk to her," Gaurangi said and went after her.

***

"Hey, can I talk to you for a minute?" Gaurangi asked politely. Raylina opened the door. Gaurangi sat with her. "I know why you are here. Ablina and Grandpa are enough. I don't want you added up in the list of pep talkers," Raylina said. "No... I am just here to say that you are becoming a pain in the ass," Gaurangi said gently.

Raylina's jaw dropped; she had never imagined that Gaurangi would talk to her like that. "We are not on a picnic, Raylina. The war is coming, and we are already outnumbered. Luckily, that day, we didn't die. Although you both girls are special, our knowledge and experience is older than yours. So you are going to do as I say, or else... well, don't let me complete my sentence," Gaurangi glowered. "Okay... Okay. I will go, but I am not going because you asked nicely. It is because I know I was wrong," Raylina frowned. Gaurangi and Raylina went in together.

CHAPTER 19

THE KANCHENJUNGA

King of the empyrean, the Sun, sent his first ray to mizzle upon the peak of Kanchenjunga to mercifully take down the unyielding snow of the mighty mountain. But despite the Sun's every effort to melt it down, the Kanchenjunga stood still and undefeated. Raylina was captivated by the spectacular amalgamation of fire and water. It was beautiful, dangerous, enthralling. Parts of her were drawn to each element—air, water, and fire.

Raylina curled her frosty lower lip watching the sunrise, pondering about how it takes only one person to change your perception about life and people. "Raylina… breakfast's ready," Ablina called, and the spell broke. One last time, Raylina glanced at the view, capturing the glimpse of cold paradise forever in her heart. For some reason, she felt that things were going to change from this moment on.

Raylina headed inside the cave, and she saw Artha and Aamirah on the little table. "Ahh... Ray... eat up. We are leaving for the peak," Artha informed. "Why are we going to the peak?" Raylina asked. Artha didn't reply and continued eating his breakfast. Raylina rolled her eyes at him but left the topic for the time being.

Everyone finished breakfast, grabbed their hiking gear, and started walking towards the mountain base. Raylina and Artha walked together quietly, ahead of everyone, while Ablina, Visac, Avyukt, and Manashaya followed behind.

***

The people with whom we enjoy silence are keepers. Artha and Raylina liked each other's company. The age gap between them was not just based on age; it was more like a hundreds of decades scenario. Artha already spent more than a millennium in this world. And, Raylina's journey was just getting started. But, from the moment they met each other, their bond began to sew. Their familiarities made it clear that they were meant to be an epic granddaughter–grandfather duo. Parents try hard to be friends with their children, but they cannot be their best friends like grandparents can.

The connection between children and their grandparents is always unique and the most effortless relationship in this world. It's mostly smooth because they both have a common enemy: the parents. And in this case, Artha and Raylina lost their equally loved common enemy, Amaraya. The depth of their grief was far beyond their understanding. All they could do in that time was to be there for each other.

Everyone started preparing for their climb; meanwhile, Artha instructed them about hiking routes. They all dressed up in their hiker suits and began tightening their ropes.

"Raylina," Manashaya said. "What?" Raylina said, focusing on buckling her backpack. "Take care of yourself," he said, trying to avoid eye contact. "Yes, you too," she replied, still striving to buckle the straps. "Bye," he said in a firm voice. Raylina stopped and looked at him. They stared at each other; they felt the change, but neither dared to talk about it.

"Feelings" are the perfect ingredient God added while cooking us up. And all they do is bring complications and chaos to our lives. Raylina Bayer was a masterpiece of complications; the word "sorted" never existed in her entire life. "Thank God," Raylina silently prayed. "Thank God! I didn't fall for that jerk," she mumbled and started climbing up.

***

"War is on our heads. Why are we climbing this stupid mountain, Grandpa?" Raylina yelled, plodding herself up with the help of the ropes. Artha ignored her and kept on moving forward.

"Manashaya, are we there yet?" Ablina cried as she dragged herself up. Manashaya gave her a death stare and didn't say anything. He turned a little to check Ekani's head and gently tapped her frozen hand wrapped around his neck. "Abby, if you ask him one more time, he will kill you," Visac said, looking at Manashaya haul his frazzled body up the arduous slippery mountain with Ekani on his back. "Sorry… Okay… V, but why is he coming with us?" she whispered to Visac, glancing at Avyukt with sour eyes. "Artha's orders," Avyukt barged in to their conversation innocently.

The funny thing about good equations is that they are always astoundingly unequal. Avyukt hated it. No matter what he did, Ablina reacted the opposite to it. His only intention was to be in her good books, but his actions made everything go astray. He understood that it was time to let it loose and stop making countless efforts to make things right.

They all were climbing at different distances, at their own pace. After every minute or so, they felt like giving up because their bodies were writhing in immense pain. But it's dumb to climb back when you are already halfway there. So, they kept on marching up.

Raylina was crawling behind Artha like a lump of dead meat. But when your best friend is given a task to prove your worthiness, they make sure you die a little every time you take a step ahead. She realized that her grandfather was testing her. "Grandpa, this is it. I can't do this," she winded, holding on to the rope.

Artha looked down at her dead freezing face and exploded, "You want to kill the man who killed your mother like this? That man happens to be the most powerful man walking on Earth, and this is how you plan to fight back?" "Come on, Ray… don't be a fragile princess. Be a queen," he roared. Artha's words pumped Raylina's Śirā (veins) with a will of retaliation, and she commanded her legs to start walking.

***

Every step Raylina took, she prayed for the next to be her last, but her sheer determination didn't let her give up. Artha and Raylina arrived first at the peak. Raylina gawked at the untouched nature's wonder. And her tantalizing wish to stay there forever made her a little sad. An absolute beauty of solitariness allured her; she couldn't keep her eyes off it. The peace she was looking for was finally in front of her, and all she had to do now was embrace it with open arms. But, rather, she stood there thinking about the thrills chaos offered to her. "No one thing for me," she smiled, breathing in the cold air of Kanchenjunga.

"Finally! We are on top of the world," Ablina screamed. "Ray…" Ablina shrieked in an enthralling voice. She ran towards her like an erratic bull and hugged Raylina from behind. "Abby, relax," Raylina said and removed Ablina's embrace from her. "She's an alien. Look at that energy, man," Raylina said to Visac. "I have been asking the same question," Visac panted, resting his hands on his knees.

We don't trust people; we never do; we trust their actions... temporarily. Raylina saw Ekani on Manashaya's back, and the band-aid on her invisible scar ripped off. A person's coping system improves after every loss; we become harder, stronger, and stone-like. The things which used to hurt us become less hurtful, but it stings— the sting remains! Raylina wanted to turn her face away from reality, but things like that are hard to ignore and live with. She walked towards Manashaya and helped him lay Ekani on the sleeping bag.

Artha kindled the glaciated ground around their tents. Everyone gulped their cheese sandwich like a ravenous beast and headed inside their tents, except Raylina. "Grandpa, now may I ask you, why are we here?" Raylina demanded in a firm voice. "It's late, Raylina. I need rest. Good night," Artha said and went into his tent.

Raylina sat there for a while, gazing at the stars with vivid thoughts running at the same time in her head. She went into her tent and fell asleep within a second.

***

"Wake up, Ray," Artha said nicely. Raylina could barely keep her eyes open; she ducked her face into the sleeping bag. "Wake up," Artha yelled like thunder. She quickly came out rolling from the sleeping bed, and stood there like a soldier on command. "Damn, man, you are strict," she said, still half-asleep. "Raylina, we have one day to save the world, so get your head here," he cautioned. "Aye aye, Captain," she saluted.

Artha and Raylina stood on the edgy rock. As she rolled her eyeballs down, she saw the white clouds covering the view below. She comprehended that one wrong step, and she was going straight to heaven. Artha sat cross-legged on the ground, and Raylina followed him vigilantly.

"What do you see?" Artha spoke without wasting any other second. "Mountains, obviously," Raylina replied in a spot. "No, what do you see," he asked again. Raylina took her time to think, but nothing came up. "Wrong answer it is then," Raylina thought in her head and loudly said, "Vulnerability." "Look at this high… mighty mountain… but think about one little landslide or snowstorm, and it gets scattered like a joke," she answered honestly.

Artha looked at her with his proud eyes. "Vulnerability," he quoted. "Its vulnerability which makes this mountain so lively; think about it being strong and undefeatable, no one likes that," he explained softly. Raylina nodded her head like she understood what he meant.

"A person's vulnerability is a two-way weapon; it can either destroy things on the inside or demolish the outer world. It's up to us how to handle it," Artha said, gazing at the daybreak. "Grandpa, I get your point, but I am only hurting right now. I am not vulnerable," Raylina argued.

"You're hurting because you gave him the power to do this to you. I am not asking you to conquer your vulnerability because I believe it is not wise to use your vulnerability as a weapon, or anything else, for that matter. It's like becoming a suicide bomber with only one mission, to kill yourself and everything around you," Artha explained.

Artha's warning was crystal. Raylina understood that her vulnerability was the reason why they climbed up 15,000 feet. "We could have done it on the ground, Grandpa," she smiled. "Yes, but then it would have been more like a boring lecture to you, just like the hiking instruction I gave, which you boldly ignored," Artha winked.

When you see something, knowing that you won't ever see it again makes it deeply interesting and beautiful. Artha and Raylina sat there, gazing at the mountains, spending some time in peace before going to war, which no one knows if they'll survive or not.

"Do you believe what Sangul said? About Śirā Ragata," Raylina asked, her eyes still glued to that fascinating view. "I am more of a realist, Raylina, and what happened eons back is not my top concern right now. I just want Vaylar not to open that portal again on my watch and save as many of us as I can," Artha answered.

"Abby believes in this crap. She always clings to the most impractical stories she can find," Raylina said. "There is nothing wrong in believing something your mind couldn't understand. It's all about faith, Ray. Somehow, your mother and Abby tend to have that faith," Artha stated.

"Can we win this?" Raylina asked. "I don't know. The Graymanos are all pitching for you girls, but…" he hesitated. Raylina broke her eye contact and asked, "But what?" "Ablina's powers only work when she is emotional. And yours, if I am right, I have never seen you doing magic of any kind. Also, Aamirah and Gaurangi are just basic witches, and I never actually taught them the real deal. None of you guys are combat warriors," Artha said darkly.

"Yes, we are a pack of a dysfunctional family of witches. I like that," Raylina laughed, trying to lighten up the tension. "Yes," Artha chuckled. "Grandpa, why hasn't Vaylar attacked us yet?" Raylina asked. "Vaylar is waiting for a full moon. His powers are fading too, and he is waiting for the right time when the moon has neutralized all of our powers," Artha answered.

"No, I mean, he can kill us, right? Without magic?" Raylina said. "Yes, of course, but he won't. He is waiting for you to find the Śirā flower, as this time, he knows how to permanently consume the magic from Darno without any side effects," Artha explained. "Why didn't anyone of you kill him? It's been ages," she questioned. "He is a brilliant disguiser. No one knows how he managed to pull that off," he said sadly. "Anyway, it's time," Artha said and stood up from the edgy rock. "Time for what?" Raylina asked. "For training," Artha said.

***

Artha and Raylina walked back to the camp and saw everybody enjoying the morning breeze. Artha gathered everyone around him and said, "You all are standing here because you all aren't lucky enough. Most of you will die on a full moon's night when that door opens. One day… We have one day to learn everything," Artha informed, staring at their blank faces.

Ablina couldn't bear the thought of learning jujutsu, martial arts, and every form of combat in an hour. It was the craziest thing to do, but they had to start somewhere, she thought and controlled herself from freaking out. Manashaya, Raylina, Visac, and Ablina stood there in a line. Avyukt and Artha stood on the opposite side, facing them. "Artha, you were right. They are really good at taking things their way," Avyukt laughed, and so did Artha.

Artha showed them the steel flask and said, "We will drink this potion." "What are you saying?" Visac gasped. "Visac, that's how things work around here. We use our magic to make things simpler," Artha said and handed him the flask. "But we thought we were actually going to learn to fight," Raylina said with disappointment. "We are not in the movie, princess," Avyukt taunted. Raylina ignored him as she felt that he was not important enough to be considered, but somehow his smug smile irked her.

"What if it wears off," Ablina inquired doubtfully. "One drop of the potion will work for a month or so," Avyukt said confidently. "What? Month… or so. What do you mean by that?" Visac questioned. "It's a new invention, Visac. We are going to test it on all of you," Artha said hesitantly. "What?" Raylina yelped. "Well, it's everyone's first time," Artha said. "We are deeply fucked," Raylina murmured. Visac heard her, and said, "Definitely."

Turn by turn, Manashaya, Raylina, Visac, and Ablina each sipped the scary-looking nasty potion from the amber-colored steel flask. The disgusted look on everyone's faces stated that they hated the potion. In the future, they would prefer to die instead of swallowing that bitter venom. "Time to test," Avyukt said.

Raylina headed first as every inch of her body wanted to punch Avyukt's smug face. And she did exactly what her heart desired. Raylina threw a robust punch on Avyukt's face. "Eureka… It works, Grandpa! Well done," Raylina applauded, watching Avyukt on the ground.

In seconds before Raylina could understand what had happened, she was lying beside Avyukt on the icy floor. "It's all about technique, Princess," Avyukt said, staring back into her eyes. Raylina thrust her palms onto the glacial ground and stood up, giving him a baleful stare.

"Magic in the potion gives us additional power, but how to wield it requires a technique. Raylina, come here," Avyukt ordered. "What?" Raylina gasped in surprise. "I need assistance to demonstrate," Avyukt requested with a tight expression. "Okay," she said and moved in front of Avyukt.

"The most basic defensive techniques are Blocking, Locking, and Grappling," Avyukt stated. "Raylina, hit me," Avyukt asked. "Gladly," Raylina said and raised her fist with full power to strike him. Avyukt blocked her punch smoothly with his forearm, "Blocking," he said.

"Our joints are the submissive points of our body during a fight," he said and suddenly, held Raylina's wrist, and bent it. "Ahh," Raylina screeched in pain. "Always remember," Avyukt cautioned, still holding Raylina close, listening to her every breath.

"It's not even full power, Princess," Avyukt whispered in Raylina's ear tauntingly and let her go. He wrapped his one foot around Raylina's, which destabilized and made her trip on her face, "Sorry, but this is what we call the Takedown," he said, reaching his hand to help her stand up.

For the rest of the day, Avyukt thoroughly demonstrated the basic handy defensive techniques, and they kept on practicing till evening.

***

Cold evening spread its deadly chills to steal the warmth of their skins. Ablina saw Raylina walking into the tent, hiding a silver flask inside her lavender muffler. "Not now, Ray," Ablina mumbled and followed Raylina into her tent.

"What on earth are you doing, Ray?" Ablina attacked her from behind. Raylina was caught red-handed. "It's medicinal," Raylina said plainly. Ablina silently watched her sister bravely gulping the next sip of Cognac from the silver flask. Raylina felt the angry stare of her sister, but she continued with her I-don't-care act. But after the fourth sip, it was hard to ignore Ablina's disappointed face. Also, it was different in taste than she expected. It was bitter. "What, Abby?" she asked.

"What is wrong with you? I know that Alisar is a monster, and Manashaya is... well, you know, but that doesn't justify your drinking. You are doing everything opposite of what Ma and Papa taught us," Ablina said, trying not to be harsh on her sister. Raylina took a breath, slipped her hands inside the blanket to warm them, and said, "They are gone, Abby. And in the middle of this entire BS, nobody seems to care about it. Everyone is busy handling their own pain."

Ablina sat beside Raylina and said, "You remember, the night before dad died? He said, 'You both have to hold on to each other no matter what. When one falls, the other should always be there by their side to help them get back on their feet.'"

Ablina intertwined her fingers into Raylina's and said, "I need you, Ray. I am falling, and you are losing right now." "And this is not going to help me stand up... the way you are handling things will make us both fall, and, Ray, we don't have Ma or Papa to help us this time," Ablina said and started crying. "Abby, please don't cry. I just can't seem to bear this weight on my chest. It hurts, it really hurts," Raylina said, keeping her hand on her aching heart, holding it from falling back into the dark pit of sorrows. "You need to stop, Ray. Every time you run away from this pain, the closer it will get to you," Ablina said in a hurtful voice.

Raylina was baffled to see her mother's wisdom reflecting in Ablina. "No matter how far I go, Ablina will always be there looking out for me," she thought, and a little smile broke out on her glum face. "I am sorry, but Abby, I don't have the strength to stand up. Losing Ma destroyed me. I have become oblivious. I don't feel anything. I try to react like the old me, but the truth is, I have changed into something completely out of the way. It's like I burned with Ma in that fire," Raylina spoke, letting Ablina in through the high walls she built around her to keep her heart, or, what's left of it, safe.

Ablina leaned her head on Raylina's shoulder and said, "Even I am lost, Ray, but this is not the time to weep or throw tantrums because we lost that one person who tolerated our endless weeping and cribbing." "Ma," they said together. "I miss her," Raylina hugged Ablina. "Me too," Ablina cried and hugged her back. "Now, let's go before that irritating Avyukt walks in," Raylina said, and they headed out.

***

Artha was sitting afar on the rock; his eyes watched them carefully, learning and testing their powers, but his mind was huddled up with thoughts of putting the kids at risk. "Kids, get back here," Artha called.

They all gathered around Artha. He looked at them one after another. Their innocent faces made him feel guiltier. He lowered his head to gather the strength he needed to face them again; slowly, he looked up and said, "It's time to learn some real magic. But before we begin, I want you all to close your eyes." They all followed his orders. "Raylina, Ablina, you both are born with magic. Visac, you were injected with it, and Manashaya, you learned it with time. Now, I don't want you all to focus on how you have it, but to focus on how you will use it."

After a few seconds of pause, Artha resumed, "Vaylar wanted magic at any cost, but he never cared about what he would do after he had it. Now look at him. All set to destroy the world again." Artha paced around them, thinking about putting the chaos of his mind into words; it was difficult for him to explain them in words. "Kids, you have a choice to choose the reason to go in this battle. Think... Think carefully about that reason because there is a thin line between bravery and foolishness. I want you all to give me a firm reason for why I should let you go to this war, and trust me, I need a pretty good one."

"If the world is really ending, then I am not the type of person to sit around and watch TV," Raylina spoke first. "We promised Papa to never leave each other's side, so I go where she goes," Ablina said and held Raylina's hand tightly. "You both don't have an option to opt-out, girls," Avyukt sniggered.

Ablina stared at Avyukt and whispered, "His annoyingness is increasing every second." "Happy to kill him for you," Raylina said in a hushed tone, throwing a fake smile at Avyukt.

"According to you all, the man who is going to bring this dreadful calamity upon our world is my father, and if it's true, I have to stop him," Visac said firmly. They all looked at Manashaya and waited for him to give his reason.

Manashaya was staring at the tent. His eyes said it all. "Ekani," Raylina said in her head. "His predictability is becoming more and more predictable," she mumbled. "Manashaya, son, speak up," Artha said softly.

"It's been 10 years. And I still remember the feeling of being lost and scared, sitting on that bench at the police station for stealing a cycle, horrified by the thoughts of never getting out of that place. Then, you came… You came and took me home. You just didn't shelter an orphan boy that day; you saved me. You showed me a way… You showed me 'my way.' You corrected me and set me on the rightful path. So yes, I want to fight along with the man to whom I owe my life," Manashaya affirmed. Artha proudly looked at him; he was happy that he raised him right.

CHAPTER 20

MAGIC

Artha gazed upon the waxing crescent glowing amid infinite stars agglutinated on the sky's blackboard, feeling nervous and terrified to teach the next generation of young witches and warlocks. Artha was a teacher first and then the world's most powerful warlock. But the burden of teaching the right things creates a certain amount of tension on teachers because they can never predict what the child will perceive from their lessons.

The concept of Śirā Ragata was deeper than anyone could understand. Unlike any other witch, Artha knew a little more about the ancient magic, but not everything. Like every other witch, he, too, was searching for answers.

Artha took out a dark brown cigar from his pocket and lit it with his expensive silver-plated lighter. He sucked the white fumes inside him, hoping to calm his nerves. Rather, the burning smoke intensified his stress level. Artha looked at the group and said, "Alright... Let's begin."

"The men who claimed that Magic was just the subject of dreamers' fascination were often found praying in temples, churches, and mosques. Our world works on two principles—Input and Output. Or that is what all humans believe. But what they often dismiss is the middle. The middle, well, no one cares about it, and that's where the 'Magic' lives. And Magic doesn't live there alone. It lives with a companion called 'Faith.' And together they make us. We are the middle, each one of us, and the fun part is even God is like the rest of us, a middle person," Artha winked.

Artha glanced at their innocent faces staring at him with curiosity-filled eyes. It made him a little jumpy. Their expressions made him wonder whether to continue or not. Artha followed his instincts and continued, "There are three types of magic known to our kind. First is the one which Graymanos have, the natural form, the 'Ragata Magic.' Then there is the second type of magic, which anyone can learn with time and patience. It includes spells, plants, potions, etc., which have infinite other subdivisions. The third is the magic that came from the other world, Darno, which Vaylar carries inside of him."

"We are going to rule out the first two, as the oldest form can only be used by Graymanos, and it's hard to learn it in a day. And the second form is also a bit slow; it requires years and years of practice," Artha said. "You mean we are going to use the third form, but... but how will we do that?" Avyukt asked curiously. "We will use... Śirā magic," Artha answered.

Avyukt was shell-shocked. He was hesitant at first, but Artha's idea was ludicrous. "But it's the purest form of magic. It will be the biggest felony of all time, corrupting something so old and pious," Avyukt said, trying to put some sense into Artha. "We don't have a choice. We use it this way, or die without trying," Artha said with a straight face.

"I think we should take a chance," Raylina interrupted without thinking it through. "Do you even understand what you are saying? You will be the one pulling the trigger," Avyukt said furiously. "That's not your call to make," Raylina said harshly. "Avyukt, this is worth the risk. And I am saying this because I have witnessed something truly divine, something which never often occurs in our world," Artha said in an unhesitant tone. "What?... What happened?" Ablina asked.

Artha blankly looked at his granddaughters. He hated his situation; he never imagined that he would have to be the one to tell them about that awful incident. But the clock was ticking much quicker than he expected.

"Ragata magic was born out of the dark emotions of Mother Nature, but it still had some light in it, as both Śirā and Ragata magic came from her. Mihira knew that it would require more than simple darkness to abort the Graymanos child growing in his wife's womb, so he specifically used his dark Ragata magic to inoculate the darkness he consumed from Darno into Ablina. Mihira wanted to save your mother, but before he could completely kill you, your mother found out about it, she called in the favors to save you, and the news spread to Vaylar," Artha said.

"Unaware of the monster Vaylar was, your mother called him her knight in shining armor; as for her, he was the man who was there to save her child's life from Mihira. Vaylar got what he wanted—the location of Mihira Adivaraha. Without wasting any moment, he murdered his biggest enemy. He left thinking that Mihira's child was worthless for him, as the child would eventually die because Darno's darkness had already deprived the child of its Ragata magic, making the child intensely weak to survive," Artha said.

"By the time I reached there, it was too late. Your mother was dying, and the only way to save her was to cut you out of her, but she asked me not to. She begged me to keep you alive. I... I didn't listen. I cut you out... at that moment I thought that a child who is going to die anyway doesn't need saving... but fate had other plans for you. You lived Ablina, and your mother died. And you know, I gave you to Amaraya under the pretext that she had twins," Artha said dolefully.

Ablina was shattered from the inside, but she didn't let it reflect on the outside. Though her blank face managed to deceive everyone, her eyes spoke the truth. Raylina caught her act and held Ablina's hand firmly to let her know that she was not alone and that she never will be.

Artha sighed deeply, staring at Ablina's fallen face, feeling guilty of being the one to wound her heart, once again by telling her the truth. He gulped his pain and continued. "After a few years, when you were around 7, your dark Ragata powers started to emerge, but they were corrupted by Darno's dark magic. You carried an extreme amount of darkness inside you, which disturbed your dark–light balance. And after a while, you were neither light nor dark. It was all messed up. And one day, what I feared happened."

"As I remember, it was a fine October evening. You and Raylina were playing catch in the meadows of wildflowers. While running to catch the ball through fields of wildflowers, suddenly, you fell unconscious on the ground. Your entire body was frozen, just like the bodies in Yana village. It was the same poison that had comatose you. Raylina came rushing towards you. She thought you were bitten by a snake, so she began sucking your blood out of your neck. Slowly your body started to recover. Raylina drank every drop of that poison from your body till you became conscious. All of this baffled George; he couldn't understand what he saw. He ran towards both of you, and Raylina fell into his arms. Raylina's lifeless body numbed him," Artha said.

"As I recall, two days before the incident, I felt that something was going to happen. So without wasting a moment, I ran to check on Amaraya, but when I reached the town, I found out that Amaraya was frantically searching for all of you. Due to the protection lockets, none of you were traceable, not to Amaraya or to me. We were searching for you like maniacs… separately, of course. Not to brag… but I was older and smarter, and I found you all," Artha said.

After halting for a whole minute, Artha said, "I found George sitting on the ground, holding Raylina's dead body, turned blue, in one arm, and Ablina sleeping in his other. I stood there, rooted to the spot, watching George wailing—thinking about what I have just lost, thinking how I will never get to hold my granddaughters or how I will never be able to teach them Niyate magic or any magic for that matter. The sun came up, and nothing changed. George was still there holding his children in his arms, and I was standing behind the willow tree, paralyzed, watching all of this."

"Amaraya came running… yelling your names… I saw her reaching closer to George, so I quickly hid behind the tree. I was standing there, with a fallen heart, waiting for my daughter to start mourning her loss, but I heard nothing but silence. I peeked through the creeping shrubs of bushy willow, and what I saw next… really… pardon my language… fucked me up. I saw… Raylina, moving, breathing! After that day, George and I started to look for answers," Artha said.

"But how come we don't remember anything, Grandpa?" Raylina asked. "George and I took care of it. We erased both of your memories," Artha replied.

"The reason why Raylina is Śirā in Śirā Ragata is that she lived after consuming Ablina's Ragata (Blood) befouled with the darkness of Darno. Her Śirā (Veins) holds the power of light, which counterpoised the poisonous magic of Darno," Artha explained.

"So, if Raylina can consume Ablina's darkness, she can withstand the third form of magic inside her?" Avyukt asked to confirm. "Theoretically, yes, now we just have to check whether it works practically or not. And that is because she consumed that poison in the presence of Ragata magic. But this time, we have to inject the pure form of Darno's magic into her system," Artha said. "But Artha, the people who consumed that magic, barely lasted for a week. This is suicide," Avyukt warned. "I know the risks, but we have to try," Artha said.

"No… No. My sister is not pulling this crazy stunt. I don't care if the world ends, but I cannot let my sister be part of this stupid experiment," Ablina declined firmly to their lunacy. "Abby, please," Raylina said. "What… No, you shut up, Ray, and no, you are not going to be part of his insanity," Ablina said sharply. "Artha, I think Abby… Ablina is right. We shouldn't do this. Raylina is important for closing the gates of Darno; without her, the power of the Crystal Rose is useless," Avyukt supported Ablina's point.

"If we kill Vaylar before opening the door, the entire thing will not happen," Artha said. "Śirā magic is way more powerful than you all think; if she can actually use it to control the third magic, she can save lots of lives," Artha argued.

Artha and Raylina were determined to convince all; the flow of optimism blurred the chances of failure. "Artha," Avyukt said in a serious tone, "Vaylar enslaved more than half a million people just to pass on his magic, and after a week, they died a very horrific and painful death, except his own kin. The people who lived for more than a week were never able to use it, it's dangerous, and we shouldn't do it." "I think it's my decision to make, and I want to take a chance," Raylina said stubbornly in a stern tone.

Ablina spent the whole night restless, thinking about Raylina's decision to consume the magic from Darno. Raylina, on the other hand, slept peacefully, like a warrior, knowing that any day could be her last.

***

The first ray of doomed dawn didn't bring any peace. Raylina's decision to take the risk was still on, and Ablina's straight 'no' for it created a never-ending conflict between them. "I am in," Visac said coldly. The self-destruction was contagious. Visac and Raylina were desperate to stop the door from opening that their own lives didn't matter to them.

Ablina saw the calm in their eyes which frightened her. "Don't do this," Ablina beseeched. "Avyukt, I want you to take Ablina and Manashaya back home," Artha ordered. "No... No... I won't be leaving them," Ablina resisted. "Avyukt now," he roared like a lion.

Avyukt forcibly took Ablina out of there and returned back to Yama Castle.

***

Visac lay next to Raylina and Ekani on the icy land. Raylina tilted her head a little on the left side to move away from the pointy snowflakes numbing her neck; she rolled her eyes upward to see Artha and asked, "Now what?" "Now you both wait," Artha said. "Kidding, right?" Visac said. Artha laughed. "The thing is, you do nothing," Artha said. "What do you mean by that?" Raylina asked in confusion. "The process is simple. You both die... naturally. The ice will drop your body temperature, which will cause heart failure, and it's done," Artha revealed. "Die? What? Grandpa... you got to be kidding," she quickly stood up. "What the hell? Artha, you are crazy!" Visac said furiously and stood up.

Artha knew what was at stake, but he was resolute to test his theory. "Well, just so you know, I know how things work, you both get your asses on the snow and freeze yourselves to death, and the magic from you will be transferred to her, and we will see from then," Artha said lightly. "What about Ekani? Is she still in a coma?" Raylina asked. "She died 5 minutes ago," Artha revealed.

"Died?" Visac gasped in shock. "Yes, but I have trapped her soul in Raylina's body, and when she dies, their souls will be released together," Artha said. "That doesn't make any sense," Visac said. "I am risking the entire human and witches race on you two, so stop behaving like children and lie down," Artha said, trying to sound rude.

***

The coldness swallowed Raylina's body bit by bit. She smiled a little, as she always thought that her coldness would be the bringer of her death, and it was finally happening. The icy bed on which she lay engulfed her inside. Visac, on the other side, felt a little different. His body rejected the cold; he wanted to get up and run into the fire, but Artha held him to the ground.

Death took them slowly, steadily. Ironically, arriving into this world is always confirmed with a loud cry and bright red blood rushing through your veins; departure, on the other hand, is quiet and pale. Watching them like this, broke Artha's heart into a million pieces.

After an hour, Artha cleared the snow and found Raylina, Ekani, and Visac's bodies caged together in an ice cube. They were lying down together, holding each other's hands. Artha waited for hours for them to wake up, but they didn't. The experiment failed, but Artha couldn't accept that. Devastatingly, he stared at their bodies; he touched the cube and howled, "No."

The intensity of Artha's grief cracked the ice cube. He dragged their bodies out of that ice tomb. "Ray, get up," he cried. He kissed Raylina on her forehead and said, "I will carry you home," and gently put her head on the icy bed. Artha went into the tent to fetch sleeping bags to carry their bodies back home.

***

Artha returned home with the news of Raylina, Ekani, and Visac's deaths. The weeds of sorrow spread all over the Yama Castle like wildfire, burning down everyone and everything in agony and despair. "Papa, what did you do?" Aamirah demanded indignantly. "Their bodies... I couldn't find their dead bodies," Artha wailed in agony. "You murdered my Ekani, Papa," Aamirah muttered, lost in his grief. "I just thought it would work," Artha stammered, ashamed of what he had done, falling down on his son's feet.

The hurt and anger mixed in Aamirah's eyes said that he was ready to destroy his father, but his conscience stopped him. He drank the pain of losing his daughter and said, "I need some air." Gaurangi resented Aamirah's obedience towards Artha. She held his hand violently and said, "Stop. I have been with you, stood behind you... forever. I never said no. Hell, I never even raised my voice. I stayed. I obeyed, but this is it, Aamirah. Your father took away our child for his stupid theory." "It's my fault Gaurangi," Artha spoke with guilt. "Yes, it is! How dare you play with my daughter's life?" Gaurangi bellowed.

Gaurangi held Aamirah's shirt collar wrathfully and said, "I am done with you and your father. After all this time, you both repay me by taking away my only daughter, and for what… Oh, I get it now. Who cares about Ekani, huh? She is not as special as Ray and Abby. We struggled for ages to have a kid, and finally, 17 years ago, we got our baby girl. For what? Huh… for this maniac to give her away like an empty box. I don't care that you throw Raylina away, but you had no right throwing my daughter away like this." "Enough," Aamirah said furiously. "Go to hell!" Gaurangi cried out, furiously pushing him away.

We all lose the things we love at some point, and we all know that, but despite knowing it all, we are still hurt. After all, the obvious circle of death and life isn't that obvious when it gets mixed up with feelings. Ablina's wounds were drilled deeper. She was traumatized by Raylina and Visac's death. A step away from a mental breakdown, peering at everyone with her vacant eyes. "No matter how much you try for them to stay… when the time comes, they leave," she thought.

Ablina flipped her hair on the other side, subconsciously imitating the picture of Raylina running in her head like a GIF. As time passed, her dizziness intensified, and the visuals of Raylina became blurrier. She felt wobbly on her legs and fell onto the ground. "Abby," Artha ran to her rescue.

Artha's tears dribbled on Ablina's bloody forehead. His hands trembled as he touched her bleeding scar. Ablina's outer wounds healed with magic, but the wounds inside her heart were yet unhealed, irreparable.

CHAPTER 21

GLIMPSE

Raylina opened her eyes to the sound of billions of souls lamenting in eternal agony. "And here I thought the chaos ended," Raylina said to herself in a hushed tone, feeling a little dizzy as she stood up from the slithering ground. The pale, haunting sky above and the slithering land beneath made her feel sick as she walked towards the oval-shaped black pit. She pondered if she was standing at the entrance to hell.

The moment Raylina went closer to see what was inside the pit, someone grabbed her hand and pulled her away. "Avyukt," Raylina whispered with relief in her eyes. Avyukt looked at her like he was meeting her for the first time—without repugnance or any hate.

Avyukt grasped Raylina by her waist, pulling her close to him, listening to the music of her beating undaunted heart. Her brunet strands hindered his gazing into her beguiling eyes, so he tucked them behind her ear. Avyukt softly pinched her chin and maffled, "Ange." His actions baffled Raylina. She looked back into his grey eyes, and at that moment, her hatred started to melt away.

Raylina's delusion broke as the memory of him calling her a 'Bitch' quickly flashed in her mind; she pushed him back and said, "What the... What is your problem, Avyukt? Are you high?" "How do you know me, Ange?" Avyukt gasped in surprise. "You... whatever, I don't have time for this, Avyukt," she irked and pushed him aside.

Raylina saw Visac and Ekani lying dead next to each other. "V, oh my god, Ekani... you guys wake up," she said worriedly. "Are they your friends, Ange?" he asked. "For the first and last time, my name is Raylina Bayer," Raylina rebuked roughly. "Raylina," Avyukt beamed like a lunatic, saving her name forever in his memory disk.

Avyukt stood there silently, watching Raylina implore the dead bodies of Visac and Ekani to come back to life. "Avyukt, please help me," Raylina begged him. "They will wake up, relax," Avyukt said calmly. "V... Ekani," Raylina whimpered and shook them harder this time. "Ouch, Ray, it hurts," Visac said as he opened his eyes. "Corrupt," Avyukt roared, and he took out his sharp sword and put it on Visac's neck.

"Whoa, stop Avyukt! He's a friend," Raylina said and threw her hands in front of Visac, shielding him. "What is up with him? He is acting a little strange," Visac asked in puzzlement, staring at Avyukt. "I don't know," Raylina said blankly, releasing her arms from Visac, stepping forward, keeping Visac behind her. Avyukt stepped closer to Raylina and said, "Ange, you should not be with the corrupt. He is dangerous and evil." "He is my friend, and you are not," Raylina spoke harshly and moved away from Avyukt.

The brawling went on between Avyukt and Raylina. Visac tried to neutralize them, but the fight was getting bigger and bigger. "Guys, hello," Ekani slowly murmured from behind, weakly standing on her feet. "Ekani!" Visac and Raylina said enthusiastically, shifting their attention from the crazy, strange Avyukt. "Oh… Thank God, Ekani," Raylina said cheerfully, pulling her into a warm hug.

Ekani being healthy and fine made Raylina and Visac forget their pain and purpose. Raylina repeatedly said how happy she was to see Ekani alive, and Visac was glad that their ritual worked. However, Ekani was worried. She was a keen observer and thinker. The first thing she noticed as she opened her eyes was that the world around them differed from the one they used to live in. In her world, the sky never looked fallen, painted in pale red, and the land was fertile, brown and intact, not like the one slithering underneath her foot. Something was wrong.

Ekani scratched her head in confusion and said, "Guys, I think we are dead." "Even I think so," Raylina said hesitantly. "No, I don't think so," Visac denied. He then looked around, not finding a world similar to his. "Really?" Visac asked, staring at Ekani and Raylina's horrified, perplexed faces.

Their plan had misfired. Ekani, Raylina, and Visac were literally and actually dead. They stared at each other for a minute as the deep shock shook their sanity. "I get it why I am here, but what sin did you guys commit," Raylina spoke without thinking.

"Ange, this is not hell," Avyukt said assuredly, out of his turn. "Avyukt, what do you mean by that?" Visac asked. "Who is he, and what is he doing here?" Ekani said, referring to Avyukt. "Oh, he is Avyukt, leader of the sidekick club…," Raylina began mocking him. But suddenly, something popped into her head, "Wait… we three are here because of the ritual…. What are you doing here, Avyukt?" At that moment, Raylina wondered why she never paid attention to all the important details or asked the right questions like Ablina.

"Right… And he is behaving weird," Visac added, staring at Avyukt, glaring at him for no reason. "Yeah… Definitely. He didn't even respond back to me for calling him a sidekick. Like he doesn't know us, or me," Raylina agreed, feeling a tiny sting in her heart, wanting Avyukt to fight with her like always. "Guys, one more thing, look around, there is a big hole, also these horrifying voices," Ekani pointed them to the pit. "No! We time-traveled," Raylina gasped, gawking at the pit, talking complete nonsense.

"What? How?" Visac asked, gawping at Raylina's disconcerted face. "I think we are at the place where all of this began," Raylina said, looking around. Ekani scrutinized the place all over and said, "You mean we traveled back in time." "It looks like it," Raylina said unsurely. "Gross, I hate time-traveling," Visac said. "Me too," Raylina said. Ekani looked at them with amusement. Their enhanced imagination about the situation enlivened her. Ekani's life had been good but never been more entertaining as after Ablina and Raylina showed up. "Your minds, I love how they work," she laughed livelily.

Avyukt kept them ongoing; he was savoring their childish conversation. The trinity was adamant about their "stuck back in time" theory. "Then what do we do now?" Ekani asked tensely. "Aren't you supposed to know everything?" Raylina said. "What do you mean by that?" Ekani asked. "Hello... Book nerd club," Raylina said sarcastically. "Ray, I think this is not the time," Visac said, looking at Ekani's bursting expressions.

Avyukt was done with the drama, so he decided to tell them what was going on there. He walked towards them and said, "If I may?" Raylina looked at Avyukt with irritation as his mere presence made her infuriated, "Yes, my lord," she said hotly. He smirked. "You guys are not time-traveling or at the gates of hell. You all are at Darno. This oval-shaped pit hole you see is a prison. It's bigger than you can imagine. This prison is like a pipeline; it opens up into two places, one in Darno, where we all are right now. And the other half opens in a whole different place called the Door, or Maori, as they say," he explained.

"Daro... Darno? How did we land up here?" Raylina stuttered in shock. "Darno," Avyukt said again, clearly. "I heard it clearly the first time," Raylina irked. "I was really rooting for the time-traveling thing," Ekani said. "Thank God! Not a fan of time-traveling," Visac panicked. "Guys, just so you know, we are on a fucking different planet. And that, too, in an open jail," Raylina shouted, unable to control the sudden rush of fear.

The big revelation turned normality into abnormality. Their perfectly amazing plan to 'kill and conquer' was diverted onto a whole different planet. Raylina blamed herself for being an idiot. "Vaylar... to Śirā Ragata... now this... a whole different planet," Raylina shrieked with frustration. "I wonder if anything is left." "Ange, don't worry, I will take care of you," Avyukt said. "No... No, I am not whatever that means," Raylina said loudly. "It's Angel in French," Visac said teasingly. "Don't," she warned. "We need to go back," Ekani said.

Visac held Raylina's hand and said, "Sorry, Ray." Ekani sympathetically put her hand on Raylina's shoulder and said, "We will find a way." "Cut," the hushed voice whispered. "What was that?" Raylina said, swiveling her head around to search for who whispered to her. "What?" Ekani questioned with surprise. "The voice," Raylina said. "I... Don't hear it," Ekani said. "Wait, I know this voice," she said, her brows frowning as she tried to concentrate on listening to the whisper. "Ange a Śirā Whisperer," Avyukt smiled with pride.

Though Raylina was Ekani's cousin and had a good heart, the facts stated otherwise. Raylina was wild, outspoken, arrogant, stubborn, sometimes cruel, untrained, and with zero knowledge of ancestral roots. The question haunted Ekani how a person with such traits could carry the sacred magic of Śirā in her veins? How could she be the chosen one, Ekani thought, and muttered angrily, "No way." "Look, I don't know what that is. I always hear these voices, even when I saved Grandpa," Raylina smirked. "Hear what they are saying and they will guide you," Avyukt said. "I know that part," Raylina said while nodding her head.

Raylina began to focus. Fortunately, this time, in flashes, the voice reached to her. "Right in front of you," the message delivered. "Okay," Raylina said, understanding the whisper. "Guys, I know how to get us home," Raylina responded out loud, smiling at her palms. She took Avyukt's sword from his scabbard, slicing her arm. "Ah," she moaned. "Your turn," Raylina said, handing him the sword. Avyukt did it in a blink of seconds.

Avyukt placed his bleeding hand on Raylina's, and as their blood met, a shiny magical green light sprang out of Raylina's fingertips and slowly started to encircle around Raylina and Avyukt. "Take my hand now," Raylina said to everyone. They took Raylina's hand, and quickly embraced her. Avyukt wrapped himself around them as their shield.

The bright green light knocked everyone down, and as they opened their eyes, they found themselves on the snowy bed of the world's third-highest mountain—Kanchenjunga.

"Home," Avyukt smiled, gazing at the breathtaking view of the wild mountains. A tear fell from his magnetic grey eye onto the icy white ground, and a beautiful lemon-touched little flower bloomed on the barren snow ground. The exhilaration of coming back home after fighting the long war on his face was priceless. Raylina was amused to see him truly happy, "Wonderful, isn't it?" Avyukt fondly gazed at her and said, "Yes."

***

Avyukt saw Ablina sitting alone, lost in grief, thoughtlessly plucking the leaves of clivia lined up on both sides, covering the doorsteps of the Yama Castle. His heart put a spell on his lower limbs, and they walked towards her against his mind's reasoning. A part of him wanted to embrace Ablina in his arms, to wash away her pain, but his courage sneaked out in the hour of need. He sat beside her.

"Ablina, it will get better," Avyukt said genuinely. "It won't, Avyukt," Ablina answered gloomily and landed her weary head on his shoulder. Avyukt cloaked her in his arms; his wild, bloody red eyes stared at the brightest star shining in the night sky, thinking, "What do I have to offer?" He was far from normality. He was cursed. "Nothing!" he mumbled, and pulled back his arms from Ablina with a heavy heart, with one he believed he didn't have. With closed eyes, they sat there for hours.

It was nearing sunrise when Ablina and Avyukt saw three shadows walking towards them. They were gobsmacked to see Raylina, Ekani, and Visac walking towards them. "Abby, I am not a ghost," Raylina beamed at Ablina's shocked face.

Ablina was more than surprised; she was petrified and angry. She clenched her fist tight and tried her best not to hit her, but Raylina's puckered brows provoked her. She opened her fist and glued it to Raylina's face sharply. "Ahh… Abby," Raylina said in agony, holding her aching jaw. "I thought you, damn you, Ray," Ablina rebuked and hugged her.

"Abby, I drank a little before the ritual, but I don't think I am still under its influence," Raylina whispered, staring into Avyukt's wild, red eyes. Ablina frowned at Raylina and said, "You are unbelievable." "Abby, I am serious. I didn't drink enough to be seeing two Avyukts… One with red eyes and the spooky one with grey eyes. Or it might be some sort of side effect of the ritual," Raylina gabbled in confusion, not sure whether it was really happening or it was all just in her head. "Visac…" Ablina called, cutting Raylina's drivel, running into Visac's arms.

"Still crazy… huh!" Avyukt taunted her. "My normal sassy sidekick's back!" Raylina exclaimed and hugged

Avyukt with wild, bloody red eyes. "Glad to have you back," she murmured in his ears, wondering why she had just said that. "What is wrong with you, Raylina," Avyukt piqued and removed her hands from him. "Wait, if you are original, then I am not hallucinating," Raylina quavered in horror, watching blankly at the Avyukt standing behind Visac.

"Ekani," Manashaya screamed and rushed towards Ekani. His scream alerted everyone on the inside and distracted Raylina from the "Avyukts" situation. "Manashaya," Ekani smiled and hugged him. Manashaya shyly held her tight in his arms and pecked on her forehead.

Artha, Aamirah, and Gaurangi came rushing out. Ekani caught a glance at Aamirah, glaring at her and Manashaya hugging, so she quickly stepped back and ran into Gaurangi and Aamirah's arms.

Artha sighed loudly, holding his knees, staring in disbelief at Ekani and Raylina, alive and breathing. "Grandpa," Raylina grinned, and she moved towards him. Artha affectionately touched Raylina's face and mumbled, "I knew. I always knew." Artha heartily embraced his granddaughters. "But it didn't work," Raylina said sadly. "Ray... What matters is you are both back," Artha said, tears breaking out of his sharp black eyes.

Raylina was emotional to see everyone happy around her, especially Ablina, but she always aced the

I-am-too-cool-to-give-a-damn task. Avyukt saw her rolling her teary eyes away from everyone hugging each other, "Ange, it will be fine," he said and slid his fingers into hers. "Wait, why do I see two of you," Raylina spoke with terror and stepped away from him.

Raylina fearfully walked towards the normal Avyukt, who loathed her, the one with the wild, red eyes. "What?" Avyukt spoke with attitude. "Why are your eyes red and his grey?" Raylina babbled in confusion, pointing to the man standing beside her. "Whoa," Raylina said and fainted. She fell down on the stairs and hit her head hard. Manashaya ran towards Raylina to help her get up, but before he could reach there. "I'll take her," Avyukt said and carried her in front of everyone.

Raylina peaked at Avyukt with squinted eyes. He seemed different, normal; all the hatred for her was still there in his wild red eyes, which was both comforting and scary at the same time. Raylina was concerned about him being a schizophrenic. She wondered how to fix a dark Graymanos gone mad. However, she doubted the possibility of him actually being sick.

***

Raylina opened her eyes and saw both of the Avyukts standing near her bed. "Ohh lord, the world was already bearing one. Why… Why did you have to send another one?" She cried dramatically. "Look, I know you're twisted, but I expected you to be a little sane and stable," Avyukt responded angrily. "I am sane. Tell your doppelganger to fuck off," she said rudely.

"Raylina, there is no one here. You nearly died and hit your head. I guess this is the whole post-traumatic thing," Avyukt said in a serious tone. "Ohh, really," Raylina jumped out and put her hand on the Avyukt with grey eyes. "Then who is he? Oh, yes, and why the hell does he keep on calling me... Ange?" she asked roughly. "It's air, it's an element, and it has no gender," Avyukt answered wittily, looking at her with surety that she had turned into a complete nut case. "Do your mojo and deal with your duplicate," Raylina warned.

"Ange, I think I can fix this," Avyukt, with grey eyes, said. "Aon anima mea," he roared, and both Avyukts exploded. Raylina was unable to figure out what was going on as she was blinded by the glare coming out from the explosion. It all felt cosmic. As the light was deemed, she saw Avyukt lying unconscious on the floor.

"Hey. Don't die on me... hey, wake up," Raylina said and splashed Avyukt's face with water. "Raylina," he said, waking up gasping for air. "Shhh... It's alright... It's all fine... Breathe," Raylina said, worriedly rubbing his back to calm him down. "I... am... Good," Avyukt said, catching his breath. "What was that?" Raylina asked, lost, looking into his charismatic grey eyes. His gaze made her nervous and fluttery, like a dark, sensual nightmare ravaging her.

"I know what happened to me," Avyukt spoke politely. "All ears. Shoot!" Raylina said agitatedly, trying to look away from his naked neckline. Avyukt stood up and sat on Raylina's bed. She glowered at him for sitting on her bed without permission, but she chose to hear him out first, as it was important to know whether he actually needed a shrink or not.

Avyukt bent and rested his head on his palms; his elbows pinched his thigh, which gave him the strength to speak up. "My duplicate was not actually a duplicate... that was me, the part of me..." he paused. He sighed deeply and continued. "The part of me which I traded back when the door was opened, my light traveled there... to Darno, and my darkness stayed behind," he tried to explain.

The moment of silence made Raylina and Avyukt uncomfortable. It was like the first forced setup dates, where the only way out was to go through it. "Oh, so that was you. I can't believe that part of you liked me," Raylina chuckled, breaking the silence, wandering away from the main topic. "Don't flatter yourself, Princess. That's not me. That's light. It always thinks good of people," Avyukt said, fake glaring at her charming face. "Very funny," she frowned.

"Greatest screw-ups are always self-created," Raylina thought while dodging Avyukt's constant fan-like stare. Raylina wanted Avyukt to hate her because the hate was easy to take. For her, it was okay to be unloved than to carry the burden of love. Just like Raylina, Avyukt, too, was not ready to let his guard down.

Despite being brave and powerful, Avyukt was afraid to show his true self out in the open. But whatever we decide to do, whatever path we choose to walk on, it will always be rigged by our hearts to make our journey more difficult and our destination unreachable. And even after being completely aware of this, the entire universe will always ask us to 'Listen to our hearts.' Why is it so? Why? Because our hearts know how to decipher the code language of the universe, and it's challenging, definitely, but it's all worth it.

"You know something, I started to fall for you, Avyukt," Raylina said flirtatiously. Her words stunned Avyukt, but he quickly gathered his emotions and said, "You know, you suck at banter."

Raylina rolled her eyes and stared outside her window to avoid Avyukt's new deadly grey eyes and also the fact that she accidentally flirted with the man she loathed. The sudden change in the course of her heart made Raylina wonder how quickly one's heart changes from hating someone to liking them. How we all are solely driven by waves of emotions.

Manashaya saw Raylina and Avyukt sitting on her bed close to each other. It irked him. "Artha is calling you two," he said rudely. Raylina hurriedly stood up and walked out of her room.

Raylina and Avyukt exchange looks while walking together down to the main hall, finding ways to explain the interpretation of Avyukt's grey eyes to everyone.

***

"Grandpa, I have something to tell you," Raylina said. "What is it, Ray?" Artha asked concernedly. "Something happened…" Raylina stammered. But before she could tell, Avyukt draped his hand around hers and said, "We think Vaylar should be punished, and for that, I believe we are wasting time. We should attack before he does." "Ya, Avyukt is right," Raylina said and played along.

"What is wrong with you?" Raylina asked in a hushed tone, staring at him with her eyes wide open in fright. "Trust me," Avyukt mumbled and patted her hand with his thumb." "Okay, now you can let her hand go," Artha said in vexation.

"Grandpa, I need to talk to him," Raylina said and dragged him upstairs by his hands. Everyone was startled to see them like that. Especially Ablina, she never thought that Avyukt, the man who despised her sister, would suddenly talk to her like she was one of his best friends.

***

"Why are your eyes red again?" Raylina angrily demanded an explanation. "Keep your voice down, you idiot," Avyukt stormed and pulled her closer. "Listen to me carefully. I think there is something wrong going on here," Avyukt said genuinely. "I know," Raylina agreed and seductively slipped her hand inside his white shirt, caressing his chiseled chest. Her touch was making him lose control over his mind, letting his heart take over on his balanced world, setting his soul free to run in the fields of wild desires. Avyukt wanted to move away from

Raylina, as he knew what consequences waited for him at the end of the road, but he was powerless, paralyzed. "I know," Raylina said again and pushed him away, "You are."

Avyukt pulled her back in his arms and led her to the wall. He fenced her way out by keeping his hands on both sides. Avyukt was losing it, and Raylina was testing him terribly. The strange feeling igniting between them was driving them crazy. Nothing was in control, their actions, their hearts, their bodies, nothing.

"You don't understand. We have a mole," Avyukt said haltingly, blocking out the 5 feet 5 distraction. "What?" Raylina spoke in disbelief. "The first time when the portal was opened, there was someone who tipped off Vaylar about the door. And that person is our main suspect. I think he is the one who is controlling this whole thing," Avyukt explained in a serious tone.

Raylina took her time to respond. She recollected the information in her mind and said, "But it was Lais who told Vaylar about the Darno." "Yes, Lais narrated the story about the place, but he never told Vaylar where the door was, and for that matter, he never mentioned what to do once it's opened," Avyukt said.

Manashaya walked in unannounced and looked at them with raised eyebrows. "Am I interrupting something?" Manashaya said, scowling at Avyukt and Raylina standing close to each other against the wall. Raylina wrapped her fingers around Avyukt's neck and said, "Yes, you are." Avyukt aggressively removed Raylina's hands from his neck and said, "Raylina Bayer, I am not your patsy." And he furiously left the room.

"You," Raylina fumed, glowering at Manashaya, trying to keep her calm. Manashaya kept quiet as her anger was justified. "Sometimes, we realize things late. Who I am to blame you," Raylina said, gulping the little hurt. "I never wanted things to end this way," Manashaya said sadly. "Things are over now, and plus, I am glad that it never actually started," Raylina smiled. He nodded, smiling forcefully. "You take care of her," Raylina said.

An amicable separation is a sensible way to bury the feelings for self-betterment. But if we have to bury something inside us, that means it is still there. Manashaya walked out. Raylina held the pillow tight against her chest because she feared it might explode.

CHAPTER 22

PHILOSOPHIES OF A MORTAL MAN

Raylina curled herself up in bed, trying to cut off the problems around her. She inhaled the cold air, and it somewhat soothed her burning head, but the squeaking sound of windows forced her heavy eyes to open. She felt the breeze on her skin. To hear what the gelid air had to say, she closed her weary eyes. ***"The characters will change from time to time, but the outline of the story shall remain the same," the Whisper whispered."*** "Thank you! To whosoever, airing live," Raylina said, and rushed out of her room. She bumped into Avyukt, and before he could speak, she dragged him along by his hand.

"Raylina Bayer, I am not your servant," Avyukt said rudely and stopped walking, jerking his hand away out of her grip. "I-I," lost in his irresistible grey eyes, she stuttered. "I am sorry," Raylina said with the utmost genuineness. "What I did in front of Manashaya was not right and amateur, but I need your help, Avyukt." Her apology sealed Avyukt's lips, he wanted to walk away, but he couldn't.

"What?" Avyukt asked nonchalantly, not ready to give up easily. "I heard the Whisper. And I think I have heard this line before from Ablina, perhaps, so we should check out her favorite place," Raylina informed. "Okay," Avyukt instantly agreed and started walking. Raylina followed him to the library of Yama Castle.

***

"Ablina's residence, Nerdbrary," Raylina mumbled, staring at the enormous library stuffed with a million words of the world's written wisdom. Red-and-green-themed opulent bookshelves, consecutively arranged, towering up the high ceiling of Yama castle. Although the room was built before ages, it seemed to keep up with the pace of the modern era.

Avyukt and Raylina decided to scatter in the library to search for answers. Avyukt commenced with red-colored shelves, and she went through the green ones. Their hunt was becoming more and more tedious as time went by. Raylina sat down on the floor and gave up first. She closed her eyes, resting her head on the wall of the bookshelf to laze a little, and suddenly a book fell on her head from above. "Ahh," Raylina yelped. "My God, what is wrong with you?" Avyukt peeved, with his face buried in a book.

Raylina glared at him and said nothing about his unnecessary attitude. She stretched her hand a little to reach to the book which fell on her head, "*Philosophies of a Mortal Man*, By R. Iris," Raylina read in her mind. "What is it?" Avyukt asked, still surfing through his pile of books.

Raylina opened the book and read the only line written on the first page. "***The characters will change from time to time, but the outline of the story shall remain the same.***" Raylina gasped, rereading the lines which whisper whispered to her. She turned the page to read. "It's blank," Raylina said with disappointment. "What kind of book is this?" Raylina inflamed and shut the book furiously. "What happened?" Avyukt said and sat beside Raylina. She handed the book to Avyukt. He flipped the pages, and suddenly a letter fell off.

"*Many men have come in search of the 'Śirā Ragata.' For most of them, it was a key to it all, an ultimate power, or a power of the universe, while some thought of it as a land where magic breathes. They all believed in the tales they were told. But few actually figured out that it was nothing. It was just two simple words which meant 'Vein (Śirā)' and 'Blood (Ragata)' penned down together by a Nepali philosopher,*" Aryaraj Saud.

"Another riddle, seriously, why can't people talk, normally," Raylina piqued. She pulled her phone out of her maroon-colored jogger's pocket and called her sister. "Abby, I am in the library, sitting right in front of a red picture of a strange man. Come ASAP, I need your brain," Raylina commanded in one breath and hung up her phone.

***

Ablina rushed inside the library. "Thank god!" She sighed with relief to see her sister alive and in one piece. But the view petrified her. It was the first time she saw Raylina sitting on the floor surrounded by thousands of books. The view was worth capturing. Ablina quickly took out her phone and took Raylina's picture. "Abby, not funny. Tomorrow is judgment day, and you are doing this," Raylina said in an irritated voice. "It's begun already," Ablina said mockingly, justifying her actions. "Now if you are done making fun of me, can you please check this out," Raylina asked tiredly.

Ablina sat on the floor alongside Avyukt. "I got this," Raylina said and handed a poorly conditioned letter and the book. "Archaic," Ablina said, closely examining the letter. "Genius, I thought so," Raylina said in a sarcastic tone.

Ablina thoroughly read the lines written in the book and the letter which fell from it. She felt like she had read this somewhere before but could not remember where. She opened a folder stored on her phone and started scrolling through the lines she had noted on her phone

one by one. Avyukt was astonished to see Ablina restlessly going through her phone.

Raylina briefed him about Ablina's obsession with storing the best lines from the books she read. She also told him that before mobile phones Ablina actually used to write them manually. To which Avyukt quoted, "Such a nerd." "Right, I told you," Raylina smiled. As they diverted their heads from what Whisper said to Ablina being epically nerdy, Ablina was, in fact, jogging her memory to remember where she read the lines.

"I got it, Ray," Ablina said excitedly and ran out of the library, which left Avyukt dumbstruck. "Is she okay?" Avyukt stammered. "No, it's her eureka thing. She'll come around," Raylina said casually, unmoved, with Ablina running like a lunatic.

Ablina came back, running. She confidently threw the book up in the air and caught it with even more confidence, like she knew the solution to all their problems and looked down smugly at them. "Yes, Yes, genius, maybe you would like to fill us in with whatever discovery you have made," Raylina said. Ablina rolled her eyes at her sister's tactics and opened the book to the first chapter and started reading it aloud.

We had walked miles into the forested hills of Nepal in midsummer to meet him, my Father's favorite author, and his best friend. I was eager to meet the man who had managed to impress my Father. After wandering for hours, my Father pointed at the abandoned hut in the middle of nowhere. It was our destination.

My curiosity stepped up with every second as we marched towards the tiny shack covered in green creepers. I wondered what type of man my Father's best friend was who would choose to live like that, alone in solitariness. Years later, I realized I would give anything up to live the same way, the solitary, peaceful way.

"Comin," the old man replied in a raspy voice, as we knocked on the door. 5 minutes later, he opened the door, and without saying hello or welcome, he simply walked into his kitchen. The old man's wrinkly unwelcoming face and grumpy expressions instantly made him unlikeable in my view. I looked at my Father, waiting like a boss for an explanation. "The greatest mind works better in isolation," my Father said to me, and we went in.

My Father and I sat on the old man's dusty, unclean floor. After 20 minutes, the old man finally came out of the kitchen holding two glasses of water in his hands with his fingers dipped inside them. It was the day when I learned my very first lesson about patience.

The old man handed us dirty, unwashed, cracked glasses. And what my Father did next shocked me; he took the glass without any hesitation and actually drank from it. Father looked peaceful. He was comfortable there like he was home. I felt a little left out until my Father's best friend became my best friend.

After eating a whole sugar cube, I fell asleep in my Father's arms. It was more than a 10-year-old could ask for. My Father laid me down on the old rustic couch, locked me in, and went outside with his best friend dressed in an old coat and pitiful holed pants.

Years have gone by, but I still haven't forgotten those old weary eyes—the eyes that battled a long war—the eyes of my Father's best friend—the eyes of my best friend.

Decades have passed, of me replaying the foggy fragments from the meeting a zillion times. I was too little to understand all the things they discussed from their conversation I overheard, but his words still ring now and then.

"In the end, the good in us will always be standing against the tempting evil, and the evil will always rise back because they are like; 'Śirā Ragata' ('veins and blood'). They give each other the meaning of their existence. As there is no good without evil, and there is no evil without the goodness."

Like Day and Night.

R. Iris.

"R. Iris," Ablina gasped in shock. "Why didn't I figure it out earlier?" Ablina said angrily, stomping the book into Raylina's hands. "That R. Iris is my alias," Raylina said blankly, touching her name on the tainted, smelly page. "What! You had an alias at 10!" Avyukt spoke with amusement. "To be clear, it was a joke," Ablina mentioned.

Raylina was speechless, staring at the book that she had written, which she did not remember. "What led you to this?" Ablina asked impatiently. "She was sitting here, and it just fell off from the top," Avyukt informed. "Nothing just falls off. Not in here," Ablina said, confused and unable to make sense of everything happening around them. "Easy," Avyukt said to calm her down. Raylina struggled, she tried harder to remember, but it didn't work. She felt that the part of hers was erased. "Aryaraj Saud," Raylina mumbled as she read the name written on the letter.

Ablina typed "*Philosophies of a Mortal Man*, By R. Iris" over the internet, and what she found made her brain dead for a while. "What is it, Abby?" Raylina asked fearfully. "This book is not published. It does not exist out in the world," Ablina said dreadfully. "From where did you get this book?" Avyukt asked calmly. "I found this book at Desovir Public Library. I took it because I liked the sentence from the prologue, '*The characters will change from time to time, but the outline of the story shall remain the same.*' Plus, Aryaraj Saud was mom's favorite author. Ma was deeply fond of his philosophies, and Dad was too," Ablina answered.

Raylina turned back to the first page. "How!" She gasped in hysteria. "I don't remember Dad taking you anywhere. And what does Aryaraj Saud have to do with any of this?" Ablina began bombarding her with questions. "Me neither, Abby. I don't know," Raylina said vacantly.

"Abby, I think we can be mistaken. There might be someone else, whose initial is R and surname's Iris," Raylina said to justify otherwise. "Ya, and it can be a complete coincidence that someone happens to know your signature," Ablina said firmly and showed Raylina her signature. "But... We never heard about 'Śirā Ragata' before we came to India," Raylina protested.

"What if the book was written during our magical cryosleep years?" Ablina asked suspiciously, trying not to upset her. "You think... I got out?" Raylina yelled angrily. "You were pretty much determined to go after the killer," Ablina reasoned lowly. "I cannot believe this is coming out of you," Raylina rebuked.

Avyukt sensed the tension building up between the sisters. "Let's not jump to any conclusions," he interrupted, before it could turn into a big brawl. "Oh, you are the new referee now, huh," Raylina said in a fake calm voice. "What if someone pulled you out of it and put you back when the time came?" Avyukt said cautiously. "I think it might be possible," Ablina agreed instantly.

"I can restore your memories," Avyukt suggested. "Wait, you can't. You'll kill her," Ablina said. Avyukt smirked, closing his eyelids. "I can," Avyukt said and gently opened his eyes. "What happened to you... your eyes?" Ablina gulped her saliva, staring into his enigmatic grey eyes. "Long story," Raylina said, breaking Ablina's awe.

***

300

Raylina laid her back on the backrest, letting her soft brunette hair fall down on the turquoise armchair. Avyukt stood behind the backrest, extending his fingers to cover Raylina's brain points like the EEG wiring. It seemed like a "finger helmet." "You... sure this hypnosis will work, Dr. Freud?" Raylina asked nervously. "It's not hypnosis. It's 'Gehir,' the Ragata magic of the mind. Ragata magic is the magic of blood, where the power resides in one's blood. Each one of us Graymanos has distinctive traits serviceable for mankind and the Earth. My Gehir Ragata magic gives me control over anyone's thoughts, emotions, memories," Avyukt explained.

"What about me? What kind of form do I have," Ablina questioned curiously. "'Akavaprigoni,' the magic of the elements; your blood holds the energy to control the elements of the Earth. This type of power is rare, as it controls the primary life source of this world. It's powerful, yet dangerous for the man or woman conjuring it. Even Lais could not conjure it up fully. I remember once he said to me that he was afraid of bursting into flames," Avyukt politely answered.

"Who else can conjure Akavaprigoni?" Ablina asked. "Until now, the only man who could fully conjure this magic was your father, Ablina," Avyukt answered in riddles. "Dad?" Ablina uttered. "No, your birth father, Mihira," Avyukt replied softly. "And now the only witch who could conjure 'Akavaprigoni' on this planet is you."

"Still, it's hypnosis," Raylina said playfully, trying to annoy Avyukt and to distract Ablina from falling into the pit of overthinking about Mihira. "It's the awakening of the subconscious," Avyukt ire. "One and the same thing," Raylina smirked. "And I thought you guys were getting along," Ablina said, shaking her head left and right in disappointment.

"I hope this works," Avyukt mumbled seriously as he kept his fingers on Raylina's head. "This might sting a little, Raylina," Avyukt said, staring distraughtly at Raylina's bright-lined forehead.

"Ahhhhhh," Raylina yawped as she clenched her fist tightly. "Ablina, hold her down," Avyukt ordered. Ablina held Raylina's hands tightly. As Avyukt dug deeper, Raylina's scream intensified. The unbearable pain rushing in her body urged Avyukt to stop, but he kept on continuing.

Avyukt's body started to writhe in pain, just like Raylina's. He attempted to peek into her memories, but the darkest corners of Raylina's mind were harder to reach. Though he was unable to witness the details, he was able to feel them with her.

***

Raylina's pain suddenly vanished, and she jerked open her eyes. The windy night started to reset the moments. A few moments passed when Raylina realized that she was in her memories, the memories Avyukt had put her in. She saw herself in a beige frock coat, black bottoms, and mustache on, dressed like a man. She saw herself walking vigilantly in the alley like she was on some sort of secret mission.

"Mr. Iris," a deep, raspy voice spoke from behind. Raylina stopped walking at once and turned around. "I have seen him somewhere," the unseen Raylina said, looking at herself, talking to the man with familiar, weary eyes. She collected her fickle thoughts of knowing the tall old man and focused on listening to the conversation happening in her memories.

"Evening," Raylina said in a fake man-like voice, looking at the tall man wearing a long, deep grey overcoat, with his face masked with a white cloth. "I have the information. I must warn you. Don't make the mistake of going alone," the tall old man said. He handed the envelope to her and left. Raylina saw herself opening the envelope.

"I got you," Raylina, dressed like a man mumbled wickedly, as she pulled off the hat out of her head and let her long hair fall down, covering her tiny waist. She quickly hid behind the off-white bedsheets hanging outside a dry cleaner's shop to change her clothes. "Wow!" Raylina exclaimed as she saw herself dressed in a dark purple Victorian-style dress.

The long dark alley raised Raylina's heartbeats. She clung to her silky purple pearly dress as she took every step. Raylina watched herself, wiping the dripping drops of her sweat as it kept on falling down her head. After following herself for 7 minutes, Raylina saw herself entering a majestic castle through the long, ghastly-looking gates. "Holy shit, it's the Duke's Castle," Raylina gasped, walking behind her.

Raylina walked fiercely like a queen heading to her coronation. Her beauty made every woman in the room envious, and some of them jealous. The men watched her like they had seen a masterpiece of God's creation. She was breathtaking yet simple. Her presence created the unique blend of melancholia and euphoria in the evening.

Though every eye was on her, Raylina avoided attention and admiration, aiming her stellar eyes at something else. Her ball gown elegantly brushed off the ballroom stairs as she hurriedly went after the mysterious man rushing upstairs. Raylina followed herself up and saw herself unlocking the golden doorknob. They both walked in, one visible and the other not. And witnessed something gut-wrenching.

***

Raylina's body jerked up and down in distress; it was worse than an exorcism. Like she was having a million convulsions at the same time. "Raylina," Ablina screamed horridly. "Hold her tight," Avyukt ordered loudly. "It's not over," he informed, as he sniffed his nosebleed inside, attempting to stop it from dropping on Raylina's forehead.

Raylina went back into her memories instantly and saw herself again, but she was not at the castle. This time she found her 10-year-old self standing in front of the tiny shack, clutching to her father's index finger. Abandoned, rustic, centuries-old, creeper surrounded, exactly like she wrote in her book. "I can't believe that's me," she murmured with a smile as she saw her little version walking inside the house, holding his father's hand.

Raylina walked near the home and peeked inside the old man's house from its window. She watched her little self sitting on the old rusty sofa with her father, keenly listening to the old man narrating the story of Iraja, creating the profound magic of Śirā Ragata. "The story… I knew it all along," Raylina said, staring at her little self fall asleep on the sofa.

"We have to protect her at any cost," the old man with weary eyes said in his deep, raspy voice, heading out of the door to fetch the firewood from the porch area. "I am afraid," George said, stepping out to help the man. "You shouldn't be, George," the old man said, handing him the log of wood.

"Do you think she can hold on to that amount of power?" George asked worriedly, watching his little girl dolled up in a rose pink dress, sleeping on the old couch peacefully looking like an angel from the window. "Have faith in your daughter," the old man with weary eyes reassured.

George and the old man with weary eyes went inside the shack, and their voices woke up the little Raylina. George lifted little Raylina into his arms, and she quickly fell asleep on his shoulders. "She mustn't remember this, George," the old man with weary eyes said gravely. "Goodbye, Aryaraj," George bid adieu to his best friend and left.

***

Forgotten memories were coming back. The scenes of memory retrieval shifted in front of Raylina's eyes like a projector changing slides. She found herself in the basement, vacantly staring at her, Amaraya, and Ablina's coffin. "Raylina," a deep, raspy voice called her, and they both turned around. The unseen Raylina recognized the old man with weary eyes walking towards the coffins, but the visible one didn't.

Raylina stepped back cautiously, "Who are you?" She asked in an unwavering tone. "I am a man with answers," the old man with weary eyes said. She was intrigued by the old man. The fear of the unknown persisted in her heart, but the time demanded courage, and it was the only way out. The old man asked her to follow him, and she obeyed without asking any questions, which was unlike her.

"Abby was right. I did come out of the tomb. And he pulled me out," the invisible Raylina said, following Aryaraj and herself walking out of the basement.

Raylina saw the world around her change. It wasn't like the one she left. "We don't have time. My magic is fading off," Aryaraj said and headed to a strange-looking object with four wheels. "100 years have passed; humans have made some inventions," he said from inside the shiny black four-wheeled car. Raylina courageously sat in the strange-looking vehicle.

"Have we met before?" Raylina charged fearlessly. "Raylina, you will get all the answers you are supposed to know, including the ones you never asked for," Aryaraj answered calmly. There was something about the old man with weary eyes, which gave Raylina an assurance that he meant no harm, and that she could trust him. He spoke to her like he knew her well, which made her feel safe. While unseen Raylina knew the man; he was Aryaraj Saud, her best friend.

***

In a flash, Raylina found herself standing at the lakefront, watching herself lost in the mesmerizing view of the day. Aryaraj stood patiently alongside her, letting her live in the moment.

Like a father protecting his newborn, the dense forest and the huge mountains encircled the glorious lake carrying heaven's elixir at its bottom. The golden fallen leaves floated like a weightless golden pearl on the water's surface. "It looks like Mother Nature spent extra hours building this specific piece of art on God's demand, customized just for him," Raylina thought.

"Śirā Ragata," the old man with weary eyes said in his deep voice. "What is that?" Raylina asked in confusion, feeling that she had heard this from somewhere before. "The third universe," he answered. The Raylinas perplexedly stared at him, hoping for him to enlighten her. "What does it mean?" Raylina asked curiously.

"One day, Lord Krishna was playing in the sand. He, like every other child, tried eating the essence of sand. Maa Yashoda caught him eating the sand. She tensely ran to her little boy and asked him to spit the dirt out. Little Krishna, the mischievous being that he was, smiled his adorable secret smile and shook his head in denial. Maa Yashoda scolded him and called him a liar. But little Lord Krishna refused to accept that he had lied. Finally, after adamantly asking, little Krishna opened his mouth, and what Ma Yashoda saw next made her eyes go round. It was a glimpse of the multiverse. Everything from galaxies to little ponds, everything existed in her son's mouth," the old man with weary eyes narrated the story again, the one Raylinas already knew; however, this time, the title of the story changed, and it was mentioned under a different name, the "Third universe."

"This story is one of the most loved bedtime stories in Indian families. It has both fantasy and magic. I have been obsessed with this story since I was a child because the idea of seeing the universe in a child's mouth was both fascinating and empowering. The obsession grew as I got older," the old man with weary eyes said.

"But what does any of this have to do with me? And is this even related to Śirā Ragata?" Raylina narked, almost on the verge of losing her temper at the old man for diverting from the topic. "Raylina, to understand the depths of Creation, one must understand the importance of 'Seeking.' You possess great abilities, but you lack the patience to seek them. Because of it, you create more trouble for yourself," The old man with weary eyes said calmly. "It's true. I do sometimes lose my patience," the visible Raylina admitted lowly.

After a moment of deeply ingesting her greatest flaw, Raylina spoke, "What about the first and second universe?" "Well, the first universe is what we live on; we can touch it, can see it. The second is a universe of intellect. This universe is based on our perception and imagination, which most of us really live in; the universe of our dreams and desires, the one we spend the rest of our lives building. And the story of the third universe points us in the direction of what I call the 'True Universe or God's Universe. The one who wishes to see the True Universe... God's Universe must align their first and second universes. And when one succeeds in doing this, they obtain the ultimate magic of creators," He explained. Both Raylinas were quiet and confused, trying to understand the profound wisdom of the world the old man with weary eyes was preaching on.

"A few centuries back, something happened, something which shook the world to its core. My friend

Mihira and I somehow managed to stop it, but I am afraid it will happen again. And this time it will destroy everything… perhaps the universes too," the man with weary eyes said in a serious tone. "You said *you* managed to stop it," Raylina said, coming straight to the point. "I am Aagney Shaurayaveer. I am your great-great grandfather," he answered.

"Aryaraj… Aagney, this family has a thing for alias," the unseen Raylina said loudly, and no one heard except her.

Aryaraj touched Raylina's forehead with his thumb and index finger. Suddenly, a white light passed on from his hand to her head. It was like magic data transfer. "Śirā… It's us," Raylina said with fascination. "Little Queen," Aryaraj called her affectionately. Her faded memories started becoming more lucid. She remembered everything, the extra sugar cubes, butterflies, the dirty glasses, the abandoned shack, her father taking her to meet his best friend in the forested hills of Nepal, Aryaraj narrating the story of Iraja and Śirā Ragata. "Uncle Aryaraj," Raylina said with tears in her eyes, remembering it all.

"I have to teach you before I die," Aryaraj said, trying to get hold of the emotional reunion. Raylina nodded. He looked at her with pride; the glimpse of George and himself was comforting. Aryaraj sat on his knees and began, "Our body holds everything. We can conjure it. The Crystal Rose is not an object." "It's us," Raylina completed his sentence.

"Yes. Little Queen, you and I, we are the Crystal Rose. We are the Śirā. The story of Iraja growing the flower out of her veins is true, but the Śirā flower was used as a metaphor for light, not an actual object. The light which gave birth to our clan, and the darkness born before which creates the Ragata line refers to Graymanos," Aryaraj stated. "That means no Ragata flower?" Raylina asked. "No, the Ragata flower does exist, in reality. And it was made to distract people from the truth," Aryaraj answered.

"Truth?" Raylina asked, trying to figure it out. "It all happened because of the power struggle," Aryaraj answered. "Power struggle?" Raylina gasped in wonder. Aryaraj took a deep breath and said, "The story of Iraja creating Śirā Ragata was limited and confidential to the firstborns of Iraja—Graymanos, as it held the magic behind creating nature. But it all went haywire when Lais fell in love with a human. The desire to take over the 'Māyākāriya throne' started a war amongst the witches."

"The descendants of Iraja—Shaurayaveers and Graymanos, born to protect the Earth, started fighting for a worthless throne. These fights started a never-ending rift between the two clans. So, Lais shared the story of Śirā Ragata with little alterations to unite the two clans. To make them understand the importance of each other. Lais told everyone that like our bodies carrying souls till their purpose is served, so do the veins in our bodies, carrying blood to all the places (organs) where it needs to be. Likewise, Śirā is a carrier, and Ragata is that purpose; both are useless without one another. There is no Śirā without Ragata and no Ragata without Śirā. Your sister Ablina and you coming together is not just a coincidence. It's fate," Aryaraj said, staring at the fallen golden leaves in the lake.

Raylina watched her reflection scatter away as she dipped her legs into cold water. "Yet to know more," Raylina mumbled, raised her eyes, and turned them to Aryaraj. "How do I become you, the Śirā?" She asked. "We all carry the energy required to be magic, the only difference is some of us are born with a little extra, not the energy, but the thing called 'Will,'" Aryaraj answered, watching the dark night take over the pink sky.

Aryaraj gazed at the stars shining brightly in the black sky, smiling back at him. He smiled faintly and said, "Your father used to say that the concept of magic is misunderstood. Magic is nothing but a person's will for something. Magic lives inside us, every one of us. Yes, even the humans. You don't need spells or power to wield that kind of magic. All it needs is to let yourself trust yourself and believe that you can do it. And when you do it, all three universes will be one, and you will become what you were born to be."

"What about the other world… that lies behind that Door? Raylina asked. "It needs something our world has, but we cannot give them that," he answered. "What is that?" Raylina said, narrowing her brows in great

312

curiousness. "I don't know. I don't have an answer for that," Aryaraj said sadly.

The unseen Raylina, Aryaraj, and Raylina headed back to the Bayers' home's basement. But before going into the tomb, Raylina went into her room to fetch out the papers. She came hastily and dragged the dusty chair from the corner. She made the coffin's top her desk, tied her hair into a tight bun, and started writing.

On the last page of the first chapter, Raylina watched herself write;

"Each day, I wake up in the search for the answers, but everyone has different things to say. Every religion has its version of the story of creation. The deeper I go, the deeper it gets. But one thing I strongly believe is that there is more to it than it seems. All these stories are narrated with a common goal. And it is to make people believe that good and bad both live within us."

Like day and night.

They both are right.

Each with their own purpose to serve;

One to spread the darkness, and the other to fight it,

But light is all we need, though the darkness will always be supreme.

~R. Iris.

Raylina watched herself, asking Aryaraj to make sure it reaches her, and only to her when she wakes up again.

CHAPTER 23

DAY OF EPIPHANIES

With a wet cotton cloth, Avyukt caringly wiped Raylina's sweaty forehead. At the same time, Ablina sat beside Raylina, anxiously waiting for her to wake up. Though multiple near-death experiences made Avyukt a daredevil, the fear of death persisted in his heart, and watching Raylina lying unconscious increased that fear.

"A… Abby," Raylina moaned tiredly, supporting her elbows on the arms of the chair, standing up. "Ray… Ray… thank god," Ablina sighed in relief, shaking off her fright of losing Raylina forever, and pulled Raylina into a tight hug. "Are you okay?" Avyukt asked, masking his clear concern for Raylina. "I know what happened," Raylina said, trying to catch her breath. "Ray, take 5 if you need to. But we'll need you to be very specific," Ablina asked.

Raylina looked at Ablina and said, "You were right, Abby. I did come out. I am sorry." She exhaled the guilt, bit her lower lip, and continued, "Uncle Aryaraj and I met each other first when I was 10." "Wait, Uncle?" Ablina interrupted. "Ablina, please; let her focus," Avyukt miffed. "Thank you," said Raylina with a huge win smile on her face.

Before Raylina could speak up about the actual reality she had learned, a thought crossed her mind. "If Abby realizes the truth, she won't think twice about sacrificing herself instead of me. No, the fewer people know, the better," Raylina thought to herself.

Raylina knew that telling Ablina about her being a Śirā was not a wise thing to do. Ablina was too smart to figure out the rest, which was if something went wrong, Raylina had to immolate herself to save the world. So she lied about the Crystal Rose and told them that it was hidden in the base ground, and she had to find it alone.

"Details make a story easier to imagine for the people hearing or reading it. But when the world is at stake, you don't go all into the details, especially the one which creates panic in the crowd," Raylina consulted with herself, justifying that she had lied for Ablina's safety.

Ablina trusted Raylina instantly, but Avyukt didn't. Avyukt trusted Raylina's ways, but he didn't trust her words. His suspicion grew deeper when Raylina asked them not to tell anyone about the Crystal Rose. "I'll check on Visac," Ablina said and left.

Avyukt stared at Raylina with suspicion, waiting for her to drop the act. His wide eyes bothered her, "What?" Raylina irked, avoiding eye contact. "You are lying," he said straightforwardly. Based on past experiences, it was a risk of telling Avyukt about everything, but he was the only person who could actually do some real magic on the team when needed. "I know who the mole is, Avyukt. I saw him in the ballroom; he was there, and all this time, it was him. The whole Vaylar thing was a decoy. He was just the hitman, a servant," Raylina spoke with a burning hatred. "Who?" Avyukt questioned in a serious tone. "Sangul," she revealed.

Avyukt was baffled; his face turned blue. Sangul stabbed them. He stabbed the whole mankind. But the question remained as to why he did it. Raylina understood Avyukt's state, as getting betrayed was something she was used to. She gently kept her hand on his shoulder and said, "Stabbers are always the ones whom we dine with." "It's not making me feel any good, but thank you," Avyukt laughed softly. "You're welcome," Raylina chuckled.

Raylina was delighted to make a truce with the man she thought was her enemy. She started seeing Avyukt differently. The curtain of his I-am-a-bad-boy charade show was finally slipping away, revealing the real Avyukt hiding behind the curtain, the real Avyukt who cared, who, like any other person, sought love and believed in giving chances.

The change of heart was mutual. Avyukt, too, had started liking Raylina, even though Raylina was not the ideal person according to his list of favorable traits. Her bratty mood swings, her sass, how she always said inappropriate things at all times, insulting him for no reason, her randomly picking fights were somehow starting to grow on him. And just like that, in the middle of all the chaos, Avyukt and Raylina became something; it was undefined, but it was there, and it was innocently beautiful.

"There is something more," Avyukt said suddenly, bringing his focus back from Raylina's face to the story. "Have you ever heard of the third universe?" Raylina questioned.

Raylina narrated the third universe story and everything else Aagney told her to Avyukt on their way to the dungeon. "So you are going to play them," Avyukt said in a low tone. "Yes, I have to. It's the only way out," Raylina said adamantly, not thinking it through. "Raylina, that place is cursed and dreadful. I was a prisoner there; it felt full of pain. If you go there, I don't think you will survive," Avyukt said to convince her, hoping that she'd change her mind about throwing herself in the mouth of danger.

"We don't know what this whole fuss is about. The fragmented theories and the awful people narrating them have created a big bang of confusion. We will create the replica of the rose, like the one Sangul is after, which will lure him to us, and then we kill him before he opens that stupid door. If it doesn't work, if the door opens, then I go down with him, and you and Abby shut the door forever," Raylina said, nutshelling her plan with confidence. "Bam," she clapped.

Raylina's plan was flawed from all the angles; in fact, there weren't any angles to her plan at all, Avyukt thought. But then he trusted her whimsical way of handling things, and sometimes the best thing to do something is just to do it. "You think killing him would be easy, and what about Vaylar, his lapdog? Huh... how will we pull that off?" Avyukt asked worriedly.

"One thing at a time, Baby," Raylina said coolly. "Baby, Huh?" Avyukt grinned mischievously and moved closer to her. "Grow up," she helplessly blushed, standing there, unmoved. "How? You just called me a baby," Avyukt said flirtingly. "Don't start," Raylina said, breaking into a sly smirk. "We should..." Raylina said, coming back to reality. "Ya... definitely," Avyukt agreed, taking his eyes off her tempting lips, and hurriedly stepped away from her.

"Avyukt, add a little red in it," Raylina demanded while examining the rose. "Really, Raylina... now?" Avyukt galled, staring at Raylina's glinting eyes. Avyukt grudgingly moved his fingers like he was sprinkling something on the crystal rose, and the tips of the flower changed its colors from colorless to slightly spruce.

"Why is it green?" Raylina said, not approving of the green color. "Because it is my favorite color," Avyukt said. She sneered and said, "Green; really? I thought you were more of a black guy." Avyukt laughed softly and carefully gave her the rose, leaning closer to Raylina, and said, "First, not every guy is into dark black shades. And second, there are lots of things about me that you don't know."

"Ray," Ablina came shouting and hindered their conversation. Avyukt and Raylina moved away swiftly from each other. There is beauty in incomplete and interrupted moments; it keeps one hanging.

"What happened?" Avyukt asked, looking at Ablina's horror-struck face. "They are gone, all of them... He took them... Raylina," Ablina said painfully. "20 minutes, freaking 20 minutes," Raylina said, and kicked her leg against the wall in frustration.

"You are hiding something from me, Ray. You asked us not to come along with you for the Crystal Rose, now what the hell are you doing with Avyukt?" Ablina asked furiously. "Abby," Raylina stammered. "No, not now, Ray, if you lie, I will kill you, trust me on this," Ablina warned in a serious tone.

Raylina's perfectly vague plan just fell apart, and she now had no choice but to tell Ablina the truth. Her master plan had involved only two people, but this untimely abduction messed things up for her.

"How do we find them?" Ablina asked Avyukt, ignoring Raylina's glum-crushed face. "We can," Raylina started but stopped as she saw Ablina's angry face, "No comments," Raylina withdrew from talking. "They are in the castle. Because the door is here, so they won't take a risk going anywhere else," Avyukt assured.

Ablina and Avyukt began searching for them. Raylina silently trailed behind them, lost thinking about what Aryaraj said. Again, she felt directionless as Aryaraj's incomplete guidance didn't tell her how to activate the magic inside her. The whole "person's will, and the story of the third universe" talk was more like a motivational lecture, which motivated her, but didn't show her the way. She felt that it was more than she signed up for.

"Do you know, guys, we haven't slept for the last 72 hours," Raylina said. Ablina turned around, glaring at Raylina, and said, "It's not important, Ray." "Have you looked at your dark circles? Man, you look like a baby raccoon," Raylina said tiredly. "I have a great idea, Abby. Let's run away," Raylina said and started laughing crazily. "This all began because we woke up from that stupid tomb. We are the fuss. No us. No opening. The world is saved!" "Vaylar has people we care about, Ray," Ablina said, trying to make Raylina understand. "WOKAY," Raylina said and started walking again.

Raylina was walking ahead; this time, Avyukt and Ablina were tailing her. "Do you think she is okay?" Avyukt asked Ablina in a hushed tone. "No, she is not," Ablina replied worriedly. Raylina stopped walking, turned around, and said, "Let's blow up the door," she said in a serious tone. All three looked at each other, their heads processing the insanely rash idea and their hearts liking it.

"We can't do that," Avyukt spoke first to Raylina's insane thought. "I have been thinking the whole time… us going to that place. And I have realized that our light part is still there. 199 Graymanos are still alive, and if we blow up the door, they also get blown up," Avyukt said. "Yes, I agree, but before blowing up, I can do the dead thing again and bring them back," Raylina suggested. "No, it's not possible. Because to do so, you have to die 199 times to bring them back, which your human body cannot withstand," Avyukt said.

"But I am Śirā and a witch," Raylina said, jazzing her hands in the air. "You are mortal, Raylina," Avyukt said as he kept on walking deep into the castle, searching for others. "Guys, I am sorry, but can you both shut up for like two seconds?" Ablina asked politely, annoyed with their constant chit-chat, striving to create a better logical plan with at least an 80 % survival rate.

Raylina and Avyukt were busy pointing out the chances of failure while Ablina was doing her own evaluation, as her genius mind liked exploring all the points before jumping to any conclusion. Ablina, being a true believer, preferred thinking the best out of the worst situation. For adults, tooth fairies aren't real, but they're as real as the moon and stars for a child, and Ablina was like that child who had faith in everything. She saw hope in hopelessness, love in the unlovable, and magic in normality, making her one of a kind.

Ablina stomped her leg out of excitement and said, "There is always a way out, even when you are sealed in the brick wall without windows or doors." "Let's open the door," Ablina said happily. "I think she has lost it just like me," Raylina muttered to Avyukt. "Bad, I was counting on her," Avyukt sighed.

Raylina and Avyukt were still unconvinced, but Ablina was determined to follow through with her plan. "We are wasting time, and this castle is so colossal that it will take days to find out where he has them. Instead, let's open the door, and let Vaylar and Sangul come to us," Ablina explained. "Who will drink the darkness," Avyukt questioned seriously. "And light, what about that," Raylina asked. "Guys, you don't understand, do you?" Ablina asked dismayingly.

Ablina breathed out her annoyance and said, "Ray, you said that Avyukt had two versions of him; that his light part was in Darno's prison, and the dark part was here with us all. Now think for a moment that when the door opened, nothing came out of it; no darkness, no light, or anything for that matter. But it looked like it did. Fumes and everything were orchestrated to fool us. In fact, I think Sangul is not a Graymanos. I think he is from Darno." "Did you get any of this?" Avyukt asked Raylina, who was staring at Ablina with her mouth hanging open. "Yes… No… Not at all," Raylina answered hesitantly, nodding her head.

Ablina smiled, knowing that she had to explain things in a much simpler way. "Okay. Avyukt, what did you do when you saw it coming, the darkness?" Ablina questioned calmly. "I thought that it would swallow the world and that I would have to save the world at any cost," Avyukt answered. "Exactly, at any cost, and at that moment, you unintentionally, gave up the light in you," Ablina said.

"Sorry, but still not getting any of this," Raylina said, furrowing her eyebrows in deep confusion. "Ray, we are both dark and light in equal amounts, not one less, or the other more. All this time, we thought that Vaylar sucked the light, and Graymanos sucked the darkness coming out of that door. But in reality, everyone just expelled their light out. And now I know you both will be thinking about how Vaylar ended up expelling his light. The answer to that question is simple. He wasn't thinking about the magic that lived inside him, as he was so desperate to get the power from Darno; he forgot to protect the light that already resided within him," Ablina said.

"Vaylar gave up his light to get Darno's magic... how?" Raylina jabbered. "How Vaylar acquired Darno's magic is unclear. But I am sure of one thing that everyone standing there, their light, including Vaylar's light, got soaked away into Darno for some unknown reason. And only darkness stayed behind," Ablina replied.

"So, if I am getting this right. Avyukt and all the other Graymanos transferred their light to Darno. And for Vaylar, who thought he was getting some real stuff, stupidly gave up his too," Raylina repeated to confirm. "Correct," Ablina said. "So if your theory is true, then Sangul managed to fool the greatest minds of history," Avyukt said, praising Sangul. "Including yours," Raylina scoffed. Avyukt ignored her.

"So if we open the door, this time without Sangul's presence, it will be just the door to another world, no light, no dark, nothing," Avyukt asked again. "And if not, we all die. Let's do this, people," Raylina said and marched towards the main hall, before anyone could come up with something new.

All the stories of myths and facts were badly intertwined. The whirlpool of confusion was sucking them dry. The myths were paradoxical, and the facts were stories. In short, there was no way out. It was like testing a nuclear bomb above the ground without any precautions. But then, if we don't try it, we'll never know it.

"How do we open this?" Ablina asked Avyukt, staring at the huge, thick trunk of the Banyan tree. "Your Ragata (Blood)," Avyukt rumbled with dramatic pauses. Ablina understood what Avyukt meant; she sliced her arm and dropped the blood on the Ragata flowers. Her boiling pure dark red blood burnt the poisonous magic of the Ragata flowers bedded around the Banyan tree.

Ablina touched the wrinkled bark of the Banyan tree and commanded, "Analaka." A little crack appeared in the center of the Banyan tree. The crackling sound of woods breaking intensified, and suddenly the trunk shattered into pieces. The pathway to the other world was open, wide. The web of lies Sangul had spun backfired. Nothing came out of it. No light, no darkness. It was all staged. But why? The question remained. "Now what?" Raylina asked. "We wait for them to show up," Ablina said.

In just a minute, Sangul came furiously storming into the main hall, "You fool. What have you done?" He roared. "We have opened the door," Raylina laughed devilishly. "You fuck up kids, you all are fools. You think you can outsmart me," Sangul hissed. "We just did," Ablina said sweetly. "You," Sangul swung his hand in rhythm with the wind, and Ablina was thrown, swirling away in the air. "Abby," Raylina screamed and ran to her. Sangul ferociously clenched his fist, and Raylina, before she could reach Ablina, hit the floor.

As Avyukt stomped his hand in the air roughly to attack Sangul, Vaylar entered the hall with style like he was entering a nightclub. He nonchalantly waved his hand, and the branches of the shattered Banyan tree curled Avyukt up tightly. "Guys... Raylina," Vaylar acknowledged everyone by glancing.

"Sangul, let's not act like hooligans. We are civilized enough to talk," Vaylar said, trying to stop Sangul from acting violently. "What kind of asshole are you," Raylina asked harshly, glaring at him with pure hatred. Vaylar ignored Raylina's comment and continued as if she hadn't spoken, "I have your entire family and friends, and, of course, my son in captive," Vaylar paused, glancing sideways at Ablina. "You have seen what I'm capable of, so don't try anything on me," he growled at Raylina.

"Girls, let's not waste any time further. Give us the Crystal Rose," Sangul threatened. They all stood there, silent and unmoved. "Vaylar, bring them," Sangul ordered. He whirled his hand in the air, and Ablina and Raylina saw their weakness—their family members chained up on the wall. They were there the whole time, in the main hall.

"Give us the Crystal Rose, Raylina," Vaylar pleaded rudely. "Or what," Raylina dared. "Or I burn every last one of you," Vaylar said restlessly. "Where is Astor?" Ablina asked concernedly. "He paid the price," Vaylar said lowly, not looking eye to eye. "You took away his magic. You killed your own brother," Ablina cried. "Yes, I killed him, and now if you don't give me what I want, I will kill you all without any hesitation, including my son," Vaylar warned, watching Visac tied up in chains.

"Is power greater than your own son, Vaylar?" Raylina questioned boldly. "Give it to me, and this ends now," Vaylar said, his words trembling like they were under someone else's control. "Okay, Alisar. I can show you. It's in the ground," Raylina said in a low tone. Hearing his name from Raylina's mouth weakened him. "Let's go," Vaylar said vacantly.

***

"You know, everyone out there is perfectly capable of killing each other," Raylina said while removing the dirt from the tiny burrow. "I know, and I am trying to avoid that," Vaylar replied forlornly, his grueling eyes fixed on her, urging to talk to her but not being able to. "Why did you kill her, huh? I suppose you guys were friends. I thought—we were friends," Raylina said scornfully.

"There is too much at stake here, Ray. I am at a bigger loss here," Vaylar said, masking his pain from Raylina. "Like your daughter," Raylina spoke unflinchingly to the man who could finish her in the blink of a second. The ice broke harder than she expected. Her words shattered the most powerful man on Earth into a million pieces. He looked at her with teary eyes, begging her to stop.

Who said cruelty didn't suit women? Raylina Bayer proved them all wrong. "Here's what we are going to do. You are going to pretend that this is the real flower. And I will do my best to bring her home. But when she's back, I will hand you over to Graymanos," Raylina promised. "Ray," Vaylar stammered. "Don't. You lost that right when you killed my mother," Raylina said strongly and handed the fake Crystal Rose. "Before we go, tell me where Astor is," she demanded. "He's alive," he said ashamedly.

***

"Sangul, my dear friend," Vaylar came walking along with Raylina into the main hall and showed him the Crystal Rose.

"Finally... the little glitch of our perfect plan. This flower had burnt many lives, but now it's over," Sangul said gaily, taking the Śirā flower from Vaylar and holding it in his hands with hubris. "We thought that Mihira would be the one, but that bastard Aagney, he was the one carrying you all this time. Now that we have Śirā, nothing can stop us. We will rule the worlds," Sangul said, unleashing his true intentions.

"You know, one thing this world taught me is that you all can be easily destroyed by just two words, love and friendship. Your kind might be a tad superior to humans, but you all are still weak, as you will always be slaves to materials and emotions. Unlike our world, which has moved beyond the bars of right and wrong," Sangul said haughtily. "Yes, that's why our world has something you don't have, Sangul. Light... which comes from these flimsy words like... Love... Hope... friendship," Ablina answered, staring him in the eye.

"You got what you wanted. Now let them go and get lost," Raylina said furiously. "Raylina... my darling, dumb Raylina, you know what? I never really liked you. You are so full of yourself; you think the world revolves around you. Well, guess what, it doesn't!... Thank god! We found a way to conjure its power without your help. Anyway, Goodbye, Raylina Bayer, until we come back and obliterate you all," Sangul said and waltzed back to the door with his victorious, smug face.

Raylina nudged Ablina's shoulders, and she promptly understood what it meant. Ablina drove her hand in the air, vigorously pushing the invisible air, commanding it like a common slave, and the little hurricane started to build in the room, swirling Sangul and Vaylar up in it, choking them on their own magic.

Ablina's little hurricane started to increase in size. Its shape was slowly turning into a giant, darksome, virid octopus-like structure eddying Vaylar and Sangul in it. "Avyukt," she yelled for help, struggling to endure the air pressure. Avyukt ran and stood next to her. He touched Ablina's shaky hand and roared, "Nisgaiss."

The hurricanes began to settle down. Avyukt steadily brought the flying men, Vaylar and Sangul, to the ground. "My powers got a little rusty, but it's good to be back," Avyukt said, wearing his I-win-smirk. "Ablina, do the honours," Avyukt said aloud, holding Vaylar and Sangul tied to the ground.

Ablina pulled out the dagger from thin air, the same dagger which Vaylar used to slit her mother's throat, and jabbed the dagger through Sangul's heart. His blood splattered all over the ground, breaking the magical chains which held everyone captive into a million pieces. Sangul died quickly. It was a mercy kill; as for Ablina, there was still some compassion left in her heart.

Vaylar saw a glimpse of his death in Ablina's eyes. "To new beginnings," he uttered, closing his eyes, waiting for Ablina to end everything once and for all. "End him," Ablina said, handing the bloodied dagger to Raylina.

CHAPTER 24

THE RETURN

Millions of reasons crossed Raylina's mind and reasoned to her, and the infamous question 'why not' kept roaming on her mind. Why not end the man who caused her pain? Pain which would never be over, and she had to carry it forever in her heart. At that moment, Raylina felt like she was offered everything. The perfect revenge was served on a platter, but she resisted the most tempted moment of her life.

Raylina closed her eyes to ask her heart, to hear what it had to say. In a trice, a gust of wind grazed her ears and whispered in a deep voice, "Little Queen. Though the world runs on the profound magic of Śirā (Veins) and Ragata (Blood), our hearts carry the magic of kindness, humility, love, the magic beyond this universe, the magic which created this universe. The magic of your heart is more precious than the magic flowing in your veins.

Don't let revenge destroy the goodness in your heart. You are like day and night, dark and light." "Stop," Raylina ordered calmly. And at her behest, Avyukt freed Vaylar.

Raylina's action flummoxed everyone. "What are you thinking? Just kill him," Ablina demanded Vaylar's blood furiously. Raylina nodded her head like she was listening to some kind of music, music of the gusting waves of wind. "Abby, we are not like him," Raylina spoke slowly with great calm, staring at Vaylar lying debilitated on the same ground where he had slaughtered powerful witches and men like pigs. "Stop blabbering, and kill him, or I will," Ablina warned bitterly.

"Girls look," Manashaya said timidly, pointing at something back, fear evident in his eyes. "We might have a bigger problem here."

An army of 199 dark Graymanos lined up one by one like tamed monsters to retaliate on Yama Castle for stabbing their chief—Sangul. "They all seemed to be in some kind of trance," Ablina said, looking away from their dark, bloody red eyes glued on to her. "They are. Sangul charmed them. That's how we never knew what he was doing behind our backs," Avyukt replied. "How do we stop them?" Raylina asked, staring at the dark men walking closer to them. "Only the next leader of the Graymanos can," Avyukt answered.

"Ablina killed Sangul, so that makes Ablina their next leader," Artha said. "We are not barbarians, Artha. We don't kill and take places... it doesn't work like that," Avyukt explained. "Yes… very noble of you guys. So, you all guys vote?" Raylina asked sarcastically. "We are doomed now," Ekani said, watching the army of Graymanos marching inside the main hall.

***

"Rudhh (Stop)," the man bawled in a terrifying bass voice, turning every eye to him. In a flash, the army of most dangerous creatures, Graymanos, ever walked on the Earth, kneeled one by one as he walked by.

"Unbelievable," Artha gasped, gawking at the man who once saved the world from dying, returning back to the place where it all began. "Am I hallucinating? Can we all actually see him?" Avyukt gasped in astonishment, kneeling down in respect. "Yes, he is totally visible," Visac said. Raylina confirmed by nodding her head cluelessly. "Who is he?" Ablina asked. "Mihira Adivaraha," Vaylar spoke in terror, sitting down on his knees as well.

Mihira's dark, dense black hair and godly giant body structure made everyone's eyeballs pop out in a poetic sense—enthralling every soul present there with his oneiric appearance. "There is a great difference between conquering a kingdom and building one." Mihira Adivaraha was the king of the world, awakened after a long sleep, coming back to save his kingdom—the world which he built.

Everyone except Raylina and Ablina kneeled down. "Are we really all alive, or are we in a movie, where resurrection is a common thing," Raylina joked nervously, looking at the terrifying man standing in front of her. "No," Mihira answered with a smile. "You were dead," Raylina asked, the first question popping into her head without thinking. "Ablina woke me up," Mihira said, looking at the expressionless face of Ablina.

Raylina courteously bowed her head down and said, "Sir, nice to meet you." "My child," Mihira replied affectionately and gave his blessings. He waited for his daughter to respond, but Ablina didn't. Instead, Ablina stood there, clenching Raylina's hand, staring at the man who was supposedly her father, a father she never knew; a father who wanted to murder her in her mother's womb.

No matter what Mihira's intentions were, the crime of killing a child before she could breathe in her mother's womb was inhuman, unjustifiable, and he very well knew that he was guilty of committing that crime. But, despite all this, Mihira came back in the hope of getting one more chance. To do right by Ablina. After all, that's all we live for, to do right by the people we love. And he was not going anywhere until he had won Ablina back.

After a moment, Mihira's attention moved from his daughter to the man who was the root cause of all. "You're dead," Mihira said, pointing towards Vaylar, and walked towards him. Mihira picked up Vaylar like a little pup from his collar and gave a sharp blow on his face. Vaylar was on the ground, blood spurting out of his mouth and nose, breathing heavily, weak, begging for his life.

Mihira once again picked Vaylar up to brutally kill the half-dead man, but this time Raylina stopped him. "Sir, we can't kill him," Raylina spoke politely. "This man killed my parents, my daughter's foster parents, my Graymanos brothers, and many innocent people. He is the reason why my wife is dead. Moreover, he also tried to kill me. I won't let this murderer roam free. And that's final," Mihira ordered stubbornly, passing his death sentence. "Forgive me," Vaylar begged faintly. "Never," Mihira said and punched him hard again.

Mihira's rage was beyond anyone's control, and the only way to stop him was to ask someone he would listen to, and Raylina knew that person was Ablina. "Abby, please stop him," Raylina pleaded. Ablina moved forward and held Mihira's hand. "I don't know why, but I trust my sister, and if she wants him alive. Then he lives," she said gently, and just like that, Mihira cooled down, shoving Vaylar to the ground.

Ablina's beaming face gave Raylina the confidence she lacked for the next move. "Okay," Mihira agreed. "Sir, there is a way to bring your brothers back," Raylina said positively. "How?" Mihira asked. "We figured out that the half-souls of Graymanos are still in the long pit," Raylina answered. "What half-souls? I don't get it, Ray," Artha asked, trying to make sense out of Raylina's jabbering.

"And here I thought Raylina Bayer can do it all," Avyukt said in a sarcastic tone. "What do you mean?"

Raylina irked. "You have a serious communication problem," Avyukt answered boldly. "You two, please don't start again," Ablina barged in to stop their heating quibbling. Ablina, with all the calm in the world, began narrating everything to everyone.

Vaylar was silently watching them, letting them make the world's stupidest plan to save the 199 Graymanos. He wanted to tell them there was no way of getting everyone safely home without a real battle. He knew what lived behind that door, only him. But he was ready to risk everything to bring his daughter back home, so he waited for the right moment to pitch his idea to make sure they all agreed to go there.

Vaylar waited for everyone to complete. He very well understood that one wrong move, and Mihira would happily tear his head apart from his body. But as time passed, he started to lose his patience. Vaylar gathered his courage, and asked "May I?" All looked at him hatefully, except Raylina. "Yes," Raylina said.

After a vicious struggle, Vaylar stood upon his wounded knees. Mihira wanted to kick hard on his gashed knees, but Ablina was more important than Vaylar, so he let the man live for a few more minutes on his loaned breaths. Grudgingly, they all gathered around in a circle to hear what Vaylar had to say.

"Raylina, the pit is just a small part, a glimpse, a prison, where they kept our souls. The door is bigger than this whole continent. And on the other side of the door lies Darno. The place is uninhabitable for humans and witches or anyone from our world," Vaylar said. "We know that. We have been there. And thanks to you and your pal, Sangul, I lived there in that prison," Avyukt interrupted rudely, staring at him with pure hatred, cooking up ways to torture his blackened soul. "You are right about that, but you were locked up. And you don't know the story like I do," Vaylar said calmly. "Just go on," Raylina said wearily, not looking at Vaylar.

"There are multiple universes, and life exists on a few. Our world is well created, and that's why envied by everyone in the universe. Our universe was created with the idea of creation. It has everything, stars, planets, galaxies, black holes, and many other things beyond our imaginations. One must need multiple lives just to study it, and I think even after this, they will still never completely know what our universe holds. But Darno..." Vaylar paused. "Well, Darno is different. Darno is like an abandoned child. No stars, no galaxies, no planets, no black holes, nothing. A part of the universe, still not part of it."

Vaylar looked at their confused faces and said, "Not fair, isn't it? Let me draw it." He picked up the small burnt, broken banyan branch from the ground and waved it like a wand, bending the wind's course, manifesting its power in the burnt branch. After that, he held the branch like he was holding a pen, and a bright sparkly blue light started to emit out of it, like ink. Magical it was. It was 'Dreamlike.'

That's the beauty of enchantments; it makes evil look angelic. Vaylar painted the image of the two worlds with his magic. Two globes linked by a huge bridge, one world within the universe and another without, abandoned yet part of it.

Vaylar saw their wowed faces and smiled a little, "Mama Nature was bam-dazzled with God's creation. The sight of God's creativity stuck in her head like she wanted to create more than just nature on a plain globe. At the end of her device, she decided to add a little... what's the term... Yes! Evolution, which God well appreciated and decided to plant in humans and everything. And like everyone else, our Earth decided to evolve and created Darno... no one knows how it happened, but Darno was created," Vaylar unraveled.

Vaylar pointed to the line drawn between the two circles and said, "This long line, you see, it's a 'door or a bridge' whatever you call it. People of Darno call it the 'Maori (Starless Sky).' The people of Darno created this for their survival, but it was hanging. Every time it came closer to us, the bridge was pushed away due to our gravitational force. The history is unknown even to the people living there," said Vaylar. "Wait, Gravity pulls. Where is your logic, Vaylar?" Ablina asked with irritation. "Ablina, I said, the abandoned child. Our Earth does not consider Darno as part of it, and neither does our universe," Vaylar responded calmly.

The profound abhor for his father was making Visac unhinged, "Enough," Visac yelped like an explosion.

"This story is a gimmick. He is just stalling us all. Let's go inside and get our folks," Visac said rudely. "Son, it's not safe," Vaylar said lowly. "Don't… call me that," Visac rebuked angrily, raising his fist to hit Vaylar on his face, but Raylina prevented it. "Back off, Ray. This man killed your mother. At least show some respect to dead," Visac said furiously. "Easy boy," Manashaya said and held him back. "I am out of this shit. Call me when we have to go in to fight," Visac said and left. Manashaya wanted to go after him, but Raylina stopped him.

Creases of tension hounded Raylina's milky forehead, and it was the 200th time she thought about running away. But she couldn't. She had to carry the burden of being selfless. She sighed and asked, "We killed one of their own. Why aren't they coming back?" "Because they won't… Why do you think they are so worked up about finding the Crystal Rose? Their world is dying, and they are more focused on surviving," Vaylar answered.

"Why can't the people of Darno just come and live with us, like in our world," Ablina asked bluntly. "They cannot. Their bodies are not designed to sustain our environmental conditions," Vaylar answered. "How do we defeat them?" Mihira spoke in a despised tone. "We kill the main man, the Prince of Darno," Vaylar said.

***

With magic and other weapons, the army of 199 Graymanos fastened their combat boots, and headed towards the darkened passage inside the great Banyan tree

338

leading to the Maori (Starless Sky), to bring back their lost selves, with Avyukt leading them. Raylina, Ablina, and the others walked behind him.

With each step, Avyukt could feel his heart thrust through his chest. He felt like it would rip out, and the reason was he was afraid to lose Raylina. Avyukt knew what she was planning and knew there was nothing he could do to stop her.

"Marching through the dark door, straight into the arms of chaos," Raylina said dramatically to lighten the mood as they walked through the narrow passage. "Shut up," Ablina said in annoyance. "Why are we not killing him, Ray?" Ablina asked in a serious tone, glaring at Vaylar being dragged by chains. "I am doing this for someone we all care about, Abby. Trust me on this," Raylina said, glancing at Visac.

***

"Ahah... Goiytjokru Veen Veri de Aerderdeyer ignar utehw Maori (Here comes the Śirā Ragata of the Earth marching under our starless sky)," an old lady screeched with joy. *Thousands of yearning eyes glanced in the direction the old lady pointed to and felt the propinquity of Suglavosf de Veen (Light of Veins) Nychnok de Veri (Nights of Blood) walking their way.*

***

Aerderdeyer Narod's eyes (People of the Earth) rolled in all the directions to study the Maori (Starless Sky) they were walking into. It was absolute nothingness. There were no walls, no floors, just a tremendous black void, and a big, bright chandelier-like thing hovering in the dark to lighten up the place; Raylina felt the magic of her veins drawn towards it, the calm wind and earthly smell made her think of a regular night in her homeland. On the other hand, Ablina's feet were sweating, burning up, like she was walking through hellfire.

"Stop," Avyukt ordered, and the troop stopped at his leader's command. He rushed back to Raylina.

"We are just a mile away from the pit. This is where we take a different path," Avyukt panted and looked at Raylina like he was looking at her for one last time. "The strangest emotions rushing in her at the strangest time," Raylina thought and kissed him on his cheeks, not realizing that her Indian grandpa and the rest of her family were standing right next to them.

"Take care," Raylina muttered. Avyukt tucked a strand of her hair behind her ear and said, "I will." Ablina teasingly coughed, which reminded Avyukt to come back to reality. Artha stormily pulled Raylina back from Avyukt, "You will need these," he said and handed him the potion. Raylina sighed and moved back with Ablina, and while doing so, she caught a glimpse at Vaylar staring at her.

As planned, Mihira, Avyukt, Vaylar, and the rest of 199 headed towards the pit bravely.

***

"It's unbreakable," Avyukt spoke, judging by the looks of the warding surrounding the pit. Mihira first moved forward and pinned his finger in the warding protecting the huge sinking inverted hole. As his fingertips touched the warding, peculiar dark-red straps appeared.

"Magic is deep. And eerie," Mihira said frightfully. "We can mix it up," Vaylar suggested with hesitation. "I am not corrupting my magic with yours," Mihira stated clearly. "Look, I know you will never get over this, but light and dark is the way out, and we are running out of time," Vaylar said impatiently. "Chief, I think he is right," Avyukt said calmly.

The bubbling rage on Mihira's face gave Avyukt a clear answer, and that was not to test the man. "But I have an alternative way," Avyukt smiled wickedly. "What?" Mihira asked curiously. "Our little team of 199 dark Graymanos can use their dark magic. Ragata magic was born out of our maker's dark emotions," Avyukt said. "Ragata as the darkness will always lead to the creation. Brilliant!! Where were you all this time?" Mihira said happily. Avyukt raised his eyebrows to control his volume, but it couldn't stop him from saying, "Cleaning your pots," Avyukt mumbled. "What," Mihira asked. "Nothing," Avyukt murmured. "Anyway—let's begin," Mihira commanded to army of 199 dark Graymanos.

In unison, the army of 199 dark Graymanos chanted, "Lumina si întunericul Forjat împreună Pentru a Rupe Necunoscut," and the giant dark waves of Ragata magic started coming out of their fingertips, spreading over the warding, leeching on it.

"Visaras Vanikya," Mihira and Avyukt thundered together, releasing multiple white flares of Ragata magic from their eyes, falling upon warding, blending with the dark Ragata magic of the army of 199 dark Graymanos that leeched on it.

Ploddingly, the warding started to burn, like a paper tearing down into pieces in slow motion. The deep power from the other world failed, just by the simple mixture of light and dark of our world.

The army of dark Graymanos hooted with pride and danced in the shower of the warding ashes. Their gallant hero, Mihira, raised his foot and kept it across the warding line; He walked in, unburnt, and hailed his clenched fist up in the air, pompously smirking to his instant win.

"Crumbling of the wall is just the beginning," Mihira bellowed. "Yeahhhh…" the army of 199 dark Graymanos howled and walked towards the pit.

As the army of Graymanos got closer to the pit, the painful cry of their other halves became audible. The Graymanos' darkened hearts sank, hearing the painful wailing of the tortured souls. Seeing them in pain broke Mihira's heart. He wanted the screaming to stop, so he pulled Vaylar by his chains and ordered him to raise them without wasting any second.

"Dìrich àradh Dorcha," Vaylar intoned the spell, and the walls of the pit began throbbing as the other halves of the Graymanos came crawling out of it. The Graymanos' darkened halves standing up on the ground of Maori (Starless Sky) heard the cry of freedom as their lost halves came climbing up.

"Gavaertianot Chveni Gakhekhili Sulebi," all the dark 199 Graymanos bellowed together. And suddenly, numerous explosions occurred simultaneously, like hundreds of suns blasting at the same time.

The half-souls of the Graymanos united. Their light blended with the darkness inside them like a lost part of it, and slowly their red eyes returned to their original colors. Till now, darkness held the command over their hearts and veins, but now the light was back to question and argue.

Watching the light and the dark unifying, becoming one whole eternal soul, made Mihira speechless. He couldn't stop his tears from breaking out of his amber, touched eyes.

***

Unaware of what's happening at the pit, Raylina, Ablina, and everyone waited for Avyukt's and everyone's return, sitting distantly from each other, except Ablina. "Something's wrong," Ablina said, pacing around Raylina. "I feel it too," Raylina said, listening to the mixed voices coming from the direction where Avyukt and his army headed.

"Grandpa, I think we should go and check on them," Ablina spoke softly to convince Artha. "Grandpa, Abby is right. Please let one of us go and check," Raylina asked nicely. "No one is going, and that's final," Artha scolded them and shooed them away.

Every hour felt like a death hour. Raylina and Ablina were sensing that something was off. Their bodies were alarming them about it, but Artha was sitting on their head, hindering them from doing anything. He acted like a grumpy old teacher for whom pin-drop silence in a class was above everything. And this made them more agitated.

Manashaya saw Raylina freaking out; he went and sat next to her, "Ray," he said lowly, to avoid Artha's rage. "What?" Raylina attacked impatiently. "Are you okay?" Manashaya asked. "No, I am fine, absolutely," Raylina said bitterly. "These days, I am working at how your ancestors fucked up things private Ltd. They pay me 3 panic attacks and 0.5 anxieties per day. Man, it's a dream job!"

After a minute of silence, Manashaya said, "I'll mail my resume. Forward it to HR." They looked at each other and suddenly burst out into helpless laughter. "We must go. I feel like they need us," Raylina said seriously. "Let's go then," Ablina chimed in. "You sneaky little kid," Raylina smiled, looking at Ablina's face flooding with faith and positivity. "I am your sister. I have a free pass to spy on you," Ablina chuckled. "So, how do we do this?" Visac jumped in the middle of their conversation. "Count me in," Ekani joined in.

***

Seeing Ablina holding Visac's hand and coming towards him frightened Artha to his core. "Not again, last time I stopped myself from killing George, this time, I will kill Visac," Artha thought. "Grandpa, we need to talk to you," Ablina said. Her flushed face scared him more. "What?" He asked. "We are getting married," Ablina exclaimed. "No," Artha denied stubbornly at once. "Cadal Agus Bruadar," Manashaya muttered from behind, and Artha fell on the ground, to which Visac applauded, "Perfect!"

Aamirah and Gaurangi came rushing to check on Artha. "Cadal Agus Bruadar," Visac read from Ekani's little grey spellbook, and they fell on the ground too. "Fear mixed with surprise, classic Ekani," Raylina said cheerfully. "My spell always works," Ekani said with pride. "Okay, now let's go, we have only 30 minutes," Ablina said tensely, casting a protection spell on Artha, Aamirah, and Gaurangi lying unconscious on the black floor.

***

Death visited them again. And as a parting gift, it left hundreds of Graymanos' bodies gutted out, lying in the river of their own blood. The view didn't startle their eyes, "Déjà Vu," Manashaya said with terror, remembering the horrific night at Yama Castle. Raylina tittered dementedly, staring at the bloodied field like she was expecting this to happen.

Raylina was fidgeting and was about to collapse any minute. "It's just 'Death,'" she muttered under her breath, reminding herself that death is a phase and soul is eternal. She sighed deeply to gather her shaken heart and started to look for Avyukt's dead body.

"It's all him. He once again betrayed us all," Visac enraged, accusing his father, Vaylar, for the deaths. Ablina was quiet, watching Raylina walking through the bloody corpses, Visac angrily venting out his hatred for his father, and Manashaya and Ekani, trying to calm Visac down. The hope Ablina had clung to was gone this time, and she felt like there was no way to bring it back to her. She believed she was now broken.

With tears drying up on Raylina's cheeks, clothes soaked in deep, red blood, she stormed out of the dead pile and walked towards Visac, looking like a zombie. She gently took Visac's hands and hauled him with her through the mutilated dead bodies. Ablina, Ekani, and Manashaya followed them.

"He didn't," Raylina said, to answer Visac's allegations, showing him the dead body of Vaylar, the man everyone profoundly despised, lying underneath the mangled bodies of two Graymanos, with his heart mercilessly pulled out, eyes popped out yet still attached to his head with a thread of muscle, his dislocated jaw, and chopped leg. Visac puked, watching his father like this. Ablina dragged Visac away from there, and Raylina resumed her search for Avyukt's body.

Ekani was terrified from inside. A part of her was thinking about her grandfather and parents, who were lying unconscious and defenseless. The other part of her was numbed, watching Raylina and Ablina, losing their heads in this unknown place. But Ekani was not the kind of person who would run away when things got harder, so despite being terrified, she decided to help her cousins in any way possible.

Ekani walked along with Raylina, knowing that Raylina was strong but not strong enough to do it alone and that she would never ask anyone to help her. Manashaya tailed Raylina and Ekani silently, doing what he did best, protecting the Shaurayaveers. They walked for a mile but couldn't find Avyukt.

"Raylina," Ablina screamed. They all turned around and saw Visac and Ablina getting captured by a group of men dressed in bright red robes. They ran to fight, but the men threw a snake-like rope which circled to their wrists and tied them.

"Levdinta," Raylina shouted, struggling to get away from the men clasping her, but nothing happened. "Silly parlor tricksters," the man holding Raylina said in derision. "We have what we need. Throw them in, except this pretty princess," the captain of the group ordered his men in his thick, guttural voice. His men did as he asked and dragged Ablina out of the cage while locking the others in the levitating cage and ignited the fiery cages.

CHAPTER 25

ONE MORE STORY

The unbearable wretched heat of the fiery cage slowly burned Raylina's upper layer of skin, waking her up from the tormenting pain. After an immense effort, she managed to open her steely, tired eyes, but they instantly shut down. Then suddenly, the loud cheering of the audience woke her up again.

Raylina faintly moved her eyes down and saw women dancing around the fire, graciously, men drinking from large silver bowls, hymning something in an alien language, and Ablina chained in, standing in the corner, surrounded by the men in red ropes. She moved her eyes back to the women dancing around the fire and looked closely. She saw one old lady rigorously carving symbols in a strange language on the archaic throne kept in the stand.

"Śirā Ragata," the old lady carving the throne said, staring back at Raylina, licking the blood dripping out of her fingertips. Raylina was petrified about how she could hear the old lady from such a huge distance in the middle of all that noise. She quickly looked away from the spooky old lady, and this time, her eyes traveled to the thousands of silky red tents surrounding the gigantic golden tent, which ruled out two things: they were not at Darno, and it was obvious that the golden tent belonged to Darno's Royal family.

Raylina wondered why everything and everyone was in red. "Darno's people didn't believe in diversity of colors," she thought, and laughed forcefully, looking at Ablina standing alone, weak, and defenseless.

"Ray," a familiar voice called her. Raylina turned her weary head and saw Avyukt's beaten to death, barely functional, swollen face covered in blood. "Don't…" Avyukt spoke dimly with his mouth, the only working part of his body which was also on the verge of exhaustion. "Avyukt," Raylina said, breathing heavily, extending her hand through her fiery cage to touch his face. The fire of the fiery cage ripped off the upper layer of her skin, turning it into brown ashes. The excruciating unendurable pain woke her up completely. She saw her entire family lined up in adjacent cages, and then she passed out again.

***

"Magic comes from within… within… within…" Raylina chanted the words repetitively, like a madwoman in her sleep. "Raylina," an angelic voice whispered in her ears. She woke up aghast and found herself floating on the lake in the fiery cage. "Who is it?" she asked with terror, turning her head in every direction to inspect the place from her fiery cage.

"No need to be scared, Raylina," the voice whispered again, and a gale of wind flowed through the cage and blew out the fire of the fiery cage. Raylina thought all of this happening around her was a mirage projected by her enervated mind, so she dipped her fingers in the cold water of the lake to confirm that she wasn't dreaming. "Oh, I know… This ain't spooky," Raylina mumbled sarcastically, gawking through the web of the fiery cage at the place where Aagney recited the story of the third universe.

After a minute of pause, the voice whispered again, "I am Iraja," in a soft tone. "Iraja, as in the maker of Śirā Ragata… the whole 'Nature' stuff," Raylina gasped in surprise. "Save Darno," Iraja said, and in a glimpse of a second, Raylina was back hanging under the Maori (Starless Sky).

***

"Ray, what is wrong with you?" Avyukt asked tensely, squinting his beaten eyes to clearly see her face. "What happened? Back at the pit," Raylina didn't answer but asked a question instead. "We burnt the pit's warding, but it was a trap. It took away our magic. And before we could understand, their men attacked us, they killed everyone and left Mihira and me for the public execution," Avyukt answered gloomily. "How? Is it even possible? Taking away our magic?" Raylina asked in disbelief. Avyukt nodded his head in pain.

"So now you all are just some random magic-less humans?" Raylina asked to confirm. "Yes, we are, and— these sons of bitches—they somehow reversed our immortality spell," Avyukt replied, with anger rising in his voice. "What?" Raylina gasped fearfully. "And these snake-type ropes are some magic-restricting devices," Avyukt said, looking dejected. "I figured that part out when they abducted us. Also, I think the walls of these fire cages are in some way blocking our powers," Raylina said.

Raylina battled with her wounded body, and after moments of the fight, with the support of her arms, she sat. "Venus. Visac's sister... They have her," Raylina disclosed in pieces. "Vaylar dragged us all here. He was well aware that there was no way we could have survived. He gambled with our lives to save one person, and you let him do that, Ray," Avyukt said bitterly.

Raylina looked at Avyukt with her weary, sorry eyes and said, "I did this to bring back your brothers, and I once again trusted the wrong man. But he is dead, now, and the good part is I have a plan." "What?" Avyukt asked vacantly. "The plan is simple, so when the red robes lower our cages to the ground for our execution, I will somehow go and get Abby, unleashing her crazy power, and then we bargain. And all you have to do is fight with red robes. I know it involves some manual labor, but it's effective."

"Just don't get killed," Avyukt said grimly and smiled at Raylina with astonishment in his eyes. He didn't speak, argue, or advise after that, as he knew that Raylina was perfectly capable of doing things as she narrated. "I am going to get you all out of here," Raylina said with sheer grit, gazing at Ablina bound in chains.

Ablina's precious tears came rushing down her cheeks as she felt useless. "All this power, and still powerless," she mumbled, staring at men in red ropes holding her prisoner. She tried invoking the Ragata magic flowing in her blood for the nth time, but it didn't work. Nothing worked; the snake-rope in her neck inhibited her magic.

Ablina looked above, praying for a miracle, and there she was, her sister, Raylina, staring at her from the burning cages hanging in the Maori (Starless Sky) in a line. "I love you," Ablina mouthed, smiling, with her eyes filled with tears. Raylina understood what her sister meant, and she replied to Ablina's message with a flying kiss.

***

"Kill them all," the mass wrathfully clamored. Men in red robes pulled Raylina and the others out of the levitating cages, tying their hands back with the snake-like ropes, and inhumanly started dragging them to the execution ground.

Raylina's eyes fell on a tall man dressed in a black robe who was sharpening his butcher's knife on a huge black stone. He seemed experienced and well-prepared. "They even have uniforms for their hangmen. This place is lit," Raylina joked in fright. "Real mature," Avyukt said. "You two, stop talking," the guard groaned. "Why aren't they killing us?" Ekani asked fearfully. "They are waiting for the Queen and the Prince," Gaurangi replied. Raylina took a deep breath to lessen the stress, as the wait was killing her.

"Long live the Queen," the thousands of men, women, and children hauled as the Queen of Darno entered. The Queen of Darno gracefully walked towards the small podium swirling her radiant black gown in the air in style, like she was walking on the ramp of an elite fashion show, showcasing her golden choker with an oval-shaped bloody ruby in the middle wrapped around her perfectly swan-like neck. Her long blonde hair bounced every time she stopped to wave at the crowd.

The Queen of Darno swiftly climbed the steps of the podium and took the chair at the podium. Her posture and body language oozed power and coldness. She slightly inclined her head towards the guard beside her and nodded, giving him permission to commence the execution.

"These guys are still stuck in medieval times," Visac said, watching in horror at the men in red ropes dragging Aamirah and Artha for their execution. "Totally," Manashaya mumbled.

The intensity of screaming amplified as an extremely tall, heavenly gorgeous man walked in. "Prince of Darno," the crowd screamed. His divine charm took over the thrones in their hearts as he walked past them. The Prince of Darno's blessed, glorious abs flaunted well in his sensational black attire embroidered in lavender. The light golden blonde, messy, quiff hair added magic to his perfectly handsome face. His blue eyes added a marvel factor to his beastly personality.

"Fantastic," Ekani said, staring at the Prince of Darno, awestruck by his charming looks. "I would totally... Ahh... I forgot the word," Raylina said, gawking at the Prince of Darno. Manashaya and Avyukt looked at them odiously. "What? He is hot," Ekani protested. Raylina raised her eyebrows and pouted. Gaurangi gave a death stare to them as if she was the executioner.

Prince of Darno sat alongside the Queen, and he waved his squire to initiate the execution. The cheering began as the man dragged Artha onto the ground to the execution stone. "Wait... if you touch any of us, you will all die," Raylina screamed, and the eyes turned to her. The Prince of Darno non-verbally ordered his squire to bring her up at the podium.

"What she's doing?" Manashaya asked worriedly, staring at Raylina, prancing fearlessly towards the stand, past the rabid crowd. "Trust her," Avyukt murmured, wondering why he trusted Raylina so much despite knowing that she was a *'Chaos Magnet.'*

A man from the crowd threw a little bag filled with stones at Raylina, which hit her head, and blood started oozing from her head. "Kill them," the man from the crowd demanded, and the screaming began. Artha roared but couldn't move as the executioner held his head down on the stone. "Careful asshole," Raylina grunted as the Prince's squire dragged Raylina up by the snake-rope. They started walking again.

This time, Raylina purposely tripped herself exactly where Ablina was standing. Ablina rushed to save her sister, but chains restrained her. "Within you," Raylina said to Ablina and winked as the Prince's squire heaved her away from Ablina.

As the Prince's squire and Raylina climbed up the little podium, she turned back and smirked at Avyukt. Ablina watched it all, but she couldn't figure out what Raylina meant. The Prince's squire threw Raylina at the Prince's feet. "Really... That's how you treat the only person who can save your asses," Raylina barked at the squire, staring right at the Prince and Queen of Darno. "What do you mean by that? What do you have?" The Prince of Darno asked in his deep voice. Raylina smiled broadly, eyeing the Prince of Darno, and said, "Something which you don't have, and I do."

Raylina's audacity irked the Prince of Darno. He controlled his anger and asked again, "What?" "Śirā," Raylina answered spiritedly. "And I know why you need it." The Prince of Darno leaned closer to Raylina and said, "We have the Crystal Rose, and we don't need you to summon its power."

Raylina chuckled softly, not intimidated by the Prince's attempt to scare her off with his massive, mountain-like masculine body. "The Crystal Rose you collected from Vaylar's dead body was a fake. My friend and I made that rose and asked Ali…Vaylar to carry it with him into the door. The Crystal Rose you have is just like the one Aagney created to fool your dumb asses," Raylina said. "In fact, he never had it." "It shines, bright… like the…," the Prince of Darno said, trying hard to wrap his brain around. "Bright? Like the last one, Vaylar stole from us," Raylina laughed sarcastically.

"Within you," Ablina mumbled and closed her eyes for quick flashbacks, as it was the only thing that could save her and her family. She stormed hundred percent of her brain, going through every part of it, making sense of what her sister said. "Third Universe," the answer reached, right through her worried mind, ripping away thousands of negative thoughts. "You have all the magic you need, not given, not born, the one inside you," Ablina said gleefully, and yelled "Ray…."

Steely snake-ropes crackled like a fragile vase from Ablina's delicate hands, shattering into pieces, swirling around her like a rising tornado. She felt the pure strand of Ragata magic awaking in her tiny teen body, converting her into a deadly weapon of destruction. "It's my turn," Ablina smirked, unclenching her fist, releasing the ethereal wave of the howling wind from her delicate hands, beginning the destruction of the Maori (Starless Sky)/the Door.

The Queen of Darno, like a true Queen, quietly watched Ablina conjuring the oldest magic of the Universe. On the other side, the Prince of Darno was terrified to see Ablina summoning such freakish magic. "And that's my sister, screwing up this creepy Door," Raylina smiled wickedly at the Prince of Darno, holding all the aces in her hands. "Darno is dead without me. Only I can save you all," Raylina spoke with a swagger. "How?" the Prince asked, with his eyes still glued to Ablina slowly obliterating the door.

Raylina held the Prince of Darno by his arms, pulled him aside to talk. "What," the Prince of Darno growled, jerking his hand away. "First, you send my family back to Earth safely, including Venus," Raylina began the bargain. "And why would I do that?" The Prince of Darno piqued. "Because… You Royal son of a bitch. I am the one you have been slaughtering for," Raylina answered seriously.

Prince of Darno was vulnerable, his mind stopped working, his well-planned plan was failing, and for the first time, the unbeatable was losing badly, "No, but Vaylar told us that the Crystal Rose was…," he mumbled in confusion. "You are funny," Raylina chuckled in wonder. "I mean, I thought the way Sangul sang the glory songs of Darno, it's hard to believe that you all got easily played by the world's oldest deceiver." "I cannot do this, my mother… she will not let this happen…" the Prince of Darno said, tensely brushing his golden blonde hair back with his fingers. "The choice is yours," Raylina smirked, folding her hands around her chest.

The Prince of Darno disliked the idea of surrender. But he was a wise man; watching Ablina destroying the door, killing his men by a simple touch, and the panic-stricken crowd screaming was enough to consider Raylina's proposal. Without saying a word, the Prince of Darno rushed to the center and yelled, "Stop… We surrender." And Ablina stopped the destruction.

The Prince of Darno ordered his men to release the prisoners. "What are you doing, son?" The Queen asked furiously, still sitting unmoved on the chair. "What we wanted from the beginning, saving our world," the Prince of Darno answered politely. "You know, these are all parlor tricks," the Queen said in an unhesitant tone, not affected by what was happening around her.

"Mother, for once, don't think about yourself, and think about the people you want to rule," the Prince of Darno begged. "Fine. Go ahead—be the coward little lamb your father raised you to be," the Queen of Darno said, shrugging her shoulders in hopelessness.

***

Ablina ran to Raylina and hugged her. "It's all over, kids," Artha said and hugged his granddaughters. "Yes, it is," Raylina said, hugging them back tightly.

"I am sorry," Aamirah said with tears of regret in his eyes, reaching out to take hold of Gaurangi's hand. "Love you," she said, interlocking her finger with his, accepting his apology. Aamirah and Gaurangi joined in a group hug while Avyukt stood there with Manashaya and Visac, watching the family reunite.

"Visac," a girl called his name in a low voice. "Your sister... What he did... It was all for her," Raylina said, putting her hand on his shoulder. "Venus?" Visac asked in a shaky voice, staring at his sister in disbelief. "Yes," Venus cried and hugged her big brother. He was shocked to see his sister alive and all grown up. "Forgive him. He did all of this for me," Venus cried softly, wiping her nose on Visac's hoodie. He hugged her back.

"Avyukt," Raylina called softly. Avyukt turned and walked to her. "When I first saw you, I hated you," Avyukt said. "And now," Raylina asked, trying to be brave. "Now, I just hate you more," Avyukt said and pulled her in his arms. Raylina wrapped her hands around him, holding him tightly, and said, "When I am gone, you take care of her and the others."

"I want to be by your side, Raylina," Avyukt uttered seriously in her ears, still holding her in his arms, not wanting to ever let her go. "Don't tell me you are in love with me," she laughed and pulled back her arms. He laughed, tears rushing in his grey eyes, knowing what Raylina had put on the stake, "You really think you are special, right?" "Yes... I am," she smiled faintly and kissed him on his cheek.

***

359

Avyukt tensely watched Raylina walking alongside Ablina, holding her hand. Out of everyone, he knew what Raylina was going to do to get them all out of there. He wanted to stop her, but it was the dead end. Raylina caught his dim grey eyes staring at her, and she quickly wore her confident, fake smile to make him believe that she was doing okay. They both looked away with their worried hearts still fixed upon each other, pretending that they would make it through.

Raylina's plan was short and clear, to stay and save Darno, while Avyukt and Ablina blow up the entrance from Earth's end, permanently deleting the umbilical cord (Maori) between Abandoned Child (Darno) and Earth. Both of them were completely clueless about how to do it, yet stupidly faithful.

The dim, faint blue light coming out of Earth's door became brighter with each step they took towards their home. Unaware of Raylina's master plan, Ablina felt that it was the beginning of her happily ever after. The happily ever after, that she had been waiting for a long time.

"Hey," the Prince of Darno said, walking over from his side to Raylina's. Raylina and Ablina stared at him. "What?" Ablina said hatefully. "Ablina, you have all the right to be angry at us, but we did all of this to save Darno," the Prince of Darno said. "You killed millions of us to save thousands of yours. Ya, all forgiven," Ablina said sardonically. "Our world is running on a ventilator.

Whatever we did, it was all for survival," he tried to justify in his deep voice.

"Ablina, could you please excuse us," Raylina said. Ablina frowned and walked away. "Cut to the chase. And tell me what's going on," Raylina said with suspicion. "My mother, she holds every soul in this place," the Prince of Darno said softly.

Raylina's eyes squinted in disbelief, "What?" The Prince of Darno held her right arm and dragged her aside. He moved his hand in a pendulum arc and said, "Every soul, from Aerderdeyer (Earth)… I mean, your planet, Earth, is compounded here in this door." Raylina looked closely at where the Prince was directing and saw millions of inert dark mahogany-colored balls stacked together, forming a perfect floor of Maori (Starless Sky) beneath her light blue shoe.

The Prince of Darno raised his wrist upwards, and pointed to the chandelier-like thing hanging in a starless sky, and said, "That bright middle cluster over there, it's 'Mirisiyasos,' means a 'Ray of Soul' in Daroan language. These are the purest souls from your land." "The 'Banyan tree'…" he said, taking a long pause and continuing, "Whose roots are spread all over your world, is not just some common magical prosperity tree—it's a 'Soul Carrier.'" "Soul what?" Raylina asked.

The Prince of Darno surveyed around with his dazzling eyes to make sure it was safe to continue the conversation. He leaned in and said, "The magic that

361

runs in the veins of your world is different than the magic that breathes in ours. You have a balance of Dark and Light, the balance of Day and Night, the Sun and the moon. The balance we lack because we are not part of the universe God created. Centuries ago, our ancestors tried something to make our world similar to yours. To do so, they made a huge mistake that led to Darno's apocalypse."

"To save our people, my father made Maori (Starless Sky) between the two worlds. And just as we wanted, Aagney and Mihira unknowingly created a link between Darno and Earth. The intent was to create a route diverting all purest souls from Earth to rebuild our world. We only needed the light of the purest souls to sustain. But both Pure souls and Evil souls started to flow in through the Maori to our world. And soon, because of the darkness the evil souls carried, Darno started to fester faster than we expected," the Prince of Darno explained.

With both hands, the Prince of Darno flipped his dense blonde hair back. He took a deep breath and said, "We knew that the daughter of Mihira was the answer to our troubles, that if we use her magic, her light will be like a sun for our world, but what we didn't know was that Aagney's bloodline held far more power than any Graymanos." "Śirā," Raylina said. He nodded.

"When things started to go wrong, my father sent Vaylar in search of Śirā Ragata, whatever comes first. But Mihira and Aagney knew what could happen if the power of Śirā Ragata falls into the wrong hands... especially in

Vaylar's hands, so they hid themselves and made sure that every child born from their bloodline didn't hold the great magic of Śirā Ragata. And they started harvesting their own magic in the oceans of Aerderdeyer (Earth) to become ordinary witches so that no one could ever misuse their power. But Aerderdeyer (Earth) needs Śirā Ragata, as, without it, the Earth is just a barren land, so Nature chose you two as her next successors," the Prince of Darno said.

"We gave Vaylar what he wanted," the Prince of Darno said. "Power," Raylina interrupted. "Vaylar pledged his fealty to us in return for the magic we gave him. He even gave his only daughter as an assurance of his loyalty," the Prince of Darno said. "You bought his loyalty, classic," Raylina chuckled sarcastically. The Prince of Darno glared at Raylina, trying not to say something to upset his only chance to save his empire, and continued, "Vaylar befriended Artha as Alisar Vasaga, from where he came to know that the thing he was looking for was right there under his nose—you and your sister."

"Meanwhile, my mother and father were fighting a different war. My father wanted peace, but my mother wanted power. My father was the only one keeping everything together and civil between the worlds. All he ever wanted was to save his people. He never meant to harm anyone. But my mother disagreed. She wanted to crush your world under her feet. And she declared her disagreement by giving orders to Vaylar to kill every last one of you. She directed the whole massacre that happened back at Yama Castle. When my father came to know about that, he decided to execute her. But my mother was one step ahead of him. Right at the time of her execution, she summoned the dark souls coming from your world, consuming them in her body, and killed my father. Raylina, she wants nothing but the dead bodies of your people. She even killed Vaylar for failing her. And if I am not wrong, she is planning something. She won't let you all go so easily, especially you," the Prince of Darno shared gloomily.

Raylina, still not completely trusting the handsome Prince, raised her eyebrows and said, "Why are you warning me?" "Because. She came into my dream last night and asked me to trust you," the Prince of Darno answered subtly. "Who?" Raylina asked. "Iraja," he replied.

Raylina stared back into his eyes with contempt. He looked away and sighed deep, "Raylina, I don't trust you either, but I am running out of options here," he said. "And I am desperate to save my world." "Your people are more messed up than ours," Raylina smiled and walked away without saying anything.

Raylina ran a little to match up with Avyukt. "Hello," Raylina said. "What... you Bffs with the baby devil now?" Avyukt huffed. "No, but it seems like Iraja is visiting us at night," Raylina said. Avyukt was dazed by what Raylina had said to him. "Wait, that sounded right in my head," Raylina said, scratching her nose. Raylina clutched Avyukt's jacket and pulled him aside to talk. "You know you have some serious mental issues," Avyukt said, removing her hold from his jacket. "You know, calling people crazy is not cool... but... whatever. Now, taunts apart. I need to tell you something," Raylina said in one breath.

Raylina elucidated Avyukt about everything that the prince told her. They were again in a great dilemma. "She won't let us leave," Avyukt said tensely. "And it's not safe for you all to stay cause our evil Queen D is on a murder spree," Raylina said wordily. "Let's destroy the door from inside," Avyukt suggested. "We can't put innocent lives at risk. No more bloodshed, not on my watch," Raylina said clearly.

"Ray, what's going on?" Ablina came in and asked directly. Raylina was a creative liar, and to be perfect and believable, she always planned it before saying it—but the spontaneity ambushed her. "A-b-by," Raylina stuttered. "Enough of your lies," Ablina said tiredly. "We are planning to blow the Mari... Maori... ahh... the Door from our end. Your sister is planning to give herself up in order to save the dying world of Darno, and Queen is a soul sucker," Avyukt summed everything up quickly. "You traitor," Raylina said furiously.

"So you plan to send me off and do this all alone... without any magic? Can you even conjure simple magic? And don't tell me you can. I highly doubt that Ray,"

Ablina said seethingly. "Ouch! That's deeply offending. But I can... No... Abby," Raylina stumbled for words as deep down she knew that she was running out of ideas. "No, you can't. And Avyukt isn't a traitor; you are. Ray, you are my sister... my family... and I respect your thought of saving the people you love, but this is suicide. We are Śirā and Ragata. We need each other. And you know I am the strongest between the two of us. I can conjure Ragata magic... Avyukt can... you need us. And we are not going to just destroy the Door from our end. We are completely destroying it," Ablina said.

"What? You... Graymanos people don't have a heart! Seriously, Abby, there are more than 100 little witch kids here. We cannot do that," Raylina said strongly. "Yes, Ray, I know. And I am not heartless. We take them back to Darno," Ablina said. "But it's dying," Avyukt said. "It's not dead yet. Anyways, they are taking Raylina back to that place... so carrying a few thousand won't be an issue," Ablina said, smiling broadly.

"But what about the Queen," Raylina asked tensely. "We snatch the souls out of her and make her powerless," Ablina said wickedly. "Snatch... what? How are we gonna do that?" Raylina said anxiously. "Remember when we were kids. Papa used to have that dream catcher thingy... to make my nightmares go away?" Ablina asked. "No," Raylina said. "Ray, the dreadful-looking thing hanging behind my bed," Ablina simplified for her. "Oh... Ya, I remember... I threw it away a thousand times. It was ghastly," Raylina recalled finally.

"Now step away," Ablina said and magically pulled out the Catcher from thin air. "Sgàil," Ablina yelped loudly. "How did you? What are you doing?" Raylina said, screaming, awed by what Ablina was doing. "Some of us actually listen... Now go," Ablina yelled, holding the Catcher expanding in size. "You should have warned first," Raylina yelled. Raylina and Avyukt rushed to the family and asked them to start running back to the tents.

The Queen understood what was happening there. She chuckled wickedly, impressed with Ablina and Raylina. "You fool," the Queen mumbled, glowering at her son, the Prince of Darno, for betraying her. She lifted her arm and grasped her fist, "Jkoi," she thundered. And her high-pitched scream throttled the oxygen out of the Maori (Starless Sky).

It's not always the power that makes one victorious, but the way to use it does. The Queen was not consuming the souls, but she was harnessing its power in her. The Queen was making them part of hers. She knew everything about them, their weakness, fears, desires, everything. She knew that Aerderdeyer Narod (Earth people) needed oxygen to survive, so she made oxygen her weapon.

Raylina saw her family dying of choking. Their lungs started drying up. The Ragata magic was enlarging the Catcher, but it was not working. "I can't hold it, Ray..." Ablina screamed, asking for help.

Raylina crawled her way to Ablina and held her leg. Raylina took Ablina's support and stood up, breathing barely. "Peaches and Pumpkins," Raylina said and kept her hand on Ablina's, and suddenly two huge light balls came out of each of the Bayer sisters. The light balls went straight into the huge dream catcher, awakening its sleeping magic and transforming it into a shiny, magnetic device. The light of the Catcher's web reached every nook and corner of the Maori (Starless Sky).

Dark and white fumes started creeping out from the Queen and getting absorbed into the strings of the Catcher. And finally, the Queen fell down. The Prince waved his fingers, and the oxygen was restored. He threw the snake-rope on his mother and imprisoned her in a moving cage.

"We have to hurry... now this Catcher is sucking the souls from Maori (Starless Sky)," Ablina said. "What do you mean by that?" The Prince asked. "When this stops glowing, we all are gonna die, so we should head back to Darno," Ablina replied seriously. "No, that place is not survivable," the Prince of Darno opposed. "That's why we are here, now move your ass. We don't have time," Raylina said harshly. "We will not make it," Prince of Darno said. "We will," Ablina said in a calm voice, looking at her sister's face one last time, not voicing her 'I love you Ray' and 'Goodbye.'

Raylina understood what her sister was trying to imply, "No, Abby... no way," Raylina cried in despair. "Ray... Don't. Go, and save them," Ablina said. "Artha, you take your family out of here, back to Earth," Mihira said. "No way… I am not leaving my granddaughters here," Artha resisted. "I am not leaving Abby here," Visac said. "We all are staying," Ekani said firmly.

"Fleòdradh Talamh," the Prince of Darno said, making everyone except Ablina, Raylina, Mihira, and Avyukt fall asleep, and their bodies started to float back towards Earth's Door.

***

Their fate took a cruel turn. Raylina left Ablina and started heading back to Darno with the Prince as she promised. She constantly cried, thinking about giving up on Ablina.

"I have to go back," Raylina said to the Prince. He tightly held her from her shoulder and growled, "No. You gave me your word that you'll save my world." "Trust me—I will come back," Raylina said, giving him her word of honour.

The pain in Raylina's eyes made the Prince of Darno take the bait; he released her from his clasp, "If you don't come back, trust me, I know where all of your family went," he warned. "Thank you!" Raylina said and she ran back to Ablina.

***

Raylina saw Avyukt lying on the ground unconscious, Mihira trying to channel his lost powers, and Ablina barely holding the sky from falling. "Abby," Raylina called, staring at them with terror on her face. "Ray… what the hell are you doing here?" Ablina rebuked angrily. "Uncle Mihira, you have to go back," Raylina yelled, ignoring Ablina's wrath and running towards them. "No, I am not leaving my daughter again," Mihira resisted. "You have a duty to our land. There are no Graymanos left to repair the hole Maori will create. It's only you. Get your powers back and protect our world," Raylina commanded.

Mihira looked at Ablina for one last time as he knew there was no way back. "Ablina, you reside in my heart, and I will find a way to get you back home... both of you," Mihira said, looking at Ablina and then at Raylina. "Take care of Visac," she paused... and yourself," Ablina said. Mihira ran back towards Earth's door.

"Śirā and Ragata," Ablina said, with tear-filled eyes. "Śirā and Ragata," Raylina echoed back Ablina's words.

"So it's two of us then," Ablina said nervously. "Three of us," Raylina chuckled and kicked Avyukt's unconscious butt. "How do we pull this off?" Ablina asked. "Well, I got us a car," Raylina said. "Wait how?" Ablina asked curiously. "I asked the Prince to make us a convertible car, and Tada...," Raylina pointed to the parked white car.

"Why didn't I notice it earlier?" said Ablina, gliding in the back seat, still holding the humongous Catcher. "Happens," Raylina comforted as she dragged Avyukt into the car. "My brain works fantastic under pressure," Raylina appreciated herself and started the engine.

Raylina saw the starless sky collapsing in the rearview mirror. "Drive faster... we don't have a speed limit here..." Ablina screamed horridly. "Shut up," Raylina said nervously, speeding the car above 200 km/h.

Ablina's arms were aching badly, and her body was slowly shutting down; the spell was gradually burning off her magic. "I never thought it would be this dramatic," Ablina said, panicking as the destruction came closer and closer to them.

"Look at me, driving a car into a door made up of souls," Raylina shouted with exhilaration. "Forgive me," Ablina muttered, looking at the starless sky turned into ashes, consuming everything into it, listening to the agonizing screams of souls annihilating into dust.

"Abby," Raylina gasped, looking at the diminutive burrow, leaking little red sparks out from it. "The Door," Ablina said vacantly, thinking about the lost souls. "Let's get in..." Raylina said and stomped the accelerator with full power. The car jumped through the door, and they landed in the abandoned world—Darno.

CHAPTER 26

THE ABANDONED CHILD

The "Defeaters" of the "Color War" claimed the "Welkin of Darno." The unsettling, faintest yellow and the bloody red—the champions of color war—painted their firmament in the color of the mother's womb. "Welcome to Darno," the King of Darno greeted and opened the door for Ablina, and Raylina helped herself to get out of the car.

"Magnificent," Ablina said, gaping around like a fool. The Bayer sisters looked down and saw the green branches slithering all over the dead land of Darno. "Birds," Raylina said, rubbernecking at a colony of strange-looking massive birds that flew by right above her head.

The King of Darno gave a small purple tablet to each and told them to swallow it. "What is it?" Raylina asked loudly, like an ill-mannered 5-year-old. "It's oxygen. This tablet will work longer than the magic spell I have cast upon you all," the King of Darno said, trying to hide his disgusted look. "And I always thought oxygen was tasteless," Raylina said, gulping the sour purple tablet.

"His Highness," the Squire interrupted. The King of Darno gave him a death glare. The Squire quickly apologized, rectifying his mistake of addressing him as prince, and said, "His Majesty. People are getting impatient," he said, looking down, fearfully. "Take them all to the castle," the King of Darno ordered. "What about the Queen?" Squire dared. "Lock her up," the King of Darno commanded, with his heart shattering into a million pieces.

The King of Darno dragged Avyukt out of the car and laid him on the slithering ground. "Venika Revivara," the King of Darno cast a spell, and Avyukt woke up. "I thought I would never see you both again," Avyukt panted, gazing at Raylina standing alive in front of him. "I saved you again," Raylina bragged, hugging him.

Avyukt cried softly, embracing Raylina into his bruised arms. At that moment, Raylina realized that he deeply cared for her and would go to any extent for her. She rolled her lower lip inside a little to moisten them and quickly stood up. Avyukt saw Raylina hiding the blood rushing to her cheeks and looked down, shyly, smiling.

The pale red color of the sky morphed into dark blue, like an ocean at night. Horrendous howls raised the temperature, and slowly the ruthless heat started to burn their flesh. "What is that?" Ablina asked horridly. "Apirdovko," the King of Darno gulped. "What?" Raylina asked. "We have to go now," the King of Darno said tensely. They all sat in the car and headed to the castle of Darno.

"Strangely, what we feel affects our heads, and what we think affects our hearts. And this happens because our hearts are entwined with our minds," Ablina recited the quote in her head from her mother's favorite book, *'The Tour to Nightmare'* by Aryaraj Saud, observing the people of Darno walking towards the castle on their foot, traveling here and there like refugees, with no place to call home. She empathized with their situation, as she knew the pain of leaving home.

Ablina closed her eyes and rested her head on the car's headrest to bury her thoughts away. But they kept on overflowing, causing a severe headache. "Abby, wake up," Raylina said loudly. Ablina opened her heavy, tired eyes to see what happened.

"Woahhh…" Raylina and Ablina said in unison as they saw an unconventional acropolis in the hills. The water-like red-colored liquid flowing through the sky-scraping, golden conical towers made the view gothic yet cultivated at the same time. As they drove near the castle, the infinite, glorious glass windows all over the castle became more visible.

"Home," the King of Darno said, looking at a sigil carved on the walls of Darno's Royal castle. They followed him. "If something goes wrong, how many people will die?" Ablina abruptly asked, staring at the Red and Green dragon wings clasping the pentagram statue on the entrance post. "We have five thousand of us left, including me, the Queen, and you three," the King of Darno answered humbly.

"Enough of all this; let's check out the castle," Raylina insisted gaily, offending the brand-new King of Darno already. "Yes," the King of Darno said and started walking ahead with his guards. "Real insensitive," Ablina murmured. Raylina ignored Ablina's comment and went in. Ablina and Avyukt silently followed her.

***

Ablina, Raylina, and Avyukt walked through the corridor made of glass mirrors, entering the main hall of the Mekmerios (Wonder) Castle of Darno. A magnolious, dense, dark green-colored tree stood tall at the center of the hall, gyrated all over the walls and floors of the Mekmerios (Wonder) Castle, slithering, except for the gold-dipped Royal throne on a black dais.

"We call her Maniyari, the first tree, the only tree of Darno. This tree is a source of light for our world and for all the magic of Darno," the King of Darno enlightened them. "Just like our Banyan tree," Raylina said, studying it closely. "Yes. But it's not Banyan tree," King of Darno said, grinding his teeth, oppressing his urge to kill Raylina. "We've figured that part out," Raylina said.

"How much time is left, till... till it all dies?" Raylina asked, lost in her eccentric cranky zone. "2 months... roughly," King of Darno answered. "Your majesty, everyone is settled," the Squire informed. "Tell Sinya to escort our guests to their chambers," the King of Darno ordered. "Chambers," Raylina cackled with laughter. The King of Darno stared at her with a blank face and rolled his eyes.

A slim, beautiful tall girl entered the hall and bowed at the Prince. The King of Darno beamed with light blush at her. "Beasty likes someone," Raylina whispered to Avyukt. Avyukt sneered at her. "You seemed intrigued by him," Ablina said in a hushed tone. "Why do you care, you have Visac," Raylina said.

Visac's name narrowed down Ablina's smile. A little water droplet came out of her eyes, recalling the moments she spent with Visac, adjusting to the fact that she might never see him again. "I am sorry, Abby... I didn't mean that," Raylina said, realizing the mistake she had just made. "You want me to jump for you, Abby? Tell me, and I will... But please don't cry." "You know you are bad at this, Ray," Ablina said in a dejected tone, burying her hurt under a fake smile and left with Sinya. "You should think before you speak," Avyukt said, trying to keep the disappointment out of his voice, and went after them.

"Hey, majesty…" Raylina called the King of Darno harshly. The King of Darno asked his Squire to start the preparations for dinner. He took his time with instructions that annoyed Raylina. "And they call me rude," Raylina grumbled. "What?" The Prince glowered. "Look, I don't give a rat ass about you. I am here to save your world even though your mom murdered my parents. I am not a manipulator or a killer like you. So throw that attitude out of this shitty window, and tell me your name," Raylina asked in the most disrespectful way possible.

The King of Darno's lips sealed, finding ways to counterattack, stood there, insulted, glaring at Raylina. "Organ Defius Vedilious," the King of Darno answered, gulping his pride. "I just asked for your name," Raylina said sarcastically. He wanted to stab her, but instead, he gave her a tight-lipped smile and left.

***

"Ray… get up, supper is ready," Ablina said. "I had enough madness for today. Tell that Gorgan… to eat good food, and relax a little bit," Raylina said, lying in a huge king-size bed. "Oh wait… It's Organ," she laughed at her own statement. Avyukt, with vacant expressions, said, "What are you saying?" "It's his name, Organ. Can you believe that? Now I know why his mother is in prison," Raylina joked. "Will you please stop this, Ray, why are you behaving like a child?" Ablina said in an annoyed tone.

Avyukt and Ablina's doleful faces made it clear that they were having difficulty adjusting to the new planet. Raylina stood up from bed and sat. She crossed one leg on another, widened her eyes, and said, "What is wrong with you two? Why are you all so stressed out?" "Sit down," Raylina ordered, miming them to come and sit beside her.

Avyukt and Ablina sat alongside Raylina. "Look, worrying and yelling in anger is not going to help us," Raylina said calmly. Ablina broke out first and said, "I feel hopeless. Dead inside." "Ray, I have all these superpowers inside me, and all I did was nothing... nothing at all," Avyukt said in a low voice.

Raylina held their hands and rubbed them with her thumb to comfort them. She wrapped him with one arm and said, "Let me tell you this. You are not useless. Avyukt, you practically saved our asses from the beginning. Without your little dramatic, scary act, we would have never come to India. Or I would have never regained my memories which helped us reach here. You are the reason why both of the worlds have still not turned into dust."

Raylina side hugged Ablina, and rested her head on her shoulder, and said, "And you can't be hopeless, Abby. You are hope itself. You are my hope. Good to my bad, and you always will be. Plus, the way you used your brain about that Catcher thing was pure genius. If the roles were to be reversed, and you would have given me a hint, we all would have been dead by now."

"I love you," Ablina cried and wrapped her hands around Raylina. "Guys, we all played our parts well, that's why most of us are alive, and that's a win for me," Raylina said with ardor, jumping out of the sofa. "Now, let's go to that stupid dinner."

Sinya came in with a rolling hanger overloaded with dresses. "Don't bow. It's ridiculous," Raylina said harshly. "Sorry, Sinya… I mean, no need for all this." Sinya smiled and said politely, "His Majesty has asked all of you to join us for dinner." "Oh, we didn't know that," Raylina laughed scornfully.

"Thank you, Sinya," Avyukt said flirtatiously. "Oh my God," Raylina mumbled with clear disapproval. Sinya giggled and left the room. "Let's dress up," Ablina said cheerfully. Ablina started picking out a dress for her and Avyukt. Raylina poured the juice in a silver glass, took the first sip, and said, "I should have let them be doomed," swallowing the bitter sip.

***

Ablina looked at herself in the mirror to tuck her wavy hair into a loose updo; she swiped her hands gently on the skin-tight grey dress, which perfectly objectified her curves. She smiled and said, "Perfecto."

Avyukt and Ablina sat on the sofa and waited for Raylina to come out of the bathroom. "Is she always like this?" Avyukt asked, busy adjusting his emerald-green cufflinks. Ablina threw her hands up in despair and said, "Don't ask me. I am done."

An hour went by, and Raylina was still in the shower. "Something's wrong," Avyukt said. "Why are you so desperate," Ablina said, winking teasingly. "What if she is sleeping in there? Avyukt said. "That can be a case, definitely," Ablina said and knocked on the door. "Ray… Ray… I am coming in," Ablina shouted. Ablina opened the door and screamed. Avyukt ran in and saw an empty shower, windows opened, and no sign of Raylina.

***

Myriads of howling sounds woke Raylina up. She vigorously rubbed her eyes to make sure she wasn't dreaming, "What are you?" Raylina gasped in terror, staring at the man's lower body smoldering in fire. "Voskresna," the man hauled, and suddenly thousands of men and women appeared out of thin air, each with their lower bodies burning in fire.

"So they have managed to bring Śirā, at last…" the woman sitting on a throne made of burnt Maniyari said in her charming voice. Raylina gazed at her fiery, rosy bottom, finding logic in why everyone's lower half was on fire. "Where are your legs?" Raylina asked incautiously. "Iraja always chose the stormy ones," the woman said, smiling at Raylina.

The woman stood up from her throne, walking towards Raylina, burning the slithering ground with her fiery cape. Her long, scintillating braided hair covered her breasts. Her smooth, spotless skin wore night with sheer elegance. Felicity, in her bewitching eyes, was enough to make her likable. "What are you?" Raylina reframed her question in her head. "We are called 'Eunopsia.' First people of Darno. The creator of 'Third Magic,' 'Magic of Darno,'" the woman answered. "And here we go again," Raylina said.

Raylina scratched her head and prepared herself for one long story. She folded her hands and waited for the woman to speak. "Here," she said and gave her a scroll. Raylina took the scroll in her hand, confused. "Come on, open it," the woman said.

Raylina opened the scroll, and the smooth wind touched her ears softly. The wind felt like home, a wind sent from Earth. "Save me," the wind whispered to her. The message was loud and clear. "It's Iraja," Raylina said, recognizing her voice. "Iraja asked me to save Darno, now she is asking me to save her. What is going on?" Raylina demanded answers. "No more stories, Raylina... only answers," the woman promised charily.

The woman whirled her fingers in an uncanny motion in the air, and chairs grew out of the burnt Maniyari. "I am not going to sit until you tell me what is going on," Raylina spoke in a firm tone. The woman bowed slightly and began, "When we were born, our bodies were full, like yours, like the people you already met. Eunopsias were powerful—magic unbeatable, doing wonders. This land you are standing on was not there before. With our powers, we surfaced Iraja's abandoned child. All was easy and possible, but it's said in our world that 'Aezdis

Kaosa Nema Mira,' meaning 'Without Chaos, there is no Peace.' So we created our chaos by making numerous attempts to create humans, but we forgot that one must be God to make his creation."

"We spent eons working on our desire to make our own Darno human. And finally, we successfully made the first human baby on our planet. Sadly, the baby died in 5 seconds. We dug a little deeper, and then we realized that we don't have the basic elements to keep a human alive, as the ingenious plan of God involved Iraja's nature for humans to survive, without her birds and plants, the whole system dies in a day or two." "Also the oxygen," Raylina spoke in-between. "Yes. We changed our prototype, and we decided to create elements first," the woman said.

"We managed to get metal to some level, but fire, water, earth, and the wind were impossible to create," the woman said. She paused for a while, as she was worried that the information she was about to give to Raylina was more than her earthly stomach could digest. "What? Why did you stop?" Raylina asked. "We decided to conjure the lady herself," the woman said with valiance. "I-raj-a," Raylina stammered.

The vacant expression on the woman's face tensed Raylina. "You sick people, you all conjured God's assistant," Raylina shrieked in shock. "We did, and by mistake, now Iraja is ensnared somewhere in these dense woods. Raylina, we never meant to harm her. We just needed her help to make our world whole like yours. But unknowingly, all this happened. Help us... please," the woman said apologetically, clasping her hands together, begging. "And I thought I was the crazy one," Raylina mumbled.

"Raylina, we are on the verge of extinction because of our mistake," the woman said wistfully. "Why don't you all just go and set her free from the trap," Raylina asked sensibly. "We tried Raylina, but the deeper we go into the dense forest of Maniyari, our magic weakens. Maniyari is not just a forest. It holds the magic of the Universe, God's magic. And only Śirā Ragata can free her from this magic, as you and your sister are part of the universe this magic flows in," the woman answered.

"But she made us... why can't she help herself?" Raylina asked, scratching her nose in confusion. "I don't know... Only Iraja knows," the woman said, genuinely lost.

"What is your name, and why did you kidnap me?" Raylina asked straightforwardly. "My name is Elora," the woman replied. "And we kidnapped you because we have some trust issues with the Royals," Elora answered. "And don't worry, we have already sent the message about your whereabouts to the castle." "They must be on their way here," Elora added. "What's Apirdovko?" Raylina asked bluntly. "Soul of the child who died," Elora said horridly.

"Ray," Ablina yelled from the entrance of the tribe. "Let them in," Elora ordered. Ablina and Avyukt stared with wide eyes at their bottoms covered in flames. "No wonder you both sisters attract chaos," Avyukt said nervously, ducking the glower of men escorting them to the stand.

"Not you," the guard said to Organ, the King of Darno. Elora nodded, and the guard let him in. He walked up to Elora, and they glared at each other, Organ restraining himself from not killing Elora and Elora trying her best not to spite the King of Darno.

"You played big-time," Organ said in an angry voice. "Don't start," Elora cut him. Organ rolled his eyes and started walking. "We confessed," Elora said. Organ stopped and turned back. "Ha…" he grunted. "We tried your way, Organ, now no more manipulations," Elora said in a serious tone.

From inseparable lovers to sworn enemies, Elora and Organ looked at each other with hatred in their eyes and hurt in their hearts, still trying to find ways to resolve their irresolvable disputes. Organ held Elora from her shoulder and maffled, "Look at them. They are frozen teenagers. One can barely hold her magic, and the other… Don't get me started with Raylina, Elora. She is a complete, messy menace."

"And yet you brought them here. You know what your problem is, Organ? You lack faith, I know this word has no meaning in our land, but faith is all we can have right now. Faith is always risky, but it's worth trying. Our ancestors messed up enough. Let us not spoil it anymore," Elora answered, looking away from his gorgeous face.

***

"Who are these people, and why did they kidnap you?" Ablina asked in shock, glancing at the King of Darno and the woman with the fiery rose bottom arguing over something. "Calm down, Abby. They are called the 'Eunopsia'... The first folk of Darno. And that lady talking to me was Elora, kinda a queen of this tribe, or she is the highest authority," Raylina answered with her mind still reeling with what she had discovered.

Every time Raylina thought that the story of Śirā Ragata was solved, and the mystery was over, it brought them deeper and deeper. She cleared her mind and filled Ablina and Avyukt with all the details she had found out about Iraja and Elora.

"What do you think?" Raylina asked after explaining everything to Avyukt and Ablina. "I do not trust them," Avyukt said. "Me neither," Ablina said. "I find their story with infinite flaws, but I trust the voice, which saved us multiple times. And we burnt our only way back home, so freeing Iraja from that cage is our only way out," Raylina said to convince them.

Ablina listened to Raylina making one more dangerous plan of getting them all killed. But she knew Raylina thoroughly, and stopping her from doing it would have only provoked her.

Raylina pulled her lips back, and opened them rigorously, and said, "Also...., there's a catch." "The power of Iraja is way beyond our imagination. The last time these folks tried conjuring her, their bodies were cut into two halves. Plus the forest of Maniyari is filled with all types of deadly night-ma-res," Raylina stammered.

"It doesn't matter now, Ray," Ablina said and stopped talking abruptly, quickly ending her conversation as she saw Elora walking towards them. The answer was finalized despite her muddled mind. For once, Ablina decided to follow the path of free-thinkers and not the analytical ones. With confidence on the outside and insecurities on the inside, like any other human being, Ablina said, "We will do it."

Raylina was fazed by Ablina's decision. Ablina mostly spent her life being nothing but a perfect planner, and being reckless was not in her DNA. A minute ago, she was indecisive about the whole thing, and now she spoke for all three of them, which made Raylina distraught.

"Abby, can we talk?" Raylina asked, furiously dragging Ablina aside. Avyukt followed them. "Before you say anything, I had a vision," Ablina said. "Vision... What? How?" Raylina asked perplexedly. "A micro-second flash-like picture of Iraja. Ray, I saw the place where Iraja is trapped. Elora is not lying," Ablina said.

"It's impossible. Graymanos or witches can never... we can never see the future. Precognition is an ability of Saith hunters," Avyukt said. "Like our father?" Ablina asked. "Yes," Avyukt said, still trying to get hold of this. "But Mihira… is Graymanos," Raylina hesitated. "That means… Aliha… your mother was a Saith hunter," Avyukt said vacantly, trying to digest the truth. Before Ablina could react to the newfound fact about her birth mother, she saw Organ marching towards them, so she concealed her emotions like nothing had happened.

"As my sister has promised, we will go and fix the mess you have created," Ablina said in an unshaken tone. "Well, you never had a choice, to begin with," the King of Darno said and handed them an old dusty brown parchment.

"Why are you giving us this stuff written in your language?" Raylina asked, studying the words written in a peculiar language. "The stuff you are holding is a map of Maniyari forest. It's almost accurate as per my knowledge," Elora said, walking in. "Almost accurate?" Ablina asked. "These marked points are the areas we had traveled so far, but the forest of Maniyari is deeper, beyond our imaginations," Elora answered, trying her best not to scare them. "It can't be that bad," Raylina said, sighing, conjuring up her buried courage.

"Kinezjok Harin Lajabda," Elora spoke, gazing at Ablina and Raylina's faces. Raylina simpered and asked, "What does that mean?" "It means 'she has faith in you,'" Organ answered skeptically. "And you don't," Raylina asked teasingly, to purposely annoy the King. "Okay,

Ray, enough," Ablina said and switched her place with Raylina, stopping her sister from doing anything silly.

Elora bowed her upper half to Raylina and Ablina. And every other member of her tribe followed her. "From the moment you both decided to save us, we see the light, the light our world has never felt or seen before, the light of 'Hope.' Our heads and lives are yours."

Elora took Raylina and Ablina's hands in hers and bowed again. "We trust you with all our hearts and what's left of it," Elora howled, and the crowd howled. "We are not God, but we will try to save your world," Raylina promised and started walking towards the dense forest of Maniyari with Avyukt and Ablina.

"But you're his Child's Child," Elora shouted. Raylina and Ablina turned around and smiled.

Elora thundered the prophecy as Raylina, Ablina, and Avyukt disappeared into the dense forest of Maniyari.

Vaniyaos, Vankemiya de ehe Boris Veh

Varukh Oste Sorao

"Her child will bring us out of the night,"

"Sun and Blood will come and fight."

To be continued…

ABOUT THE AUTHOR

Dr. Meera Vyas is a regular doctor by the day and a crazy hustling philosopher/writer by night. She completed her Doctor of Pharmacy from KSV University in 2019 and joined a corporate PV firm right after graduation. After working for two years, she decided to take the "Road not taken" and became a full-time writer.

Dr. Vyas is a 90s kid who grew up watching all the best content they had to offer. She is currently residing with her parents, and she spends most of her time in her sanctum, her room, which she calls the hub of all the amazing books, shows, and movies. And she only crawls out of it when there is a new release and for food.

Vyas calls herself a "Reality Escapist,"
with the belief that "One day, I will be gone, but, my words shall remain." *Śirā Ragata and the Abandoned Child* is her debut novel.

ACKNOWLEDGMENTS

Any foundation has 4 pillars to strengthen its clasp on this world. But fortunately, I have 6 pillars holding me and my book, ***Sirā Ragata and the Abandoned Child,*** strong.

My 6 pillars are:

The first and second pillars are my parents, who doubted every decision I ever made and pushed me to an extent where I almost dropped my career as a writer, but who somehow still managed to support me (miraculously) in every aspect of writing this book. It's the blend of their criticism and the love they showered on me that made me who I am today.

The third pillar is my sister Suchi Patel, one of the forced financial investors of this book. It was Suchi's impeccable efforts that convinced my first and second pillars to let me do what I want and justified my every rash life decisions to the world ever since the day I was born.

The fourth pillar is my brother-in-law Aditya Patel, who is also a major financial investor of this book. I would like to thank him for being an eternal Swiss bank for ***Sirā Ragata Series***. Also, for teaching me that hard work is the only way.

The fifth pillar is the man who has been with me for 9 years, tolerating me, listening to my every BS, bringing me my midnight snacks, taking me on enormous coffee dates. Thank you, Pranav Gadhvi, for making me a non-quitter and bringing out the best in me.

My sixth and final pillar is Aarushi Shukla. The girl who taught me what 'power' means in 'empowerment.' Who stood by me as my personal cheerleader and made sure that I completed the story I was born to tell. Aarushi, a zillion times—Thank you! for editing and reviewing my book at night after working two jobs in the day. Aarushi Shukla, from this day forward, I am booking you forever as my best friend (which happened years ago, just officiating it) and beta editor **of** *Śirā Ragata and the Abandoned Child* series, and many more for life.

Once again, thank you, my pillars, for doing all you can and for the things you can't. Also, I am grateful to everyone else who has believed in me and supported me in any way they could.

Most importantly, I would like to thank you, my readers, for picking up **Śirā Ragata and the Abandoned Child,** for giving me and this book a chance. I have poured my soul into this book in the hope that you'll thoroughly enjoy it and fall in love with the world and characters of **Śirā Ragata,** just as I did.

SPECIAL CREDITS

Ever since I was a little girl, I loved sneaking out to my quiet place and cook-up amazing stories in my head. But as I grew up, my wild and wide imaginations narrowed, and they dissolved with time. And the condition worsened when I lost my best friend/grandfather—my Dada. Dada and I were kindred spirits. From reciting complicated slokas to understanding their meaning, Dada taught me everything about my culture and religion.

The story of Maa Yashoda seeing the glimpse of the universe in Little Lord Krishna's mouth is close to my heart. And the reason is that it was the story my Grandfather used to read when I was little before bedtime. This story opened the doors of imagination in my mind; it inspired me and made me into the dreamer I am today.

I surrender myself at the feet of Lord Krishna, and I thank him for becoming my 'Sarathi (charioteer)' on the journey of self-discovery.

I am endlessly thankful to my Grandfather for helping me realize my true passion—writing.

RESOURCES

Bhagavad Gita: Chapter 2, Verse 19,

Translation: Bhagavad Gita, the Song of God Commentary by Swami Mukundananda,

"Ya Enam Vetti Hantaram Yash Chainam Manyate Hatam. Ubhau tau Na Vijanito Nayam Hanti Na Hanyate,"

from https://www.holy-bhagavad-gita.org/chapter/2/verse/19.

"In Love with **Śirā Ragata And the Abandoned Child**?"

Then go and yelp to the world about it.

Shower your reviews about the Book on **Amazon**, **Google Books,** and **Good reads**.

For more updates on the upcoming series, follow Author on Instagram.

@meera_starunicorn

Made in United States
North Haven, CT
24 November 2021

11468958R00240